CRAZY PAVING

CW00954004

Gillian Griffiths

ISBN: 9798421454694

Cover design: Dave Lewis

For Jonathan Livingston Seagull
and all who have the courage to follow.

CHAPTER ONE

'Get out of here you lame brained son-of-a-bitch.' My voice sounded fish-wife shrill even to my own ears as I shouted at the buzzard circling above me and lobbed another pebble in its general direction. It mewed contemptuously at my efforts.

It had never ceased to amaze me how such a large, impressive-looking bird, with its voracious appetite, a nut cracker for a beak and meat-hooks for talons, had such a pathetically weak cry, like that of a new-born kitten. He and I had, for a long time, had a difference of opinion, which sometimes bordered on outright warfare. Okay, okay, I know. Buzzards are all part of Mother Nature's rich tapestry, but you have to admit that they are far from cuddly. And I accept that, like all of us, they have to eat. But I'll be damned if I am going to serve him up one of my poor, helpless, gentle, adorable, little domestic bantams on a platter. Free-loaders are not welcome at my house, unless I say so. He has no excuse. He lives in an area of wide open countryside of diverse flora and fauna in which he may practise his good old-fashioned hunting skills to his heart's content, though preferably somewhere out of my sight and hearing. I had always been squeamish when it came to entrails and bloody bits. But this one in particular had found a softer target – my chickens! It has become a battle of attrition.

It dipped lower.

'I'm not telling you again. Next time I'll nail you dead centre. Chicken is off your wish-list, for breakfast, dinner and supper, so get used to it. Cop this, dick-head.' I cursed my own rather down-market phraseology, but it was early in the morning and I am always a bit cranky before my first cup of coffee.

I took another pebble off the little cairn of beach pebbles stacked beside the chicken run for this very purpose. I shaded my eyes against the brightness of the clear morning sky. I threw it. It missed by a mile. The buzzard's mewing was by now veering towards laughter. I had been pretty good at throwing when I had played in the school rounders team, but that was over sixty years before and now old age had decimated what little kinetic power I had ever had. But it wasn't the result that mattered: it was the process of fighting back, which made me feel a whole lot better. I found that lobbing pebbles into the sky satisfied a deep-seated primeval need in me to protect what was mine. I liked to think that the buzzard understood this and respected me for it.

Privately I admired and envied the old devil. He rose high above me, gliding effortlessly on invisible thermals rising off the crest of the bluff with hardly a flicker of movement in his entire body. I could feel one beady eye keeping me in constant sight. Oh, to be able to soar like that and feel the lift of the wind under my wings taking me higher and higher, my vision crystal clear for miles all around, master of my element and magnificently free.

To be honest with you, if I ever managed to hit him, I would be devastated. If I injured him, I would probably end up nursing him back to health or driving miles to take him to the nearest vet, with the subsequent massive bill. I just wanted him to get the message and go somewhere else. I didn't want to hurt him.

The chickens had adopted a much more pragmatic approach and had retreated to the safety of their five-star coop, their breakfast postponed until the danger had passed.

'Dora?'

I froze, my arm raised to send another missile in the general direction of the circling bird. I squinted towards the direction of the voice, somewhere below me, down the slope. The morning sun was bright in my eyes plunging everything into deep shadow. Did I just hear my name being called? No, I must have been imagining it. I did not have casual visitors. I did not have visitors, period. It had probably just been some noise carried up on the breeze. Without my hearing aids in and with two different tinnitus noises competing in my left ear, I could no longer be sure of anything.

'Dora. It's me, Elizabeth Henshaw.'

Damn, damn, damn – (you will possibly appreciate that that's the polite way of describing my actual thoughts). How was I going to get out of it this time? Elizabeth bloody Henshaw! She was a newish arrival in the village and I had scrupulously avoided bumping into her for all the months of her residence. I was aware that my dislike of her was totally irrational since I had never met the woman, but even living up here in my splendid isolation, word about her had trickled up to me. Her reputation in the village was that of a meddlesome do-gooder, an officious WI type of woman who thought the rest of the world should be just like her and whose life's purpose was to mould everyone into clones of herself. She was the type of person I did not like. Her name alone was enough to send shivers through me.

I turned around slowly and shaded my eyes against the glare. My ears had not been deceiving me. Below me, grouped together on the uneven paving slabs, which served as a patio outside my kitchen door were three of the village's worthies, dressed immaculately in all their frills and fancies, while I by contrast was in scruff-order in my old working clothes. They had me at an immediate disadvantage. I had heard all about them: they had formed a clique of busy-bodies (I wonder what the collective noun is) who felt it was their duty to stick their multi-ringed, manicured and varnished fingers into other people's lives and stir things around. All done for the most altruistic of reasons, of course, but I was someone who subscribed to the view that people should make their own decisions in life, rightly or wrongly, and live with the consequences. It was a tenet I was proud to live my life by.

I rearranged my face to give what I hoped looked like polite indifference tinged with a touch of petulance at being disturbed but in reality it probably looked more like I had an attack of wind. 'Mrs. Henshaw, how nice to finally meet you,' I lied. 'And to what do I owe this unexpected visit?'

Anyone with a hide less thick than that of a rhinoceros would have noted the bite of acid on my tongue. On a good day, it could strip paint at a distance of ten feet. Elizabeth Henshaw did not notice. Need I say more?

'We called at the front, but couldn't get an answer, and we really wanted to have a word. My husband, the vicar you know, was

3

adamant that I should call on his behalf. To be perfectly honest, my dear, we are all worried about you.'

For a full five seconds I was speechless.

'Why?' I asked incredulously. 'I don't even know you, and you most certainly don't know me.' A sudden image of myself as Maggie Smith as the Dowager Countess of Grantham popped into my head, but with a supreme effort I managed not to sniff. She was such a splendid role-model for me: she used her carefully chosen words like ballistic missiles, which were always dead on target. But I couldn't claim to be that sharp or that clever; well not on first acquaintance, anyway. They had taken me by surprise and I was a bit shaken. I needed time to work up to pithy sarcasm.

'Oh, but you are quite a celebrity in the village, Dora. I have heard so much about you.'

I raised a quizzical eyebrow. I had practised that look in a mirror for hours when I was younger until it had become second nature; a well-placed eyebrow can speak volumes. It gave me a spare moment in which to ponder this unprecedented event. The word 'celebrity' was certainly a misnomer. If it had been 'batty old biddy living on her own up on the bluff', it would have been far more realistic and acceptable. I wondered if it was possible that I might have committed some inexcusable *faux pas* against polite society which had brought them to my door ready to issue me with some sort of reprimand. Nothing came to mind immediately but these days I often wondered whether I hadn't forgotten to do something vital like forgetting to comb my hair or to change out of a pair of old gardening trousers with my arse hanging out of the seat or even to have gone shopping in my pyjamas. I had taken to checking that the doors are locked at least twice, if not three times, before going out, and still managed occasionally to forget altogether. Had somebody reported me to Big Brother and were these women the advanced guard, minus their white coats, coming to take me away?

Not a tremor of doubt creased Mrs. Henshaw's unfurrowed brow. She was in full command mode. 'Could we go inside, do you think?'

Ah! Slight problem, I thought. I couldn't let them enter through the kitchen as it was a total mess. I hadn't got around to tidying it for a couple of days as I have always believed that just about anything is more interesting than housework. In my opinion it was much better to have a thorough clean all in one go when the end result was noticeable and a source of satisfaction of a job well done rather than to spend hours every day tidying up what doesn't need tidying. Also, I had had other more important things on my mind lately. And anyway, everybody knew that, according to the unspoken rules of etiquette, visitors should enter via the front door – not that I am a great devotee of etiquette in any form – and that the kitchen door was for tradesmen only. *Do I sound terribly snooty? How wonderful.*

'If you go around to the front, I'll open the door for you,' I said as forcefully as I could. I disappeared inside and closed the back door behind me, practically slamming it in their faces. Mrs. Henshaw and her entourage were left with no choice.

CHAPTER TWO

I charged through the kitchen like a cannonball, and into the dining/sitting room. One look told me it wasn't much better than the kitchen. I quickly dismantled the ironing board that was propped up in the window from the night before and threw the ironed laundry onto the dining room table where it teetered perilously alongside my laptop and bundles of papers and files. I swiped the knickers, which had been drying on the radiator into the half-full basket of washing, which was still awaiting the attention of the iron, and kicked it behind the sideboard.

You might think I wouldn't care what people thought about me, and you would be right and you would be wrong. As an abstract, I didn't care what the wider world thought of me, but when three women such as these were about to enter my house, I did have enough self-pride left to want to make a reasonable impression.

I opened the front door, only slightly breathless.

'I do admire your courage trying to grow anything up here. You are so exposed to the elements,' Elizabeth Henshaw said as she looked down her long, sharp nose at my stone planters flanking the doorway. 'It must be so disheartening trying to get anything to thrive in all this salt air and wind.'

I looked reproachfully at my planters. They had contained a fine display of Tete-a-Tete jonquils only a few weeks before: why couldn't they have lasted a while longer? The flowers had miraculously survived the once-in-a-generation storm of early March but now their wilting leaves flopped untidily over the edges. All the gardening books and television programmes recommended you allow the leaves to die down naturally, and that was as good an excuse as any for me to let them go on another week, or so. Later on in the year, after the next once-in-a-generation storm, the planters would be beautiful again with a riot of summer flowers. I felt the hackles rise on the back of my neck at Mrs. Henshaw's gentle scorn of my gardening skills. She had already wrong footed me once with her ambush in the back garden. Enough was enough.

'Correct me if I am wrong, Mrs. Henshaw, but as you've only been in the village for a few months you don't have the experience yet to make such assumptions. We gardeners have to learn to adapt to nature, not the other way around. There are many fine gardeners in this village, as I'm sure Mrs. Anthony will agree. She had a most wonderful display of osteospermums and irises last year.'

Mrs. Anthony simpered a small smile in my direction. I thought Mrs. Anthony, a timid widow who had lived in the village since her conception, was an unlikely choice to be part of this delegation.

I ushered them into the living room and I took a quick look around. It is a strange but by no means an unknown phenomenon, that a person who lives alone and discourages callers of any pedigree, can cheerfully ignore things they would rather not be bothered with until such time as they are screaming for attention. I was one such person. But, introduce another person into the equation, and every bit of tat or smear of dust, cobweb or pile of old newspapers jumps into prominence. The bright sunshine streaming in through the big front window highlighted every misdemeanour quite spectacularly. I could only hope that their eyesight was not too good and that they might think that the matt surfaces were original and not the accumulation of a couple of days of dust.

I straightened my back and told myself to embrace my shortcomings. If they didn't like it, they could leave. And quickly, I hoped. 'Please, sit yourselves down and tell me your concerns, ladies, as I am rather at a loss,' I said waving a gracious hand towards the three-piece suite.

Mrs. Henshaw hesitated as she decided which of my mismatched pieces of furniture she would choose to rest her posterior upon. She finally sat gingerly on the three-seater settee and I noticed that the muted chintz pattern on the arm nearest the window had faded almost to oblivion. I had not noticed it before. *Head always in the clouds,* my brother used to say. *You really ought to take a leaf out of*

Helen's book, Dora. Our house is always neat as a pin, just as I like it.

My brother and I saw eye to eye on just about nothing.

'Can I get you tea or coffee, or perhaps you would prefer a cold drink – a glass of elderflower cordial perhaps?'

'Home made?'

'Green bottle from Asda. Keeps longer, I find,' I answered breezily. 'Of course, like everyone, I have made elderflower "champagne" in the dim and distant past, but since it makes gallons of the stuff at a time, I soon got tired of drinking it. It's just not worth the bother.'

Was I laying on the perfect hostess bit rather thick? I noticed that, alarmingly, I had developed a slightly English middle class accent, which made the whole thing rather surreal, but they didn't seem to notice anything amiss. Perhaps to them it was normal – I didn't have a great deal of experience of entertaining – but I found it rather worrying, all the same. Could I have become contaminated in just a few minutes of encountering members of genteel society?

'A cup of coffee would be delightful, thank you Dora,' chirped up Mrs. Flo Jenkins, a rather plump lady who had sat besides Mrs. Henshaw on the settee. The seat cushion had sagged under her weight and tilted her towards Mrs. Henshaw, who had taken avoiding action and, with difficulty, had shuffled herself a few inches away. I hoped the settee would survive.

I left them and fled to the kitchen. I filled the kettle and took down my mother's best china from the cabinet. It hadn't been used for years, so I gave it a quick rinse under the tap while the kettle boiled. I silently chided myself for pandering to these women by using the delicate cups (but I could hardly blame them for my not using my usual mugs which were rather pretty and all porcelain as I couldn't abide thick earthenware) but the cups and saucers would be my only nod to gentility. The coffee would be instant Gold Blend and the biscuits Bahlsen Choco Leibniz, dark chocolate, which I buy in bulk when they are on offer.

By the time I carried the tray in, the three women had had a good chance to swivel their restless little eyes into every corner of my sitting room, without actually having moved from their seats. It was a pleasant room and was one of the main reasons I had fallen in love with the house. It was subtly split into a lounge in the front and a dining area at the back, which I used as a work area instead of for eating my meals as I preferred to eat off a tray. I don't think the dining table had seen the light of day since the celebrations at the turn of the century when I had given it an airing and a polish. The front window looked out on a stunning panoramic sea-view, which was a constant source of pleasure to me. The light was immense and as pure as clear spring water, even on the dullest of days.

The room did look rather cluttered now, but I told myself that it was a comfortable lived-in look. What's the point of living in a show house fit for *Homes and Gardens* if there was nobody else to see it? I may have only been one person, but I made full use of every room of my house and I valued my comforts. It was a house for living in and working in. They could like it or lump it.

Now that the initial shock of their invasion – sorry, visit – had worn off, I sat back in my chair and assumed an air of slightly amused calm, waiting for them to tell me what the hell they were doing in my house.

'Such pretty china,' Mrs. Henshaw finally remarked to break the awkward silence. She lifted the cup to her lips, little finger elegantly poised in a fair imitation of Hyacinth Bucket.

I had to admire her acting ability – Mrs. Henshaw's, that is. There was only the slightest suggestion of a grimace and a shudder as she sipped the instant coffee, and quickly returned the cup to its saucer. She was every person's stereotypical vicar's wife: austere face immaculately made up, with lavender tinted white hair tightly set and heavily lacquered into obedience and with a thin, angular figure. Her discreetly patterned dress was adorned with a double string of pearls at the neck.

'Well, Dora, as I said, we have been worried about you,' she said, dabbing at her lips with a fine lace-edged handkerchief. 'Living up here all on your own, it must get very lonely. As you pointed out I am new to the village and my husband, the Reverend Henshaw, and I are determined to bring together people from all generations and make this village into a flag-ship of what a rural community should be.'

'Well, Mrs. Henshaw,' I said sweetly, 'I have been here nearly 20 years, and it suits me down to the ground, just as it is.' Any more sugar and I would go into hypoglycaemic shock.

Mrs. Henshaw continued as if I had not had the audacity to interrupt her. I did however see the hint of a smile on Mrs. Anthony's lips, but she hid it immediately by taking a sip of coffee. She didn't seem to mind instant. I immediately warmed to the woman.

'I haven't yet seen you at any of the new activities we have been organising in the village and I thought perhaps that you didn't know about them. Tonight, you might like to join us at our bridge night down at the village hall. You will be more than welcome, and it is a very pleasant atmosphere, not really competitive at all.'

'I don't play bridge,' I answered.

'Oh, that's not a problem,' Mrs. Flo Jenkins said eagerly, first looking in Mrs. Henshaw's direction as if seeking permission to make a comment all of her own volition. That surprised me; I had not thought she was the type to play second fiddle to anyone, but she seemed content to defer to Elizabeth Henshaw. She was a fat woman and like all well padded people, had a smooth seamless skin and rich colouring. She and her husband owned the Seaview Hotel down on the main road.   She continued. 'Beginners are very welcome.'

'I not only don't play bridge, but I have never had any inclination to learn,' I answered sharply. 'If that is why you are here, Mrs. Henshaw, I am afraid you've had a wasted journey.'

'Call me Elizabeth, please,' Mrs. Henshaw graciously answered, her smile having become rather fixed on her face. She did not seem to have anticipated my resistance. Had she bothered to ask around, she would have been better prepared, but women like Mrs. Henshaw only ever listened to her own advice, it being so far superior to anyone else's. In their opinion.

'I would prefer surnames at this early stage of our acquaintance,' I responded. 'Maybe we will be on first name terms some time in the future, Mrs. Henshaw, but I'm afraid I am rather old fashioned in that respect. I use Christian names for friends and family, and this is the first time we have met. I do think that there is a presumption these days that everybody from toddlers to greengrocers are at liberty to use one's Christian name, without so much as a by-your-leave. I do find it so demeaning.'

In actual fact, I didn't give a fig, but there was no harm in asserting myself in my own home. I tried hard to maintain my crusty persona while Mrs. Henshaw's mouth worked out its correct response.

'I quite agree, my dear,' she managed, her strained smile still just about in place. *Wara teg,* fair play, she was holding up well. 'But the bridge was not the only reason we called. My husband says he hasn't seen you at St. Hilda's since we arrived and he would so love to welcome you into our congregation for the Easter celebrations,' Mrs. Henshaw continued.

'I don't do churches either, Mrs. Henshaw,' I answered. 'My beliefs are my own, and they are not open for discussion. So again, I must decline your offer, thank you.' I was becoming tired of the woman. She hadn't picked up on my subtle hints as not being welcome, and I didn't want to be outright rude to her. She thought she was doing the right thing, after all.

As Mrs. Henshaw breathed in noisily at my dismissal of organised religion of any denomination, Mrs. Anthony, the little mouse sitting separately in the armchair, took up the baton. She was dressed just like a character from Beatrix Potter, all frills and sweetness. I have never known her Christian name. 'We don't like to think of you up here all on your own. You must feel terribly isolated. I know I did after my Trevor passed away, and I live in the heart of the village.'

I sighed theatrically. None of these women had the faintest idea that life could be lived very successfully and enjoyably beyond the confines of being a wife or a mother. They would never understand that some people had absolutely no wish to partake of husbands, screaming brats and soft furnishings or had a burning desire to spend their lives attending what they considered to be worthy charities and sitting on socially acceptable committees where local windbags droned on for hours while nothing ever got done. There wasn't a snowball's hope in hell that any of them would understand me, or people like me, even though in this age of greater freedom and choice, many more were taking to the single life, and enjoying it. Fringe benefits like sex and the occasional meal out were optional and available when needed, though these days it was definitely the meals which were the priority. I felt I had to take a stab at educating them.

'It's Mrs. Anthony, isn't it?' I asked. The lady nodded. 'Well, you see Mrs. Anthony, I chose to come and live here and since the village is only half a mile long I do not feel "isolated" as you put it. I enjoy living alone. I find great peace in living alone, and if I find I want company, I have many friends who have similar interests to me whom I can visit, if I wish.' Major exaggeration! 'For twenty six years I spent my life working in pokey little offices with people with whom I had nothing in common and didn't particularly like. To be fair I think the feeling was usually mutual. When I took early retirement – nearly twenty years ago now – I chose to live my life the way I had always wanted and I must say, I have enjoyed every minute of it, just the way it is.'

Mrs. Henshaw sat up even straighter. I did admire her back strength, very Victorian. 'Well, the offer still stands, Dora,' she said stiffly. 'One day, you may be grateful for our help.' *Pigs may fly*, I thought. 'It doesn't do any good to vegetate at our age. We need to keep the body and brain active as long as we can.' The proverbial lace gloves were off and her tone was icy.

'I quite agree,' I said, my own temper hovering just below the surface. How dare they! The arrogant presumption of these women who knew nothing about me, but had bulldozed their way into my life, implying I was too feeble to make my own decisions. How dare they! But I smiled back with what probably looked like the rictus on a death mask. 'It was very kind of you all to call, but I really have quite a lot to do,' I said, rising to my feet and staring down at them, leaving them with little option but to rise too.

After I had ushered them out of the front door, I stood in the hallway and roared out my fury. *Count to 10 old girl*, I told myself. I had read somewhere that to allow oneself to be angered by other people was to let that anger, and consequently them, win. They were winning! Number crunching was not having the desired effect either. Deep breathing just left me feeling dizzy.

I left the cups where they were, scooped up a couple of the untouched biscuits, put on my walking shoes, and locked the back door. I needed air and vigorous exercise to wipe away the acrid taste of that woman's patronising, overweening do-gooding, interfering … My vocabulary failed me, which was unusual but testimony to my agitated state of mind.

The buzzard mewed overhead, its strange cry mocking me. 'And you had better make yourself scarce if you know what's good for you,' I shouted at it. 'Or I'll be back with a shotgun.' It mewed again and with the merest flap of its wings hitched a ride on a thermal and glided off inland. My anger obviously had more effect than my pebbles. For now.

CHAPTER THREE

I strode across my front lawn, which sloped steeply downwards, and stopped for a moment to look at the view before me. The combination of the slope and the steep drop beyond had the same effect as that of a manor house ha-ha; but instead of rolling fields dotted with sheep and trees, I gazed out over a vast stretch of sparkling grey-blue sea. I breathed deeply of the bracing air, rich in salt and ozone.

But that morning I couldn't appreciate any of the stupendous view before me. I was too unsettled. Why should I be so upset, you may well ask? After all it was only a brief visit by three women whom I couldn't have cared less about and hopefully would never meet again. In my younger days I would have eaten them alive, but the encounter had made me aware that I was woefully out of practice. I had been rattled. It was years since I had verbally sparred with anyone and I was dismayed at how quickly it had turned me into a quivering jelly. I realized with a shock that other than polite comments and short chats to shopkeepers and check-out staff at the supermarket I really did not have what could be called a conversation with anyone. I had no idea how long this had been going on without my noticing. It was a disturbing revelation and one to which I would need to give further thought.

I slipped through the little gate in the stone wall which had been built at the bottom edge of the garden presumably to stop it from tumbling into the road below, an event which always threatened but had not so far happened. On the other side of the wall was a set of steep stone steps which I had to take carefully, one hand hovering over the ancient rail – just in case. These days, it was always – just in case. The need to concentrate on not tripping over my own feet as I descended had started to cool my temper. It was a very long way down.

When I had first moved here, I could have run prettily down the steps and, with almost the same ease, climbed my way back up again. I could still go down – cautiously – but my knees did not take kindly to any attempt to return by the same route. Common sense and the escalating cost of large tubes of Voltarol (12 hour variety which I applied about every two hours when the arthritis was bad) dictated that I returned via the main road and up the hillside lane to reach my front door. The route took much longer, but the incline was more gradual and kinder on my joints and lungs. But each time I took that back road, I felt as though I was being forced, inch-by-inch, closer to acknowledging the date written on my birth certificate. But, like Dylan Thomas, I would 'Rage, rage against that dying of the light.' I'm probably one of the few Welshmen (women actually) who would admit to not understanding the majority of Mr. Thomas' writings, but here and there a nugget shines through and speaks to my heart.

I smiled as I descended, and spoke his words to the breeze, one arm raised in an eloquent salute to the bard, the other clenched firmly on the handrail – well, let's face it, if you are going to be viewed as being batty, you might as well enjoy it.

> *"Do not go gentle into that good night,*
> *Old age should burn and rave at close of day;*
> *Rage, rage, against the dying of the light."*

I was starting to feel better. My raised blood pressure, racing pulse and high dudgeon were indicators that I was following Mr. Thomas' advice and not going gently anywhere in the immediate future.

I crossed over the main road at the base of the steps and on to the low dunes, which fringed the car park. It was a stupid thing to do, as just there the main road curved around the crag upon which my house stood in a dangerous blind bend, but I was still feeling reckless enough to risk playing Russian roulette with the traffic. The wind at this lower level had been chopped into a pleasant breeze and the sun had already warmed the patches of exposed sand and short sheep-cropped turf. I headed off, at a brisk pace through the car park to walk across the cliff-tops, which stretched for mile after mile along this beautiful coast where the southernmost end of Wales butted up against the Bristol Channel.

Well, it would be beautiful if it wasn't for the people – myself excluded, you understand. I was still too fired up to care about the papers blowing around, the crisp packets, empty plastic water bottles and the general rubbish, which had escaped from the overflowing bins which would normally have had me straight on the phone to the council. There were not many cars parked up, which was pretty normal for the middle of a working week. They would be mostly dog walkers and retirees who got away without paying parking fees and bagged a fine sea view for themselves. Some chose to just sit in their cars with a flask of tea and the windows half down, enjoying the bracing air and saving themselves a bit of legwork. A few children ran around screaming at the tops of their piercing little voices and somewhere the blare of a car radio thumped monotonously. My bad mood was straining to return.

I was not looking where I was going – after all these years I knew every dip and fold. I had my head down and was walking quickly through the remains of the parked cars when a group of boys, whooping and laughing, charged down the path towards me. They were totally oblivious to any cars or people who got in their way as they chased after an orange football. Before I had time to sidestep them they barged into me and knocked me over. I landed flat on my back in an undignified sprawl. The noxious smell of dirty old sand filled my nostrils. It was a mixture of thousands of feet, sheep droppings and old fag ends and was grey and smelly, not like the golden beach sand, which was cleaned and purified twice a day by the tide. As I struggled to my feet, I was determined to blast them with both barrels. First that damned buzzard, then Elizabeth Henshaw and now this!

'I'm sorry, miss,' one of the boys said, trying to help me up and nearly dislocating my arm in the process. He was laughing at his mates with the blunt thoughtless cruelty of the young and didn't look in the least bit sorry. 'It was Mikey's fault. Are you hurt anywhere?'

The four boys gathered around me. I was only 5'2" tall and

they were big brawny lads, full of testosterone and energy, and I felt intimidated by their size and their pent-up ebullience. Well, if I am honest, I was intimidated full stop. The truth is that young people *per se* terrified me. I did not understand them, this modern generation. They were like alien beings to me and they spoke in an alien language and did alien things.

They all looked much the same – short back and sides hair with an unruly thatch falling over their eyes and spray-on jeans. They were all grinning inanely.

I wasn't going to show my fear. I straightened up to my maximum height and looked them in the eye. 'Shouldn't you lot be in school instead of running riot in car parks?' I asked angrily, making a great display of brushing the dirty sand off my clothes.

'Inset day, miss,' one of them smirked.

'When isn't it?' I answered acidly. 'Why don't you go down on the sand to play your puerile games instead of creating mayhem where people are trying to walk?'

'I am sorry, miss,' the boy Mikey said, grinning widely. 'Look, there's a van over there, let me buy you an ice cream, as an apology, like. We can all chip in!'

That completely took the wind out of my sails. 'No thank you,' I gabbled, all of a fluster now at this unexpectedly kind offer.

'We were going down on the sand, miss – but we've got to wait for the tide to go out,' one of the boys said and the others giggled.

I could feel my face burning. The balloon of my anger had deflated and I just wanted to get away. People were looking. I felt a fool. 'I accept your apology,' I said with wavering confidence. 'Just be careful in the future, or it will cost you a fortune if you have to buy ice creams for everyone you barge into.'

I stalked off with as much dignity as I could summon and made a quick exit through the opening in the old stone wall which marked the boundary of the car park and which helped to muffle some of the boys' laughter. The breeze helped cool my burning face and I was disgusted to find that I was trembling. And my bum was starting to feel sore from where I had landed. I would probably have a spectacular bruise in the morning.

As I walked on I could feel tears of anger and frustration building up behind my eyes. I just wanted to be left alone! Was it too much to ask?

Slowly, very slowly, I felt the tension of the morning leach away. A person would have had to be brain-dead not to be affected by the beauty all around them. Spring was swelling fit to burst. The sun sparkled playfully off the gentle sea and had coaxed the coconut scent out of the gorse flowers, masking the greasy smell of the sheep who constantly grazed these cliff-tops. Virginal primroses peeped shyly from the edges of the gorse or were tucked safely inside tangles of rusty old bracken fronds. Up ahead a ewe called for her lamb. Seagulls heading inland screamed noisily to each other. Overhead a kestrel hovered motionless in search of prey. In my childhood they had been a common sight, but they were rare now, and I watched his mastery in awe.

'Good morning,' a passing walker said in greeting. I had seen the man out walking the cliffs before, but couldn't have told you his name, but his little Cavalier King Charles spaniel was called Monty. His coat was the same colour as marmalade.

I returned his greeting and continued on.

It may seem a small thing to most people: a casual greeting from one stranger to another, but for me it epitomised the reasoning behind my having moved into the countryside. When I had lived in the nearby town I had felt as if I had lost my identity, even to myself. During the working week old people populated the town, and I found myself being carried along in a flood of equally anonymous elderly people who studiously ignored each other and who were increasingly viewed by everyone else as a drain on the resources of the country. One felt as if one should apologise for having lived so long and confessing to being responsible for the crisis in the NHS, social services and the world economy. People under pensionable age walked

18

around, head down, wires dangling from their ears, eyes glued to their smart phones, oblivious to everything around them. For me town living had been a different kind of isolation; cold and depressing.

As soon after retirement as I could I had escaped to this small seaside village on the edge of the wild, only five miles from town but a universe away in spirit, where I could be myself, loud and proud. Nobody in town would ever dream of passing the time of day with a stranger. Here, it was unusual to be ignored.

The kestrel broke away and relocated to a more likely patch.

The further away I walked, the more the tension in my stomach from the upset in the car park eased. The sun was deliciously warm and the peace and quiet set me to pondering the strangeness of the day. The whole morning seemed to have been one long battle and I wondered if it wasn't one of those days when it was best to turn around three times, get back into bed and rise again as if it were a new day. Though my reactions to the day's events may indicate to the contrary, I usually steer clear of any conflict, preferring to keep my own counsel and I never ever get myself embroiled in village matters.

So why did I now feel so shaken up and unsettled? It was totally unfair to blame the buzzard. Was it because of the visit of that woman and her minions? Was I, as Elizabeth Henshaw had implied, stuck in a rut and deep down was hurt by the truth of it? Had the woman been pitying me!

The word curmudgeon popped uncomfortably into my head. So much meaning in a single word I thought – cranky, crabby, a cross-patch, a boor – nothing quite had the colour of the word itself. Perhaps I was morphing into one. That thought did not appeal to me and I wasn't at all sure that it was how I wanted to see myself, let alone how I wanted other people to see me. I constantly told myself that I didn't care what other people thought of me, but maybe I did.

Or was it more likely that it had nothing whatsoever to do with any of them, but was rather a deep anxiety about the contents of that envelope sitting on my mantelpiece? I felt suddenly cold and brushed the thought away.

CHAPTER FOUR

I was approaching the rear of the Seaview Hotel, where Mrs. Flo Jenkins and her husband were the proprietors. It was the only one left in the village now, catering for the much-diminished domestic tourist trade. Towns like Barry Island or Porthcawl still managed to scrape by, their fairgrounds being the main attractions, but Sutton had nothing to offer but an unspoiled coastline and a few small shops. The other two hotels had long ago been converted to *des res* apartments for the well-to-do, who rarely visited and when they did, left no footprints in the sand: holiday lets – the scourge of rural Wales. The hotel itself sat on high ground next to the main road and its garden swept steeply down to end at the stone wall. The word "garden" was printed in the hotel brochure in defiance of the Trades Description Act. In actual fact it was no more than a long arid stretch of thin sand-blasted, sun scorched scraggy grass where only musk thistles and gorse bushes could survive. But the holidaymakers didn't seem to mind. They still came and drank warm beer or ate tiny sandwiches and stale dry cakes served on fine gold-edged china, pretending perhaps that they had been transported back to the days when high teas were the height of fashion. They did have a magnificent view which possibly made up for its other shortcomings. I put my head down and marched past.

The dry stone walls at this southern side of the village had been built down to within a dozen yards of the cliff edge. They had collapsed in parts, aided and abetted by roaming sheep and small children and, with the increasing erosion of the flaky limestone cliffs themselves, it would not be many more decades before the two shook hands.

The path split two ways just beyond the hotel boundary; one continuing along the cliff top for a couple of miles towards the next bay, and the other to a stiff trudge uphill, through yet more banks of gorse bushes and up to the main road. My bad temper had gone. My breathing was only slightly ragged, and I had a million things I should be doing. I refused to give my temper another minute of my time. The germ of a brilliant plan had been hatched in my brain as I had been walking and I was eager to see if it would work. I often found that a brisk walk in fresh sea air would wake up the few grey cells I had which remained in working order.

I followed the steep path back to the main road and was perspiring profusely and gasping for breath by the time I got there. I took a moment to recover my decorum before continuing back through the village in the general direction of home, carefully sidestepping the liberal scattering of sheep poo that always covered the pavements. So far, human ingenuity had failed to outwit the canny Welsh sheep; cattle grids and fencing were no barrier to them.

I stopped at the local general store which stood not a stone's throw from the lane leading homeward. There had been a Hardy's Store somewhere in Sutton village for as long as anyone could remember, passing from father to son for three generations. The current incumbent, Alf Hardy, sometimes spun a tale to gullible day-trippers that his family's ancestry went right back to the Normans who had built a castle a mile or so up-river. Some even believed him – tourists I mean, not locals, and he did add a touch of local colour, especially when he broke into a chorus of *Calon Lan* in his fine tenor voice. It didn't do his profits much harm either. His shop catered for everyone, at a cost. Well, these days we have become resigned to having to pay for convenience, and his shop was like an Aladdin's treasure cave, everything from ice-cream to shoe laces and it was even rumoured that Alf had a stock of condoms under the counter. Though, I couldn't possibly comment.

There were no other customers inside the shop when I got there, only Mrs. Hardy busying herself dusting the sand off her tins of peaches and baked beans on the stacked shelves. She twisted precariously on the rickety old steps as she saw me enter. I swear the woman had antenna in the back of her head.

'Dora,' she said, a genuine smile on her face. She was one of the very few people who, over the years, had earned the right to call me by my first name. 'I can't for the life of me fathom how the sand manages to get into every crack and crevice. I swear it comes up through the floorboards as well.'

'I know what you mean,' I commiserated. 'But I only bother clearing it up after we've had a stiff westerly, otherwise I'd be cleaning all day.'

Mrs. Hardy stepped nimbly down from the step-ladder and turned her attention to me, hitching up her wrap-around pinnie and settling her well padded bum on the edge of a high stool, ready for a chat. 'I noticed you had a visitation from The God Squad earlier on,' she said.

Nothing in the village passed Mrs. Hardy's notice. Gossip was the lifeblood of any village shop and she was an expert at winkling out the merest scrap. She was pleasant to everyone and kept her own views private, but if you wanted to know what was going on in a five-mile radius, Megan Hardy was your woman. The bottom of my lane was opposite the large front window of the shop, directly in her line of sight, and she would have seen Mrs. Henshaw driving up it to my house.

I smiled at the name. 'Did you give them that name or is that what they call themselves?' I asked.

Mrs. Hardy scoffed dismissively. 'They are far too much on their dignity that lot. No, it was Alf,' Megan answered. 'One of the things we Welsh are good at is giving nicknames to all and sundry. If you don't qualify for one, then you are just not worthy of being mentioned.'

'I remember when I was in Grammar School I felt so left out because I didn't have one – well not one that I knew about anyway,' I admitted. 'I'm sure Alf has one for me, but I won't embarrass you by asking what it is.'

Megan tapped the side of her nose and smiled. 'Best not to know, Dora. The only thing I will tell you is that it is not nasty and it shows you are a person who has definitely been noticed.'

I was intrigued, but took it no further. 'Well, I hope that was the first and last time I encounter The God Squad; nothing but a bunch of interfering busybodies,' I said firmly. 'But, down to business, Megan, I have got something to ask you. I was wondering whether you have any of those long strings of bunting with the colourful little flags on them. They were all around the village green (a major exaggeration if ever there was one) for the fete last year and I was wondering if you had any left over.'

A village shop gets many strange requests, and Mrs. Hardy did not flinch at mine. She narrowed her eyes, raised a finger to her lips and considered for a moment, mentally running through her extensive stock. 'You know, Dora, I think I do,' she said, triumph in her voice. 'If you'll mind the shop for me while I have a rummage in the back, I'm sure I can find what you want. Any preference as to colour?'

'No, I'm sure the chickens won't mind. Aren't they colour blind, anyway?'

Mrs. Hardy froze half way through the storeroom door. 'You're decorating the chicken coop now?' she asked incredulously, pencilled eyebrows rising to her hairline. She chuckled to herself. 'What's next? A crystal chandelier? Fairy lights?'

She set off without waiting for an answer while I hovered, self consciously, behind the counter praying that no-one would come in, as I had no idea how to use her computerized cash register.

A voice sounded from deep inside the storeroom. 'Those eggs of yours must be the most expensive ones in the whole of Wales, and your chickens amongst the most pampered!'

'Don't be daft, Megan. It's my latest deterrent to keep the buzzard away. He took Vera, my pretty little golden bantam last week.'

'More work than the worth of them, if you ask me,' the distant voice said. 'Ah ha! I knew they were here somewhere.'

Megan Hardy reappeared, dishevelled and flushed, a great jumble of brightly coloured plastic flags in her arms.

'How much will you want, gal?' she asked.

I hesitated. I had not thought out the details of my brilliant idea that far. Mrs. Hardy summed it up immediately. 'Take the lot and bring back what you don't need when you've done. We can settle up then.'

'Do you think it will work?' I asked, doubt starting to creep in.

'Only way is to try,' Mrs. Hardy said. 'Do you want my Adrian to come up and help?' Adrian Hardy was her thirty-seven year old son, six foot two, piercing blue eyes and gorgeous.

'Very kind of you, but I think I can manage,' I answered, my first reaction always being to assert my independence, though a visit from the delightful Adrian never went amiss. 'If I fail, I'll give you a ring.'

'What did The God Squad want?' Megan Harding asked. Her need to know the details must have been eating away at her all the time she'd been searching.

I laughed. 'They wanted me to join the bridge night. Me! I'll paint them a bridge, but I certainly am not going to try and play it as entertainment – with that lot! Thanks for this Megan. I hope it works, and maybe you are right. Once the last of my little chucks has passed on, I'll probably not get any more. I'd miss them though. They are something alive about the place.'

'You'll have to get yourself a cat, girl,'

'Never!'

I left the shop, wrestling with the bundle of flags which, even in the light breeze, threatened to break loose and take to the skies. The plastic was slippery; it was like trying to hold on to an armful of live eels. I suppose I should have asked her if she had any made from cotton, what with plastic being the current public enemy number one. Living above a beach and an estuary, there was always an abundance of plastic trash washed up with every tide and once a week, I joined a local clean-up group to scour the river banks and beach. I had done it for years, and we got on well together, though they were mostly much younger than me. I think they looked upon me as a rather sprightly if eccentric grandmother. Not surprisingly, I hadn't seen the likes of The God Squad there.

When I finally got the squirming bundle to the house, I

dumped them on the kitchen table where they slithered slowly onto the floor and finally came to rest. I made myself a reviving mug of Earl Grey and took it out to the front of the house and sat down on the wooden bench, bleached silver by sun and wind and old age.

The view was spectacular. Even after all this time, seeing it every day, I did not know of any to surpass it.

The headland on which my house was perched rose almost a hundred feet straight up from the beach, cark park and road below and gave me a panoramic coastal view. To the west, on the other side of the river estuary which cut into the flank of the Downs were the high dunes of the Merthyr Mawr Warren curving around the bay for miles toward the seaside town of Porthcawl, whose small iconic lighthouse stuck up like a needle to pierce the skyline. To the east, mile upon mile of limestone cliffs stretched into a hazy infinity, their edges being nibbled away more and more after every winter storm.

Of course there were penalties to pay for living on such a chunk of rock exposed as I was to the constant battering of the wind and the roaring westerly gales, but it was never, ever boring. No two days would be the same not even hour by hour. The colours and the light were constantly changing. Sometimes the sea could be a bruised purple with storm clouds lowering and brutal winds rattling the airborne sand against the windows like grapeshot. Or it could be sullen, sulking underneath a grey cold blanket of fog, the waves flattened as if coated in oil. Or it could be benignly beautiful like today with the sun shining warmly out of an azure sky and the sea playfully breaking onto the wet sand in sparkling little wavelets as the turning season slipped gently into spring.

I wondered if the boys had finally managed to play their game of football.

I wandered to the edge of the lawn and gazed down over the car park far below. More people had arrived to take advantage of such a clement day. I could make out the black dots of a few brave souls who were taking a paddle in the shallows, shoes and socks off for the first time that year. The water would have been freezing. Sometimes, when the weather was right, I would spend an hour watching the surfers and be amused by their antics but the sea was too flat today, and I must confess to often spying on the day-trippers through my binoculars. It was surprising what people did when they thought no-one was looking. Better than any telly.

Megan's talk of nicknames came back to me as I gazed down from my lofty perch onto the people below. I wondered what the locals did think of me – a batty old biddy, vegetating away all on her own, swearing at buzzards and talking to her chickens? I suspected the children of the village had me marked down as a witch, just as we had done in our time of any old woman who happened to live on her own. All of it was true of course (other than the witch bit) and I secretly revelled at this image of myself. I felt it gave me an air of mystery, of someone who could not be pigeonholed into any normal category, perhaps one of the last of an almost extinct breed of eccentrics. I thought of myself as enigmatic and mystical.

Nobody suspected the truth about me, and I fully intended it to remain that way. My life was nobody's business but mine and I think that perhaps over the years I had encouraged that image of the ancient Welsh recluse living on the top of some remote mountainside (or in my case a bluff on the edge of a seaside village but you can only stretch imagery so far) which was so much at the heart of the Welsh psyche. Only one person knew who I really was and she lived hundreds of miles away in a foreign land called London. My secrets were safe with her, but closer to home I gripped my secrets tightly to me like a child with a scrap of old blanket as a comforter. After this morning though, I was starting to wonder if I might have taken it too far and was being absorbed by my own creation.

I hauled myself to my feet. Next on the agenda was some lunch. Then I would lose myself for a couple of hours in the painting I had on the board. It had reached that easy stage where it was almost finished, just needing a couple of tweaks here and there. After that, perhaps I would play with my latest attempt at improving the fortifications around the hen house.

CHAPTER FIVE

Painting was one of those secret joys and I had dabbled in it since I was a small child.

Just after the war, there had been a shortage of everything and rationing had gone on until the early fifties. As children, we knew no different; after all, everybody was in the same boat and I remember a thriving 'swapsy' market amongst school friends for everything from comics (so well read they would be falling apart) to cotton reels and glass beads. The few children's books we managed to scrounge were illustrated with simple line drawings then but they were exquisitely done and, though I was no great reader at that age, I memorised all the pictures and could still remember some, even seventy years later. Occasionally there would be a coloured plate printed on shiny paper of a scene from a fairy story or the adventures of Aladdin or Robin Hood. We had so little colour in our lives then that they captivated me and I fell in love.

My mother had been scathing at my first attempts at colouring-in some of the illustrations. 'Do you think money grows on trees, child?' she had said snatching the book from my grasp. 'Have you so little respect for what your father and I give you that you can deface these books like this? I won't allow you to have them until you can prove to me that you can colour them in properly instead of scribbling over them any old shape. Only then will I let you have them back.' I was four years old!

In defiance I worked hard to improve my artistic skills and have continued painting as a hobby throughout my adult life. It had become my passion and my obsession. I read a quote in a novel once and I remembered it to this day. It was a story about an artist – Hogarth I think but I can't really recall the name of the author or the artist – *"The goaded servant of creative work."* I so understood that statement, then and now. To create something from nothing, something that is entirely born of your own inner vision and that is unique anywhere in the world, becomes a compulsion that does not diminish with the years or with fading eyesight.

People sometimes asked me why I hadn't gone to art school. I would fob them off with some lame excuse or other. But it wasn't that unusual then in the south Wales valleys; there was little spare cash to throw away and you had to be either very brainy or have parents who were loaded. These days youngsters expect to go to university or college as a rite-of-passage and feel hard done by if they can't go, but in my day it was the exception rather than the rule. It was just not done, but that wasn't the real reason.

I had put the suggestion out there to my parents after my art teacher in school had been going on and on at me. I had not had much in the way of expectation and I wasn't disappointed. My father had flown into a rage and my mother, taking her cue from him as always, had backed him up.

'You! An artist! Don't be daft, girl. You needn't think for one minute that I am going to shell out my hard earned cash so that you can go off for four years putting childish daubs of paint on paper and getting involved with boys and drugs. I know what goes on, my lady, I read the newspapers. It's disgraceful,' he shouted, angrily waving a finger in front of my nose. 'If anyone is going to go to university, it will be your brother, so that he can get a good job to support himself and his family. In my opinion it is a total waste of time educating girls beyond a minimum requirement. You only ever think about marriage and having babies anyway, and you don't need a college education for that! Women don't have the intelligence or the temperament to cope with anything more. A total waste of time!'

My mother bit her lip and said nothing. It was still many years away from any sort of women's lib.

'Art school, my eye! You can go and get yourself a proper job, in an office or something and start paying your mother and me back for all the years we have kept you.'

I remember my brother sniggering in the corner. I never asked again.

I had had to wait until my early retirement before I could

follow that dream. You may think I was not serious enough about my art or else I would have tried to make a living at it no matter what. But I was serious, and I became a lot more serious as the years went by, but I was also a coward. There was little or no money in art, especially in the Welsh valleys, unless you knew someone who also knew someone, and so on. I was not one of those *avant-garde* people who could live on lentils and wine and believed that the world was out there waiting to applaud me for my genius. I was a conventional soul and a pragmatist and liked my creature comforts. And I was a loner even then, and the Bohemian life is just plain ridiculous if you live it on your own.

But I learned my craft during those arid years and now I think I have earned the right to call myself an artist, even if it is only for my own pleasure. I have made a separate space in my home in which to paint. A more pretentious person would call it their studio but I think of it simply as my painting room. It was my sanctuary and my joy. Well, in reality it was a corner of one of my two spare bedrooms, which also doubled up as junk room, storage space, filing room, and library and just happened to be the place where I painted. It was cluttered and comfortable and I could leave all my work in place at the end of the day and just close the door on the mess. I sorted it out twice a year or sooner if my junk started to get out of hand and meet me at the door. There was a large window facing northwest with a panoramic view over the river and estuary and out towards the dunes and it gave me a constant clear north light. It also had the advantage of being too high up for me to get distracted by people-watching.

I settled comfortably into my second-hand typist's chair and started mixing some colour for the next part of the painting.

While I did so, I checked my inner calm. A quick assessment told me that I had put behind me the upsets of the morning and was able to concentrate fully on my painting. Sports people, I believe, called it 'being in the zone' and it was an absolutely necessity if I wasn't going to ruin all the work I had already put into the painting. It could happen so easily and I had learned by painful experience never to paint when I was upset or angry.

I was quietly pleased with the way my current painting was progressing. I had started it many days before and had been in two minds whether to use acrylics or watercolour. In the end I had plumped for acrylics. I wanted to illustrate a tidal rock pool, stitching together a dozen or more photographs I had taken over the years so that my super-pool would be jam-packed with different seaweeds and anemones, barnacles and shells and a miscellany of creatures. By using acrylics I could add extra bits as I went along – a starfish here, a shrimp there, maybe a tiny fish stranded by the tide – without having to work the whole composition out in advance. It needed to be full but not messy.

Acrylics allowed me more flexibility but it was not as good as watercolour for capturing very fine detail. *Horses for courses,* as they say. In the end I had decided to compromise by painting the rock pool in acrylics and, if I wasn't thoroughly bored with the whole subject by the end, I would do small extra watercolour studies of anything which had more interesting minute details. One of the disadvantages of using acrylic was that once the paint was squeezed out of the tube it would dry quickly and become waterproof. Even though I was using a wet pad, I was approaching the time limit before this latest palette of colours went into the bin. I needed to finish it soon.

'Well, Herman, old chap, it's time to finish making you a super star and then I can take you back home,' I said, addressing the hermit crab scuttling around in his plastic aquarium by the side of my work table.

It wouldn't have been fair to keep him for much longer despite his being housed in luxury accommodation, in sea water laboriously lugged up from the beach, and surrounded by rocks and seaweed and with a nice sandy bottom. I had been feeding him on gourmet scraps of defrosted king prawns and had named him Herman, as in Herman's Hermits, (you'll only understand the relevance of the name if you are of a certain age). But he needed to go home soon so that he and I could get on with the rest of our lives.

I only had the fine-tuning left to do on the ridges and striations of the whelk's shell inside which Herman currently lived. It was beautifully gnarly and covered in barnacles and with a tiny plume of red seaweed attached to the top, which I looked forward to working on. If I could finish it that afternoon, I could take him back home before the next high tide.

Barely an hour had gone bye and I was completely absorbed in my painting when the doorbell rang. I mouthed various unladylike expletives and tried to ignore it. It rang again. It was too late to be the postman who sometimes called for a buckshee cuppa at the end of his rounds and I wasn't expecting anyone else to call (not that I had been expecting The God Squad earlier!) and the days of having groceries delivered to the door had been relegated to ancient history, although the modern equivalent of on-line shopping meant it was making a comeback, but that only worked if you were on-line, which I most definitely was not. Casual callers, Jehovah's Witnesses or double glazing salesmen hardly ever puffed their way up the hill to my door and I hadn't heard the straining of a car engine. Whoever it was seemed to have got their finger jammed in the doorbell and it was impossible to ignore it any longer. I washed out my brushes and put the top back on to the wet tray, and stomped heavily downstairs.

'Alright, alright, I'm coming,' I shouted irritably.

On the doorstep was a girl I didn't recognize, though it was a bit difficult to tell whether I did or did not as her face was half hidden inside a grubby grey hoodie. She just stood there, silent and very still, as if she had used up all her energy on the doorbell and had nothing left in reserve. She hadn't even looked up when I had opened the door.

I waited for her to speak. Nothing. After another minute of silence I thought that if one of us didn't break the silence soon, we could both have been standing there at the dawn of the next millennium. 'Yes?' I asked. 'What do you want?'

I didn't think I had said it in a particularly threatening manner.

Abrupt maybe, but not aggressive by my standards, but the girl took a step back and looked up startled, almost afraid. I caught a brief glimpse of enormous dark eyes and a surly down-turned mouth. She mumbled something, which I didn't catch.

'I'm sorry, child, but I can't hear you. Could you speak up?'

She gave a long sigh of martyr-like proportions as only bored adolescents, especially girls, can carry off to perfection. Modern youngsters seemed to me to be constantly teetering on the edge of resentment with a world which only they were made to endure. But why I should be the recipient of such from a total stranger, I had no idea. She kicked languidly at a stone. She sniffed loudly. 'Have you got any jobs for me to do? Like, for money.'

Well, I must admit I liked straight talking and I couldn't fault the girl in that respect. I studied her more carefully but still couldn't penetrate the gloom of the hood. If she was doing bob-a-job (I had no idea whether they still did it) then the girl-guide movement must have fallen on savagely hard times. From the bit I could see of her face, which was extremely dirty, she was very young, perhaps only in her mid teens. She was as thin as a stick and her clothes, which I think were black with an overlay of dirt, were wrinkled and filthy. Strapped to her back was an equally dirty backpack, its original colour lost. She was tall, a good four inches above my squat five foot two and the rather pungent odour of a body that hadn't seen soap or water for many a day wafted off her.

I had no time for beggars or idlers who could be seen in increasing numbers on the streets even in our local small towns. They sat on grubby blankets with an emaciated dog on a lead and their hands held permanently outstretched. Most collected more in a day's begging than an old age pensioner got in a week and probably went home to a nice little council flat with a takeaway and a beer. The girl wasn't quite as bad as that I had to admit, as she had offered to work for any hand-out, but I didn't want anyone thinking of me as a soft touch. I was about to send her away, when Mrs. Henshaw's ghost tapped me on my shoulder. Damn the woman – was she becoming my second conscience now? All morning I had been raving about her holier-than-thou interference, her do-gooding and aggressive form of charity, but here I was, about to send this poor child from my doorstep with nothing more than a few sharp words. *What did that make me?* I thought ashamedly.

I was torn. One half of me felt sorry for the poor scrap (and I hoped I wasn't feeling that just to raise a finger at Mrs. bloody Henshaw) while the other half resounded with warning bells clanging silently in my head. Weren't we constantly being warned to be on our guard for anybody out to dupe us poor old age pensioners and separate us from our cash? And didn't we tend to look pityingly down on those who had succumbed, certain that we would never fall into such a trap? They were clever though, these scammers, and I, like the rest of the country, had had my quota on the telephone, but so far I had managed to escape being caught out. Beware scammers, cold callers and the great unwashed. Well, she certainly qualified for the last, but she looked as far removed from a professional scammer as I could imagine.

I had been dithering for so long that the girl had turned her back, a dejected slump to her thin shoulders, and she was walking away.

'Hang on a minute, lass. There is something you can help me with,' I said much to my surprise. 'I want to string some bunting over the top of the chicken coop, and you are just about the right height to help. How about it?'

I think the girl was as stunned to get a positive response as I was to have given one. She had probably knocked on every door in the village and I was her last resort. Well, I must have been to drag her all the way up the hill as there was nothing but rabbits beyond my house.

'Have you got any food?' she asked after another lengthy pause. She sniffed and dragged her filthy sleeve across her nose.

The words *Waifs and Strays* popped into my mind. When I was a kid, my brother and I were 'volunteered' every year to go around the houses selling little paper badges of yellow daisies in aid of

Waifs and Strays, but up until now I had never met one.

'Go around the back, and I'll fix you a sandwich,' I said, shutting the front door. I shook my head in amazement. It seemed that Mrs. Henshaw had got further under my skin than I had realized and here I was, a couple of hours later, acting totally out of character. Caution was my middle name and my dislike of strangers, especially teenagers, was legendary. I always felt they were mocking me and they made me feel old and inadequate. They lived lives so alien to anything I knew, and they spoke in a language, which I could make neither head nor tail of. I knew more Klingon than what came out of their mouths. For most of my life I had successfully managed to steer clear of them. And here I was, inviting one in for lunch!

I ushered her around the side of the house. 'What's your name, lass?'

'Jan,' she answered quietly.

'I'm afraid you are going to have to speak louder than that,' I said as we got to the outside seating area – two plastic garden chairs which were so old they were by now dangerously brittle and about to collapse. 'I'm afraid I'm a bit deaf without my hearing aids in. I don't wear them when I'm in the house, as I like the quiet. If I want to have an intelligent conversation or hear the birds singing or listen to the television, I suffered them.' *Why was I explaining myself to this stranger?*

'It's Jan,' the girl said, louder than before. 'Or Janine, if you want.'

'Good, that's fine. Now you wait here and I'll make you a sandwich. Tomato, cheese and lettuce do you?' The girl gave a slight nod. 'And would you like a cup of tea or a soft drink?'

'Tea, please.'

I gave her the sandwich and mug of tea, and took the other chair, placing it upwind of her while I tried to untangle the yards of bunting. The girl had pushed back her hood and I watched her out of the corner of my eye. Her dark hair was – I think the best description would be – chewed. This could have been a fashion statement, or on

34

the other hand she could have taken a blunt shears to it without the aid of a mirror. Beyond a polite 'thank you' for the food, she made no attempt at conversation, but sat completely fascinated by my three remaining chickens as they scratched around in their run. She shovelled the sandwich into her mouth without even looking at it and seemed surprised when it had all gone.

'Don't you let them out?' she asked in a hard flat voice, which had none of the inflections and cadence of the Anglo/Welsh. If anything, I would have said there was a hint of Cardiff or Barry.

'I do when I am out here to keep an eye on them,' I answered. 'But between the buzzard, the foxes and once I even had a grass snake taking the eggs, they like to have the security of their coop. That's what the flags are for, but no predators will come whilst there are people around.'

The girl continued to stare at them. I don't think I had ever seen such focussed attention before as if she was memorising every feather and tuft. I know I was biased, because they were pretty, my bantams, with their plumed heads and fluffy feet. The chickens ignored her.

'They can come out while we put up the bunting,' I said, finally separating the strings. 'They won't go far. The white fluffy one is Cilla; the lavender one with the feathered feet is Sandi and the one with the fluffy head and attitude is Shirley. They are all named after famous singers,' I explained.

Janine looked blankly at me. Way, way before her time! I didn't bother to clarify.

Working in almost total silence other than for a few brief instructions, it took us quite a while to get the flags all tied securely in a criss-cross pattern across the top of the wire run, but it did look quite festive by the time we had finished. I was quietly pleased but what the chickens would think of it was another matter. I had been so proud of my solution to give them 24/7 security, which did not involve me being a human windmill, that I hadn't considered the possibility that they might be terrified out of their wits by the bits of plastic fluttering manically above them. I called them in. They clucked warily at the edge of the gorse bushes – you may have gathered gorse was prolific on our sandy windswept coastline – and appeared to be completely underwhelmed by my efforts, even with a bribe of some extra corn and a chopped apple.

'I'll get them,' Janine said, suddenly as animated as if someone had flicked a switch. But instead of charging up the steps and scattering them to the four winds as I would have expected, she climbed the back steps slowly and crept towards the cowering chickens making comforting cooing noises in the back of her throat. The chucks looked balefully at her and finally, as if by some form of chicken telepathy, seemed to make a collective decision and sidled towards her. She scooped up all three of them and settled them into her arms. Without as much as a squawk or a ruffled feather, they allowed her to deposit them in the coop and pecked contentedly at their extra rations while she closed and latched the gate.

'Well done, lass,' I said. 'I couldn't have done better myself.'

She gave me a sour look, which spoke only of suspicion and a great weariness, which should not have been on the face of any child. She sniffed loudly and turned away.

'Just wait there, and I'll get you your money. How about some cake as well? I only baked it yesterday – banana and date.'

'Ta.'

She stuffed everything into her filthy backpack and walked off down the lane without another word. After she had gone, I realized that I knew no more about her than when she had arrived. If it hadn't been for the bunting snapping in the breeze, I could almost have believed that I had dreamt her up.

CHAPTER SIX

With all the physical activity, I knew I couldn't return to my painting as my hand would not have been steady enough for doing the remaining fine detail. I had already finished painting Herman, so I decided to use this unexpected free hour to return him to the sea and the remainder of the flags to Megan Hardy all in one go.

I popped Herman into a battered child's bucket which I had picked up on one of our group litter-picks, and stuffed the flags into an old plastic carrier bag – three times reused in case you are wondering – closed the back door and locked it. It was only as I got to my front gate that I heard the purr of a car coming up the steep lane towards my house. Not another visitor! Could the day get any weirder? I thought. I certainly wasn't in the mood for more people but there was nowhere to hide as whoever it was would have already seen me. So I stood and waited for the inevitable, like a condemned felon awaiting their sentence.

Go away world! I want some peace.

To my absolute horror, my brother stepped out of a gleaming dark blue BMW and strode through the front gate towards where I was standing. Come back, Mrs. Henshaw, all is forgiven, I muttered under my breath.

'Hello, Dora. Long time no see,' he said with a forced attempt at cheeriness.

I was in a state of shock. It must have been at least ten years since we had last met and before that I could count on one hand the number of times he had deigned to visit me since I had moved in, over twenty years before. They had been quite enough and I had never wanted more.

'Every agonizing moment of our last encounter is still engrained on my soul, James,' I answered. 'If you need reminding, the last time we met was at your home after we had had mother cremated. Helen served cups of weak Typhoo tea and fish paste sandwiches to the few of us who felt obliged to attend the wake at your house.'

I thought for a moment he was going to keel over. His usual grey colourless skin had flushed an unhealthy purple like a cuttlefish flashing out a warning colour code.

'How dare you, Dora! As always when you try to take a swipe at me, you end up making yourself look ridiculous. It just goes to show your total lack of a refined palate when you cannot tell the difference between common fish paste and *cordon bleu* salmon paté from Giovanni's delicatessen in Cardiff, or builder's tea from Earl Grey Special Blend. I had hoped that as you had aged you would have gained some wisdom and just a touch of finesse, but it appears I was wrong. You have gone backwards: you have let yourself go.'

I smirked at his attempt to belittle me. At one time, long ago, it would have reduced me to tears and chronic self doubt, but it had lost its sting decades ago. 'You haven't the slightest idea who I am, thank God!' I muttered under my breath. 'But, enough of these pleasantries. Why are you here, James? Have the little green men invaded from Mars or perhaps you need a kidney transplant and were hoping for one of mine? Because I can tell you now, you can't have one.''

'You do talk such drivel, Dora,' he replied with a brittle smile.

'Then, for the love of god, what is it that you want?' I asked snappily.

He laughed humourlessly. I think the comedy gene had been mislaid when my brother's DNA had been compiled. I don't ever remember him, in all our childhood together, having a good honest laugh. 'Really, Dora, can't a person visit his sister without an ulterior motive?' he replied with a lame attempt at looking affronted.

'If the "person" is you and the "sister" is me, then the answer is no,' I said. 'We do not socialize. We do not talk on the telephone, and we do not ask or care about each other's health. The obligatory Christmas card once a year and the cost of the stamp are about as far as I am willing to go to acknowledge any blood ties between us. So, once again, what do you want, James?'

His face darkened for a moment with a rising temper, which he tried to hide but which only make him look like a rebellious child whose new toy had been taken away from him. It was rare for my brother to attempt to communicate politely, especially to women. I had always thought he was a man born out of his time. He should have lived back in Victorian days or earlier when he could have been the squire of a small manor where every man would doff his hat to him and no woman would ever have had the temerity to answer him back.

'Tongue still as sharp as cut glass, Dora,' he sneered. 'If you are not careful…'

'…I'll cut myself,' I finished for him, wearily. 'And that wisecrack hasn't changed since you were eight years old either. Well, what do you expect? Who wouldn't be suspicious at this sudden appearance after years of mutual acrimony and total indifference? Now, for pity's sake spit it out. I want to catch Mrs. Hardy before she closes.'

All the calm I had managed to achieve after the morning's confrontations had deserted me and my loathing for my brother had gathered into a pain in my nether regions, like trapped wind.

A nerve twitched at the side of his eye while he thought up a response. He resorted to his usual arrogant bluster. 'If you'd stop sniping at me for just one minute, I will,' he answered.

'I am sorry, James,' I said with total insincerity, 'but you do bring out the best in me.'

He took a deep breath and attempted to dredge up a smile but his mouth did not seem to recognise the concept and failed miserably. 'I don't see why we have to discuss our business on the doorstep as if I were some brush salesman. How about a cup of tea?' he asked. It came out more as a demand than a request.

'To be honest, I would be more likely to invite in the brush salesman than you, James,' I said.

But he had planted his feet firmly on my doorstep and was not for moving.

There was definitely something up. James was not a man for prevarication, but here he was, cane in hand beating his way around the proverbial bush.

I capitulated. 'Oh, alright, you can come in, but as I've told you, I am going out. There's no time for tea,' I said and reluctantly let him in through the front door. I put the bucket containing a disgruntled Herman down on the doorstep (admittedly it was hard to tell his facial expression as he had withdrawn into his shell – sensible crab!). James cast a withering look in his direction and then entered without a word. He had always chosen his battles carefully and when they could do the most damage but from long experience I had learned that I could avoid a serious tongue-lashing if I went on the offensive as soon as possible, thereby pre-empting any attack from him. 'Should the occasion ever rise again, you need to ring before you come, otherwise I might not be in at all and you'll have wasted all that petrol and increased your carbon footprint for nothing. I'm sure that monstrosity of a car must drink petrol, especially on short journeys.'

We lived six miles and a universe apart.

James snorted. 'I need a big car for my height,' he huffed. 'And I am always prudent with petrol consumption. I only use it for essential journeys, especially in out-of-the-way places where there is no public transport.'

I was five miles away from a busy town!

'We have a bus twice a day, James, and you could have saved even more by using your Bus Pass, though you probably wouldn't recognize a modern bus even if it ran over you.'

'Wishful thinking, sister dear?' he said with a sneer. 'Once again, you are wrong. I caught the bus into town only last week.'

'Car in being serviced, was it?'

He glowered at me as my guess scored a direct hit. He barged his way into the living room and stood there, hands on his hips, scanning the room for something to criticise. His nostrils flared with distaste at what he saw, which gave me a little tingle of malicious delight. I still hadn't got around to clearing away the cups and biscuits from the morning, the ironing had finally tumbled off the table onto the floor and the settee seats still held the imprint of Mrs. Jenkins' ample behind. James had always been fastidiously tidy, even as a boy.

He used to throw a tizzy if the vegetables on his plate were not properly separated. As he had got older, he had got worse. His books were all aligned and colour co-ordinated, pencils in a row, carpets straight, tea cups matching, and trousers pressed to a knife edge every morning after a night under the mattress, and that was as a teenager! These days he would be diagnosed with some posh-sounding medical disorder but when we were children he was called anally retentive (only put less politely) and a weirdo. He had always demanded constant attention and admiration and expected people to obey his slightest whim. My parents had obeyed; I had not. Needless to say, he had never had any friends.

'You could take some tips from my Helen,' he said, eventually sitting down. I was surprised he didn't take out a handkerchief and dust the seat first. Perhaps he was mellowing with old age. 'She may have her faults, but she is an efficient housekeeper and an excellent cook.'

'You are talking about your wife here, not the hired help!' I answered sharply. Helen Cummings was a timid, nervous lady, who jumped to obey my brother's every wish. When they had first married, I had had high hopes for her but he had finally worn her down and she had long ago lost the ability to think for herself. She had become a nothing person whose only purpose in life was to serve my brother. Poor Helen. I did feel sorry for her, sometimes.

'Don't be facetious, Dora. Is it surprising I don't visit more often when this is the reception I get?' His moustache, which I swear he trimmed with the aid of a ruler, quivered with indignation.

'I'm glad you get the message,' I answered shortly. I was growing bored with sniping at him and hadn't the energy to fight any more: I had had enough for one day, and I knew that as neither of us would give ground, it could go on for ever.

'So, let's just get this charade over with. You want something, so for God's sake tell me what it is. Neither of us have so many years left that we can afford to waste them waiting for you to come to the point. So hurry up and then I can get on with my day – come to think of it, I do need to clean the toilet.'

He silently chewed around the possibility of storming out in an almighty huff, but whatever it was he had come for was important enough to keep him seated. Despite myself, I was becoming intrigued, and his next words caught me completely by surprise. 'I want to borrow mother's old photograph albums, if you haven't chucked them out already,' he said tersely. I could see it was like fire on his skin to have to ask me for anything. I wondered idly how many weeks or months it had taken him to work himself up to this visit. 'I need them to include in the book I am writing of the family's history. I have plans to get it published one day.'

A snort of laughter escaped my lips before I could stop it. 'Published!' I burst out. 'Who on this benighted planet would be interested in our family? You have to be either famous – or infamous – to get anything published these days, and our family is neither; unless you were thinking of becoming a mass murderer, child molester or killing Helen off, burying her body in amongst the petunias and marrying a member of the royal family – which in our age group would have to be Her Maj? Confessions of one kind or another seem to be all the rage these days.

Livid spots of colour had risen to his cheeks. 'You can be so crass, Dora. And you are once again showing your total ignorance of anything going on in the real world,' he snapped back. 'Today it is an easy matter to self-publish. Anyone can do it – except those who are still in the dark ages scratching away with a quill pen and rolls of parchment like you. I feel it is my duty to devote my time to recording our family history otherwise the stories, which have made us who we are will be lost forever. It is a moral obligation as well as a labour of love and I am well advanced with the research but I need to have the photographs in order to illustrate it.'

'Self publishing is nothing new, James, it used to be called "vanity publishing" in my younger days,' I answered. 'And even if you do spend a fortune on producing something, I still don't think anybody would be in the least bit interested in reading about the tedious minutiae of our lives.' *Especially told from your narrow-minded point of view, I thought but did not say.*

Had my parents been alive, no doubt they would have stumped up the necessary cash and applauded his efforts from the highest roof-tops. James was two years older than me and had been much loved by our parents, in whose opinion he could never do any wrong. He was the son they had wanted and I was the mistake, as they so often reminded me. I was swept into the background and made to feel that I owed them for being such an unnecessary encumbrance in their lives. But they had both passed away and our family had never been a prolific one – a distant cousin or two, twice or three times removed. I doubted if anyone with even a thimbleful of Cummings blood in their veins would be daft enough to fork out real money just to see their names in print.

'I don't really care what you think, Dora,' he huffed. 'Tiffany would definitely be interested.'

Now, that would surprise me, I thought. Tiffany was his only child. She was a lovely girl in her mid forties, the child they had given up hope of ever having. But she had escaped from the smothering tensions of her parental home as soon as she had been legally able and she had lived the cliché and ran away to London where she had made a success of her life. Though her father and I had been estranged since our teens, she had never held it against me and we had always kept in touch. As she had got older, we often had long conversations on the telephone. To hear us you would think we were a very close mother and daughter. She had even stayed with me on a number of occasions, and especially when she had had to come down for her annual Christmas visit to her parents. Dutiful daughter she was, but she could only take so much of her mother's neediness and her father's pomposity and by Boxing Day she would be ready to flee, blaming pressure of work for having to leave so early when in fact, she would come here for a day or so and stay in the little self-contained annex tacked on to the side of my house. She and I would spend the evenings sitting on the settee, gazing out at the sea and the sunset, a bottle of wine beside us, and we would set the world to rights. Her father knew nothing of our closeness. Neither did he know that Tiffany was married to a beautiful Italian girl, Gina, and they had been together for nearly four years. He would never have recovered from the shock.

'The photographs?' James asked in an exasperated voice, which dragged me back from my wool gathering.

'Stay there, I'll get them.'

The old albums were somewhere in my painting room, and it took me less than ten minutes of rummaging through the clutter to find them. The room may have looked chaotic to an outsider, but there was a degree of method and order to it and though I hadn't looked at them for donkey's years, they were almost exactly where I thought they would be, once I had moved everything else out of the way.

As I carried them downstairs I could hear James ranting down below. I couldn't make out a word of what he was saying, but he seemed to be quite content to continue his argument with himself. At least that way he would be getting the answers he wanted, I thought.

'I've put them in a bag for you,' I said breezing into the sitting room. It was empty.

His voice thundered from the kitchen. 'Have you completely lost your senses, woman? Now I know that it is time you were certified, for your own good. First you play with buckets and spades, in public, at your age, and now this!' he shouted. 'You've turned this house into Porthcawl fairground and yourself into a laughing stock, woman!'

He was glaring out of the kitchen window as the freshening breeze made the bunting flap playfully above the chicken coop. The red temper patches on his cheeks had spread over the rest of his face which was turning a rather alarming puce colour, or to be more exact, rose madder with a hint of Schminke brilliant purple.

'As you very well know, James, I have given no explanation for having a child's sand bucket, but as usual, you cannot resist embroidering the facts. In actual fact, I was taking my hermit crab for a walk. And since it is only myself, the buzzard and the chickens who can see the bunting, I really do think you are blowing everything out of proportion,' I said. I cocked my head on one side and put my finger to my lips as if I was studying the coop, just to annoy him, you understand. 'I really do think that they add a touch of panache to what is otherwise a rather mundane feature.'

James' eyes were bulging, and I did think for a moment that I may have pushed him too far. I was getting too tired to fight our childhood battles any more, but James seemed to have other ideas. He turned away from the window, oblivious to the unruly state of my kitchen, and marched back into the sitting room.

'And, what's more, Dora, who was that scruffy individual I saw leaving your house when I arrived? She looked as if she had been dredged out of the bottom of some ditch. It's typical of you to encourage shiftless strays off the street. Don't you realize, you stupid woman, that people like that target vulnerable people living on their own, and here you are inviting them in! Why don't you just package up your silverware and leave it on the doorstep for them? You have always been so naïve but I thought in your old age you might have learned some sense. Once again, it seems I was wrong.'

I didn't think I had ever been called naïve before. I knew that he meant it as an insult, which was how I took it. It was only later when I had time to think about the conversation that I realized he and the girl could not have crossed paths. She was long gone before he had turned up on the doorstep. The only explanation could be that he had been parked at the bottom of the lane for ages before he found the courage to come up to the house. *Did I scare him that much?* I wondered. Oh, goodie.

'I am not answerable to you for how I order my life, James. And anyway, you know very well that I have no "silverware" as you took everything of value when you cleared out mam and dad's house. I was glad really, as it's such a pain to have to clean it all the time, but then dear Helen is so house-proud, isn't she?' I answered, evenly and calmly. I opened the front door and picked up the bucket and the bag of flags. 'Now, you've got what you wanted and I have things to do.

Perhaps you could return the albums eventually – anytime in the next millennia would be fine.'

He left, muttering under his breath. I closed the door behind him. I looked down at the crab scuttling unhappily in the bottom of the bucket. 'Sorry, old boy, but I'm too exhausted to take you home. And Mrs. Hardy will have closed up by now as well. I promise I'll take you tomorrow morning. How about a whole prawn for your supper?'

Now I was talking to a crab! Chickens, yes; crab, no. Which only went to show how rattled I was by the whole confounded day. I was feeling every minute of my seventy-four years. I needed a drink and some chocolate, in that order. It couldn't get much worse, could it?

Within twenty-four hours, I would come to regret having had that thought, even in the privacy of my own mind.

CHAPTER SEVEN

In a slight alcoholic haze I crawled up to bed just as the last of the light faded out of the distant horizon. I had hoped that the sherry would have dulled the nauseous churning in my stomach and the fizzing in my brain but it hadn't worked. Today had thoroughly upset me. I couldn't remember the last time I had felt so utterly out of kilter and I was struggling to cope with it.

I stared at my image in the bathroom mirror, my mouth rimmed with white froth as I scrubbed uselessly at my yellowing teeth – no matter what the adverts said, they still hadn't invented a toothpaste that could reverse the ageing process and return them to gleaming white gnashers. Not that they had ever been that good in the first place. I stared at the image that stared blearily back at me. The light caught the hairs sprouting on my chin. I needed to see to them before I morphed into the bearded lady. I sighed. It was just another of the indignities of old age that one's hair thinned on top and in areas where it should have been and sprouted happily in one's nostrils and on one's chin. At least I hadn't been burdened with the problems of incontinence – yet!

'Who are you, Dora Cummings?' I asked my reflection. 'I don't recognise you any more. You sort of look like me, I think, but I'm not even sure about that any more.'

I had thought I knew myself well, both inside and out. I prided myself that unlike many people I had always been completely honest with myself, warts and all. *To thine own self be true* – and all that. But the person I thought I knew had disappeared overnight and left behind this stranger who was staring back at me with a puzzled expression on her face. It wasn't the physical appearance that bothered me: I had never been vain. I rarely looked in the mirror especially now in my more mature years – I mean really, really looked. I was old and I knew I was old. So what? I didn't need a mirror to remind me and my reasoning was that if I couldn't see myself, then I could happily create my own image of myself, like a child who puts a paper bag over their head and thinks nobody can see him. My fantasy version would not look as if it had been moulded of melted candle wax, scored through with creases and wrinkles and with dark smudges under the eyes, which became positively panda-like when I was really tired. I had been prettyish once, when the jaw-line was taut and the skin was young and fresh. My blue-grey eyes had perhaps been my best feature, but they were too deeply set to ever be described as beautiful. By avoiding mirrors or any such reflective surfaces, I could retain the illusion of just a smidgeon of my younger self and be contented in my ignorance.

It was easy to hide from one's outer self, but impossible to get away from what was inside.

There was no way I could ignore the inner stranger who had appeared during the past twelve hours. It was not somebody I recognized. Where had she come from? Why? What had shaken my usual calm to create such a nasty, mean-spirited person? It was so unlike me, wasn't it? What had triggered it? The only thing that had changed that day was the unprecedented influx of people who had swept like a flood-tide to my door. Compared to my usual smattering of visitors, which could be counted on one hand per month, I had been fairly inundated with them. And I had not handled any of them well.

I was appalled by the sheer spite, which had surfaced inside me, starting with Mrs. Henshaw, a woman I had never even met before. (The buzzard didn't really count as he was a regular visitor and was way ahead of me on points.) I had taken an instant dislike to her and her minions and hadn't hesitated to show it. I had been sharp-tongued and dismissive of her good intentions. She hadn't deserved that.

The boys at the car park I felt I had treated relatively well in the circumstances. After all, they had knocked me over and if I had fallen on anything harder than sand I could have done some serious injury to my brittle old bones.

And the girl? Well, nothing much in all honesty. She had come and gone, leaving nothing more behind her than a half a dozen words and the stale whiff of an unwashed body.

Then there had been the crowning glory – my brother. I had held nothing back from the moment I had clapped eyes on him and had laid into him with a-vengeance. I had been brutal and spiteful, sarcastic and mocking, all the things that I had always accused him of being and had prided myself in being so much better, a superior person in every way.

My God! I was turning into my brother!

But why on earth had I suddenly felt the need to launch myself at him as if the past seventy-odd years had never existed and we were back in our childhood, fighting our endless battles? He had absolutely no part in my life now, yet within an instant it had all burst to the surface like a volcano erupting. I had lost control – and over what? A request to borrow old albums I hadn't looked at for decades!

I knew I would never get to sleep with my insides all churned up, so I went back downstairs and made myself a mug of Horlicks and wrapped myself inside an old blanket I kept to cover my feet when watching television. I didn't put on any lights; there was sufficient coming from a thin sliver of moon, and the unpolluted starlight casting its own soft silver glow.

I was disgusted with myself. This was not the Dora Cummings I thought I knew. It felt as if I had been possessed by some parasitic creature who had been slowly eating away in secret at the person I had so carefully spent my life crafting. I had always thought of myself as calm and collected, able to be at one with the world around me while not needing anyone else. I was the centre of my universe, safe in my own little spaceship and had never felt the need to open the airlock to the outside. It was not a conventional life, but I was comfortable with it, happy and fulfilled. It had suited me and I had spent the past fifty years quietly being me.

I sipped my Horlicks and gazed out at the stars. Had I got it so very wrong? Over the years I had enjoyed a deep contentment with the way my life had progressed since retirement. It had more or less followed the course I had planned and up until now things had worked out far better than I could ever have dreamt of. I suppose it was because I had not expected anything significant to happen beyond my own enjoyment, so I had been pleasantly surprised when it had. Anyone who believed that the world owed them success in life was destined for major disappointment and depression. I think in many ways that was my brother's problem. He had always had an elevated sense of his own worth, even as a child, and constantly needed someone to be pandering to him and polishing his ego. First our parents and, when they had died, Helen had taken on the role. He had never amounted to anything special. He had risen slowly in the managerial ranks of the N.C.B. offices and had retired before the entire mining industry had collapsed in the eighties. But retirement had been such a shock for him. In one fell swoop all his little empire and status had disappeared and there had been nothing but poor Helen to take its place. It had made him resentful and envious.

I had no such excuse. I had done what I had wanted to do and didn't want to change one little thing. I neither expected nor sought other people's approval or disapproval. I had worked out what I wanted out of life and had worked hard towards those goals.

My mind drifted back to my younger self. There hadn't been many options open to me. I had seven mediocre 'O' levels in subjects I would never ever need again and had done a year afterwards in a technical college gaining good speeds in shorthand and typing. In those days – the sixties – the main choices for girls were either factory work, working in a bank, as a nurse, behind the counter in Woolies or in an office. I had done enough factory work during school holidays to know that I would never be able to stick it; blood made me feel faint; my brain turned to jelly at the mere thought of numbers, and the humiliation of working on the sweet counter at Woolworths propelled me towards the only alternative left - life in an office. With my qualifications I got a job as a civilian with the South Wales Police. It offered a guaranteed pension and endless boredom. But besides learning my trade, I learned also to be self reliant, and to ignore the straying hands, filthy language and sexual harassment from the police officers with whom I worked, men and women. In those days there was no opportunity to complain. Civilian staff were the lowest of the low and if you played awkward, you would be out on your ear. Life was very different in the seventies and eighties.

I had left home immediately I got the job, which was one of my better decisions. My colleagues spent their salaries on foreign holidays, fashionable clothes, jewellery and nights out. I put mine into investments and savings and even managed to get a mortgage on a little semi-detached house on a new housing estate. Everyone thought I was mad. I had never seemed to have the same hunger as my friends for boyfriends and weddings and children. I guess I was blessed with a low libido and certainly nobody ever came along to sweep me off my feet and persuade me to change course. I tried the usual dating game but mostly I got bored with the available men. I would hold the prospect of a future with them up against my own plans for myself and always found them lacking. I knew I could never spend my life with any one of them, no matter how secure that life would be. They seldom lasted more than a couple of weeks. I wanted nothing less than total freedom to do and be whatever I wanted.

And I had achieved it. And it was marvellous.

Current indications were that I may have taken it too far. This cantankerous old crone had deftly and insidiously slipped into me when I hadn't been looking and the worst thing was that I hadn't even noticed. Until now. Mrs. bloody Henshaw had been right!

So, that couldn't have been the reason for my bad temper either.

There was only one other reason, which might have contributed in part to my uneasy mind. The proverbial elephant in the room, one might say. My mind shied away from it even now in the wee small hours of the morning when I was trying so hard to understand why I seemed to have lost myself. I shuddered at the thought and banished it firmly to the back of my mind – again. I had a few days' grace yet.

Change was coming whether I liked it or not. If I could be this upset by a few unexpected visitors, then I needed to give myself a stiff talking to: pull up my socks: gird up my loins: stiffen the sinews and all that stuff. I had nobody else to lean on which was entirely my own choice – so deal with it, Dora Cummings. Sort yourself out.

CHAPTER EIGHT

I awoke feeling refreshed, renewed. My soul-searching of the evening before had cleansed my soul and I was raring to go.

I peeked through the bedroom window. The sun was rather brittle and out to sea there was a suspicious haze sitting on the horizon, blotting out the distant hills of Exmoor across the other side of the Bristol Channel. It was not a good sign, not this early in the year.

I fed the chickens and made myself a mug of Earl Grey and a bowl of my own mix of muesli, sprinkled with a generous handful of blueberries and raspberries on top. I tried not to think of the air miles and carbon footprint for these out-of-season pieces of fruit; I was feeling in too good a mood to burden myself with global angst this early in the morning. As I ate, I planned my day ahead. I wanted to do all the things I had failed to do the previous day and looked forward to a serious dose of normality.

I put on a warm sweater and an old pair of jeans. If that mist did come inland, I knew from experience that it would be as cold as if I was standing inside a refrigerator. But for now the sun was shining and I wanted to take advantage of it.

Once again I transferred the much-travelled Herman into his bucket and scooped up the bag of flags. As an after-thought I grabbed my sketching satchel, which I always kept by the back door, ready packed. If I was lucky, I would have the chance of a good walk across the cliff-tops before the mist rolled in.

I wandered down to the main road. Alf Hardy was manning the shop that morning.

'Morning Dora,' he said cheerfully. 'The wife said you had nothing but visitors all day yesterday; even a male visitor in a swish BMW. Got yourself a fancy man have you? And there was me thinking I had a chance.'

He was as big a gossip as Megan, but they were always quite open about it, nothing behind your back or malicious. I suspected they were also very good at keeping a secret, if asked.

'You can tell Megan she won't be seeing him again in a very long while,' I answered with a laugh. 'It was my brother, and we do not like each other. So, maybe you are still in the running Alf, once you get rid of Megan that is. Mind you, these days I don't think I'd have the energy anyway – rather read the Echo with a mug of cocoa.'

I paid what I owed for the flags and set off for the beach to return Herman to his home. The tide was just on the turn and the rock pools were full to the brim.

I found a large one and slipped Herman in, with a word of thanks for being such a patient model. To take his place, I found a pretty little starfish and an interesting cluster of mussels, their blue-brown shells studded with tiny barnacles, which would keep me happily occupied for the rest of the day. I knew just where to place them in the painting.

I wasn't going to carry the bucket with me on my walk, so I tucked it inside a stand of gorse scrub so I could collect it on the way back. Hopefully I would remember which gorse bush it was under!

I had it in my mind to wander over to the little quarry, which had been gouged out of the top of the cliffs about half a mile away. It used to be a magnet for fossil hunters. Most of the high cliffs in the area were made of crumbling carboniferous limestone, which rose up in towering layers like slabs of golden shortbread and were lethal. Every year more great chunks fell away but people would insist on scrambling over any falls of rock in search of spectacular finds, oblivious to the precarious layers perched above their heads. The little quarry was a much safer bet. I had my own modest collection of ammonites and shells and devil's toenails edging my flower borders. My best fossil was a perfect imprint of a feathery coral set in a slab of limestone almost a foot in height and which stood against the wall beside my front door.

I thought it was high time I recorded the place for posterity. I could include my own fossil collection in the painting along with any others I could beg or borrow and I had the advantage of not having to work at lightning speed because they were most certainly not live or perishable goods; they would probably hang on for another few million years. I could use the quarry itself as a back-drop to the paintings of the individual fossils. It was an easy walk across the short turf, but I hadn't been there for ages and it took me a while searching through the overgrown scrub of brambles and bracken, hawthorn and elder – and of course, gorse – before I finally found the entrance.

The light inside was perfect, slanting down in a great wedge to illuminate the back wall while plunging the rest into fascinating purple and blue shadows. I picked my way carefully through the detritus of used needles, glue sniffing canisters, crushed beer cans and used condoms to reach a suitable slab of rock on which to perch. I snapped a load of reference photographs from various angles so that I could choose the best for the painting, but there was nothing to beat a quick sketch or painting to cement the scene firmly in the mind. I would use the photographs as an *aide-mémoir* when I came to the final composition.

I became absorbed in sketching. It was almost totally silent inside this secret place except for the distant boom and shudder as the waves crashed into the cliffs below, and up above me a stonechat scolded me with a harsh *tsak-tsak.* It did fleetingly occur to me that this was not the most sensible place for an old age pensioner to be sitting alone and unseen. I sketched faster.

I nearly jumped out of my skin when the quiet was shattered by stones rattling down behind me. 'What you doing?' a voice asked.

I clutched my heart and waited for the pounding to calm. 'You nearly gave me a heart attack!' I said sharply as a boy, no more than seven or eight, clattered over the rubble. 'Be careful where you put your feet. There are all sorts of dangerous things littering the ground.'

'Didn't mean to scare you, miss. Didn't know anyone was here,' he answered, taking no notice of my warning and leaping sure-footed over the cluttered ground. He looked over my shoulder at what I was doing. 'Can I have a look?'

I gave him a quick appraisal for threat level. He was rake thin, with skinned knees and a thin grubby face, which was already starting to show some summer freckles. His fair hair had been cropped so short, he looked almost bald. Threat level low, I decided. He was just nosy.

I patted the rock next to me. Strangely enough, I felt safer with this two-pint scrap as my companion. I explained that I was drawing the little quarry.

'Why? There's nothing here 'cept rubbish.'

'Today's rubbish, tomorrow's treasures.' I explained about the fossils. 'They are the image left behind from creatures which lived and died here millions and millions of years ago, when all of this land was actually under the sea.'

The boy's eyes grew as large as saucers as it sunk in what I had said. He screwed up his face and gave me a suspicious look. 'You're having me on; the sea don't come up this high even after a storm.'

I gave him a smile and carried on sketching. 'This was in a time long before the dinosaurs, when the only life on earth was under the sea, which covered most of the planet. If you look carefully, you might be able to find a fossil or two amongst the rocks at the back. Sometimes you have to smash a rock open to find them.' He looked sceptical. 'Try bashing one down against the edge of another one so they split open. You may find ammonites or shells. They look like this,' I said as I did a quick sketch in the corner of the page.

While I continued with my sketching, the boy warily approached some of the smaller rocks. He started tentatively and then seemed to enter into the spirit of it and crashed stones into each other with great enthusiasm, chunks flying off at all angles. I had probably infringed untold reams of health and safety regulations by suggesting it to him, but you only get one childhood.

'There's nothing here, miss,' he said sullenly after a few energetic minutes.

I started packing my things away. 'Oh, they won't appear just like that. You have to remember they have been hiding in these rocks for a very, very long time. You have to persevere. One will find you when you've worked hard enough for it.'

Kids these days wanted everything now.

As I turned to leave, the sun caught the back wall of rock at an interesting angle and I took a quick photograph.

'Will you take my photo, miss?' the boy asked.

Cheeky monkey, I thought, but he was rather an engaging lad enthusiastically smashing away at the rocks, his face intent with concentration least his promised prize escaped.

'Okay, but keep still,' I said.

He struck an arrogant pose on top of a small pile of rubble, a rock in each hand and a broad grin on his face. Only the future would know if this moment would lead him on to other things – perhaps he would be the next David Attenborough – or maybe he would simply remember a fleeting moment on a sunny morning grubbing for fossils. This was the sort of brief encounter I preferred for any social interactions: a pleasant exchange without any obligation or confrontation. Yesterday's mayhem had been an aberration.

'When I eventually get these developed, I will leave yours with Mrs. Hardy down at the shop. It won't be for a few days though, so don't go bothering her all the time.' I may have been trying to become a friendlier and more benevolent me, but there was no sense in letting him know where I lived so that he could trash the garden or nick my own fossils. Rome wasn't built in a day, you know.

'Ta, miss,' he said and returned to his rock pile. I was forgotten.

I waved him goodbye and headed home. It was only when I was retrieving my bucket that I realized I didn't know the lad's name but undoubtedly Megan Hardy would recognize him and could probably recite his lineage going back three or four generations.

The day was shaping up very well. The real Dora Cummings was back.

CHAPTER NINE

I watched the sea mist roll closer to the shore, filtering out the warmth from the sun. As long as it didn't get too thick, I would still have good enough light in which to work, but there was no time to lose. I hurried up the front path to my house and for some strange reason I felt compelled to look down into the car park below. Some cars were starting to leave as the mist slithered closer, but other people still hung around the hot dog van and the ice cream kiosk. Someone caught my eye and though my long sight wasn't as good as it used to be, I could have sworn that one of those people was the girl who had visited me the day before. It was quite a long distance off, but she appeared to be begging off people in the queue, but I could have been wrong.

I shrugged and went into the house. *It's not your problem*, I told myself. *Keep your nose out of it*. Today, once I had painted in the starfish and mussels, I would have finished the picture. Any smaller illustrations I decided to paint of the more detailed items could be added at any time using my copious study worksheets but the major illustration for the seashore section of my work would be completed. It had been a delightful project.

I settled myself down in my painting room, away from any distractions, and lost myself in my miniature underwater world. Since retirement, painting had become one of my main passions and I had made a serious commitment to myself many years before to paint the flora and fauna of the area surrounding my home. It had slowly but inexorably taken over a great chunk of my life. The scope of my interest had expanded enormously, and now covered an area which started at the sea's edge, up the shoreline and the headland and the sandy downs beyond, before following the river inland past the ruined Norman castle and up to the edge of the town, five miles away. I had also got seduced by the terrain on the other side of the river, where the sand dunes stretched for miles and boasted one of the highest dunes in Europe. There was such a wide variety of dune plants that it had been designated a SSI with rare protected orchids flourishing in the slacks, and the place was alive with birds and animals. The area was for the most part untouched and unnoticed as few people ventured that far out. I doubted I would be able to do more than record a tiny fraction of what was there before global warming changed it forever or I was ready for my coffin, whichever came the sooner. The task was enormous. The more I looked, the more I found, and sometimes I doubted the wisdom of having started such a massive body of work. But I was never a person to wallow in "what ifs". I would do as much as I possibly could, and that would have to suffice.

I had had no expectations of my paintings being of any worth after my day, but rather than let them be tossed into a skip, I had left the whole collection to the National Museum in Cardiff in my will, whether they wanted them or not. My enjoyment was in trying to render everything as accurately as I could, to capture their image for one fleeting moment in time before they and I were gone forever. Perhaps the paintings would give us both, Herman and I and all the rest, a kind of immortality, but then none of us would be around to check.

In complete ignorance of the fact that this would be the last day of my freedom, I settled into my chair and started painting. Behind me, I played a CD of mellow classical music. I knew the melodies so well that, though comforting, they did not intrude upon my concentration and I became lost in an oasis of calm. Don't get me wrong. I enjoy loud stirring music, but in the past it had led to some disastrous mistakes coming out of the other end of my paintbrush, so I kept those CDs for when I was doing boring household chores and I could let rip. Then I was free to prance up and down the sitting room, brandishing my iron or conducting an imaginary orchestra while I pushed the cleaner. I could grieve with Roy Orbison as he begged his latest ex-love to *Walk On* or ride the high seas with the theme tune of *Pirates of the Caribbean* or soar through the heavens with the Valkyries. All far too much emotion, high and low, when trying to paint the long antennae of a common shrimp with a 0000 brush.

I broke off for a quick lunch at one o'clock. Sometimes I had to force myself to do this, especially when I was 'in the zone', when all my creative juices were flowing. But a break served three purposes. One, it stopped my stomach rumbling and distracting me; two, it rested my eyes and got them back into focus and three, it put some distance between me and the painting. When I returned, I could look at it with fresh eyes and mind and any glaring mistakes would be instantly obvious. There had been a few times, when I could genuinely say that I couldn't remember actually painting a picture, as if some divine hand had taken over and done the work for me, probably before I made a hash of doing it myself. This didn't happen often; two or three times in my lifetime was about it, but the hope was always there that the next one would be the masterpiece.

I ate at the kitchen table so that I did not catch sight of the envelope on the living room mantelpiece. I had a few days' grace, and I did not want to spoil my sense of wellbeing by worrying about it. Everything was going along too well for me to sabotage it now.

By mid afternoon, the sun had burnt off the sea mist and I had put the finishing touches to the picture. I was pleased and exhausted. When I was younger I could paint for five, six hours a day without a problem. Now my back was aching, the arthritis in my hands was throbbing and I was almost seeing double. It had been a marathon, but it was done.

I took the starfish and mussels back to the seashore, restored myself with invigorating gulps of sea air, and treated myself to a soft ice cream as a reward. I felt on top of the world.

The next morning, still in my pyjamas, I popped in to my workroom to check on the painting. I took off the protective sheet of paper and looked at it with a critical eye. First impressions were always the best and after a night's sleep, any anomalies would be the first to hit me. It gave me a quick overview of the whole painting without getting bogged down on the detail and if something bugged me, then it had to be changed. But it looked good. Nothing glared at me. It was finished. I let out a great contented sigh, and toddled off to the bathroom to wash and brush my teeth.

Before I sat down to breakfast, I went outside to let the chickens out into their run and give them their food. I had to smile at the flags. They really were cheeky and would lift most people's spirits. I could just imagine them on a grey winter's day; they would be even more delightful.

I unlatched the door of the coop. 'Come on girls,' I said. 'Breakfast time. And, Cilla, I hope you've finally decided to produce at least one egg today, this strike of yours is going on for far too long.'

All three of them hurried out and started pecking at their food, clucking contentedly. I went confidently into the dark interior in search of eggs. I could have found my way around blindfolded but the tiny slivers of light which squeezed through gaps in the warped boards of the coop were usually enough to light the interior. Today there were none. It was completely black – 'bible black' as Dylan Thomas would say. Ice water shot through my veins as tiny pinpricks of light blinked on and off and the darkness appeared to move. Whatever it was, it was big and dark, and coming towards me. I shrieked and stumbled back outside into the light.

My heart was racing and my breath was caught somewhere in mid windpipe as a shape appeared in the doorway. My overactive imagination had conjured up zombies, crazed murderers and creatures from outer space within the span of a millisecond and I would have stood on a witness stand and sworn that that was what I saw. It took me a few moments for my brain to reassert itself and interpret what my eyes were actually seeing. Relief and anger flooded through me. It was the girl from yesterday but she was barely recognisable. She had straw and feathers clinging to her, and there was something unmentionable smeared down the side of her face. Her clothes were liberally splattered with dollops of white chicken poo, and she stank worse than ever.

'What the hell do you think you are doing here, girl?' I demanded, anger taking the place of my fright. 'Just because I helped you out yesterday, it doesn't mean than you have *carte blanche* to have the run of my house. This is private property. You have no right to be here. And if you've harmed one of my hens…'

'I haven't hurt anything. And I haven't broken any eggs neither,' the girl answered sullenly, head hanging.

'That's not the point. This is my house, not yours.'

'You don't live in a hen-house,' she said. I looked for scorn but there was only a look of bewilderment in her eyes. 'So why can't I? The chickens don't mind.'

Her simply statement stopped me in my tracks. It hadn't been said impertinently and from what I could see of her face, she seemed genuinely puzzled that I should be making such a fuss. And I suppose she had made a valid point. 'That's not the point,' I repeated, flustered. Any clever Maggie Smith put-down had escaped me for the moment – well, it was early in the morning!

'It was warm, and the chickens like me,' she said.

'But it's not your house. You have no right to be in here.'

'It was nice,' she answered simply.

It was like having an argument with a wet flannel. She did not argue back, was not rude or sneering like youngsters can be. She really seemed to be bemused at my objecting. And she was right - all three chickens were happily pecking around her shit-laden shoes and were ignoring me completely. How was that for treachery? She seemed to be totally without guile and plainly saw nothing wrong with bunking down on someone else's property. But if she thought my chicken coop was an improvement on previous residences, then where in the name of God had she been living before? I suddenly felt churlish and mean. Poor kid, I thought, remembering my resolution of the day before to be a kinder person.

She pre-empted my kindness.

'Have you got anything to eat?' she asked.

I am seldom lost for something to say, but on this occasion words deserted me and I simply gaped at her. I held open the outer gate to the coop and waved her out, like an usherette in the cinema. 'Out!' was all I could come up with. I was seriously losing my touch.

62

My brain seemed to have atrophied.

The girl did as I asked and stood outside, looking wretched. 'Is that a no, then?' she asked, still not able to look me in the eye.

I felt ashamed of myself, it was as if I had just crushed a butterfly with a sledgehammer.

'It is not "no",' I said, recovering my linguistic skills. 'But you are not coming near my house smelling like that. I might not be house-proud, but the smell of chicken poo will hang around for days.'

She looked more whipped than before.

'Go around the side of the house, and take off your shoes, then wait for me,' I said. Oh, God, I thought, what am I getting myself into?

I went back into the little utility room, which was off the kitchen. It was another room, which seemed to accumulate junk at an alarming rate and required regular sorting. I kept odds and sods of old clothes, wellies and gardening clogs in there which I could grab quickly for use in the garden or for mucking out the chickens. I think posh people called them "mud rooms". The clothes were nearly clean (well compared to hers, they were immaculate), and they would have to do for now until I could rummage upstairs for something more wearable. The girl, Janine I reminded myself, was much taller than me, and, though I was not fat, I wasn't as skinny as her either. With a sixty-year difference in our ages, I very much doubted that any teenager worth the name would accept the offer, but otherwise she would have to strut around naked. I only possessed one dressing gown, and I was not letting this scruffy kid anywhere near it. She must be crawling. For now, my old gardening clothes would have to do. They were due for a wash.

I grabbed the key to the annexe off its hook and went around the side of the house to find the girl. In my heart of hearts I hoped that she had gone, but no such luck. She was exactly where I had told her to be: standing in her bare feet, shoes by her side, waiting patiently like an obedient dog. 'Let's get one thing clear,' I said to the top of her bowed head. 'This is a one-off. I don't want you coming around here again, do you hear?'

Janine nodded miserably.

I unlocked the door and motioned her in. She took a timid step inside and stood still, as if afraid to go any further. She peered around the room, uncertainty in every inch of her body.

'There's a bathroom just through there,' I said pointing to a door to the left. 'You can have a shower and wash your hair and there are towels and toiletries in there that you can use.' Mentally I gave myself a reminder to disinfect or bin everything once she had gone. 'You can put these things on when you've done,' I said. I put the old sweater and jeans down on a chair. 'These will have to do until I get your stuff washed and dried, if my machine can cope. Oh, and if there's anything needs washing in your backpack, they might as well go in at the same time. Have you got any clean underwear, lass?'

She looked shyly at me out of the corner of her eye, and shook her head.

'I don't think I can help you with a bra, it would go around you twice,' I said as she continued to look sideways at me, her wariness now turned to puzzlement. 'But I've got a new pack of pants upstairs. I'll get it for you. They'll be far too big and are hardly sexy, but they'll be better than nothing. Now, off you go and get clean.'

'Why are you doing this?' she asked suspiciously. 'What do you want from me?'

'I don't want anything from you, child. I'll get you sorted out for now and then you can leave. That's all I ask. Okay?'

Janine shrugged her thin shoulders. I had a growing suspicion that she may have been what they euphemistically call today a 'special needs' child, or someone with 'learning difficulties.' How wrong I was!

I opened the door of the tiny bathroom and showed her how to operate the shower, and then left her to it.

I let myself back into the house using the connecting door, which led from the sitting room of the annexe into the hall in the main house and was fitted with locks and bolts on both sides. At one time I had rented the annexe out to holidaymakers, but I had always been uncomfortable with having strangers just on the other side of the door and, no matter how nice some of them were, I found that I valued my privacy more than their money. It was rarely used now, other than serving as Tiffany's Christmas bolthole and then the door was never locked.

I found the pack of M & S pants (which I'm sure would be described as granny knickers by anyone from this girl's generation) and knocked on the bathroom door. 'I'll leave the pants outside the door. When you've finished, bring your dirty clothes around to the kitchen. I'll put them in the machine and they should dry well on the line as there's a good stiff breeze getting up.'

I returned to the house and locked and bolted the connecting door. What on earth are you doing, Dora? I thought to myself, shaking my head in bewilderment.

Since when have you become a Fairy Godmother? This is taking things just a tad too far. And you don't even like kids.

CHAPTER TEN

The girl was absent for so long that I had almost started to believe she was a figment of my imagination, but finally I heard a faint tap on the kitchen door. She was a moving mound of clothing on legs. *That backpack must have been a portable Tardis,* I thought. The smell was beyond ripe and I wasn't keen on touching them and perhaps contaminate myself with whatever else lived in that particular midden heap, so I showed her where the machine was and she stuffed them all in.

'At least we don't have to worrying about the colours running,' I said as I tossed in a detergent tablet and on second thoughts added a second. 'Grey on grey on black would be the outcome whatever I do.'

She stepped back, arms hanging at her side, uncertain as to what to do next. My old jeans started slipping off her non-existent hips, and she grabbed the waistband before they fell down completely. I gave her a length of garden twine to tie them up. 'It's just until your own clothes are clean - ish,' I told her reassuringly. 'I'm afraid you now look like a very young bag lady, but there's no-one to see you.'

She sat down at the kitchen table and waited silently while I cooked her a full English breakfast – two eggs, bacon, beans and sausages, which she packed away with alarming speed. She refused to eat the eggs. 'It would be like eating a friend,' she explained when I asked why she was wasting good food.

'What about the pigs for the bacon and sausages?' I asked once I had realized what she meant.

Her answer was simple. 'I didn't know them.'

I started to laugh, but quickly choked it back into a strangled cough. The girl was serious. From the look on her face I could see that she had meant what she had said, quite literally! As I sipped my coffee, I watched her eat. Now that the several layers of grime had been removed, I could see that she was really a rather pretty child. She had an elfin face with skin so white it was like alabaster, enormous dark eyes, black curling lashes which I would have died for at her age, and her short hair feathered delightfully to frame her face. She was so very young and she really was rather enchanting, vulnerable and fey, and even though she looked as if the downdraft from a bird's wing could knock her over, I suspected she could hold her own far better than I could. There was a knowing weariness in the dark depths of her eyes.

'How old are you, Janine? Where have you come from?' I asked.

She ignored me and continued to eat with studied concentration, as if the pattern on the plate needed to be scraped off too. I got up to pop a couple of rounds of bread in the toaster.

'I'd put you down for 14 or 15; too young to be wandering around on your own. You should be in school.'

'I got expelled.'

She stopped eating and hung her head, closing herself off from me.

'Look, I don't want to pry into your private life, but you are living in a dangerous, unforgiving age which exploits children as well as adults.' I thought of the boy at the quarry. Perhaps this was the norm for modern kids and I was just too far out of touch, but the news programmes were full of such terrible things happening to children these days. 'Aren't your parents going to be worried sick about you? Why don't you ring them now, and just let them know that you are okay. They may already have called the police and they'll be out searching for you. At least you can put their minds at rest.' I was getting even less response from her now. I could almost see her physically winding herself into her protective shell, just like Herman (that's the crab, by the way) would have done when he was frightened.

'She doesn't care. She told me to get lost. So I did,' she mumbled, barely audibly.

She licked the last of the baked bean juice off her plate and carefully placed her knife and fork on top. Well, at least it would make the washing up easier, I thought. Then she lathered the toast with butter and my best black cherry jam.

'People often say things in temper that they don't mean,' I explained. 'I don't think your mam really meant for you to disappear.'

Silence, except for the monotonous crunching of the toast. It was obvious I wasn't going to get anything more out of her for now and I needed to have a serious think about what to do next. It was a situation I had never been in before and my brother's warning words burned in my brain. Every instinct in my body told me not to get involved, but could I be hard-hearted enough to kick the girl out of the door once I had graciously fed and watered her? Wipe my hands of her and send her on her way to who knew what fate? I needed to think through my options.

I picked up Janine's plate and mug and dumped them in the sink. 'I have to go out now,' I said. 'Your clothes will be washed by the time I get back but they'll take a while to dry. I don't have anything new-fangled like a tumble dryer, so we'll have let the sun dry them.'

In the meantime... what was I going to do with her? Once upon a time, long long ago, I wouldn't have thought twice about letting her stay for an hour on her own in the annexe, but I had become cynical in my old age and it was my belief that the younger generation these days was not to be trusted. They didn't seem to have any respect for other people's property and only thought of satisfying their own selfish demands. It made me boiling mad when I saw on the news hoards of kids gleefully marching out of school in protest – in front of cameras of course –at the plastic pollution that was killing the planet while they themselves leave tons of plastic rubbish and litter in their wake wherever they go.

They were greedy and thoughtless and usually one-step ahead of the rest of us. I did not trust them and I didn't trust this girl either. I certainly wasn't going to leave her anywhere inside the house.

'You can stay out here in the garden until I get back, or you can come with me and lend a hand – whichever.'

'Where are you going?' Janine asked suspiciously.

68

'There's an old gentleman, Ted Morris. He lives just down the lane and he's finding things a bit difficult at the moment. He's not a bad old soul. He had a heart attack a month or so back, and his garden is getting out of hand so I said I'd help him out for a bit, weeding and stuff, until he can do things for himself again. I know he likes sitting out there in the sun with his newspaper and a cuppa. Well, do you want to come?'

'Will he pay? I'm not doing it for nothing.'

I was speechless for a moment. Well, what else did I expect – really? 'You can count that enormous breakfast and the soap powder as payment, miss,' I answered shortly. 'It's not as if you are doing anything else with your time, but it's your choice.'

She shrugged her bony shoulders. Interpret that any way you want, they said.

'I'll just go in and lock up in the annexe, and then I'll be on my way. Come if you want or not,' I said, and opened the interior door. Janine was right on my shoulder, watching.

I admit I expected the place to look like a war zone; teenage girl's stereotype and all that. I was stopped dead in my tracks. It was pristine, as if nothing had been touched. In fact it looked tidier than I remembered it. The shower had been wiped down and to my utter amazement the wet towels were both flapping happily on the line outside. It was a considerate thought on the girl's part, but I would still be putting them into a very hot wash once I got back. Hanging forlornly next to them was a dripping teddy bear with one ear, one eye and one leg. I had to smile. I'd had one just like it when I was a toddler, and though it had had all its limbs, not a scrap of its fur had survived its loving and the remaining fabric was pot black from playing repeatedly in the coal bunker and from being rescued many times from the rubbish bin. He had been my comforter and my friend and I had loved him to bits.

The girl followed me silently as I locked and bolted the inner and outer doors. I collected my secateurs from the kitchen (Mr. Morris'

69

were too heavy and big for my small hands, so I always took my own), and a spare pair of gloves for Janine. They were brand new and rather jolly in bright shocking pink and black, but she didn't even raise an eyebrow when I handed them over. I would have to do with my old ones, which had a hole in the middle finger, which let all the dirt through.

I walked down the lane, which led towards the main road and the heart of the village, Janine following on about ten paces behind, scuffing her feet like a moody toddler. It gave me a bit of time to think things through and if I should inadvertently start talking to myself out loud, she was hopefully too far away to hear. The main question I asked myself was – where was I going with this? I don't like children, especially teenagers, which I think I have mentioned before. In fact, if I was being brutally honest with myself, teenagers of whatever sex terrified the living daylights out of me. They were all hormones and energy and sarcastic superiority. You could jolly along younger children by throwing a ball or doing a bit of drawing with them, but teenagers always had that bored judgemental look to them, especially girls, smirking and giggling at you and criticising everything in the entire world but themselves. I could never handle being mocked and laughed at, especially when I was young. My brother had taken advantage of that and had keep on at me with snide cruel remarks, none of which my parents ever seemed to hear. It was never their darling little boy who had the sharp tongue, it was always me who was to blame. I think my loveless upbringing was one of the main reasons that I had been put off having children for life. My parents had often accused me of being unnatural not to want children – in an era when the pinnacle of a girl's ambition was supposed to be marriage and the production of the next generation. They may have been right. I knew I didn't want kids because of the terrible responsibility of getting things wrong and messing up the life of another human being, as I felt they had messed up mine. I made my decision a long, long time ago not to have kids and I've never regretted it. I give children as wide a berth as possible.

So what was I doing helping this runaway? Admittedly she didn't seem to be the normal run-of-the-mill teenager, but she was clearly disturbed and in need of help, probably far more than I could offer. With my own woeful lack of experience and antipathy towards this particular sub-group of the species, I should have disqualified myself immediately. If I got it wrong, I could do her more harm than good.

CHAPTER ELEVEN

When I arrived at the back gate of Mr. Morris's house I was no clearer about what I should do with Janine than I had been when I had started out, so I pushed these disturbing thoughts to the back of my mind and concentrated on the job in hand. The old man – who was two years younger than me, but I always treat age as fluid – lived in a large house which fronted on to the main road. The front entrance was only accessible via a very steep flight of stone steps up to the house and sat on top of an outcrop of Sutton stone which used to be extensively quarried in these parts in past times. Nobody used those steps and they were lethal after years of neglect and an overgrowth of red valerian and bramble whips. At the side and back, the surplus of rock from excavating the house's foundations had meant that Mr. Morris had a ready-made rockery, but he had told me once that it had taken tons and tons of topsoil to cover the thin sandy soil and create his garden.

I knocked on the back door and by the time Mr. Morris had managed to shuffle his way to answer it, I had already slipped around to the shed and collected my tools.

'Just wanted to let you know I was here, Mr. Morris,' I said, glancing at the stooped figure before me. He had once been a tall man, but even before the heart attack he had started bending himself into old age. His hair, still thick, was almost all white now, and his skin was creased and creviced, but his faded blue eyes held a wicked twinkle. He was a bit of a loner, like me, so we understood each other well enough. 'I'd like to introduce you to Janine,' I said, pulling her forward. 'She'll be helping me, if that's alright with you?'

'Want a cuppa do you?' he asked me, hardly glancing at Janine.

'I'd rather get a start on, if you don't mind; that couch grass is a devil. It will take some getting out, even with two of us. I'll give you a knock when we've done a bit, okay?'

'You just let yourself in when you are ready, Miss Cummings. I'm not going anywhere.'

'Why don't I bring out a chair so you can sit outside for a bit?' I suggested. 'It's out of the wind in this corner and there's just enough heat in the sun to make it pleasant to sit out.'

'Oh, that would be grand,' he said, a broad smile reaching right up into his eyes. 'Just for ten minutes or so. Got to keep an eye on the staff, you know.' He chuckled merrily to himself while I ducked inside and dragged out a kitchen chair.

I tucked an old blanket around his knees and settled him down. He patted my hand weakly. I always found it sad when some old people willingly surrendered to feebleness and infirmity especially after an illness. They seemed to give up and wait quietly for the inevitable ending. Please god, don't let me get like that.

Janine had watched the exchange without a trace of interest. After all, what would she know of old age?

'Have you ever gardened before?' I asked her as she turned the hand fork I had given her over and over in her hands. She couldn't have looked more bewildered if it had been Poseidon's trident.

'Didn't have no garden,' she answered. 'It was just a flat.'

I carefully instructed her in the delicate art of yanking out couch grass, complete with as much root as possible, from in amongst the cracks and crevices of the rockery. 'If you see a plant with the grass growing through it, you'll have to dig the whole lot out and try and separate them. Then, put the clean plant back in. The plant, not the grass. Okay?'

She glared at me. It was the first real emotion I had seen her show and I realized that I had been more than a little patronizing. 'Sorry,' I said. 'I was just making sure you understood.'

For the best part of an hour, Janine and I attacked the rockery. She stabbed away, hacking and pulling, with not a word of complaint. Mr. Morris had sloped back inside once the wind had found him and he had started to get chilled.

I stood back and looked at the small patch we had cleared. Janine was higher up, her feet precariously straddling a couple of rocks. She looked back at me with such a joyless look in her eyes.

'You are hating this, aren't you?' I asked.

'Yer.'

'Fair enough, you've done very well, considering. Why don't we take a break and ask Mr. Morris if we can have a cup of tea, and we can make him one as well. How about that, aye?'

She scrambled easily down from the rockery and tossed her fork on the ground. I gave a tentative knock on the door and walked in. Ted Morris was dozing in the armchair next to the low fire in the grate, mouth open and snoring. It looked as if he lived mostly in the kitchen. It was cheery, with bright yellow and blue curtains, which glowed even brighter with the sunshine that streamed through the window. But if I had thought my own kitchen could do with a makeover, his was beyond redemption! We washed our hands as best we could in a sink over-brimming with used plates and mugs and pans. There wasn't a surface which wasn't stacked high.

I rummaged in his cupboards but couldn't find any clean mugs so I swilled three under the tap and put the kettle on to boil. Janine sat at the table and looked from him to me. 'He's very old, isn't he? Is he as old as you?' she said.

Mr. Morris spluttered and shook himself awake, if indeed he had been asleep at all. 'That's very rude, young lady,' he said, levering himself out of the armchair and flopping into one of the dining chairs around the little table. 'You should never query a lady's age.'

Janine hung her head. 'Sorry,' she mumbled.

He cast a critical eye around the kitchen, much as I had done in my own during the visit of The God Squad the day before. 'Sorry about the mess, Miss Cummings,' he said, running a skeletal hand through his thick mop of white hair. It stood on end more than ever. 'I don't seem to have the energy for anything right now. Full of good intentions when I wake in the morning, fairly bursting with ideas, but by the time I get myself downstairs, it's all beyond me.'

'I'm sure it's early days yet, Mr. Morris,' I answered, pouring him a mug of tea. 'You should be having some home help in, I'm sure the social services could organise a care package for you until you are feeling stronger.' I thought I sounded as if I knew what I was talking about but that's all it was. I didn't have a clue.

'I'm not having strangers messing around in my house,' Mr. Morris said with a burst of sudden anger. It was obviously a subject he had visited before. 'And call me Ted, please. We've known each other long enough for that, haven't we, even if it has only been in passing? I'm a bit of a loner, I'm afraid. I'm used to my own company and I'm happy muddling along.'

'And you must call me, Dora,' I said. 'Miss Cummings seems so B*enny Hill*. And I can sympathise completely with your wanting your own space, but you must allow people to help in times of need. Don't be too proud to ask or accept help, Mr...Ted.'

He drank his tea with a loud slurping noise. 'You've never felt the call to get married then, Dora? Or am I prying too much? Tell me to mind my own fool business if you want. I won't be offended.'

I smiled and shook my head. 'My mother always told me I was too choosy, but I knew myself better than her, even as a youngster. If a boyfriend didn't come up to my ideals, and if I could not have full trust and respect for him, I would make his life hell. I would have eaten him alive. I wouldn't be able to help myself, and I would end up terrorizing the poor creature. It would be domestic abuse from a more unusual direction.'

Ted Morris chuckled. 'I think I would have liked to try and take you on, in my younger days, Dora Cummings. We'd certainly have made the sparks fly.'

'So long as we both had our own bolt-holes where we could retreat to and lick our wounds and re-emerge when the snows had melted!' We both laughed. It was fun to speculate on fantasies from the safety of old age. Anything was possible then. 'Well, I'll do another hour in the garden, and then I'll be off. Are you coming back out Janine?'

Janine shook her head. 'I'd rather wash up some of these dishes,' she said, rolling up the overlong sleeves of her sweater.

'Ted?'

'Aye, I'd be glad of the help on the backlog,' he said. 'We'll see how she shapes up.'

I forgot all about her for well over the hour as I battled the couch grass. My mind was stuffed with memories I had not thought of for thirty or forty years. Just like all my friends when I was younger, I had had my string of boys, but the sixties with their sexual freedoms and wild living never managed to swing into my part of the world. It took a detour. By the time the flower power generation had started filtering down the M4, they had lost their initial steam and had come to a grinding halt at the buffers on the eastern side of the Severn estuary. They had never really managed to cross over, well no further than Cardiff anyway. There had been no equality of the sexes, no free love and for girls, precious little freedom. Good girls did not have fun. And with the only two male role models available to me – my father and my brother – I had seen no desire to jump from the proverbial frying pan into the proverbial fire. If I was jumping anywhere, it was to freedom.

I was brought back into the moment by the pain in my lower back having progressed from a dull ache to a screaming agony. Enough, Doris old girl, I told myself irritably, time to stop. I thought angrily of a book I had recently read which had claimed that most of elderly people's complaints and aches and pains were as a result of inactivity, overeating and smoking! It was written by a man! Well, I've got news for you mate: I don't qualify for any of those criteria but moderately clean living hadn't in any way reduced the pain I now felt in my knees, hips and back. I slowly straightened myself up and tried not to groan too loudly. As my blood pressure steadied, I started to clear the rubbish into green bags for the council collection. As always, the amount of garden waste seemed to be vastly more than the small patch of ground cleared.

I stuck my head tentatively around the kitchen door. Ted Morris was standing in the middle of the kitchen, a wide smile on his face. He looked years younger. 'You've got a rare find here, Dora,' he said, nodding at Janine who was standing shyly at the sink. 'Not many youngsters like her these days. She's a real hard worker. A treasure! She can come here and sort me out any time she wants.'

I thought it possible that, as his kitchen had been starting out from such a low baseline, the old man was exaggerating a bit, but one glance around the transformed room and I had to agree with him. The sink was empty of crockery and pans which had all been washed, wiped and returned to whatever cupboard may once have been their natural home. The table and counters were uncluttered and free of stains and grease.

'It's unbelievable,' I gasped.

'Janine says I'm out of cleaning stuff and the like, and that there's not much food in the cupboards.' He looked a little sheepish. 'I've let things slide further than I had thought. I offered her a tenner as a thank you, but she said I'd have to get your permission first.'

'What on earth for?' I asked her, rather more sharply than I had intended. Janine shrunk back from me like a startled fawn. 'Of course you can take it, if Mr. Morris is kind enough to offer. I think you have more than earned it, lass.'

'You'll come again, won't you?' he asked eagerly.

Janine quickly pocketed the money. She turned to me. 'Can I come home with you now?' she asked timidly.

CHAPTER TWELVE

The girl waited, head hanging, the very epitome of a little lost lamb, weary and abandoned who would lick you to death for one scrap of kindness – and yet... my hackles were prickling, warning me. This apparently shy, meek girl would never have been able to survive on the streets – she wouldn't have lasted a day. Of course I could be reading her all wrong and I was old enough to admit that my instincts were not always correct. But they were all I had and they were screaming at me not to trust her one little bit, to get shot of her a.s.a.p! After all, I had done my bit to help her, she was clean, had a full stomach and money in her pocket; I could walk away with an easy conscience.

However, Ted Morris was obviously bewitched with the girl and between the two of them, I felt as if I had been backed into a corner.

Reluctantly I said, 'You can come home for now, until I decide what's for the best. In any case, your clothes are still in my washing machine and won't be wearable for an hour or so yet. Just you go and wait outside for a minute while I speak to Mr. Morris.'

Meekly, Janine walked outside and I closed the door behind her.

'Have I said something wrong, Dora?' Ted Morris asked. He was holding tight to the corner of the table, shaking with the effort of staying upright in a woman's presence. It was an endearing act of old fashioned courtesy, and I was more touched than I could say.

'Sit yourself down before you fall down, Ted,' I said in a mildly teasing voice and pulled up a chair next to him. 'It's like this. The girl's a runaway, and she has been expelled from school. I don't know where she's from, but I've got a feeling she's not from around here. I have tried to persuade her to ring her mother to let her know she is alright, but so far she has refused. There's been no mention of a father, but as you've probably noticed, she's not exactly a chatterbox. Other than that, I don't know a thing about her, so you may want to think twice before you invite her into your house.'

Ted Morris put his head on one side and gave me a shrewd appraising look. 'Well, until you've decided what's best to do, I'm ready to take a chance on her,' he said. 'You have, and I wouldn't think you were an easy push-over.'

I shook my head. 'Oh, I don't know about that. To be honest, I am torn. I feel sorry for the kid but at the same time I wouldn't put it past her to clean me out when I was sleeping. But I've got no proof. She may be everything she seems, I just don't know. Anyway, it's probably all academic, Ted, as I don't expect she will stay around here long. And I certainly wasn't planning on offering her free board and lodgings.'

'Shame that,' he said shaking his head. 'I could have done with her sorting me out for a couple of days. Sure you can't be persuaded to let her stay?'

'Let her stay?!' I exclaimed. 'What on earth for?'

'Until you find out what's going on with her and get her sorted. It's too dangerous for young girls to be wandering the streets. You know that Dora.' He could see I was weakening and his argument was exactly what I had told her but I was still not convinced. 'You could earn yourself a few Brownie points with the big man upstairs. We are neither of us that far away from shaking his hand, you know.'

I laughed. 'Maybe you are right there, Ted,' I said with a wry smile. I did not add that for both of us it could be sooner than we think; it seemed like tempting fate. Perhaps it was high time I started boosting my credit score. 'I think I must be getting soft in my old age, but maybe she can stay for a day or two.' We both laughed. That was something I missed sometimes, a laugh amongst friends, especially those of the same generation who could see things from the same perspective. Hells bells, I was getting maudlin and soft!

'Atta, girl,' he said enthusiastically.

He got up from the table and straightened his shoulders. He was like a man waking out of a long slumber, peeping out at a new day. 'Can I impose on your generosity and boost those Brownie points further, Dora?' he asked shyly, obviously embarrassed to be asking for a favour. I gave him a wary nod. 'I've not got back driving the car yet and Janine says I need quite a lot of things – more than Megan stocks anyway. Any chance you could get some things for me next time you are going to the supermarket?'

I gave him a reassuring smile. 'Of course I can, Ted. Write up a list of what you need. I was going to go myself anyway in a day or two. I'll send Janine down for it later.'

As I walked back up the lane with Janine in tow, it seemed that my decision had been made for me.

I made baked beans on toast for Janine and myself for lunch, followed by bananas with Ambrosia custard. I was too tired to do much else, and it was what I would have had on my own, anyway. At least on this occasion, Janine did not lick the dishes clean.

'Can I stay, then?' Janine asked, after she had finished.

Her clothes were washed and blowing on the line. They'd only need an iron run over them and then there would be no reason for her to stay any longer. Doubts had been rushing back into my mind since I had told Ted she could stay. I was no longer certain. I would be better off keeping my nose out of it.

'I don't think you can, lass. I'm sorry.' I held up my hand to stop the objections, which I expected would burst out, but Janine remained mute. 'Hear me out, please. For a start, you are a runaway and you are underage. My guess is that you are only fourteen.'

'Fifteen, nearly sixteen.'

'Is that the truth?' I asked. She nodded gravely and some instinct told me that she wasn't lying. I took a closer look at her. She was tall, and very thin and her big eyes and perfect skin could have put her anywhere between twelve and twenty. I decided to take her at her word. 'You've said your mother doesn't know where you are, and for all we know she may have called out the police and they are searching the rivers and woods for you right at this moment. How long have you been gone?'

Janine shrugged. I was getting to know that shrug quite well; it was shorthand for *no answer would be forthcoming in the near future.* 'My mum would never go to the police. She's been in trouble with them before, ever since she was a kid, and she said they had it in for her and they'd lock her up just because she liked to have a bit of weed. Anyway, I told you, she said she didn't want me around and told me to get lost.'

She was getting more talkative, almost babbling, but it got us no further forward. 'I will do a deal with you,' I said firmly. Janine tensed as if readying herself to make a bolt for the door. If she did do a disappearing act, she wouldn't have been hard to find as she was still wearing my old gardening clothes held together with a piece of string! Not too many of those wandering around Sutton. 'You phone your mother and let me speak to her. If, and it is only an 'if', she says you can stay, then maybe you can bunk down here for a couple of days. If she wants you back, you will have to go home. Well? What do you say?'

Janine chewed her bottom lip. There were unshed tears glistening at the corners of her eyes, but I couldn't tell whether that was from the self-inflicted pain of her mangled lip or the stress of making a decision.

'You won't tell my mum where you live, will you?' she asked. 'Promise?'

'We'll do "number withheld" so that she won't even be able to tell the area code, and if she wants a return number, I'll give her my mobile phone number. Is that alright?' I sent myself a quick mental memo to turn the damn thing on and check the battery, just in case.

Janine nodded. I handed her the phone and she turned her back to me to hide what she was dialling. It rang for a long time, but finally it seemed somebody had picked up.

'It's me, Jan,' she said and without any more preamble she offered me the phone. She had fulfilled her part of the bargain, it seemed.

I suddenly felt a hundred doubts surge through me. I had no idea what to say to this total stranger. My normal behaviour was to avoid confrontation like it was the plague; always had been (brother James exempted). Some people who had come up against me in the past may have disagreed with me on that score, but I cringed from arguments and shouting matches. If I was pushed far enough, I would stand up for myself against the best of them, but usually I got all hot and bothered, my brain turned to jelly, I turned bright red and talked gibberish. But I reminded myself that I was the one who had asked for this, so I took a deep calming breath.

I spoke into the hissing silence at the other end of the line. 'Hello,' I said brusquely. 'Are you Janine's mother?' I had no idea what the woman's name was. Pretty pathetic, don't you think?

'And who the fuck are you?' a raspy voice asked. Her words were slurred, either from too many fags or booze and it was only twenty past one in the afternoon. 'What've you done with my little girl? 'Ave you kidnapped her? 'Cause I 'aven't got no money, so you can piss off.'

'My name is Dora Cummings, and I found your "little girl" eating out of rubbish bins and sleeping rough. I have done nothing more than given her food and a shower,' I answered. I put on my poshest authoritative voice. When in danger of showing your weakness, go on the offensive. I think I had read that somewhere, but I might have got it totally arse backwards 'She says you told her to leave. Is that true?'

I listened once again into the silence. Eventually the words 'Silly little bitch,' grated down the line. 'She's not right in the head, that one. She's been a weight around my neck from the day she was born.' I didn't think it was the right time to dispute her command of human anatomy. 'She's no good to anyone. I should know, I'm her mother.'

'So you say,' I answered tartly. 'Now I need to know what's best to be done. For a start, how long has Janine been missing and have you notified the police?'

'Keep your knickers on, it's only been a couple of weeks.'

I could hear a man's voice shouting in the background, loud

and angry, but I couldn't make out what he said. I ploughed on.

'So you haven't told anybody that your daughter is missing? For all you knew she could have been dead in some alleyway somewhere, and you don't seem to give a damn.'

'I've just spoken to her, haven't I? She's old enough to take care of herself, silly little cow. You want to take her on, you're welcome to her. She's a miserable little shit, and my life is a bloody sight easier without her.'

I could feel the heat rise in my cheeks along with my temper. 'You can't just turf your own daughter out onto the streets like a piece of garbage…' The line burred dead.

I stared at it in horror. What had I landed myself in? I didn't want to look after the girl *permanently*. I couldn't. I felt sorry for the kid, I really did, but I had only been an impulsive act of charity, a one-off. I didn't like kids! I had no idea what to do with them. What's more, I had my own life to lead – what was left of it – and I had it all planned, a nice comfortable dotage doing the things I liked, without interference or involvement with the outside world unless I wanted it. I didn't deserve this hassle. And I was none the wiser about where the girl lived, so I couldn't even wrap her up in brown paper and post her. I quickly jotted down the last number dialled. It had a Cardiff code, but that covered a hell of a wide area.

Janine had disappeared into the kitchen, and I could see her sitting at the table with her hands over her ears. She looked very young, her huge eyes flat with the beaten look of a life which had held too many disappointments.

'Can I stay then?' she asked. Her toneless voice was barely above a whisper. No begging, no pleading; just heart-wrenchingly sad.

Did I have any choice, really?

'Okay. I've already said you can stay a few days, and I meant it. You can have the spare key to the annexe and let yourself in and out. But there have to be rules.'

To my surprise, a look of what could only be termed hope crossed her face. It was hidden in an instant.

'You keep the music and the TV down. You don't go out at night and you do your own washing and ironing. You can come in here for meals with me, but that connecting door will be kept locked and bolted at all times. You come around the outside and knock. You don't just walk in. Do you understand?'

'Yes.'

'There are some games and jigsaws and books in there left over from when I took in holidaymakers. You are welcome to use them. And there's a travel iron in the cupboard under the sink.'

'Thanks.'

Her meek politeness was pulling down my defences better than any battering ram. I wondered if I had misjudged teenagers the world over, believing too much in the perceived hype and my own prejudices, or was this girl different, not content to follow the herd but somebody who danced to her own tune, whatever that might be?

I needed to think; to gather my scattered wits. I shooed Janine out and grabbed my painting bag. Over the years I had found that one of the best way to calm myself and work out my problems was with a pencil, paints and a sketchpad in my hand. Nothing complicated or precious, you understand, but just having something to occupy my hands and being outside under the big open skies would allow my brain to function more freely. I locked the back door, feeling a bit guilty at my lack of trust, but I hadn't gone completely loopy. I had no idea who this girl was. The nicest people in the world could turn out to be thieves, madmen or mass murderers. This one would have been a very polite one, but who knows? I wasn't yet ready to trust her too far.

I climbed up the hillside behind the house and found a good viewpoint right on top, where I had a panorama of the shoreline and the river, and with the grey ruins of the castle way off in the distance behind me. I wasn't much good at painting landscapes. I always tried to put in too much detail and colour, spoiling the overall effect. I had been toying with the idea of including a few landscapes of the area to go with my other paintings. They would put the botanical and animal studies into a context rather than some unimagined coastal wilderness. Too many outsiders still thought everything Welsh had to include coal tips and rows of grey terraced houses and hairy-arsed rugby players singing *Hymns and Arias* with a pint of beer in each hand and a fag in the other. Let's just say I wasn't expecting very much from my efforts as, with one thing and another, my head was all over the place.

CHAPTER THIRTEEN

Janine slumped on the comfortable settee in the cheery rooms that the old woman had called the annexe. She kicked off her shoes and curled her long legs under her. She couldn't believe her luck. She was almost afraid to breathe in case she broke the spell and woke up to find that everything had been just a stupid dream and that she was really huddled under a stinking old carpet in a shop doorway surrounded by puke and crap, while someone tried to touch her up or steal her backpack. She blinked rapidly until light flashed inside her eyeballs. No, the room was still there.

She had no idea why the woman had let her in. She had never been much cop at understanding other people; let's face it, she didn't even understand herself most of the time, and it didn't seem possible that somebody would do all this without expecting something in return. In her experience, life just wasn't like that.

But the old woman had said she could stay for a day or two and so far she hadn't made any demands. She really could be on a winner here. Everything was so light and clean, and she liked that. She liked the order. It made her feel calm and safe and it was a million miles away from what her mother's flat was like.

It had all happened so fast. The day before, and for too many days before that, she had been nearer to starving than she had ever been in her life. She had thought she knew what hunger was – like when her mum got hold of a fresh wrap and snorted herself into oblivion for days, but it had never been anything like she had suffered in the last few weeks. She had almost felt her belly button joining up with her backbone.

She hadn't had a clue where she was going, but she had known that she had to get out of the city. It was too dangerous. So, she had kept walking and had tramped her way down the A.48 heading west, through the last of the out-of-town retail stores and small clusters of houses until she was out in the countryside where there was nothing but trees and hedges and green fields dotted with sheep and lambs:

foreign territory. She tried begging for food in some of the villages she passed through, but the people had looked at her as if she had come from another planet. One woman even threatened to set her dog on her.

So she had headed out for the coast where she hoped for better pickings before she starved to death. She had never been to the real seaside before. The most she'd previously seen was a glimpse of the sea from Cardiff docks, the water oily and thick with rubbish and dead cats.

She had managed to beg some scraps from a pub and scavenged a half-eaten pie, which had been tossed into a bin, but the pickings were sparse and the vast emptiness of the sky and sea frightened her far more than the city streets. The openness made her feel vulnerable, naked. She had trudged on, knocking on doors and being turned away. She had been beyond hunger, beyond hope when she had dragged herself to the old woman's door. She had looked at her with the usual hostility in her eyes, but she had hesitated for a moment and that had been all Janine had been waiting for. She had been so desperate, she wouldn't have cared if it had been Count Dracula himself who had answered the door, complete with fangs. She had been tired and starving and scared and she had lived with her own stink for so long that she didn't notice it anymore. She had even disgusted herself. This was her last chance and she couldn't screw it up. She would do whatever it took – beg, cry or turn somersaults, anything the old woman wanted, but she hadn't had the energy to do more than stand there like a zombie and grunt!

She hadn't believed it when the old woman had actually given her food and paid her money to help put some flags up around the chicken thingumajig. Whilst she was there, she had sussed out the chicken house as a likely place to kip down in for the night. She had expected to be long gone before she could be found there in the morning and had been surprised when all hell hadn't broken loose. It just hadn't happened. She had been invited in for breakfast and had no idea why. And then the old woman had taken her to see some old bloke and she'd been paid a tenner to pull up some grass and wipe some dishes! The two oldies could potentially be a little goldmine for her. The man was just as good an opportunity to make a few quid out of as the old biddy, more so perhaps, as he had practically invited her to go through his house. How daft was that? Silly old sod.

Weird.

But it could all be a winner for her. If she could milk it for a week or so, she could get herself back on her feet and work out a plan. She had soon realized that running off blind like she had, had been a stupid thing to do.

It may have been ill planned but it had definitely been the right thing to do – to run away, that is, to get away from the stinking flat with her slob of a mother and her 'boyfriend'. What a misnomer that was! Hands and eyes everywhere, pretending it was all just harmless fun, chasing her and grabbing her and slobbering over her with his wet beery lips while her mother watched through unfocussed eyes, patiently waiting for her next fix. She could have coped with her mother's drinking as she always had, but this latest dickhead had introduced her mother to coke and life had turned from bad to horrendous.

When her mother had finally turned on her, she had just run and kept on running. She hadn't had any choice. She had thrown a few things into her backpack and had left. There had been no time to think. How much worse could it be on her own? She was practically there anyway. She had no money and no food and precious little else of any use and for some god forsaken reason she had put in old Mr. Boots, her teddy bear from when she was a baby. He had been through as many battles as she had but had survived. At one stage, she had even thought about eating him. Instead, she had *cwtched* him to her and cried herself to sleep.

The past few weeks had welded themselves into a long dark tunnel in her mind, filled with horror and pain and terror. She was not going home, no way, not ever, but she felt so small and alone. Even though her mother hadn't known she existed anymore, she had been a physical presence, a familiar face. But on the streets and then tramping the road to nowhere she had never known such loneliness and she had sunk into such a depression that she had been ready to give up altogether, to lie down on the warm sand in the sunshine and clean air and wait for the tide to take her out to sea. She had gone beyond fear, beyond hope. And then the old woman had taken her in.

It had left her terribly confused. The house had stood all on its own, no immediate snooping neighbours. It would have been easy to do a quick once-over of the house, nick anything she could find and leg it. Even if she had been caught at it, she knew she could overpower and outrun the old woman and she'd be long gone before the cops could show up. Even now, well fed and with money in her pocket, she could still do it. The old dear was up on the hillside, she wouldn't notice her slipping in through the back door. It would have been a perfect opportunity. Why the hell not? She couldn't understand her own reluctance, to get on with her almost non-existent plans and bail out.

The man and this woman were both very old. They wouldn't miss a couple of quid; they were practically in their graves anyway. So why was she sitting there, twiddling her thumbs. She didn't understand it and thinking about it made her brain hurt. Maybe, if she waited a bit, got herself sorted, she'd be in a better position to work out what to do for the best. In the meantime, she'd play them along and take everything these old fogies were gullible enough to give her. Why settle for just a couple of quid. These two houses must be stuffed with all sorts of things she could flog. She'd wait and watch.

CHAPTER FOURTEEN

It felt good to be simply scribbling away without thought or expectation. It was a joy to relax and just let the pencil do its own thing. Up on the top of the bluff the breeze licked at my face and the sun, warming now with the promise of summer, shone down on the top of my head like a benediction. Now I was really getting fanciful!

But not a quarter of an hour passed before Janine came scrambling up the hill and, without a *by your leave* sat down beside me. This was not at all what I had in mind. Sharing a house, even for a short time and divided by a solid wall, was obviously not going to work if the girl thought she could share my life as well. I turned to her, about to protest that I wanted space and time to think, but she turned her back to me and opened a book and started to read, without a word being said. I didn't know whether to be glad or insulted. I noticed that she was wearing her own clothes, which must still have been a little damp and hadn't even been introduced to the iron.

To an observer, it would have looked as if we were friends spending an hour together in companionable silence, albeit an odd couple, one very young and one very old; an unusual combination rarely seen today, this mingling of the generations.

I had gone up the hill to think things through, but my mind had refused to focus. It was like when I couldn't get off to sleep and my brain skittered around the edge of things or grappled with the most improbable and stupid scenarios, like reorganising the traffic system in town or creating a new variation on my recipe for banana muffins. And no matter how much I punched the pillow, got up for yet another wee, or went cross-eyed over another chapter in my book, nothing ever worked. This was the daytime version. My mind was more or less a blank. I had two problems I had to get to grips with: the girl and the letter sitting on the mantelpiece. Nobody else was going to sort them out for me and neither problem seemed ready to disappear in a puff of smoke and leave me in blissful peace.

The letter could be ignored for another day. The girl could not.

Above me a skylark burst into liquid song as it rose higher into the sky. Without my hearing aids in, its melody was lost to me long before I lost track of it as it melted into the sky. Janine didn't seem to have noticed or was monumentally unmoved, and she kept her head down as she read on in silence.

The girl discomforted me by her mere presence, even though she hadn't so much as said a word or looked in my direction since she had sat down. I was simply not used to company; to another person breathing beside me, sharing my personal space. I found her closeness to be unnerving and I was the one who finally break the silence.

'I thought those books would be too young for you,' I said after recognising the cover of the book she was reading. 'But if you want to read them you should start at the first one of the series. That's the last one.'

She didn't take her eyes off the page. 'I know. I've read all the others before.'

'Oh,' I said, and couldn't keep the pleasure out of my voice.

'I'll go back and read them all again, once I've read this one.'

I smiled to myself. Well, she can't be all that bad, I thought, as the girl obviously had good taste, well in literature anyway.

She put the book down with a long-suffering sigh. I was pleased to see her keep her page with a blade of grass and not by folding over the corner. I hated that. 'I like drawing as well. Can I have some paper and things when I've finished this chapter?' There was a pause as if she was struggling with an unfamiliar concept and then added, 'Please.'

I passed her a small sketchpad and a pencil.

'Thanks.'

She put them beside her and returned to her reading. So much for being firm and keeping my distance! I think it was the politeness that was getting to me. If she had been rude or off-hand or surly, it would have been easy to reply in kind and send her on her way. But her placid acceptance and simple gratitude was reeling me in. There was so little of it around in this mad world we lived in today and now it was coming from a source I wouldn't have expected to know the meaning of the word. My hedgehog-like defences were starting to soften, even against my own better judgement.

I turned back to my sketch, which I had barely begun. Perhaps a dab of paint would distract me. I decided to tackle the landscape before me in a loose, sloshy way – quite unlike my normal careful style of painting. The main advantage would be that anything I produced would only take a half hour or so and, if it went disastrously wrong, I would not grieve over the time wasted before dumping it in the bin. On the other hand, if it turned out to be a minor masterpiece – well, that would be in the hands of the gods to decide. If only my other decisions were that easy to solve.

The time passed quickly as I lost myself in the moment, applying great puddles of colour, and letting them mix and run and merge as they saw fit. I relinquished all control to the wind and sun and the gods of the hillside. By tomorrow, with the objectivity of enough time having passed, I would make a decision as to what to do with it – bin it or save it for posterity.

The girl, Janine, had sat sketching for a little while and had then become restless, humming something tunelessly to herself and fidgeting, so I had sent her off to Mr. Morris's to collect his shopping list. I wallowed in the delicious peace all around me. I imagined I could hear the soft murmur of the waves as the distant tide started its endless crawl upriver. Seagulls screamed on their way inland in search of better pickings. The heat of the afternoon sun released the intoxicating coconut scent that arose from the masses of golden gorse blossoms and the tiny stars of blackthorn blossom on the scrubby bushes scattered in the breeze like spring snowflakes.

I put my brush aside and lay on my back staring up at the clouds scudding across the soft blue sky.

I had finally come to a decision – to do nothing. For the time being at least. I had promised Janine she could stay for a few days and I would not go back on my word. By then I would have had to apply myself to the contents of the letter anyway, so everything could be resolved by Saturday at the latest. Who knew what would happen before then, I thought with a wry smile. Maybe the Martians will have landed!

As it turned out, it wasn't quite that dramatic but almost.

'I've got the list,' Janine announced, as she plodded back up the hill, bursting my bubble of peace. 'There's money in the envelope.'

It was time for me to shift, anyway. I was getting stiff sitting there and I had pins and needles jittering in my legs. I started packing my things away. 'I might as well go and get them now, and I can do some of my own shopping at the same time. It should be quiet in the supermarket at this time of day – after lunchtime and before the mums go to collect their little darlings from school. I'll get the car out,' I said as I slithered down the hill towards home.

'Can I come?'

'You'd be bored rigid, it's only the usual supermarket stuff. Why would you want to come?'

Janine shuffled her feet. Her brow creased in concentration as she sought for a convincing reason. 'I can help carry stuff,' she said finally.

I tried to think up an excuse for going alone, but nothing came. Grudgingly I had to admit that she would be handy to carry the heavy bags and to reach those essential products, which always seem to be stacked on the topmost shelves. No matter how much I denied the relentless creep of old age, it had a way of insinuating itself into every corner of my life and I was no longer too proud to ask a complete stranger to hand me down something I couldn't reach or to read a label because I had forgotten my glasses. 'True,' I answered. 'Go and check that the annexe door is locked while I get some bags.'

I dumped my painting bag on the kitchen table and rooted around in my overflowing cupboards for large supermarket bags, preferably ones without a split down the side, which anything small always managed to find and make a bid for freedom. I handed them to

Janine who was already waiting outside and opened the garage doors. I used my car as little as I could, but living out on the coast was tricky, especially in the winter when there were only two buses a day, one into town and one back. Anything further a-field by public transport required orienteering skills and the patience of a saint. It had been unfair to taunt my brother with that as even I baulked at taking a bus ride.

Nellie, my twelve year old mini, coughed cheerfully into life apparently happy to see me and I backed her out onto the concrete apron at the top of the drive. I looked to Janine for a reaction, but I got none. I must admit I was rather disappointed. I had once been told by a bunch of kids of about nine or ten years of age that my car was 'really cool' and I had been chuffed to bits. She was gunmetal blue-grey, and was the original little box on wheels, not like the modern ones that looked like overstuffed sofas. Janine was not impressed. Her face was blank, neither pleased nor displeased.

I drove down the lane and turned onto the main road, which ran beneath the bluff and headed inland towards the town. The afternoon sun was shining along the winding river, turning it into burnished pewter and highlighting the tiny thatched whitewashed cottage, which sat like a full stop at the foot of the ruined Norman castle.

Unlike the steep river valleys inland, the flood plains both sides of the tidal river were wide with lush water meadows, which were an almost impossible emerald green after the deluges of winter. Two rivers converged just below the castle, and after wet weather and high tidal surges, the fields would flood into shimmering lakes and leave the cottage and castle standing defiant against the torrent. It was a view, which always took my breath away.

'Isn't that a glorious sight,' I said. I would probably have said it aloud even if I had been on my own in the car, but I got no reaction from Janine who continued to stare out of the side window.

I was stupid to expect more. The girl was from Cardiff after all and they had always considered themselves to be a cut above the rabble Welsh – I blame it on the Normans. I don't think I understate it when I say that, as far as the true Celt is concerned, Cardiff is not the most popular capital city in the world. But if I had to endure her presence, then I thought it was only right that she should be introduced to some essential historical and cultural facts about the place.

'All this landscape is incredibly old, you know, much older than anything in Cardiff,' I said, establishing my own bias from the word go. 'There are Neolithic remains over in the dunes and this land was settled by native Welsh long before the Roman legionaries marched through the river marshes as they made their way west in search of gold. We have been invaded many times by people who came to steal these rich coastal lands of south Wales; Romans, Vikings, Normans and more recently the English, but now everything that could be taken has been taken, and the land has been returned to us, its rightful people. It is a land we Welsh feel in our bones, in our very souls.'

'Why are you driving so slow?' Janine asked.

I came thumping back to earth. While I had been getting myself all fired up with nationalistic fervour, Janine had apparently not taken in one word of it.

'Why do you think, girl?' I snapped.

I felt her shrug.

'Because at this time of year you have to have eyes in the back of your head when you drive down this road,' I answered. 'The sheep who live on these downs all year round have lambed and they consider humans and their cars to be the trespassers. They ignore the Highway Code. They appeared out of nowhere, waiting in ambush amongst the dead bracken before dashing straight across the road, or else they amble along, munching on the grass at the edges, their bums sticking out into the road.'

Cute little lambs, their fleeces still gleaming white, would scatter in all directions, intent on causing mayhem and the maximum frustration for anyone in a hurry. At night, with the total absence of any road lighting, they were lethal.

'I don't see any.'

'That's the point. You never do until it is too late!'

I was concentrating so hard on watching the road and the banks on both sides, that I nearly jumped through the windscreen when Janine suddenly screamed at me to stop. Automatically I stamped on the brakes. Both of us came up hard against our seat belts. (It was hard to believe that I had failed my first driving test by being too late on my emergency stop. My reflexes can't be all that bad, when I am paying attention.)

CHAPTER FIFTEEN

I waited for the thump of metal on metal as someone back-ended me, but thankfully there had been nobody behind. Nellie came to a shuddering halt.

'What the hell is wrong?' I gasped. 'Did I hit something?'

Janine wound down the window and pointed at the castle which now lay below us, almost flush with the river which coiled like a silver snake around its footings.

'That castle!' she exclaimed. 'It's the one in the books!'

'What are you talking about,' I said, though I already knew the answer.

'In the *Two Rivers* books; you know, the ones you've got on the bookshelves, the one I was reading earlier. The description of the castle is almost exactly the same as that one; the sea, the river and the valley and everything. It's the same place!'

Janine was almost breathless with excitement; gabbling, in fact. I put the car into gear and moved off quickly, less mindful now of the sheep and desperately trying to come up with some way to get her off the subject. Nothing very creative came to mind.

'No, I don't think so, Janine. That's Ogmore Castle, and I think the one in the books has a different name. Let's face it, there are so many castles in Wales of all sizes and a lot of them are similar – next to a river and the sea. It's nothing unusual.'

'It's got to be the same one! Look, you can see the stepping stones that go across the river and over there, that has to be the haunted thatched cottage, just as it's described in the stories,' she said, tripping over her words in an excited jumble as she twisted around in her seat. 'It's called Uggomor Castle in the books, but I know it's the same place. And right over there on the other side of the river, I can see a white bridge. You said yourself that there were two rivers, which join together at the castle. In the books the river serpent comes out of its lair and stands guard so nobody can cross and sometimes the bridge can disappear altogether, like magic.'

'It's just a story, Janine, a fantasy . . .'

She continued as if she hadn't heard me, words pouring out as if somebody had turned on a tap. 'And there's another castle hidden over the other side of the river in the dunes, it's called the Castle of the Red Kite and it protects the people who live in the Village of the Two Rivers. There are enchanted folk who lived underneath the dunes, and they help the villagers and Caradoc, the Prince's son, to fight against the Normans who have stolen their land and built their castle.'

'It's not real! None of it is real!' I insisted as Janine finally lapsed into a breathless silence.

She unbuckled her belt and almost climbing over the back of the seat so that she could catch the very last glimpse of the castle as it disappeared behind a fringe of trees lining the road.

I gave a non-committal grunt and a sigh of relief. But Janine was not finished.

'Can we go there? Like now,' she asked, settling back down. Her eyes were sparkling and, for the first time a smile lit up her whole face and transformed her into a different person. With her wispy black hair and small delicate features, she would easily have passed for one of the elfin folk who were supposed to guard the tiny hamlet beside the dunes. She shook my arm. 'Can we go there, please, miss?'

'It is not the same place as the one in the story, so there's no point,' I said sharply, trying to dampen her enthusiasm. 'Writers get their inspiration from all over the place, they take a bit from here and a bit there, and then use their own imagination to stitch it all together. The stories are a mish-mash of things, scraps of history and myth and fantasy all mangled together. Maybe the author came here on a holiday or lived here for a while or maybe the whole scenario is made up and it's just a coincidence that some bits fit. You shouldn't read too much into it. It's a coincidence, that's all.'

She gave me a withering look and I pretended to concentrate on my driving so that I would not have to meet her eyes. As we left the ruins behind, Janine slid further down in her seat mumbling to herself, arms folded and a furious scowl on her face. Neither of us spoke until we reached the supermarket car park.

'I'll let you do Ted's list. If you put them in the front of the trolley, I can pay for them separately,' I said, handing her the list. I wondered, briefly, whether I should give her the money too, but decided against it. Perhaps it would be putting too much temptation in her way, I thought, though I felt a little ashamed of myself for even thinking it.

Janine raised one shoulder in reply. Perhaps that was an advancement on the two-shouldered shrug.

We did the shopping in rigid silence. For half an hour we worked our way through the lists, me tossing my groceries any which-way into the trolley while Janine stacked hers carefully in the front. Damn it, the girl was showing me up to be a slob! We had nearly finished and I was aching to get out of the place but I couldn't find the damned bags of chocolate nuts and raisins which I was addicted to – I swear they moved them to different aisles every week because I always had trouble finding them and they were my weekend indulgence – when I saw Justine pick up a bar of chocolate and slip it into the pouch pocket of her hoodie.

I was horrified. I stared at her open-mouthed. She looked back at me with her big innocent eyes and a smile on her lips. 'What?' she asked innocently. 'What?'

I stepped closer to her in an attempt to shield her from the security cameras, if they hadn't already spotted her. 'You put that chocolate back right now, or I walk away and you are on your own,' I said through gritted teeth. 'What's more, I'll have a word with the security guard at the door and you can explain to them why you are shoplifting when you have money in your pocket.'

She looked at me aghast. 'You wouldn't dob me in, would you?' Janine asked, doubt suddenly creeping into her eyes.

'Try me,' I answered, staring her down. 'I might have given you the benefit of the doubt if you were still destitute and grubbing for scraps in rubbish bins, but that is no longer the case. You will be on your own, Janine. It's your choice.'

For a tense moment we glared at each other, testing each other's resolve, and then she took the bar out of her pocket and put it back on the shelf. 'I don't like fruit and nut anyway,' she said and stalked off.

I stood there for a moment, mouth gaping, speechless – at myself rather than at Justine. Dora, I said silently to myself, you are a stupid, arrogant old woman! When James had called me naïve I had been faintly amused, but now it looked like he might have been right all along. Had I really thought that by plucking this child – whom I knew less than nothing about – out of the gutter, dusting her off and giving her a few scratch meals that I could transform her from a thieving bum into an angelic little girl? Who did I think she was – Oliver Twist! Had I been so desperate to prove to the likes of Mrs. bloody Henshaw and her God Squad that I too could do my bit in helping out the less fortunate; that I was just as good a person as they were?

The girl would have to go. She was turning my life upside down and making me doubt all that I had once believed. Wasn't my philosophy to live my own life and not get involved in anyone else's? And hadn't it worked well, until now? So what was I doing with this girl? She had to go.

We spent the first few miles on the drive back in silence until I came out of the other side of the bank of trees, which bordered the road. The view beyond suddenly spread out before us, like somebody had opened the curtains. The late afternoon sun gilded the castle's craggy ruins in shocking pink and gold. Beside it, the darkening purples of the woodlands and dunes formed the perfect backdrop. It would have looked impossibly gaudy if I had tried to paint it: totally unreal. I pulled up at the side of the road.

'Wow!' I gasped.

This time even Janine was impressed. We sat is silence for a minute or two as we drank in the glorious scene, the tension that had sprung up between us slowly ebbing away.

'I'm sorry,' Janine whispered, her face glowing golden from the reflected sun. 'Habit, I guess. '

'I thought I could trust you,' I answered.

'Are you telling me you never nicked stuff when you were a kid?' she asked with a hint of defiance. 'It was only a bar of chocolate. No big deal.'

I opened my mouth to protest, but unexpectedly a long buried image of myself when I was about nine, pocketing sweets on a regular basis from the counter in Woolies made me choke on my words. I turned it into a strangled cough, but for all her surly silences, Janine was a quick kid and I knew she wasn't fooled.

She tried to hide a gloating smile. 'I wouldn't blame you if you kick me out, now,' Janine murmured, all very meek. 'I would if I was you. You can leave me here and I'll go down and explore the castle. You can dump my things out in the lane and I'll pick them up later. You've been very kind. I'm sorry.'

She had unbuckled her belt and had her hand on the handle. Oh yes, I thought, this kid knew exactly what she was doing. She could turn the charm on like a tap when she wanted. She had cleverly pushed the onus back on to me and I knew I was in danger of being manipulated by her. However had I thought she was a kid with 'learning difficulties'? She could probably eat me for breakfast.

'You can't go down there now, it will be dark soon and the tide is coming in. The stepping stones will be flooded and that river is deceptive. It's dangerous; people have drowned,' I said. I took a deep breath. 'I probably over-reacted back there in the supermarket.' *Do not apologise! I thought.* I clamped my mouth shut.

'So, does that mean I can stay?'

I put the car into gear and pulled out. 'Until Saturday.'

'So, we can come and see the castle tomorrow, together?'

'I have things I have to do tomorrow. You can go down there on your own, it's an easy walk from the house, especially if you go over the top and cut down to the road.'

'I'd rather go with you, and you can point out things. I'll wait 'til Saturday.'

I felt a momentary flush of resentment. I was the person in charge here, wasn't I?

I stopped the car outside Ted's back entrance and we hauled out his carrier bags of shopping. Ted eventually opened the door, his hair all mussed up and his eyes still unfocussed with sleep.

'Well, isn't this a wonderful sight to wake up to,' he said. 'Come in, come in.'

We struggled inside with the bags and I gave him the bill and his change.

'Do you ladies want a cup of tea?' he asked as he slumped into his old armchair beside the dead fireplace.

'No thanks, Ted. I'm a bit tired and I'd like to get off home. Janine can put your stuff away for you and come on up to the house once she's finished. Is that okay?'

He gave me a questioning look. I wondered if he sensed the frostiness still in the air between Janine and I. 'More than okay, Dora. She did a grand job on the kitchen. I've only got one complaint – I'll never find anything ever again.' He chuckled to himself. As Janine started to apologise, he waved his hand to silence her. 'I'm only joking, lass. If you'll let her, Dora, I wouldn't mind if she'd help me sort out the rest of the house, especially upstairs. Everything has got dumped up there over the years. I'd pay the going rate, of course, if you and Janine are willing.'

I shrugged. It was getting infectious. 'I told you, it's got nothing to do with me, Ted. There's no telling how long she will be staying in the area, but if she wants to do it, then I've got no say in the matter.'

'I bet there's a lot of people in the village who would welcome a helping hand from such a good little worker, cleaning and whatnot. Might be worth staying on for a while,' he said, addressing himself to Janine who kept her back turned to him, fussing with putting the groceries away in the cupboards.

'Well, Janine? What do you think?' I asked doubtfully. It

didn't seem the right sort of work for a youngster, and I didn't want her to feel she was being pressured into what amounted to skivvying.

'I'm only here until Saturday, you said so,' she answered, still not turning around. 'So I can't, can I?'

'But you've only just come, child,' Ted protested. 'Surely you'd let her stay a bit, Dora, get herself back on her feet like. If she was earning, she could pay her way, for a bit, nothing permanent if you don't want it.'

'No, Ted. I've said until Saturday. I've got things to do.'

'I could stay with you,' Janine said, finally turning to speak directly to Ted.

'That's not possible, Janine,' I answered quickly. I could see that Ted was keen on the idea, but Ted was even more vulnerable than me. So for that matter was Janine. 'I told you she's underage, and it wouldn't be right for her to be staying alone with a man, a stranger. There'd be gossip and busy-bodies sticking their oar in – I can think of three straight off. You wouldn't want that hassle, Ted.'

The excitement went out of Ted's eyes. 'Maybe you're right, Dora. It's terrible what mucky things some folk can think up. But she could stay on with you, pay you a bit of rent and the like.'

I turned my head just quick enough to see what I thought was a gloating triumph flicker across Janine's face, but it was gone in an instant. 'Yes, miss, and I could clean up your place as well. It's almost as bad as Mr. Morris's.'

Ted and I looked at each other speechless, and then we both roared with laughter.

'Well, that's us told, old girl,' he said.

Once again I had been snookered. I had a day's grace. Meanwhile, I had Friday to get through.

CHAPTER SIXTEEN

I was gazing at the pot of black cherry jam on the kitchen table, lost in thought. I chased my piece of toast round and round my plate; it was hard and cold and unappetizing. I knew I should eat it as it was going to be a long day, but the very thought of food made my stomach flip over. But Friday was here and I couldn't shilly-shally about it any more. The day had finally arrived and by the end of it I would know my fate, one way or another, and I already felt totally exhausted before it had even started.

There was a timid knock on the back door. Janine opened it a fraction and pushed her face through the crack.

'I've fed the chickens, and I've got four eggs. Can I bring them in?' she asked.

'Yes, of course. Give them a swill under the tap if they are mucky. There's a spare carton on the counter.'

Janine had successfully transported the four still-warm eggs in a pouch made from the upturned hem of her jumper. She washed them carefully, dried them off and put them into the carton.

'You can make yourself some toast if you want, Janine,' I said listlessly flapping a hand towards the toaster. 'You may need to re-boil the kettle.'

She made herself two slices of toast and lathered them with butter and jam. By then the kettle had boiled.

'Do you want another cuppa, Miss?' she asked. 'Yours looks like it's gone cold.'

I shook my head and nibbled the edge of my toast to prevent any further conversation. Janine gobbled hers down and put on another two pieces. She seemed to be making up for the times when she had been in competition with the seagulls for leftovers. The silence stretched between us. Other than that uncharacteristic moment at the castle, she was certainly a girl of few words but I didn't feel it was an uncomfortable silence, one which had to be filled with inane chatter. We both seemed to be happy inside our own heads. So we sat: I nibbled and sighed and sipped my cold tea. It was disgusting. I got up and popped it into the microwave to re-warm. It was still disgusting but I drank it anyway.

'I shall be out for most of the day, Janine,' I said eventually. 'If you want to go out, make sure you lock up the annexe. There's some bailer twine in the drawer by the sink. Make a loop and tie the key around your neck so you don't lose it.'

'Where are you going?'

'None of your business, young lady,' I answered sharply. Janine cringed and applied herself to scooping up the last crumbs of her toast with a wet finger. 'Sorry. I didn't mean to snap. I've got things on my mind. Look, I've dug out an old pad of cartridge and some pencils for you, if you want them.'

'Ta,' Janine answered, pulling the pad closer to her. 'I was going to go down to Mr. Morris to start on his house.' She had cherry jam plastered around her mouth and a smudge on the tip of her nose, and she looked so young and innocent, like a five year old on best behaviour. It made me smile.

'Before you do anything, check with him first that he does want you; don't just go barging in,' I said. I thought it was more than likely that after a night's sleep, he was having second thoughts about letting a stranger loose in his house.

'But he said I could go back at any time. You heard him.'

'He may just have said it to be polite, and I don't want you making a nuisance of yourself. If he says "no" then you'll have to find something else to occupy your time. Do a bit of drawing, you said you liked that.'

She cleared the table and started washing up our things. I just sat there, staring at nothing. Friday, bloody Friday.

The past week had been the longest and the shortest in my life. When the letter had arrived with an appointment for the Breast Clinic in Cardiff, I hadn't wanted to wait in a kind of ignorant limbo while some stranger meddled with my life. Four days had seemed an eternity then and I had wanted nothing more than to get the appointment over with as quickly as I could and get it out of the way. Now that the day had arrived, I wanted time to stand still so that I would never have to face it.

I had tried to put it to the back of my mind, but it had had the ability to creep back in when I was least expecting it. In my more lucid moments, often spurred on with a couple of sherries, I had given the letter some thought. I had never had a recall after a routine mammogram before. It hadn't said much, just the time and date. It could go one of two ways but I knew in the depths of me that it would be bad; just how bad I was about to find out.

I think what terrified me the most was the loss of control over my own body and life. Somebody else would be making decisions for me and about me. Total strangers would know more about my body and my insides than I knew myself. They would peer at me as if I was some lab specimen and tick off my life on their pieces of paper before dismissing me and waving in the next victim. I would be reduced to a number; a case; a statistic.

I was scared. I admit it. The next few hours could change my life forever.

Janine watched the mini chug its way down the lane and turn onto the main road before disappearing from sight. She perched on the wall at the bottom of the garden where it fell away almost vertically and watched the road and the activities down on the beach car park far below. There wasn't much going on that morning, just a couple of intrepid dog-walkers, as the sky was overcast and there was a chilly on-shore breeze. She didn't linger long, only until she was sure that the old lady hadn't doubled back because she'd forgotten something.

She let herself in to the annexe and rummaged around in her backpack, then took one last look up and down the road. She walked around to the back of the house and slipped the rack of lock-picks out of her pocket. She tried a couple of them in the lock, jiggling them around a bit until she felt the lock click and open. One of her mother's "admirers" had amused himself by teaching Janine, then only seven, how to pick locks. By the time she was eight, she was an adept, not quite up to safe cracking standards, but fine for most run-of-the-mill domestic locks. When the lover, whose name she couldn't even remember, had finally followed the way of all the other men before him, he hadn't noticed that his lock picking tools were missing. This old door would hold no problems. It took Janine two minutes and she was in. She shook her head in disgust. She was getting rusty – it should only have taken one.

She was already familiar with the kitchen and utility room, and so she didn't waste any time on them. She wasn't sure how long the old woman would be gone, but she thought she had a couple of hours at least. Plenty of time to do a search of the house for any cash or for anything that might be easy to flog. Older people seemed reluctant to embrace the realities of the modern world, *thank God!* They distrusted credit cards, debit cards and ATMs and were more likely to keep a stash of money hidden under the mattress or in an old jam jar to cover their everyday expenses, especially as so many banks were closing down and hard cash was getting more difficult to access. She needed to get money if she could; jewellery or any other valuables would be harder to get rid of, especially out here in the back of beyond.

After a couple of hours searching she had only managed to find six pounds 92p all in small denomination coins. There were lots of knick-knacks but she didn't think any were of much value but some were pretty enough to fetch a few bob. She had even worse luck with the jewellery; a couple of thin gold rings and a broken gold chain. It seemed the old biddy was not one for expensive jewellery or silverware, and even her electronic equipment was out of the ark. There was nothing really worth bothering with. Instinct told her that there was money in the house somewhere, but with all the junk and jumble of the rooms upstairs it would take her too long to do a thorough search. So either the old woman had a cunningly hidden bank vault or she really didn't have anything of value.

She was getting pissed off. Damn the woman! This was turning into a complete waste of time. Probably time to move on, scout

out somewhere where the pickings were better, maybe down with Ted, the old feller.

What she found in the last room changed her mind. At first sight she had only been able to take in the mess; bookcases overstuffed with books and magazines, piles of black plastic bags and tottering stacks of boxes and papers in no apparent order, old clothes and bottles. But one part of it was different. It was obviously the place where the old woman painted, but not even in her wildest dreams could it have been called a studio. It only occupied about a quarter of the room, but that part was well organised and neat, something which Janine could appreciate. There was a finished painting taped to a board showing a rock-pool with crabs and anemones and seaweeds and lots of little shells and bits and pieces. It was painted in the finest detail, and it looked so real that she felt that if she touched it, her fingers would come away wet. She sat for ages, mesmerised by it, unable to believe that it could have been done by old Miss Cummings, whom she had mistakenly thought was a doddering, ancient old trout who was overdue for a visit from the Grim Reaper. Searching further, she found large black folders at the back of the room and she opened them carefully, almost reverently. She lost all track of time as she was plunged into a miniature world of animals and birds and flowers of every size and colour. Never would she have imagined that anyone, especially the old biddy, was capable of such mind-blowing work.

She returned everything to its rightful place and went back downstairs and threw herself into the comfortable armchair in the lounge. She gazed out of the big window at the grey uninviting sea outside but she didn't see anything. Her mind was still buzzing with what she had seen upstairs.

She smiled to herself. Her favourite painting had been of one of the chickens, the lavender coloured one with the fluffy feet which looked like crazy mad slippers, scratching around in the long grass and buttercups, all fluffy and bright in the sunshine. Maybe, when she left – if she left – she would take it with her. Get real, Janine! What the hell would you do with a painting? If she was kicked out on Saturday like the old biddy said, she would be homeless again, sleeping rough in all weathers and with only twenty pounds in her pocket. She wouldn't have a pot to piss in yet alone a wall to hang a picture!

But the last few days hadn't been that bad, she thought. Why run away just yet? She had never been any good at reading other people; they always seemed to say one thing and do something entirely different. But the old woman had been kind. Why not take advantage of that for a bit longer? She had been fed and cleaned and had even been given her own little flat, at least for a few days. She'd been treated really nice, and then she'd nearly ruined it all by doing that dumb thing in the supermarket. It was hardly the crime of the century; it was only a lousy bar of chocolate! She'd have to work hard at smoothing the old lady's ruffled feathers over that one, but she thought she had got away with it. If she played her cards right, she could wheedle her way into a nice comfortable little place here and make some money at the same time. Easy money was great, but she didn't mind hard work if she was paid. She'd done enough of it for blow all when she'd lived with her mother who wouldn't have noticed if the council bin-men had dumped their load in the living room. Janine knew exactly how to play the old woman – yes Miss, no Miss, three bags full Miss. When the time was right, she'd split. But for now, she was on to a good thing and if she was careful she could spin it out for as long as she wanted.

Meanwhile, she'd earn herself a couple more quid by giving Mr. Morris a visit and maybe give his house a quick once-over while she flicked a duster. Perhaps she would have better luck there.

Time to find out.

CHAPTER SEVENTEEN

I was cold. I had been sitting still for too long. The weather all day had stayed overcast and squally and there had been no sun to warm the living room. I was exhausted too and drained of energy. I knew that I must move but I did not budge.

I was still wearing my best navy wool coat, silk scarf wound loosely around my neck and outdoor shoes that had dried on my feet. As the sky gradually darkened towards an early dusk, the chill had crept inside me and entered my bones. A sliver of gold suddenly flared at the edge of the horizon in the west, as if the sun were making an apology for having sulked for so long.

The events of the day had been lost in the fog. I realized that I must have driven home from the clinic, but I had no memory of any of it. I couldn't even remember if I had returned via the motorway or through the back roads or if I might have left carnage in my wake or been caught speeding on every single camera on whichever road it was that I had taken. It had all merged into a distant uneasiness, a generalized undercurrent of terror but nothing that could pull me out of the numbness that had engulfed me since leaving the consulting room. I felt as if my body and my brain had become separated from each other; my body functioning automatically like a robot while my cowardly brain had taken a bit of a holiday and drifted off into another dimension.

Now, as I sat there slowly turning into a human ice-lolly, memory was seeping back. I had got to the Breast Care clinic in Cardiff in plenty of time and had a bit of a wait until they had called my appointment. By then I had fully convinced myself that the recall was as a result of a malfunctioning mammogram machine and nothing more. On the other hand…! Eventually a young nurse whose name I promptly forgot, called me into an empty consulting room, indicated one of the hard plastic institution-type chairs, smiled at me and left, leaving the door slightly ajar. Another five minutes passed. There wasn't much to look at. It was a soulless, sterile room, as I supposed you would expect in a hospital clinic, but as I had never been a patient in a hospital in my life, I had nothing to judge it by. There was nothing to distract me, not even a view through a window and my doubts, long held at bay, started creeping in. I had had enough mammograms in my lifetime to know that this was not the normal procedure. If all had been clear, as it always had been in the past, there would have been a lovely little letter in the post with the gladsome tidings – *We are pleased to inform you...* etc. Not so on this occasion. Before I could talk myself into an even greater panic, a tall good-looking man, middle aged and with the sort of face you instantly trusted, swept into the room followed by the nurse, who closed the door and took the seat beside me.

'Miss Cummings, we haven't met before, but I am Mark Preston, your consultant. Would you prefer I called you Miss Cummings or Dora?' he asked, bowing low over my hand and looking me full in the eye. He must have felt my trembling, but he gave nothing away. His voice was what I would call deep brown; clear, slow and professional.

'Dora would be fine, thank you,' I answered in a croaky whisper. It was all I could manage as my voice seemed to have petrified in my throat.

He placed a buff coloured folder on the desk. 'I have good news, and not so good news, I'm afraid,' he said, not needing to open the file as he was obviously quite familiar with its contents, which was reassuring: I wasn't just a statistic. He watched me carefully with concern in his kind brown eyes.

I think it was at about this time that my heart and my lungs stopped functioning and the humiliation of losing control of my bladder was a whisker away. So much for thinking I was prepared!

'If we get the "not so good" out of the way first, then it can only get better,' he said with a sympathetic smile. 'The mammogram has shown up a small mass in your left breast. It is small, but it is suspicious. I'm afraid there's little doubt in my mind that it is cancerous, but we need to do further tests in order to ascertain the exact type.' He paused to let it sink in. 'I am sorry I don't have better news.'

I took a gasping breath. 'Are you sure?' I murmured. *What a stupid thing to say, Dora, he'd hardly say it if he wasn't.* I could feel the eyes of Mr. Preston and the nurse fixed on me, ready to act if I went into hysterics or if I had simply blanked everything off after the word "cancer" and collapsed in a heap on the floor. I jumped slightly as the nurse slipped her hand over mine and gave a gentle squeeze.

'I don't think there's any doubt that it is cancerous, but the good news is that the tumour is small and has been picked up very early which is an extremely good sign. It should be easily treatable, but we can't discuss the pros and cons until we've done a biopsy to identify the type.' He paused again. 'Would you like me to go back over anything, Dora? It's a lot to take in. Or do you have any questions so far?'

It may sound strange, but it was as if my mind had put the shattering news to one side and my main concern was that I didn't make a fool of myself in front of these professionals, people who must had broken similar news to countless women before and had witnessed just about every reaction. I hadn't wanted to let myself down. I needed to be stoical and calm and to ask intelligent questions, not mouth utter drivel and admit that I'd only taken in one word out of every four.

I took a deep breath.

'Well, obviously I had hoped for better news, but I think it is what I expected, once I found that lump,' I said cursing the tremor in my voice. 'I don't know how long it has been there, you see, but once I found it, I got it checked out straight away.' Was I talking sense or was it gobbledegook? It could have been either.

'You did the right thing, Dora. And as I said, it is in its very early stages. You may not even have noticed it before. With luck, it is so early that it hasn't had any chance to metastasise – to spread – and treatment will be straightforward. We have a number of options open to us, but we can discuss that again once we've done the tests.'

I was sure there were questions I should be asking; intelligent, informed questions that would occur to me the instant I was out of the place. The windowless room was stifling, and I could feel a cold sweat trickling down my back. White noise roared in my ears and my heart was racing. The room had started to spin when I felt the nurse's hand squeezed down on mine and I tightened my grip. *Don't you dare faint, Dora Cummings,* I told myself furiously. The moment passed and I was thankfully still upright.

'Would you like to take a break, Dora?' he asked. 'Susan will get you a cup of tea if you want, and we could do the biopsy after.'

So, that was the nurse's name. I must concentrate, I must remember things. I mustn't make a fool of myself.

I mentally gave myself a shake. 'I'm alright now thank you, Mr. Preston. Silly of me. Please, let's get it over with.'

'Susan will be your liaison nurse. She'll explain everything to you about what is happening now and in the future. We'll give you a pack of information brochures, which you can look through in your own time and if you have any questions after you leave here, just give her a ring. One word of advice. Don't under any circumstances go on-line to find out about breast cancer except from the authorized NHS sites. There is a lot of misinformation out there and it will be very frightening and confusing. Okay? If you have *any* questions, ring Susan.'

I nodded. 'I may be the only person in the whole world, but I am not online, so that particular problem won't arise.'

Mr. Preston smiled. 'If you are sure you are ready, then we can get started. It won't take long and is unpleasant rather than painful,' Mr. Preston said. 'If you'll just pop yourself up on the bed and strip down to your waist.'

Just like most women, I had got used to many undignified visits to the doctors over the years, but I felt singularly vulnerable as I sat there on the bed, naked as far as the waistband of my skirt. I couldn't bear to look down at myself. When I had been younger, I had had reasonable shaped and sized breasts which had been much admired by various short-term boyfriends (I was repeatedly told they were my best assets) but as age had advanced, they had wended their way south (the breasts as well as the boyfriends), never to return.

Around me Mr. Preston and Susan the nurse busied themselves with preparing things on trays and explaining to me what they were doing in quiet tones. I filtered the whole lot out and tried to pretend I wasn't really sitting there, displaying my sad, sagging boobs and rolls of spare tyre. I wasn't fat, but I challenge anyone over the age of fifty to sit naked without their bodies becoming an advert for Michelin tyres. When I was prompted to lie down, it wasn't much better as everything simply slipped off to the sides.

'I'll just give you a local anaesthetic. You will feel a sharp prick, and then that area will go numb. You won't feel anything,' Mr. Preston assured me.

No way was I looking. Needles and I did not get along at all. My veins tended to go on walk-about as soon as there was one within half a mile of me. It hadn't been as bad as I had expected, it never was, but that has never stopped my phobia about needles.

'I will insert another needle and take a small plug out so that we can test it,' Mr. Preston continued. Surely not enough time had elapsed? Shouldn't he wait longer... 'There, all done.'

'Already?'

'Yes, I'm all finished,' Mr. Preston assured me. 'You'll have some bruising, so don't try to lift anything heavy for a day or two.'

'Does that include the Hoover?' I asked, eager to sound normal.

Mr. Preston laughed. 'Most definitely! I'll give you a docket.'

I had walked out clutching a piece of paper with another appointment for the results in a week's time, a handful of information leaflets and a thick dressing slapped inside my bra.

I had no idea how long ago that had been. Now, the light had gone and I sat in darkness in my own front room. I felt frozen both inside and out. 'Stir yourself, you silly old fool,' I berated myself, speaking out loud so that my thoughts could not creep back. 'Sit here much longer and you'll get pneumonia to add to the list.'

I switched on the standard lamp. There was no need to draw the curtains unless I wished it, as nobody could look in – well not unless they had an extremely powerful telescope and were standing either in the car park far below or on a boat out at sea, and I hardly warranted that sort of surveillance, even stripped naked – especially stripped naked! I poured myself a large dry sherry and took a hefty swig. It burned its way down into my stomach and outward into my extremities and shot back up into my brain. The hit was immediate as I hadn't eaten since nibbling that piece of toast at breakfast. I turned on the central heating and set it up higher than my normal background heat. Well, why not?

I wasn't hungry but I topped up my sherry glass and took it upstairs with me while I changed into some comfortable slop-about clothes. By the time I reached the bottom of my second glass, I was warmer and I was rather astonished to realize that, now that the shock had worn off, the emotion I felt was one of relief. Ever since that letter had arrived with the appointment date, I had been in a suppressed state of panic, one which I had uncharacteristically dealt with by trying to ignore. There had been too many unknown factors, then. Now, I had been given a roadmap of what might lie ahead. The professionals were in charge of my body and my life. Important decisions had been taken out of my hands. Did I trust them? Yes I did. It was now over to them and I could only describe the feeling as one of relief as if a burden had been lifted. Whatever lay in the future, I wasn't going to be alone.

All my life I had been on my own, making my own decisions rightly or wrongly, and there had never been anybody to hold my hand when things went wrong or pat me on the back when I had succeeded in something. Okay, okay, it had been my choice, I knew that, and I had long ago accepted that I had to live with the consequences of my own decisions. It had all been down to me. I had never expected helping hands, but when they had been offered it had been a nice surprise. Tiffany, my niece, chided me that I was too independent for my own good, but it had been what I wanted – not what was considered normal behaviour possibly, but what had been right for me.

It felt strange now to be handing responsibility for a part of my body over to strangers, professionals who would get on with the business in hand without any histrionics. The nurse's instinctive quiet calm at my side had felt supportive without being intrusive. I liked that feeling.

As I came downstairs, I caught the lingering smell of burnt toast, and suddenly I remembered Janine. I hadn't given her a thought all day. Now, *there* was a problem that was still up in the air, and somehow or other, she had become my responsibility. I wasn't sure how it had happened, but it had.

I put on the television, but it became nothing more than moving wallpaper to my thoughts. I no longer had to fret about my own life – it was in somebody else's capable hands, but Janine's had somehow been put into mine. I saw it now from a new perspective. I couldn't just turf her out because of one misdemeanour, something which I had to admit I had done in my own childhood, and I had had no excuse. To punish her over a bar of chocolate would have been the height of hypocrisy. She was now my responsibility and I could not let her down. And it had nothing to do with trying to out-do The God Squad!

There wasn't any good reason why she couldn't stay in the annexe for a while, other than my preference for my own company. Despite the difference in our ages, I thought we should be able to rub along together so long as we kept out of each other's way as much as possible. We could exist independently of each other. She could get herself a job so that she could keep herself. Ted Morris' suggestion of cleaning for people in the village wasn't bad, but I didn't think I knew Janine well enough to hand out letters of recommendation. Let's face it, I hadn't trusted her alone in my own house, so how could I foist her on someone else? Mrs. Hardy might have some ideas. She knew everything about everybody. I'd sort it out in the morning. I swallowed the last of the sherry, turned off the television, and staggered unsteadily up the stairs to bed.

CHAPTER EIGHTEEN

The sherry had only succeeded in numbing my senses for the first hour. I had gone to sleep as soon as my head had touched the pillow but after that I had tossed and turned all night, repeatedly getting up to the toilet as that seemed preferable to lying there staring at the ceiling. Sometime in the small hours I had finally got up, my bladder empty but my stomach rumbling, and chomped my way through half a packet of chocolate digestive biscuits. By morning I was gritty eyed from too little sleep, and had a headache from too much sherry and I was none the wiser about which way I was to turn.

Only two things had emerged from the night's brain-storming: I would not tell anybody about my breast cancer, probably not even once I had had the final diagnosis – I was determined to cope with it myself and dreaded other people's pitying looks, no matter how well meant. At some time during the wakeful darkness of the night, the threads of a 1960's tune had popped up from some hidden corner of my brain and was still playing on its own loop in the morning:

> '...Yesterday's gone sweet Jesus,
> Tomorrow is nowhere in sight,
> Please help me today, show me the way,
> One day at a time.'

Forget the Divine Being bit for the moment, it was the overall sentiment which seemed particularly apt. I decided that I would make it my mantra for the foreseeable future – take everything one day at a time!

The other conclusion I had come to was that if Janine was going to stay, she needed to get a job.

I crawled downstairs as the rising sun made a dirty yellow smudge behind a thick blanket of grey cloud. In the half light I wandered around the house, touching things; things I had had for fifty years or more, knick-knacks I had become so familiar with that I would only have noticed them if they had gone missing. I lingered over a silver framed photography of Tiffany, taken last year with her Italian girlfriend on holiday in Rome. Beside it, a little Ladro spaniel puppy gazing at a snail crawling up its leg, uncertain whether it was friend or foe. I had bought him in a seconds shop in Majorca when I was eighteen; my first holiday paid for out of my own meagre wages. My mother's Indian brass bell which she had used to call us in for meals when we were children, bought on a family holiday in Weston-super-mare. The too familiar had suddenly become the unfamiliar, and I saw them all through new eyes.

Janine knocked and entered without waiting for me to call out. 'Five eggs today,' she said, and went straight to the sink to wash them and put them into an empty egg carton. 'I'll clean their house out today. It could do with fresh straw.'

'I'd better make us some scrambled eggs or we'll be getting overrun at this rate,' I said, getting up from my seat. My bones cracked and I felt every one of my seventy-four years.

'I can't eat them. I told you.'

I was in no mood to have an ethical discussion on the rights and wrongs of eating one's friends so early in the morning. 'The chickens laid those eggs for you because they like you. Since you have been here, there's extra every day. Isn't it more insulting to the girls if we waste them?'

She gave her familiar shrug, so I started whipping up the eggs for both of us. 'We can take a half dozen down to Mr. Morris later,' I said, stirring absentmindedly. 'But before then, we need to have a talk, you and I.' I felt the temperature in the room drop by a few degrees.

'Originally I asked you to leave by today, Saturday,' I said as I set our plates on the table and spooned out the eggs. 'I thought a lot about it last night, and I have decided you can stay for another week, on trial, which should give you enough time to get yourself properly sorted. I'll review it again next Saturday.'

Janine said nothing and turned to her eggs with singular concentration but not before I had caught the flash of something cross her face – I couldn't be sure whether it was a look of pleasure, calculation or confusion.

She squinted up at me sidewise. 'I can stay? Just like that!' she said, a forkful of egg half-way to her mouth. 'Why? What's changed your mind?'

'Nothing… I just have.'

How could I explain to the girl what I couldn't really explain to myself. I didn't know if I was using her as a distraction while I digested my diagnosis, or whether my sudden awareness of my own mortality had made me see everything in a different light. Things which previously would have worried me, no longer seemed to matter a jot, and I still wanted to achieve something in whatever time I had left. The world had shifted overnight. But was I using the girl for my own ends, I wondered? Probably. Possibly. Who knew? I certainly didn't.

I ploughed on. 'You can pay me for your rent and any meals you have with me by keeping my house clean and tidy. You could get yourself a little job locally, if there are any to be had and any money you make will be yours to keep. It's only for a week, and both of us can call a halt any time we want.' I took a deep breath. Well, I had committed myself now. 'What do you say?'

'Okay.'

'We'll pop in and have a chat with Mrs. Hardy down at the shop this morning. She might have some idea about little jobs going around the village. If there is anything, she will be the one to know.'

Janine's put her fork down, her mouth slightly down-turned at the edges in a pout. She hadn't embraced my suggestion of finding employment with the unrestrained enthusiasm I had expected.

'Don't you want a job? It's not conditional on you staying for the week, but I thought you might like some money for yourself until you make a decision about what you are going to do. You can't stay here forever, love. I don't really know, but I think it might be illegal.' *And I have other things on my mind, which do not include mothering runaways.*

'I was hoping to go and see the castle today,' she muttered.

Give me strength! Did modern children have no sense of perspective? Did everything have to be for instant gratification and to hell with tomorrow? 'It has been there for a thousand years, Janine, I think it might hang around for another couple of hours yet,' I said rather tersely. She picked up the fork and continued to eat. 'Let's see what Mrs. Hardy has to say first, and we can both go down to the castle after, I could use some fresh air. I can drive us as far as the river car park, and we can walk the rest of the way. I'll make us some sandwiches and there are a couple of small bottles of water in the fridge. How does that sound?'

'Okay.'

Nelly was rather surprised at being called upon twice in one week and was a little reluctant to start but she came through in the end. Janine jumped out at Ted's house to deliver the eggs while I parked the car outside Hardy's store and went in.

I explained what I wanted, and after a virtuoso performance of pursed lips and raised eyebrows, Mrs. Hardy said she would be delighted to help. When Janine entered the shop, she eyed her with suspicion. 'She looks a bit young for working,' Megan Hardy said.

'I'm nearly sixteen,' Janine answered. Her tone was rather sullen and I hoped it wouldn't put Megan Hardy off from helping. Her badge of approval would count for a lot around the village.

Mrs. Hardy looked to me for confirmation. I held up my hands. 'I've only known her a few days, Megan, so I can only go by my instincts. For what they are worth, I think she's telling the truth. She looks younger than she is because she is so petite. But I can vouch for her being a good worker. She worked like a Trojan for Ted Morris, sorting his house out.'

'Whatever a Trojan is, I'm not one of them!' Janine hissed.

I hid a smile. 'It's just a saying, Janine. It means you have been working extremely hard,' I explained.

Mrs. Hardy looked from me to Janine and back again. 'Well, as it happens, I do know of something that might suit,' she said. 'Flo

Jenkins was in here yesterday complaining that she can't get kitchen staff and now that the season is getting under way she's expecting to be busy.'

'Wishful thinking, that,' I muttered under my breath.

My heart sank at the prospect of going cap-in-hand to the Jenkinses, but I had really no reason to feel like that, other than my own prejudices against anyone connected with The God Squad. I hardly knew the woman.

'I had been thinking more along the lines of Ted's suggestion – doing cleaning around the village for a couple of days. She may not be staying long so she can't really commit to a proper job.'

'That's probably as long as it would last with Flo Jenkins anyway, as nobody seems to stay more than a week or so,' Megan said with a sniff. 'I think she only pays minimum wage to her full-timers, so it would be cash in hand and no questions asked. What do you think?'

Janine shrugged. I took that one to be a positive.

'Okay, thanks Megan. We'll call in at the Seaview sometime today and see what's what,' I said. I bought a couple of packets of crisps and stuffed them into the backpack that Janine would be carrying. *Well, why keep a dog and bark yourself?*

'You don't have to take the job, if you don't want to,' I assured Janine as I drove down the main road. 'We may be able to find something else.'

The shrug inside her seatbelt was open to interpretation. We quickly arrived at the lay-by at the edge of the river. It was an indulgence to have taken the car really as it would have been an easy walk on foot, but after such a restless night, I doubted I would have the energy to do the whole trek both ways. I locked the car, gave her an affectionate pat, and set off along the sheep track, which was just about visible through the young bracken. Janine trailed along behind.

CHAPTER NINETEEN

Janine shivered inside her hoodie. It was a grey, unwelcoming day, with a spiteful wind, which nipped every inch of her exposed skin. Tall ferns, drooping with the morning's dew soaked through the rips in her jeans and saturated her shoes, which squelched with each step. She was cold.

She jumped back startled as a sheep which had been completely hidden in the ferns, broke from cover in front of her and bolted off, her two lambs skipping and jumping along behind, their bleating sounding like malicious laughter. She watched them go, her hand clasped to her thudding heart. 'Bloody sheep,' she snarled through gritted teeth.

Janine stumbled on blindly through the sea of ferns until her foot caught in a whip of bramble that had stretched itself across the path like a booby trap, pitching her forward. She only just saved herself from a head-dive into the bracken. Up until that moment, Janine hadn't realized how much she hated the countryside. She was a city girl, born and bred. She understood the ways of the streets and alleyways. There were rules there, ways of living that everyone understood, whether they obeyed them or not; whereas here, she was at a complete loss. There was nothing familiar, no signposts to tell her what she should or shouldn't do. And the absence of noise frightened her, it was as if all human life had been wiped from the surface of the earth. At this distance she couldn't even hear the roar of the sea, and the silence was oppressive, broken only by the faint rustlings of unseen creatures through the grass and the manic screaming of the gulls.

What a stupid idea this had been! She shook her head. She had no-one to blame but herself, she thought, since it was she who had insisted on making the trip, but it certainly wasn't turning out to be any fun. And for what? She couldn't understand why she had got so excited about the grotty remnants of an old castle. She could only imagine it came from reading that *Two Rivers* book the day before which had brought back so many memories. When she had been a lot younger, she had spent hours and hours in her room reading and re-reading the adventures of the kids in those stories. She had known them so well, they had taken the place of brothers and sisters and her non-existent friends and in her fantasies she had gone off with them, standing side by side while they had fought off the invading Normans or had gone on other wonderful, impossible adventures. Sometimes she had got so involved that she hadn't been able to tell what was real and what was fantasy but she hadn't cared. The books had seen her through so many miserable times. When she had seen the castle, it had all come flooding back, swamping her with memories and feelings she had almost forgotten. Grow up, she chided herself.

'Come on, slow coach,' a disembodied voice shouted from up ahead.

There was no sign of the old woman. As Janine slogged along the path, it started slanting upward, and she realized that she had been walking in a deep gully and that the bracken fronds swaying above her head were in reality only waist high. She jogged up the trail, the bottles of water banging uncomfortably against her backbone. She suddenly emerged into the open and stopped to recover her breath. In front of her she could see the whole of the river valley. The river's muddy banks were exposed by the receding tide and were spotted white with gulls in search of a late breakfast. It meandered lazily along the wide valley floor, curving around the foot of the castle before disappearing inland. Purple clouds rested heavily on the shoulders of the distant hills.

Miss Cummings was waiting for her at the tarmac path that cut down from the main road and dipped down towards the river. They went through the small iron kissing-gate, which led up to a modern bridge spanning the dry moat. Above them rose the arch of the castle entrance flanked by a part of its one remaining entrance tower. Janine craned her head back and looked giddily up at the empty space where the battlements would have been. Ragged clouds scudded past, creating the impression that the ruined walls were about to topple down on her at any moment. It made her feel sick and giddy. A great black bird scolded her from the top of the ruined walls. Janine didn't like the way it fixed its beady little black eye on her as if it knew something but wasn't going to tell. She gave an involuntary shiver.

Miss Cummings was talking, and had been for some while, but Janine had not been listening. She filtered her voice in.

'...in wood, but in the twelfth century the Norman lord, de Londres, rebuilt it in stone and used the Sutton stone from a quarry near my house, for the decorative window and door surrounds and for the entrance archway.' She disappeared inside a low tunnel and her voice echoed back. 'Down here was... '

Janine let her hand trail across the stones, which despite the coldness of the day, felt warm to the touch. She imagined she heard the chink of metal, the scuffling of feet, the whisper of voices, and she even thought she could smell the sweat of unwashed bodies, of steel and leather and the ashes of long dead fires. No matter how many times Miss Cummings tried to deny it, Janine knew that this was the castle from the adventure books. She couldn't fathom out why the old lady was so determined to put her off. Everything fitted so well. Why make such a big deal of it?

'Come on,' Miss Cummings said, unaware that Janine had not heard a word she had been saying. 'It's low tide, so the stepping stones will be easy.'

Janine shook her head to clear it of the images she had conjured up. Thunder rumbled lazily down the valley. Miss Cummings took no notice. She had stopped at the edge of the river where a line of a dozen or more large stones were laid across it, spanning it from one side to the other. She steadied herself for a moment before leaping agilely across, stopping only to regain her balance between each one before leaping on to the next.

Janine watched her before following. Dora Cummings was a small woman, slightly chunky but neither fat nor thin. She had a lined face completely devoid of make-up or artifice, and grey deep-set eyes. Her short flyaway hair still retained some of its original blonde colour sprinkled in amongst the grey. She wore a brown shapeless sweater, jeans and sturdy walking boots. Janine had never been around any old people before, her only family had been her mother and, before he had buggered off, her father. And neither of them had been old. But she had a suspicion that Miss Cummings was not typical of what the average oldie should be like; in her imagination they had always been slumped on sagging sofas, slippers on their feet, television blaring too loud, with dribble trickling down their chins as they nodded off to the theme tune of *EastEnders.*

In a moment's clarity, Janine was surprised to find that she rather liked the old woman. She lived her life as she wanted and to hell with the rest of the world. Janine liked that about her more than anything else, in fact she had always felt the same. She had never fitted in. She was a loner too. It didn't seem possible that they could really be so alike when they were a couple of centuries apart in age, but when it came down to it, they were both just a couple of misfits going their own way. A kindred spirit? Had she finally found someone who could be her friend, she wondered. Was it such a ridiculous notion?

CHAPTER TWENTY

I stopped on the far side of the river and waited for Janine to catch up. I didn't turn to watch her. Crossing those stones, with the hypnotic swirl of the water as it rushed between them was challenging enough if you weren't used to them, and that was without having somebody scrutinising your every move. I suspected that at Janine's age, the humiliation of taking a ducking would be huge.

With my back turned to her I explained, 'This is the old track that went from the village to the castle. It crosses the other river – the *Ogmore* – which joins the one we just crossed just beyond the castle, though it has changed its course many times over the centuries. It's not tidal like the *Ewenny* and there's a pedestrian swingbridge that crosses over it. These days there's a single-track road off the main road, which comes in to the other side of the river, so only tourists and walkers use this track now. It's the back entrance to the village.'

Janine overtook me, having crossed unscathed, and ran on ahead. The track ran alongside fields of rough grass and thistles and fragments of old stone walls, most of which had long since been robbed out by the locals. I rounded the last bend and caught sight of her standing in the middle of the white painted iron bridge, which spanned the second river, a look of pure disgust on her face.

'Is this it?' she asked swinging her arms around. 'This can't be the magic bridge! It doesn't even move!'

I couldn't help but smile at her disappointment. 'This bridge is fairly new though it is still called the *swingbridge*. I remember when it was a real swingbridge,' I said as Janine tried jumping up and down in a vain attempt to get it to move. 'In my day it was suspended on ropes and the wooden planking was rotten with gaping holes where some of the planks had fallen into the river and drifted down towards the sea. It was lethal, but I used to have great fun running across it back and fro while it bounced around like the cakewalk in the fairground. I never gave a thought to its collapsing under me.'

'So this is just a modern one, then?' Janine said excitedly, her disappointment apparently having vanished in an instant. 'So I *am* right! The wooden one – that's just how it's written in the stories, about the planks missing, and that, and when the Norman soldiers chased the village children, it waited until the kids had got over safely and then would bounce all of its own accord and throw the soldiers into the river.'

'Don't be so daft,' I said tersely, kicking myself for giving the girl more fuel. I needed to stifle her growing excitement. It was all my own fault: I should never have agreed to come but somewhere in the back of my mind was the niggling thought that I may have wanted this. Subconsciously I was chuffed at her obvious delight in the books, while another part of me screamed for us to turn back – now. For a normally silent kid, she certainly got very vocal when it came to those books! 'There have been hundreds of bridges built here over the years what with rot and floods ripping them apart. I would imagine there are similar ones on every small river in Wales. Take your pick!'

I didn't want her to see the alarm on my face and walked swiftly away before she could answer. We emerged right into the heart of the village of Merthyr Mawr. On a sunny day it was a chocolate-box *Midsummer Murders* type of place of thatched cottages with roses and honeysuckle around the doors and a very rare find here at the edge of the industrial valleys. There were no modern houses, just thatched cottages of various sizes and designs from tiny one-roomed houses to the large vicarage, all built in the lovely soft creamy Sutton stone and limestone. It was a pretty, secluded village, which always seemed to me to have been transplanted from somewhere else and was a little self conscious, as if it was stuck in a time warp and didn't really belong. It attracted visitors in the summer months, but they were mostly locals or people in the know and the numbers never got out of hand.

I didn't linger, but walked quickly through the village, past the quaint little church where in early spring the graveyard was a carpet of snowdrops, and out the other side. Around the corner the road narrowed to a track with tall unkempt hedges on each side. In the summer it caused chaos for motorists and a lot of bad tempers as there were few passing points and plenty of potholes. It twisted and turned like all the best country lanes should until it ended dramatically in a small car park, which was slowly disappearing under a huge sand dune which blocked the way ahead.

'The sand is swallowing up this side of the river more every year,' I explained. 'I suppose eventually it will reach as far as the village, but that won't be in my lifetime or yours. It has almost buried the old manor house, which will be the last of the original 14th century hamlet to go under.'

'The manor house! That's where…'

'Oh, for Pete's sake, Janine, give it a rest.'

Janine turned and confronted me angrily. 'Why? Why are you trying to put me off? You know as well as I do that everything fits – the castle, the stepping stones, the swinging bridge and now the old manor house. The only thing that's missing is the cave, and I'm sure it's around here somewhere. You can tell me it's all rubbish until you are blue in the face, but I'm going to find it.'

'Good luck with that!' I countered scathingly. 'There are hundreds of caves around here because the whole area is limestone. You can choose whichever one takes your fancy. You can make anything fit if you try hard enough.'

'I don't care what you say, I know what I know!' Janine shouted back at me. Her face with flushed with temper and her eyes were unnaturally bright. 'You are treating me like I am an idiot, just like everyone else. Go ahead, laugh at me, tell me I'm stupid, I'm used to it. I thought you were different, but you are just the same as them. Well, fine, go ahead, make fun of me, but I know I am right. I know the woman who wrote the stories knew all about this place and she used it in her books.'

'You don't know that…'

'It says on the backs of the books that Anna Clare is Welsh, and I bet she came from around here. You can't say any different, so stop telling me what to think. If I'm such a pain in the arse, why don't you go back now and leave me here, I'll walk back. I'll collect my things and leave and then you won't have to listen to me anymore.'

'You are being overdramatic, Janine,' I said, shouting back at her. We were both getting angry with each other and my self control had deserted me. I had intended this jaunt to be a calming distraction for me after my hospital visit and a chance to blow away the cobwebs of my sleepless night, not to wage a war. Trying to steer her from the truth was like trying to deflect a cannon ball.

Janine was not calming down. She was furious. 'Those books were my only friends when I was a kid. I read them over and over. I know them! I could probably still quote them to you, word for word. They were safe, they were mine and I lived with those kids and joined in their adventures as if they were my own. They were precious to me, so don't you dare trash them or belittle them. You are a stupid, sad old woman without any idea of what it's like to be ignored and alone. You don't understand.'

She had started to plough her way back through the sand towards the lane and I shouted after her. 'I do understand, Janine, more than you realize. And I know all about those stories too, because I am Anna Clare,' I shouted at her retreating back. 'I wrote them.'

The instant the words were out of my mouth I was furious with myself for my carelessness but there was no way to take them back. I hoped she hadn't heard me, but I had forgotten the sharpness of young hearing. She stopped in her tracks and turned. Her mouth flopped open and a look of pure shock flickered across her face followed by one of mounting suspicion. The silence around us deepened; I could hear the rat-a-tat-tat of a woodpecker a quarter of a mile away in the distant woods. *Damn, damn, damn! Now I've really messed up!*

'You can't be her,' she stammered. 'You are a painter not a writer. You are lying!'

'I'm not lying, child; I do them both. But painting is purely visual and my eyes and my shoulders can only do so much fine work. I always needed something else, something which filled in the gaps and writing did that for me. When you think about it, it is the same thing but different – instead of using paint, I turn the pictures in my mind into words. It's fun.'

Janine shook her head vigorously. Her face was flushed red like a child having a tantrum. 'No, no, no. You can't be her, you are too old!' Her face hardened. 'You are making it up because you are making fun of me. You hate me and you are being nasty and horrible.' She turned to leave, angry and hurt.

She clapped her hands over her ears but she didn't move away.

'You said yourself you loved the books because they took you away from reality into a fantasy world where you could be an entirely different person,' I said quietly. She was listening even though she kept her back to me. 'Well, so did I. When I was even younger than you I started writing stories – total rubbish no doubt but I could lose myself in them for days on end. Nothing else mattered: the bullying from my brother and the indifference from my parents, the lack of love of any kind. I'm not saying I had it as bad as you, Janine, but I lived most of my childhood in a fantasy world. In my daydreams I could be anyone I wanted – younger, older, wiser or sillier, it didn't matter. In my daydreams I was free. I've done it all my life and it has meant that I still have a very active imagination which doesn't give a damn how old I am.'

I didn't know if she had heard me, but it felt good to have finally admitted it out loud. Her face was still ugly with mistrust but she sneaked a look at me out of the corner of her eye.

Almost grudgingly she turned to face me. 'I thought I was the only one who did that, daydream I mean,' she whispered in amazement. 'Are you saying it's normal?'

I laughed. 'Not at all. We are very special people. We create entire worlds from inside our own heads, we don't need to be spoon-fed computer games or rubbishy television programmes. The only difference is I wrote my make-believe worlds down and you could do the same. There's nobody stopping you except yourself.'

'Then why did you pretend you had nothing to do with them, that I was wrong when I said I recognized the castle and the rest of it.

You are famous. Kids love your books. They'd be coming here from all over the country if they knew.'

I gripped her fiercely by her arms and shook her. She would have bruises by the morning. 'That is exactly what I do not want. You must promise me that you will never tell another living soul who I am. Promise me, Janine.'

She seemed to miss the breathless panic in my voice.

'Why? I thought everybody wanted to be famous, and make oodles of money. They could even make them into films...'

'That is the last thing I want. My writing is my joy, Janine, nobody else's. If people like reading my stories, that's great, but they are done for my own enjoyment, not theirs. My identity has to remain a secret. You've seen the way I live. I value my privacy above all else. The money doesn't matter, I give most of it away anyway. If it got out who I was, then I would be forced to move away, to sell my home, and that is something I do not want to do. Please try and understand.'

Janine pulled herself out of my grasp and rubbed the pain out of her arms. She scowled at me. 'I don't know,' she muttered uncertainly. 'But don't you care that the people in the village think of you as just some doddering old fart...' I coughed at the bald cheek of the girl but she held up her hand. 'That didn't quite come out right, but you know exactly what I mean. They'd be chuffed to conkers to have a celebrity in the village.'

'With every horrible consequence that that would bring,' I answered sternly. 'People thinking they owned me just because they read my books, knocking on the door day and night, sending me manuscripts of their "masterpieces" to read or endorse, making a fuss all the time and me having to give some sort of polite response. I don't do polite! The local press would always be poking their noses in, picking my life apart; looking for scandal. I don't want that sort of pressure, I can't work under it and I have no intention of living under it.

'And just imagine what they would do to this place,' I continued, flinging my arms wide. My stitches pulled, reminding me that life was fleeting. 'They wouldn't have any respect for it or the village. They'd come down here in their hordes trampling all over it and taking away "souvenirs". What you see now would be destroyed. You wouldn't have to wait for the sand to take it over.'

'I wouldn't like that either,' Janine agreed quietly.

'I love this place and my home and my life, Janine. Promise me you will keep it our secret, or I will have to ask you to leave. I will say that you are making it all up, that you are a fantasist and not quite right in the head. People will believe me. Like you said, they think I'm just an old fart waiting to fall off her perch. They won't believe you. So, promise me, Janine. Not a word.'

'I won't say anything,' Janine answered sullenly.

I walked past her and down the lane. I was feeling light headed from not enough sleep and all the stresses of the past few days and now this row. And I was also angry with myself. It had only taken one careless word and I had put everything I had built for so many years into jeopardy. What a fool I was! And I was just as angry with Janine for having caused it. I heard her charging up behind me.

'Miss. Hang on a minute, Miss,' she shouted.

I rounded on her, hand on hips, ready for round two. 'Well?'

'I just want to say – thank you for writing the stories.' She gave me such a wonderful smile that I felt sudden tears prickle behind my eyes. 'I wouldn't want strangers messing around in my life either,' Janine said. 'I promise I won't say anything, ever.'

I was stunned at her sudden about-turn. Did I believe her? She seemed genuine and I felt I would be churlish not to take her at face value. 'Thank you, Janine. I'm trusting you to keep your word.'

We walked a while in a strained silence.

Janine was busy thinking. She didn't want to believe that this old woman could possibly be her childhood heroine. Just like the characters in the books, she had conjured up personalities and images of them all and somebody like Dora Cummings had never ever figured, not in a million years. But then she had to admit to herself that she had never been any good around people. Boy, had she been off whack on this one! Now she was more confused than ever.

'Miss, are all oldies like you?' she asked.

'Very few, dear,' I answered with a grin. 'Are all teenagers like you?'

Janine grinned back. 'Very few, Miss.'

CHAPTER TWENTY-ONE

We stopped at the edge of the river and sat down, gazing across at the old castle on the other side, its stone walls steel grey in the lowering light. We ate our sandwiches in silence, each engrossed in our own thoughts. A few heavy drops of rain squeezed themselves out of the leaden sky.

'Let's make a dash for it,' I said gathering up our bits and pieces and stuffing them into the backpack. 'We can finish our picnic in the car.'

Janine followed her in a quick trot across the stepping stones and back through the bracken. She couldn't get what had just happened out of her head. How could this old woman, who must be at least a hundred, know how to write such exciting books for children? And yet all her characters had been totally believable. Initially she had felt elated to be in the company of her most favourite writer in the whole world, but then she had started to feel almost betrayed, as if she had been tricked.

But the more she thought about it, the more she could see that Dora Cummings was anything but ordinary, even though she pretended to the world that she was. Not only could the woman paint exquisitely but it seemed that she was also a famous writer whom nobody knew about. She was famous within her own private world and it was enough for her. When Janine looked at her now, she didn't see an old woman any more, but someone who was exciting and interesting, someone she wanted to know. It was a new and disturbing feeling.

She had intended staying with her for only a short while, grabbing anything she could before moving on. But now? She felt that everything had changed. She wanted to stay. To stay with the one person she could respect, the one person who had ever shown her kindness. But the sudden need to be wanted and liked scared her. What if she had read it all wrong and she would be turfed out for doing something wrong and she landed back on the road on her own again. It would feel worse than ever before because this time she would have lost something precious, something she yearned for with every fibre of her body. Was she willing to risk that? Perhaps it would be best if she didn't get her hopes up, then it would not all end in disappointment.

We reached the car before the heavens opened and dived in, gasping for breath. As I drove home, I tried to understand how the ground had shifted so suddenly. I had thought that we were building something between us but somehow or other between the lane and the river it had dissipated like morning mist. That brief glimpse of mutual rapport I had felt after I had stupidly revealed myself had gone and once more Janine had withdrawn into her shell. She turned her shoulder to me and gazing out of the window with a sulky, brittle expression on her face.

We drove back in a strained silence. For a short time, I had to admit that I had enjoyed my break from my own problems, but with the sudden tension and Janine's sullen withdrawal combined with my sleepless night and the exercise, they were all starting to take their toll and the only things I wanted now were my armchair, some soothing music, a dry sherry and my own thoughts.

Janine hovered as I put the car in the garage. 'What about the job the woman in the shop mentioned?'

'I don't have the energy to do any more for now, Janine. I want my own space. Why can't you go off and see to that yourself? It's your job after all.'

A slight frown creasing her forehead and she pouted at the sharpness of my tone. I did not relent. Offering a stranger a bed for a couple of nights was one thing, but I did not intend setting myself up to be her babysitter. She shrugged, but I sensed it rather than saw it as I had already turned away to my back door.

I thought no more about her. I made myself a mug of coffee and took it into the front room. The thunderstorm was rolling off the land towards Somerset, taking its curtains of rain with it. The sea was a bruised purple colour. In the far distance, fork lightning split the underbelly of the clouds but it was moving away and losing its strength.

I awoke to weak sunshine, a stiff neck and a cold mug of coffee. I had no idea of how long I had been asleep but it must have been a while because I felt sluggish and thick-headed. I went out to check on the chickens knowing that they would have hated the storm. If they had been out loose when it had hit, they would be in hiding and it would take hours to round them up for the night.

As I opened the back door, I bumped into Janine. She had her backpack over her shoulder and even though she turned her head away quickly, I could see that her eyes were red from crying. She started to push her way past, but I grabbed her by the arm and pulled her towards me.

'What has happened? Where are you going?' I asked.

She pulled her arm free. 'I don't know what you want from me,' she said angrily. 'You pretend you care about me and that you want me to stay and then you say such horrible things about me and call me names. You say one thing to my face and another behind my back. I don't know what you want from me,' she repeated with an anguished cry. She only knew that the dreams she had dared to dream had been shattered for her.

'Janine, child, I have no idea what you are talking about? What is it I'm supposed to have said, and to whom?'

A flicker of doubt crossed her face. She hung her head and muttered to her shoes. 'I went for that job.'

'And?'

'I didn't get it.'

'That's not the end of the world. You can try somewhere else,' I said. 'But what is this about me calling you names? And to whom?'

She shrugged and clamped her lips shut.

'I told you, you could stay for another week whatever the outcome of the job hunting. You seemed fine with that. So why are you leaving? I don't know what I've done wrong.'

Another shrug.

'Janine, just tell me,' I almost shouted.

'Mrs. Jenkins was there. And she said that she didn't employ riff-raff off the street, I had to have references, whatever they are. She said I was too young and that my sort didn't know the meaning of the word work.'

'Well, that's not so bad. Anything else?' I asked as Janine hesitated and I knew there was more to come.

'I said I was living here with you, and that you'd speak up for me, and that the woman in the shop had said I should try for the job.'

I nodded but she was reluctant to go on. 'Janine, this is like getting blood out of a stone. Spit it out.'

Janine frowned. 'Stones don't have blood.'

'Tell me, for the love of God and all his angels!'

She spoke so quietly, I could only just make out what she was saying. 'She said she'd heard all about me, that everyone in the village was talking about me. She said *you* called me a filthy little gutter snipe who'd strip the clothes off your back when you weren't looking. That I wasn't to be trusted. Then she said that you were a batty old woman and that I was taking advantage of you because you were so desperate for company that you'd take in the sweepings out of the gutter.'

The whole speech was obviously quoted verbatim and fell into a deep bottomless silence.

I was stunned, shocked rigid. When I could find my voice I said, 'And Flo Jenkins was the one who said all this?'

Janine nodded. 'Did you? Did you say those things about me?'

'I have not said more than a dozen words to that woman in all the time I have lived here, other than when she and The God Squad paid me a visit earlier in the week. And if my poor addled old brain serves me right, that was before I even knew you existed. So, no, I did not say those things about you. I wouldn't.'

'Oh.'

I tried taking deep calming breaths but it didn't work. 'You turn right back around and unpack your things,' I said after a long pause. 'If you want to leave, then it obviously is your choice, but you are not going like this. She has slandered both of us and I for one am not going to let her get away with it. I'll call for you in an hour when I've had time to cool down and think things through.'

I desperately needed to get control of my temper or I was liable to blurt out things which should never be said and, once aired, could never be retrieved. It was one of my many failings and I was well aware of it. When I blew, I blew spectacularly, red mist and all. Either that or I would degenerate into a gibbering idiot and I would be proving her case for her. If, when I confronted her, I found that the battle wasn't worth fighting, then we could walk away with dignity. But I would not let Janine be used as a weapon by that the evil-minded harridan.

I couldn't think what had turned the woman so viciously against me. Was it just her or was that what everyone thought of me? But what I found most unforgivable of all was the slander she had invented against Janine using my name. How dare the woman!

I walked up and down the steep lane outside the house trying to think of a winning strategy, until I started getting dizzy and could hardly draw breath. Supporting myself against the wall with one hand, I knocked at the annexe door. Janine answered immediately.

'Are you alright?' she asked, taking in my bright red cheeks and strained breathing.

'Never better,' I gasped. 'Come on, let's go.'

Janine hesitated on the doorstep. 'You are not going to make a fuss, are you? I don't like it when people shout at each other. It doesn't matter what she said, so long as it wasn't you saying it.'

'Me? Make a fuss? Of course not!' I answered with mock innocence. 'I think I have a plan and you will go along with whatever I say. I will pretend I know nothing about what she has said to you, and say that I am merely there to give you a reference, which I was very remiss in not doing in the first place. Once I sweet-talk her into offering you a job, you can tell her what to do with it. Or you can take it – whichever you want. Okay?'

138

She raised a sceptical eyebrow. 'What about what she said about you?' she asked.

'You leave that to me,' I answered. 'I have been called far worse than that in my time. It's like water off a duck's back.' I held up a hand to block Janine's obvious questions about where ducks came into it.

I wasn't feeling as confident as I had led Janine to believe. I had been too long away from the cut and thrust of argument and debate. I would probably come out of this looking like a fool, but I couldn't let that woman get away with it. It would have festered away like a boil under my skin for months, and even if I did come off worst, at least I would have had my say.

CHAPTER TWENTY-TWO

Luckily it was Selwyn Jenkins and not his wife who was hovering in the reception hall of the hotel when we arrived. He had the flushed red cheeks, thickened purple nose and beer belly of a habitual drinker, but it was he who was the congenial host to all the visitors to the hotel. He was good-natured when sober and weepily nostalgic when drunk. Flo Jenkins was the opposite. She had pretensions of grandeur and still clung on to the delusion that her rightful place was running a swanky hotel in the heart of London and not actually in some last gasp of the tourist trade in a sleepy seaside village at the bottom end of Wales. Rumour had it that she was rather too fond of a gin and tonic or two, or three but then I was hardly in a position to cast stones in that respect.

Selwyn gave me a long hard look and then glanced at Janine. He raised both his hands in mock surrender. There was obviously no need to tell him about Janine's job interview. 'It's the wife who hires and fires, Miss Cummings,' he said kindly. 'I don't interfere. Personally, I've got nothing against the lass and we are desperate for help in the kitchen. But you'll have to take it up with Flo. She's in the lounge.'

'Thank you, Mr. Jenkins. There seems to have been some misunderstanding, and I wanted to put it right,' I said, and sailed through in what I desperately hoped was the direction of the lounge. If I landed up in a broom cupboard, my grand entrance would have been ruined.

To my horror, it wasn't just Flo Jenkins in residence, but Mrs. Anthony and Mrs. Elizabeth Henshaw as well. They were settled in the far corner of a large dimly lit room, its décor tired and in need of sprucing up. The 80s furnishings would never have been opulent enough to be able to get away with being classed as shabby chic. The detritus of afternoon tea and cakes littered the low circular table in front of them. The God Squad was holding court.

'Good afternoon, Mrs. Jenkins, ladies,' I said, walking

confidently through the otherwise empty lounge and halting in front of them. I tried to think of some pithy introduction but failed. Maggie Smith, where are you when I need you? 'I wonder if I might have a quick word with you in private, Mrs. Jenkins. I think I need to explain a few things about Janine's enquiry regarding the vacancy in the kitchen.'

Flo Jenkins was sitting in the middle of the group and showed no signs of moving. 'I have already given my decision on the matter. I have said "no" which I made perfectly clear to the child. I assume she understands the word – no?' she asked in a voice stiff with condescension. She hadn't even glanced in Janine's direction but challenged me directly.

I stared her down and let the silence stretch. Florence Jenkins was a large lady, with a heavily upholstered bosom and her white hair had recently been tinted a rather startling pink, whether by accident or design I wasn't quite sure. As with most overweight women, the natural padding on her face made it impossible to determine her age; creases, crevices and lines had no chance of survival.

'Oh yes, she understood you perfectly, Mrs. Jenkins, though I believe you said a little more to her than just a simple "no",' I answered. The other two seemed to sink further into their seats. 'You see, Janine is an extremely unusual girl. If you ask her a question, she answers with scrupulous honesty, to the point of embarrassment sometimes. And she seems to have a remarkable ability to memorize whole speeches, word perfect.'

Flo Jenkins' florid face blanched slightly. 'It is out of the question. She is far too young, and I doubt she has done a hard day's work in her life. The young are all the same, selfish and shiftless,' she said dismissively.

Not that long ago, I would probably have completely agreed with her views but Janine was slowly re-educating me. 'I think you are wrong on both points there, Mrs. Jenkins,' I answered, keeping my voice low and even. 'She looks younger than she is. She is in actual fact nearly sixteen. And as far as hard work is concerned I think Mrs.

Henshaw might back me up here,' I said, turning to the lady who so far had said nothing at all. I could use her presence to my advantage. She gave me a puzzled look. 'I believe you know Ted Morris?'

Mrs. Henshaw nodded. 'Yes, I do. I was there only yesterday in fact, to see how he was coping after his heart attack.'

Something I was well aware of as I had spotted her car parked outside when I had driven to the hospital. 'Did you happen to go into his kitchen, Mrs. Henshaw?'

Elizabeth Henshaw looked to the others and then back at me. 'Well, yes, as a matter of fact I did. He made me a cup of tea.'

'Was it clean and tidy, would you say?'

'Surprisingly so, in fact. I had expected chaos, you know – a man living on his own. They never seem to be able to look after themselves, do they, poor dears?'

'I wouldn't know if that is true as a general rule, Mrs. Henshaw, but when Janine and I called on him to do a bit of gardening earlier in the week, we had found it in a bit of a state. The poor man was only just getting around properly and it had all obviously got too much for him. Without a word from me, Janine turned too and cleaned and scrubbed his kitchen and sorted out all his cupboards. Would you say she did a good job?'

Elizabeth Henshaw looked uncertainly at Flo Jenkins. 'It was immaculate, Flo,' she said. 'I wouldn't mind her doing the same for me at the vicarage.'

Flo Jenkins huffed and puffed as she tried to think up a fitting riposte. If she had expected backup from her companions, she had been disappointed. Between us we had effectively wrong-footed Mrs. Jenkins. I never thought I would be grateful to have Elizabeth Henshaw on my side – even unwittingly. 'Well, I couldn't let her near the guests' bedrooms. The hotel is accountable for the safety of the guests' belongings. It is a huge responsibility.'

The woman was floundering and I decided to go in for the kill, with the help of just one teeny-weeny white lie. 'It is true that I have only known Janine for a few days, but I trust her implicitly. And a job in the kitchens would not bring her into contact with members of the public. Mr. Jenkins has only just told me that you were still looking for staff.'

'Yes, but…'

'How about a week's trial, Mrs. Jenkins, on basic wages of course since she is only fifteen, for however many days you want the extra help?'

Mrs. Anthony, the timid little mouse who always seemed to be nursing some hidden source of amusement, spoke up for the first time. 'You were only just saying you were worried about the engagement party booked for tonight, Flo. The girl seems to be an answer to your prayers.'

'Well, yes, but…' She was still not getting any encouragement from either side, and I could almost see the moment of her capitulation. She seemed to physically deflate. 'Very well. You can start tonight at six, on trial. If you don't come up to scratch, you are out. I will be watching very closely.' Her rolls of fat quivered.

Janine stepped forward. I had no idea what she was going to say. She fixed her eyes an inch or two above Flo Jenkins' head. 'I'll take it, Mrs. Jenkins because I don't want it to be said that I am sponging off anyone. I am a good worker and I want to pay my way with Miss Cummings. She has been very good to me and she took me in when nobody else gave a flying fuck.' She said it calmly and clearly as if talking to a child, then turned on her heel and walked away, her head held high.

Flo Jenkins opened her mouth to answer, but wisely shut it again. Elizabeth Henshaw blushed furiously and Mrs. Anthony chuckled into her lace handkerchief.

I would have to have a word with the girl about her ripe language, but silently I cheered my little protégé as we left the lounge to a thunderous silence.

Wow, Janine thought as she followed the diminutive frame of Dora Cummings out of the hotel. Nobody had ever stood up for her before, for any reason. And she had even lied for her, because she actually said she trusted her, as if that crime of the century with the bar of chocolate had never happened. Thank God she didn't know about her secret rummaging through her private things!

She was getting more and more confused, as if she was caught in a river and was being swept along without any choice. She had never been one to look ahead, into her future. As far as she could see, she had never had one worth thinking about anyway. But now? Dare she hope? She had to know if the old woman was going to boot her out in a week's time.

'Will you let me stay longer than a week if I pay you rent?' Janine asked me as we walked back up the lane. 'The old cow probably won't pay much, but like you said, I can do some cleaning for you and others and look after the chickens to make up the rest.'

How could I say no when I had just trumpeted the kid's virtues to The God Squad?

'I said you could stay another week and I will review things then,' I answered. 'I have a lot on my plate at the moment and I really can't think much beyond that. You can work for Mrs. Jenkins...' I laid particular emphasis on the lady's correct title, '...for the week and maybe Ted Morris as well. Anything you earn will be yours to keep.'

'Okay.'

'In the next couple of days, I would be grateful if you would do some hoovering around the house; I've been told not to do anything heavy. But you can only come in when I am there, and you must never enter the spare bedroom where I do my painting. Do you understand?'

'Are you ill then?'

'Not ill, no, but I have had a couple of stitches, so I have to be careful.'

'Shall I start on the house now?'

'No, tomorrow or the day after will be fine,' I said rather sharply. 'You've only got a couple of hours before you have to report to the kitchens and I could do with being on my own for a while.'

Janine disappeared around the side of the house towards the annexe. I brewed a mug of Earl Grey tea, and took it into the sitting room and gazed out over the sea whilst it cooled. Less than a week had passed and I could hardly recognise myself. Where had my peaceful life gone? I had had it all planned out and up until now it had been working out splendidly. I had passed my days in quiet contentment, with leisurely strolls across the cliff-tops, with my paintings and my writing – and by minding my own business! In the space of a few days I had managed to antagonize the powerful God Squad, been diagnosed almost certainly with breast cancer and picked up a waif and stray to whom I had blurted out one of my most dearly held secrets. I had a runaway as a lodger and I had no idea where I stood legally with harbouring a fifteen year old in my home. And now I had launched myself into a running battle with Flo Jenkins – and won! It was all getting too much for my frazzled nerves. I was exhausted.

CHAPTER TWENTY-THREE

The night had finally dragged its feet towards dawn. I had lain fully awake unable to get off to sleep, waiting for any sound that meant that Janine had got back safely after her first stint at the hotel. Every minute I had expected her to return in a fury, but the house had remained silent. There was still an old World War II air-raid siren mounted on the roof of the Seaview Hotel, and it had to be a good sign that I hadn't heard it go off.

I had squinted at my bedside clock when I heard the bang of the annexe door closing. It was 2.32 a.m. Flo Jenkins had certainly been getting her money's worth from the kid. After that, I could have sworn that I had not gone to sleep, but by the time I woke the sun was just bleaching the horizon.

I washed quickly in cold water and grabbed a jacket against the morning chill, though by the look of the sea haze it promised to be a fine day. I let the chickens out into their run and threw them a handful of feed.

I was too unsettled to stay still, I didn't even want to stop for breakfast so I grabbed a rather stale bread roll and a piece of cheese and left. I needed to walk and think.

Now that my problem of what to do with Janine was sorted for the time being, my brain had made the decision during the night to torture me with my impending diagnosis. So much had happened the previous day that I hadn't had time to think and all sorts of scenarios had worked their way into my waking dreams. It had kept revisiting the same question, over and over. What if? What if? What if the cancer was more advanced than they said and they were hiding it from me? What if I would need to have not just invasive surgery but the horror of chemotherapy treatment as well? Would I lose my hair? I was not and never had been a vain person, but I imagined that without the camouflage of hair I would be revealed for what I was – a wrinkled inhabitant of *The Lord of the Rings*. Gollum would be favourite! The final indignity would be to lose my teeth as well – boobless, hairless and toothless!

I locked the back door and set off down the lane towards the beach and the sea. All these thoughts were still crowding my mind as I stepped out briskly over the cropped turf of the cliffs. To my right the distant hills across the channel were hidden by the morning haze. The sea was a featureless flat grey calm.

'Are you enjoying this wallowing in self pity, Dora Cummings?' I asked myself and to my surprise realized that I had said it out loud. Luckily for me, at that time in the morning there was nobody around, so it was only the dawn bunnies who witnessed my embarrassing downward spiral.

I was annoyed with myself too. I thought I had come to terms with my most likely diagnosis, but it seems the night horrors, over which one can have no control, had had different ideas. They had unnerved me.

I walked on and on, desperate to outrun my tumbling thoughts.

The sun was high by the time I came to my senses and I stopped to look around. I hadn't noticed where I had been walking or how far, and to my dismay I realized that I had walked right across the top of the cliffs and was half-way down the cliff road into the next bay. What had eventually stopped me had been the amount of traffic on the narrow road, mostly heading down towards the beach, but a few were struggling to barge their way through in the other direction. It was a sunny Sunday morning, the first of the new season, and trippers were flocking there in their hundreds. They should have spent a couple of extra minutes checking the tide times before they left home, I thought churlishly. The tide was still crawling up the huge bank of pebbles which fringed the beach and wouldn't be retreating for a couple of hours yet. The tiny ice-cream kiosk would be doing a roaring trade, and trippers clutching their inflatable dolphins and lathered in sun-cream waited impatiently for the tide to turn. I turned around and headed back home.

It would be a long hot walk back, but now that my brain was

finally in gear I could shorten it considerably by following the road and then cutting across a couple of farmers fields. It had turned unusually hot for so early in the year and there was very little wind; a day stolen straight out of summer. The heat was bouncing off the pavements as I trudged down the road and the sparkle from the sea sent daggers piercing into my eyes. I hadn't brought my sunglasses and my head started to throb. Behind my eyes I could feel the first tightening as an eye-migraine started.

I slumped down on the old stone mileage marker at the edge of the village and rested my head in my hands to shade my eyes from the glare. I would just have to wait for it to take its own course.

'You okay, Miss?' a voice asked from beside me, startling me.

I squinted around the zigzag lines which by now obliterated half my sight. The boy from the fossil quarry stood there. He thrust a water bottle towards me.

'It'll be warm, but it's wet,' he explained.

I took the bottle gratefully and took a good swig. 'You are a life saver,' I said handing it back to him. 'I'll be fine now, thank you.'

'Have you done the photos yet, the ones from down the quarry?' he asked. 'I've been back down and I found a fossil but I don't know what it's called.'

I got up and carefully set off down the road, boy in tow. 'There's a couple of more photos I want to take before I get them printed, so it will be a day or so yet. I said I'd leave yours with Mrs. Hardy at the shop.'

I meandered along the pavement in a more or less straight line and at least I didn't fall off the edge of the kerb into the road.

'Shall I walk home with you, Miss. You don't look too steady.'

'No thank you, lad. I know my way. I'll be fine in another ten minutes or so and by then I'll be home. Thank you again.'

The boy gave me a dubious look and left me. Good lad; he knew when to take a hint.

As I laboured up the lane on the final stretch, desperate for

148

home, Ted Morris stepped out and blocked my way. 'I've been watching out for you, Dora,' he said. 'I saw you going out and I've been keeping an eye open.'

'Why, Ted? What's wrong?' I asked. I didn't think I could cope with any more problems.

'Nothing wrong, old girl. When I saw you earlier, you looked as if you were carrying the weight of the world on your shoulders. Come on in and have a cuppa or a cold drink. You look as if you need one.'

'I'm nearly home now, Ted. Thank you all the same.'

'I'm not taking no for an answer,' Ted Morris replied, waving his walking stick to block my way, as if he was shepherding a wayward sheep. 'Get yourself inside. You can talk if you want, or not. I know you like your own privacy but sometimes it is – like the advert says – good to talk.'

'No, I don't think so, Ted. I'll just want to get myself home.'

'I don't think I am capable of putting you in a headlock, and I know you wouldn't want to be responsible for me being rushed back into intensive care, so do me an enormous favour, Dora Cummings, and come in and keep an old man company, for as long as it takes to make and drink a cup of tea. Please?'

'I must look a terrible sight, and I am all sweaty from walking in this heat,' I protested. 'And I've got a headache…'

'It's nice and cool in the kitchen, and you look fine to me. Now, come on in out of the sun.'

Reluctantly I followed him into his kitchen, which was blissfully dark and cool. I pulled out one of the chairs at the table and sank down with a sigh of relief. Without saying another word Ted put a tall glass of water and a pack of paracetamol in front of me, and turned to fill the kettle and get out mugs and a plate of biscuits. I ached all over.

Ted was true to his word and we drank our tea in silence for a while, with only the ticking of the Westminster clock on the mantelpiece providing a soothing accompaniment. I started to feel awkward. I didn't really know this man. Our only common denominator was that we were neighbours of a similar age who seemed to have lived our separate lives in splendid isolation even though we only lived yards apart. Two stubborn, independent old stick-in-the-muds who had not known how, or had even wanted, to reach out to somebody else.

'Is it the girl that's upset you, Dora?' he asked eventually.

'Who says I am upset?' I answered sharply. I was being prickly, I knew it. It was like when you are in a bad mood and you are told you are in a bad mood, which makes the bad mood even worse. I could justify it to myself by blaming the migraine; they always left me tired and brittle.

'You've certainly got a bee in your knickers by the look of you. And that is not the Dora Cummings I know.'

'Since when do you think you *know* me, Ted Morris,' I said indignantly, starting to rise from the table.

'Don't start getting all offended, Dora,' Ted said, taking a firm hold of my hand and stopping me from leaving. 'We've both seen each other coming and going over the years, and you have been kindness itself to me over the past weeks since I've been recuperating. But since that lass has come, you have not been your normal level-headed self. I don't think I have ever seen you in such a tizzwaz.'

I sat back down and shook my head. 'It's not the girl, well not really. She's just a part of it,' I admitted. I fiddled with my empty mug, turning it this way and that.

'Those busy bodies from the church then?'

'Yes and no.'

'Was it the man in the BMW who blocked the bottom of the lane the other day? He was stopped there for a good twenty minutes before driving up to your place.'

'My brother! Oh, good God, no. I haven't given him another thought.'

'Well, if it's none of the aforementioned, then I give in. But if you want to chew over whatever is bothering you, it won't go any further than this room, I promise you,' Ted said. 'Scout's honour.'

'Were you ever in the scouts, Ted?' I asked.

'I went once, for a whole day. That was enough,' Ted laughed.

'Can we get off the subject of me, please,' I begged. 'Tell me about yourself instead. Other than that you hated the scouts, I don't know much about you, which is disgraceful after all these years. What did you do for a living – I don't even know that?'

'You are changing the subject, but that's fine, if it's what you want,' Ted said, pouring us both another mug of tea which was a bit stewed by now but it was wet. 'I worked in Safety at the NCB offices down in Tondu until a couple of years before they closed. I enjoyed the job, a good mix of office and practical, but we could all see that the mines were in trouble – it was the eighties. So I got out when I could and got a decent pension from it.'

'My brother worked there. Did you know him, James Cummings.'

Ted grimaced and stirred his tea, not looking me in the eye. 'He was the one in the BMW? I often wondered if you might have been related – Cummings isn't a common surname in this part of the world.' He squinted up at me and sighed. 'Yes, I knew him alright. He was a pernickety, nit-picking bastard who ruined anybody who went up against him or disagreed with him. He set himself up as a little Hitler and, though he may have been good at pushing paper around, he was hated by everybody. I tried to have as little to do with the bastard as I could. Sorry, Dora.'

I gave him a wry smile. 'No need, Ted. There's nothing so bad that you can say about my brother that I haven't already said a hundred times over. It's nice to know that I wasn't the only one.'

'I remember the day you came here, Dora. It was in January, and the weather was wild, force 8 gale, lashing rain and winter bleak. I half expected to see you packing your bags the very next day, but you've hung on like a native. But I've never seen you looking so down. Come on, girl, a problem shared and all that twaddle. Spit it out.'

151

And I did. Just like that. He heard me out without saying a word. I should have realized Ted would have understood. His heart attack had been a serious one and had nearly seen him off. He had been lucky that it had happened when he was out shopping and he had been rushed straight to hospital. If it had happened at home he would never have survived. Nobody would have known perhaps for days. Another of the drawbacks of living alone and best not to think about.

'So, how can I help?' he asked after I had finished. No pity, no meaningless clichés, and I was grateful for that.

'You have already, my friend,' I answered, giving his hand a tweak and getting wearily to my feet. 'I was feeling a bit sorry for myself, and everything seemed to be crowding in on me. But I do feel better now. One day at a time, like the song says.'

'No other way to live it, Dora, not at our age,' Ted said, giving me a gentle understanding smile. 'I'm here if you want me. That rockery is only half done, you know, and I really do need that lass of yours to sort the house out.'

'I'll tell her, Ted. Now I must go. I need a lie down – I'm shattered.'

As I struggled up the lane, I felt as if a cloud had been lifted from above my head and had been replaced by high clouds threatening light rain later. Maybe Ted had been right and the very act of talking through my problems had put them into perspective.

When I arrived home, I crashed out on the settee and had four hours of the best sleep I had had in weeks.

CHAPTER TWENTY-FOUR

Over the next couple of days I didn't see much of Janine, and to be honest I was too busy making up for the time I had lost while I had been in such a lather. She had popped her head around the door to tell me that she would be doing more shifts down at the hotel, mostly in the evenings. She had said she would be managing for herself for food as the chef had told her she could help herself to any leftovers, which would otherwise be thrown out. She said she would like to join me for breakfasts though, if that was alright.

And that was it. We fell into a routine without noticing. She collected the eggs and brought them in while I made breakfast. A couple of times she brought me a fancy pastry or a triangle of savoury flan, which had made their way from the Seaview kitchen. Neither of us spoke much, which suited me fine, especially first thing in the morning.

I remembered to get my photographs of the fossil quarry and the boy developed in the post office on the main road. It had its own developing machine and Mrs. Davies who ran the post office cum shop cum mini plant nursery kept it in perfect working order always. I dropped the photos of the boy off to Megan Hardy who knew exactly who it was.

'That's young Jimmy Farr. His parents leave him to run wild but he is still young and there's no real harm in him so long as I keep an eye on where his hands are when he's in the shop. He's already been in asking, every day in fact,' she said with an indulgent smile.

'I'm sorry, Megan. I told him not to pester you, but I didn't want to tell him where I lived,' I explained. 'I don't want any more waifs and strays turning up at my door. One is enough!'

My life returned to its even keel and I picked up my writing again. The chat with Ted had done me the world of good and I was fizzing with energy once more – well, at least as "fizzing" as anyone my age can be! I hadn't touched my laptop in days and I had been three quarters of the way through the first draft of my latest *Two Rivers* book when everything had ground to a halt. It was now at its most critical stage.

I worked hard for a few hours, picking up the threads of my imaginary friends again, before it became apparent that my experiences of the past week had started to colour my thinking. My original plot now seemed rather limp. I was feeling dangerously rebellious and wondered if I dared take my little characters off on an entirely different tangent, something unexpected which would make my readers sit up and think. Hmm.

A rewrite would delay my deadline and I had been expecting my agent, Melissa Sinclair, to be shouting down the phone already, demanding a progress report. Melissa was a lady with a personality as big as her voice and, though we had only met once (on my stipulation) we got on very well together. I'd have to make it good so that she would consider the wait worthwhile.

I slogged away at it for a few days, immersing myself in a fantasy over which I had complete control, though it was still lacking something, which I could not quite put my finger on. It felt good to be back at work.

But I was soon hankering for a bit of painting. I liked to have variety in my working days, to give my brain a rest and indulge in colour and paint, which seemed to satisfy both of my creative needs. The new storyline was coming along and I made myself finish the chapter before I thought about setting off on a hike up over the downs in search of the early purple orchids which should be just about coming into flower. I knew a secluded spot where they grew, sheltered inside a stand of hawthorn and hazel scrub. It was illegal to pick them, so I would have to do my initial studies in situ. The weather was rather indifferent, but a dull flat light was better for sketching or painting as sunshine tended to bleach out the details. I packed my canvas painting bag with camera, paints, pencils and pads, and was lacing up my trainers, eager to be off.

Janine gave a perfunctory knock and walked in. She made herself toast and tea even though it was by now mid morning and sat down beside me. I had learned that where Janine was concerned, it was never obligatory to enter into a conversation, but I felt guilty at having neglected her over the last couple of days.

'How is the job going?' I asked. 'Are you surviving?'

She gave me a sideways glance and returned to her toast. 'It's okay.' She sighed heavily. 'Mrs. Jenkins wants me there to help with a wedding reception on Sunday, but it would mean a late finish and you are kicking me out on Saturday, so I said no.'

Oh, definitely below the belt that one! I wasn't sure whether she was manipulating me or whether she was simply being honest. Whichever it was, she succeeded.

'I said I would be reviewing it on Saturday not kicking you out, as you put it. But since you've got a booking, I think you could stay for the weekend and we'll discuss it again next week,' I said. 'Don't forget that you promised Mr. Morris that you would do some cleaning for him as well.'

'I've already been a couple of times.'

'Oh! Right! Well, I'm off out, so don't let me hold you up.' A very unsubtle hint for her to leave.

The warble of the telephone interrupted me just as I was locking the door. I considered not answering it. I rarely got social phone calls, so I suspected it was probably a scammer, or Amazon telling me to renew my Prime account, whatever that was. I was in half a mind to ignore it, but on the other hand... twenty years of working in an office where the rule was never to allow a telephone to ring unanswered had hot-wired itself into my psyche. I went back in and picked it up. I didn't recognize the voice on the other end of the line but she quickly introduced herself as, Susan, the clinical nurse whom I had met in the clinic. My first reaction was one of cold panic, which Susan had obviously anticipated as she put my mind at rest immediately.

'There's nothing to worry about, Dora. But your results are in and we have had a cancellation for 12.30 today. If you would prefer to wait until your arranged appointment next Monday, that would be fine, but Mr. Preston thought you might like to have them as soon as possible – less time to worry. What do you think? Could you get here on time?'

Waiting was not going to alter the results of the biopsy tests, so the sooner the better as far as I was concerned. I had always been one to face my challenges head on, and there seemed no point in spending more restless nights going over and over the possibilities in my mind. During daylight hours I had already more or less accepted the fact that I had breast cancer, but without the full facts to hand, at night my imagination was working overtime. At least this way I would have no more time to speculate. In a few hours I would know for sure.

'Yes, of course, that would be wonderful,' I answered. 'I will be there at 12.30, and thank you.'

Hopefully, there would be many more opportunities to go in search of my orchids. I ushered Janine out and rushed to take a quick shower and change into some decent clothes. I knew they were clean as I had yanked them out of the airing cupboard, but other than that I didn't really notice what I wore.

I had kept my clinic documents and the leaflets they had given me tucked behind the brass candlestick on the mantelpiece, and had moved them on to the kitchen table before I went to change so that I could put them straight into my handbag. Needless to say, when I got to the hospital, I discovered I had forgotten to put them into my bag, but there wasn't really any need for them as the receptionist had been warned to expect me. Susan met me at the door to the consultant's office and I went in on the dot of half past twelve. Whether it was because of the unexpectedness of the appointment or the rush of getting there I didn't know, but I was not feeling in the least bit apprehensive. That heart-to-heart I had had with Ted may have been embarrassing at the time but it seemed to have clarified matters in my own mind and I had lost the terror I had felt on my previous visit. I was ready to listen, to put on my armour and prepare myself for the battles to come.

Mr. Preston rose from behind his desk, and shook my hand. My file lay open in front of him and I thought it seemed quite considerably thicker than the last time I had seen it.

He gave me a quick appraising look before saying, 'Well, Dora, it is as I suspected. The tests confirmed that you have a lobular carcinoma in the left breast, which is one of the commonest types. It is small and in its very early stages. I doubt it has had time to spread. Okay so far?'

I nodded and couldn't think of anything to say.

He placed a hand heavily on the top of the file. 'It is up to you how we proceed from here.'

'I read the leaflets you gave me, and really by the end I was more confused than when I started,' I admitted. 'Could you advise me, please; after all you are the experts.'

'I can lay out your options for you, Dora, but the final decision has to be yours,' he answered. 'Firstly, you could do nothing – which I most seriously advise against – it will not go away of its own accord. Secondly you could have chemotherapy alone. Thirdly, you can have the lump surgically removed, and, subject to further scans, you can opt for either a lumpectomy or a mastectomy: again, the decision will be yours. With a bit of luck, you won't need chemotherapy afterwards, but will be able to get away with taking a tablet once a day for the next five years. I would imagine you would have no objections to that?' He smiled gently at his little quip. He paused briefly to measure my reaction. 'Are there any questions you would like to ask me?'

I shook my head. 'You may think this a strange thing to say, but it is has almost been a relief to know where I stand,' I answered. 'I am grateful that it has been found early, and I appreciate that you haven't tried soft-soaping me with a bucket of platitudes. Obviously I would like to know where we go from here, but I feel very safe in your hands, and, believe me, I don't say something like that lightly.'

Mr. Preston smiled with relief as well as a slight approving nod of his head. 'You have the right attitude, Dora. Beating cancer depends as much on your own mental outlook as it does on the surgeon's scalpel. You can think over your options for a day or so and then let Susan know. Between us, I'm confident that we'll get this one licked.'

'I'd be grateful if you would tell me a bit more about what is likely to happen from here on in, if for instance I opted for surgery which I am tending towards. I live on my own, you see, and I need to know what preparations I have to make,' I said. 'I don't particularly like surprises; I much prefer to be as prepared as I possibly can.'

'That's no problem. You can have a chat with Susan before you leave and she will explain everything to you and give you more detailed literature, now that we know which variety of beast we are dealing with.

A half an hour later I left the hospital clutching a card with further appointments for various scans and consultations, which would keep me busy for the next few weeks.

We had parted almost like old friends, my bag weighed down with booklets and papers, which I intended reading carefully that evening. I probably wouldn't understand the half of it, but I wouldn't be going into it totally ignorant. I wanted to gather as much information as I could. Mr. Preston had again warned me about the vagaries of the internet and fake news. He had sounded guardedly hopeful that it was a very early, simple, tumour, and these days no doctor would dish out false hopes like that without being 99% certain of a correct diagnosis. I believed him. I had faith in him.

I wondered if I should tell Ted, but decided that it could wait a few days. I was still trying to get over the shock of my meltdown at his kitchen table and didn't want to appear to be too needy, but it was comforting to think that somebody might be worried about me.

I drove back home via the motorway, this time well aware of my surroundings and traffic conditions, but I didn't fancy going straight home. I parked for a while at the side of the road overlooking the estuary, watching the oystercatchers scampering around the seaweed and mussel-encrusted rocks in search of goodies. The tide was ebbing and the birds were dashing frantically from one rock to another as more were revealed by the receding waters, always on the lookout for something better. I knew a few people exactly like that!

I felt better than I had for days. I had been freed from all those "what ifs" and I was ready to get on with my life again. It had been on hold for too long. I decided I would grab a quick cup of tea and a sandwich before setting off in search of those orchids.

My brother's car was parked outside my house. I mouthed an obscenity, which I assure you I only used in extreme circumstances, but there was nobody around to hear me. He was the very last person I would have wished to see as he was bound to put an end to my newfound positive thinking. I pulled in beside the BMW and, as I got out of my car, I heard his raised voice coming from the kitchen. He was obviously giving somebody a tongue-lashing, and from past experience I knew that that person needed rescuing. But how had he got inside my house and who could he be berating?

CHAPTER TWENTY-FIVE

The noise – all of it my brother's – was coming from my open back door.

'I think you should turn out your pockets, young lady, before I report you to the police,' he was shouting. 'Goodness knows what will have gone missing with that imbecile sister of mine allowing all and sundry to have the run of the house, and her nowhere to be seen.'

Janine's timid voice was only barely audible. 'I told you, I've been cleaning the kitchen. I haven't taken anything.'

'And I am supposed to take your word for that, am I? For all I know you've broken in here and I have only just arrived in time to stop you from trashing the place,' James shouted angrily. Spittle sprayed over Janine who seemed to be too terrified to move out of range. 'And where is my sister? Can you even tell me that?'

James had had his back to the open doorway, blocking any means of escape, and hadn't noticed my presence. I could well imagine his face suffused an unhealthy shade of red as he whipped himself up into a self-righteous rage.

Janine however, had seen me and shot a furtive glance in my direction. James finally paused long enough to realize that they were not alone. I waited for him to turn and face me. He looked so startled that I feared for one moment that he would have a heart attack to accompany the stroke he was cranking himself up for.

I carefully and slowly placed my handbag on the table and squared up to him, hands on hips, chin out. 'Since when do I need your permission to have friends in my own house?' I asked. My voice was incredibly cool, almost to the point of icy. 'Take note, James, I said *my* house. And just in case you do not know what a friend is, James, it is someone whose company you enjoy without any strings attached and who feels a mutual rapport towards you; a person whom you can be comfortable with and who sticks by you through thick and thin, good times and bad. I am trying to make allowance for your ignorance, as I doubt you have ever had any friends beating a path to your door. But just in case the possibility should ever arise, you should know that it is not customary to have to issue them with identity papers or gold embossed invitations before they are allowed to pop in for a chat or a cup of tea.'

He ignored my sarcasm. 'Where have you been?' he blustered.

'That is none of your business, either, James,' I answered calmly. 'But now that you have had your melt-down, I think it is high time you explained *your* reason for standing in *my* kitchen haranguing a friend. A friend, I may add, who is doing something you should wholly approve of – housework! Then you can leave and I want never to lay eyes on you again.'

For a moment he was speechless. And so nearly was I. I felt so calm. I felt in charge, not intimidated or tongue-tied. If the man hadn't taken the unsubtle hints I had given him the last time he had called – was that only a week ago? – then I was happy to spell it out to him again. I looked at the man standing before me, a thin man, his face flushed with temper, his pale blue eyes rheumy with old age. He was a grey man who had lived a grey mediocre life, and who still clung to the belief that the world had been unfair to him, had failed to fully appreciate his worth. For forty years he had sat behind a desk shifting paper from one side to the other (and as Ted Morris had said, a man hated by all); a nonentity, a nobody, with nothing now left to him to justify his existence. We had fought since childhood. Well, no more. With the shifting axis of my world after the morning's revelations, I knew that I wanted him out of my life for good.

'Well?' I demanded arms folded defiantly. 'Speak now and then get out.'

His upper lip curled in a barely suppressed snarl. 'I was safeguarding your interests, you stupid woman. Obviously I wouldn't have bothered if I'd known this was all the gratitude I'd get. You should be certified. You are not safe to live here on your own…'

'If you are not going to explain yourself, then I want you to…'

'I was returning the albums, as you requested, sister dear,' he sneered. 'But there's a lot missing and as *I* haven't got them, they must still be with you.'

'There are no more,' I said holding the door open. 'As you would have known if you had helped sorting through all the clutter after mam and dad died. But no, you were too busy to waste your time with all that dross and you left it for me to sort out. You were only interested in the few bits of silver and anything you could flog.'

'That's a scurrilous thing to say, Dora. How dare you!'

'You can go now James. Anything else you want, you will have to wait until I am dead. But I can tell you now, you'll get nothing in my will. I am leaving it all to the Chicken Rehabilitation Society for Ex Battery Hens.' I have no idea where that little gem had popped up from. Janine choked. 'The rest will go in a skip.'

But James still wasn't finished. 'This girl,' he said pointing at Janine as if I had not noticed her standing there, 'I last saw her slinking away from this house after trying to get money out of you. She's not a friend of yours, she's nothing but a street bum, a piece of trash who preys on vulnerable old women. God knows what she would have taken if I hadn't come along…'

'I was cleaning the kitchen,' Janine said through clenched teeth. The skin around her mouth was white and her whole body was rigid with indignation.

'Janine is living here in the annexe and cleans the house in lieu of rent. She has got herself a job and she pays her own way. And she is rapidly becoming a friend, so I think you owe both of us an apology, James.'

'Living here…! Are you out of your tiny mind! She's a mere child, she should be with her parents, for God's sake.'

'I'm nearly sixteen, and it was my mother who told me to leave,' Janine mumbled, but I doubt James heard her through the roaring of his temper.

'You don't frighten me any more James, and if you are not going to apologise, then you will leave now before I have you forcibly ejected. I don't back down to bullies, in fact, quite the opposite,' I said. 'And since you don't seem to know the meaning of the word "apology", you will leave, now. And if you refuse to go I will have you kicked out.'

'What? You're going to throw me out?' he scoffed.

'Yes, James. I will call on Mrs. Hardy's son so that he can, literally, throw you out,' I said. 'He's a big strapping lad and it wouldn't be wise to try and intimidate him. But silly me, I forgot – you wouldn't, would you. You are too much of a coward. You only pick on children and old ladies.' (Well, there had to be a few times in my life when I can play the age card to my advantage.)

James was breathing heavily, desperately searching for some way to reinstate his authority, but finding nothing. He pushed his way past me and out of the door.

'And don't come back,' I shouted at his retreating back.

I had won the battle, or so I thought, but it had felt rather like poking a sleeping snake with a stick.

Janine gave a nervous giggle and I turned my attention on her. 'Now that that is settled, I want a word with you, Janine,' I said. 'Take a seat.'

She remained standing, her head bowed, staring at her shoes.

'Sit!' I said sternly, and she slid onto one of the kitchen chairs. 'Don't think I am letting you off the hook, my girl. I spun my brother that load of twaddle because – well because he was my brother – but now I want to know what *you* were doing in here?'

'Like I said, I was cleaning the kitchen as a thank you for letting me stay here,' she answered furtively. 'It was very dirty, and you said you wanted it done.

I glanced around me. I must admit I hadn't noticed that the kitchen was pristine and smelled of lemons laced with a slight whiff of disinfectant. The work surfaces were cleared (and presumably everything put away in cupboards so that, like Ted, I would never find anything again), the stainless steel sink was gleaming, the floor had been scrubbed and the mats were outside drying off. I could even see through the freshly cleaned windows without worrying whether I was developing cataracts.

'That is not the point, Janine,' I said. 'What I want to know is how did you get in?'

She traced the pattern in the tablecloth with her finger. Her head dropped lower. 'The door wasn't locked,' she muttered.

I shook my head. 'Oh, I think it was locked. In fact, I know it was, because these days I check everything twice, at least. So, how did you get in? And if you are not honest with me, you will be out on your ear now and I won't need my brother's prompting.'

Janine put her hand up to pull her ear. 'What has my ear got to do with it?' she asked. For a moment I was about to explode as I thought she was being flip with me, but one look at her face told me otherwise. She was serious. The girl took everything so literally.

I was not in the mood to be sidetracked. 'How, Janine?' I demanded.

'You were out, and the car was gone, so… well… I picked the lock. I wanted to give you a nice surprise when you got home.'

'You picked the lock!'

'But I never took anything, honest. It's all in the cupboards, and I've wiped them all down too. Some of the stuff in there is way out of date, but I put it back for you to sort out.' She sniffed as tears leaked down her cheeks. 'I'm sorry. I thought you'd be pleased.'

'About the kitchen – yes of course I am pleased. It hasn't looked so good for nigh on twenty years. But picking the lock is an entirely different matter!' I glared at her angrily, which had absolutely no effect since she hadn't lifted her gaze from the tablecloth. 'Have you no idea of the difference between what is right and what is wrong? This is my home and I have invited you to share a small part of it for a while. But I told you never to come in here unless I was here. Didn't I?'

Janine nodded.

I put my head in my hands. 'I feel as if my worst nightmare has just happened. My brother may have been right!'

She wiped her tears and running nose with the sleeve of her jumper and looked up at me, her eyes red and runny. 'Can I still stay?'

she asked.

My mouth gaped open in astonishment. She sat there looking like a whipped puppy but there was such desperation in her eyes that my heart went out to her. I sighed. I seemed to be doing a lot of that lately. I could feel my resolve melt. Too much had been happening, too quickly, and I needed time to think; a breathing space, a chance to step back.

'I'll give you the benefit of the doubt, this time, but it is definitely the last time, you hear? If you ever do anything like that again...' The tension left my shoulders and I was suddenly very tired. 'By my reckoning there are another five rooms to be cleaned yet. One a day will do just fine – but only when I am here,' I said with the hint of a wry smile to soften any hurt. 'Now, if you don't mind, I'd like to make myself a cup of tea in my spanking new kitchen and then I'm going to have a lie down.'

Janine left quietly through the door and closed it behind her. I lingered for a minute at the table, my fingers playing absently with the pack of letters and papers I had forgotten to take to the clinic. I couldn't make my mind up as to who was causing me the greatest seismic shift in my life, the cancer or Janine.

I settled in my favourite armchair with a mug of tea and a toasted cheese sandwich, which I didn't want now that it was made. At some time I must have nodded off, because I was rudely awoken by the telephone ringing in the hall. I stumbled groggily to my feet and picked up the receiver. Before I could say anything, a voice erupted in my ear.

'Auntie Dodo, what on earth has happened?'

CHAPTER TWENTY-SIX

My brain was mushy from napping and I wondered how on earth Tiffany, living in London, could have known about my diagnosis. I had been going to tell her, and only her, but I simply hadn't had the time. I knew she would be furious if I kept her in the dark, but it hadn't been intentional. Events had simply intervened.

'Tiffany love, how nice to hear from you,' I said slowly and with deliberation, stalling for time until I came fully awake. 'I'm not sure I know what you mean.'

'I've just had dad on the phone. Auntie Dodo, I'm worried about you.'

Only my niece Tiffany ever called me by that silly name. As a tiny tot she couldn't get her tongue around her 'r's, so I had become Dodo and the name had stuck. It was a measure of her anxiety that she had added the prefix "Auntie", which I had persuaded her to drop many years before.

'Ah,' I said. I felt a bit stupid at having leapt to the assumption that she knew about the cancer. I had only just found out myself, for Pete's sake! I blamed it on still being half asleep. 'Well, don't let that spoil us having a nice little chat. Let's start again, shall we? How are you, dear?'

Tiffany laughed. 'I'm sorry, Dodo,' she said. 'I was a bit rattled. Good evening, how are you. Now, spill the beans. What's going on?'

'Like what, Tiff?'

'I've just got off the phone with dad but he was so incoherent with rage that I could only make out about half of what he was raving on about. From what I could gather it was all to do with something you had done which he thoroughly disapproves of and claims you are in danger of life and limb,' she explained. 'You know I rarely speak to him, and he never ever rings me, so you can see why I was a bit worried.'

'Tell me what you did manage to decipher, and then I will tell you the facts,' I said. I was now wide awake.

'He says you are harbouring some runaway child who you've given the freedom of your house and that you are treating her like some surrogate daughter and that she is some tramp off the streets and that you don't know the first thing about her. He said you were being completely irrational and wouldn't listen to sense – his, of course. To cut a long tirade short, he thinks you are going to be robbed blind and are obviously not fit to live on your own any more and it was time you were put in a home. So, how much of it is true?'

'The bit about being irrational and being unfit to look after myself are definitely your father's interpretation and not mine, but as for the rest, it is basically accurate.'

'Are you serious?'

'I do have a girl living here, temporarily, in the annexe. She is nearly sixteen and when she appeared at my door she said that her mother had told her – in her own words – "to get lost", which she had taken quite literally and had done just that. I think she may be a touch autistic or something along those lines as she seems to take everything literally.'

'But . . .'

'Before you go off on one and prove to me that you are your father's daughter – how's that for an insult – just listen.' I said calmly. 'I have spoken to her mother who sounded as if she was either drunk or on drugs and she most definitely wasn't keen to have her back. So what was I to do, Tiffany? The kid was living out of scraps from dustbins and sleeping under hedges. And she wasn't begging, she was asking for jobs for money. I couldn't turn her away, could I?'

After a silence punctuated by static, Tiffany said, 'And is it true that you allow her free access to your house, Dodo? I'm afraid it's a different world today than the one when you were a kid, when you could leave your doors unlocked and toys left out in the street. It's cutthroat with everyone out to grab what they can; even when you are doing someone a good turn they are just as likely to bite you on the bum. You have to be so careful.'

A bit of a sore point, but I wasn't going to linger on it. 'A misunderstanding, that's all. Your father walked in on her before I got back and jumped to all sorts of nasty conclusions. I had gone out and can't have locked the back door behind me and the girl, Janine, decided to spring-clean the kitchen as a thank you for allowing her to stay. You know how I hate housework. Your father wouldn't listen to my explanations but just laid into her – and me.'

'That's my dad,' Tiffany agreed. 'But, it is rather uncharacteristic of you Dodo. You've never liked being around kids never mind having a teenager living with you. You do know that they are a breed apart, don't you, and even a PhD in parenting won't cut it?'

'I must admit, I'm as surprised as you,' I said with a chuckle. 'I think in some ways she reminds me of myself at that age. She wears a shell an inch thick and from what little I have gathered, she seems to have been desperately unhappy and unloved at home. She's been excluded from school, where she seems to have been left to her own devices; she had no friends and there was nobody she could turn to for help or advice.

'As you know I left home when I was only a few years older than her and I could easily have ended up like her except for the fact that I had had an education and had a hazy idea of what direction I wanted my life to go. At the moment she is a bit lost and I wanted to give her the time to work things out for herself. Now that she's opening up a bit more, I find she is bright and very willing and she already has a little job locally. She'll only stay until she is back on her feet.'

There was another long pause followed by a deep sigh. 'I trust your judgement implicitly Dodo, which is more than I have ever been able to say about Dad. Is there anything I can do to get him off your back?'

'Oh, your father will cool down and do nothing more about it, as usual. Forget about it Tiffany. I've still got all my marbles, dear, though nowadays it takes a bit longer to knock them into any sort of order. But there was something I wanted a word with you about. I was going to call you in a few days, but now that you are on the phone – '

'Now you really are worrying me,' Tiffany said. 'Go on, spit it out.'

I told her about the breast cancer. She was very quiet. I continued speaking into the silence, quietly and calmly and matter-of-fact, and gave Tiffany time to absorbed the shocking news. 'It is in its very early stages, and there's nothing to worry about. I'll be having more scans and tests done and then I will be given a date for surgery, which is the route I have decided to take.'

'I don't know what to say,' Tiffany said, her voice little more than a whisper. 'Why haven't you told me before, Dodo? I thought we told each other everything.'

'I only knew for definite this morning, Tiff. I needed time to get my head around it myself before telling you and having to cope with other people's reactions. I wasn't shutting you out, love.'

'Does dad know?'

'Dear God, no! And don't you dare say a word to him. I know he is your father, but if I never set eyes on that man again, it will be far too soon. Not a word, Tiffany. Promise me.'

'Yes, I agree. But, you sound so calm about it Auntie Dodo. Are you really okay or are you still in shock?'

'I have had a while to come to terms with it, and to be honest Tiffany, I am not as scared as I expected to be. Mr. Preston, the consultant I saw, was very reassuring that I am not going to die in the foreseeable future or anything else so melodramatic. He said I may not even need to have chemotherapy, which can only be a good thing from the horror stories I have heard. So you see, it's all fairly low-key. And to answer your question – yes, I am as okay as anyone can be after such a diagnosis. It's the unknown that has always terrified me, and now from what I have been told and from what I have read, I have at least a layman's understanding of what lies ahead. '

There was a much longer pause. 'Tiffany, are you there?'

'I was thinking. I'm going to come down and see you next

week – and before you shoot through the roof – I am coming whatever you say. I'll book into that hotel on the seafront if I have to, but I am coming. I wish I could come sooner, but I've got a few meetings that I simply have to attend. Once they are over I can take as much leave as I like, as I'm owed. I want to talk to you face-to-face, Dodo, for my sake as much as yours. Please let me come. Please.'

'I can't think of anyone I would rather see,' I answered, tears starting to well up in my eyes. I brushed them angrily away. When one lived on one's own, one rarely indulges in a good old cry, except sometimes when there's a real weepy on the television. It had rather caught me by surprise. 'And don't you dare go to a hotel, or I will never speak to you again. You will stay here in the spare room, you silly girl,' I said brusquely. 'But are you sure, love, I know how busy you are.'

'Please don't push me away, Dodo. You are my only real family, and if the circumstances were reversed, you would do exactly the same, you can't deny it. I'll give you a bell when I know dates and I'll bring the booze.'

'You could bring Gina for company. It's a long way to drive on your own.'

'I think she would feel a bit awkward with all the family stuff, but we'll both come down later when everything is more sorted and we can ply you with alcohol and real Italian cooking and smother you until you can't stand it any more and send us packing. I'll see you soon. I love you, Dodo.'

I put down the phone and wiped the tears from my cheeks. I poured myself a large sherry to steady myself. It would be so good to see Tiffany. She was the kindest, funniest, most passionate person I knew, and I had often wondered where her genetic makeup – given who her parents were – could have come from. Perhaps God did have a conscience or a sense of humour after all. Or maybe, just maybe, her mother had been playing away from home? I laughed at the thought – no, not Helen, never!

CHAPTER TWENTY-SEVEN

Janine finished making her bed and took her mug of coffee over to the little armchair besides the window. She tucked her feet under her and stared unseeingly out at the thin pearly mist that still clung to the front garden, jewelling the lawn and all the plants with trillions of tiny diamonds. The sun was no more than a yellow haze on the eastern horizon, but the mist was already thinning and it would soon burn its way through.

She had had a restless night, turning over and over in her mind what she had overheard the evening before. She hadn't meant to eavesdrop, but she had been quietly reading and had heard the telephone ring. Dora obviously had no idea how thin the connecting walls were between the annexe and the main house, nor that a ventilation grill in the same wall had been left open so that any conversation, with a little concentration, could be heard on either side. She also tended to speak rather loudly when she wasn't wearing her hearing aids and especially when on the telephone.

The letters Janine had read on the kitchen table the day before had suddenly made more sense. She had taken a quick peek – well who wouldn't? – but she hadn't understood the technical stuff and the rest had only been clinic appointment times and hadn't told her much.

When she had got up, Janine had peeked in through the kitchen window but there had been no sign of Dora having risen. It was early anyway, so she had returned to the annexe to think. As far as she could figure it, she had two main problems, three if she counted in the telling off she had had from Dora about having picked the lock, which she didn't think was anything to get so worked up about anyway. The other two were part and parcel of the same problem. She had heard about cancer before, who hadn't, but details were a bit sketchy. It was something for older people, she had always thought, and nothing to concern her. The word had always been spoken in hushed tones and with pitying sidelong looks, as if whoever had it was already in their coffin and everyone would speak quietly and respectfully as if over a corpse. Or as if they could catch it if they spoke about it too loudly. Was it catching? She didn't know.

Although Dora had said on the telephone that she was not going to die anytime soon, Janine had no idea how far in the future that would be or if she had been lying. Even before then, she could be desperately ill and the person she had been speaking to on the phone, Tiffany, seemed to be coming down to look after her.

So, where did that leave her? As Dora had said, she'd be out on her ear, and even though she still didn't understand what ears had to do with it, the meaning was clear. She would have to leave, probably by next week.

She took another sip of tea.

She had known her run of good luck was too good to be true. When had anything ever worked out right for her? But this time it was different. Of one thing she was certain – she didn't want to go. If this Tiffany had the same opinion of her as that horrible man, then she would fight to stay, if she had to. She was not going to give up the prospect of some sort of life easily.

She liked the old woman. She was eccentric and cranky and wandered around talking to herself and her chickens in her pyjamas and manky old slippers. She didn't care what she was wearing or doing, and she fiercely protected her independence. She was her own person.

And then there was the way she had stormed down to the hotel and faced up to Flo Jenkins on Janine's behalf. It had been astonishing.

Okay, she had come close to being thrown out a few times, but she didn't think she had done anything really bad. Obviously the older generation saw things differently and lived by a set of rules she hadn't known existed, so she was bound to do things wrong now and again. But she could learn. She wanted to learn.

And for the first time in her life, she realized that she respected someone, not just because she was Anna Clare who wrote the books or the woman who painted so beautifully for no other reason than because she loved to do it, but she respected her as a person. She would like to be like her when she was old – well, not quite that old, but older than now.

She didn't want her to die, not just because it would mean she would be on her own again, but because she wanted to get to know the old lady better. And yes, she thought, it wouldn't be such a bad thing to end up like her.

The sun had broken through the thin cloud and the fleeing mist revealed a blue sky, the same colour as a blackbird's egg.

I sat at the kitchen table, toying with my cup of Earl Grey and the remnants of my toast and black cherry jam. It was not my usual breakfast, but I had felt like a change and according to all the latest propaganda, at least the wholemeal bread was good for the digestion.

Janine popped her head around the door, and for once seemed hesitant about coming in. 'I'm off to see if Mr. Morris wants me to do some cleaning,' she said, rather timidly. 'I'll go and collect the eggs now, if you want.'

'I've already done them, thank you,' I answered. Both of us were still feeling awkward after the row about breaking in and were being stiffly polite with each other. 'You shouldn't go off without any breakfast, Janine. It's not good for you – they say it is the most important meal of the day.'

She shrugged. She hadn't even come over the step, but stood in the open doorway. 'I've had some left-over pizza and a cup of tea, thanks.'

If my breakfast wasn't particularly healthy, then hers was ten times worse.

'Before you go, I've got a favour to ask. I wonder if you would dust and hoover the spare bedroom for me. My niece, Tiffany, is coming down sometime next week to stay for a couple of days, and the room needs a polish and an airing. Shall we say tomorrow morning, or would you prefer to do it later in the week in case you are kept late in the kitchen tonight?'

'Tomorrow morning is fine,' Janine answered. 'But I won't come in unless you are here, I promise.'

She slipped away before I could reply. Just as well, I thought. Best we keep out of each other's way for a day or two and let our ruffled feathers settle.

Looking back, the next couple of days were like the calm before the storm. I pushed everything to the back of my mind – I had a particularly good knack of doing that with things I had no control over – and set about enjoying myself before my life became an endless round of hospital appointments and all things medical.

I should have taken the opportunity to finish writing the book, but I was still unhappy with the way in which it was progressing. Some instinct was holding me back. Over the years I had learned to trust that sixth sense and I was seldom proven wrong. I felt the need for a radical change but I wasn't sure whether I was simply being influenced by all the changes that had happened in my life in the past week or whether it was for the good of the storyline. No doubt it would reveal itself in its own good time. Best leave it alone for now.

Sometimes it also applied to my paintings – should I add an extra leaf in that awkward looking space or should I leave it alone? If my instinct said – go for it, then I would. If it turned out to be a mistake, then the most I would have wasted was a few hours and perhaps a potential masterpiece. It would not be the end of the world. But it was an easier matter to lose myself in a painting which may be no more than a couple of hours of pleasure or may occupy me for days. That was the joy of creating – you never knew.

I had been planning my next botanical masterpiece (I am being facetious here) before I had even finished my painting of Herman the crab's rock-pool. In fact it had been on my mind since the previous autumn. It was to be a study of the complete growth cycle of bracken, *Pteridium aquilinum*; a plant despised by most people, especially farmers, who thought of it as a thug, which choked the hillsides and fields every summer and became a fire hazard every autumn.

174

There was no scarcity of it along the coastline and it flourished all along the riverbanks and inland up to the next village. I love walking through the waist-high sea of fronds in the summertime, startling sheep and rabbits cooling off under the shade of its green umbrellas, and breathing in the clean musky scent of the crushed fronds. In a few months, serried ranks of foxgloves spires would march amongst the bracken while underneath slender milkmaids and bluebells, harebells and golden carline thistles and clouds of small blue butterflies would all be sheltering from the salty winds. But now, in the spring, they were only starting to spurt into growth, some still nothing more than tight green crosiers encased in bright orange fur which would slowly unfurled. They reminded me of those paper toys you have at parties where you blow in one end and a tightly wound curl of paper unravels, often with a squawk and a brightly dyed feather at the end. In the autumn, the gold and russet of the dead bracken would twist and break and lay down a protective blanket over the smaller plants sheltering against the onslaught of winter.

It would be a major undertaking and I had been looking forward to it. But I wasn't at all sure that this would be a good time to start. Hospitals, clinics, and surgery loomed on the horizon and I had no idea how much I would be able to finish before I became incapable and how long that incapacity would last. Would I be safer limiting myself to searching for my orchids and doing a bit of preparatory work instead? Nah! Safe didn't sound very interesting and usually the most enjoyable part of any painting for me tended to be in the planning stage and the first few days of painting. I felt I had earned myself a couple of days of pure enjoyment, so, the bracken it was to be.

Of course, all that depended on having a specimen to work from. In the autumn I had planted a root of bracken in a large pot so that I would have my material to hand when the time was right. I had tucked it behind the chicken coop and in the turmoil of the last couple of weeks, I had forgotten about it. Now that I was decided, I was eager to start and dashed out up the back steps to rummage behind the coop. To my delight, there were three beautiful crosiers pushing through. It was at the perfect stage for beginning my study and I eagerly grabbed the pot in both hands and tried to lift it. It didn't budge. Damn, but I was getting old!

The warnings from Mr. Preston about not lifting heavy things briefly came to mind but I decided they only related to houseworky things. Any right-minded person would have asked for help – Alf Hardy or the lovely Adrian would have come up in a shot or even Janine at a push – but I was a long way off admitting I was too weak and feeble – yet. I was too fired up with all the ideas running through my head to brook any sort of delay.

'Alright buster,' I muttered to the pot. 'If you think you can hunker down here for the rest of the year, you can think again.'

Cilla, Sandi and Shirley wandered over to check out who I was talking to and whether it augured some choice titbits or extra rations. They were no help at all, getting under my feet and flapping around as I wrenched the pot out of its winter nesting site and rolled it across the edge of the flower bed, past the netting of the chicken run, and around the stone pixie ornament until it rested on the top of the steps. As I took a breather, the doubts started crowding in. Could I? Should I? My back ached a warning and the site where the biopsy had been taken from was stinging. I took a quick peek, but I didn't seem to have popped my stitches. There were only four steps but they looked steeper than they ever had before. I took a deep breath. What was the worst that could happen? Gingerly, and with much huffing and puffing, I 'walked' it over the lip of the top step and slowly and carefully eased it down the first few steps until it rested half way down. So far, so good.

'And how do you expect to get it all the way up to your painting room, Dora Cummings?' I asked myself.

I leaned against the wall and took a moment to study it. Actually, left where it was it would be perfect. I could drag up a chair and do all my initial detailed sketches and colour swatches in comfort. No need to call in the cavalry. This was a good omen.

For two whole days I was in sheer heaven. The weather held and I managed to do enough preparatory work to enable me to start my bracken life-cycle series.

CHAPTER TWENTY-EIGHT

By the third day, my wild enthusiasm to paint bracken had begun to wear off and reality was setting in. My shoulders ached, my back ached, the arthritis in my thumb was throbbing and I had a thumping headache.

I had left the bracken in its pot in the middle of the steps and had drawn everything that was showing above ground; it had been accurately measured and all the individual segments exactly counted. As it grew, it would branch and then branch again, but for now it was beautifully compact and easy. As well as the detailed drawings, I had done some quick colour sketches to work out what colours I would need for the fresh new growth. When I was ready to start the actual painting I would be able to pop up onto the downland and dig up another specimen that I could take into my 'studio' with me and keep in a jar of water. It would probably only stay fresh for a few days, which should be enough time to paint a good portion of the study. I would not have to worry about breaking any environmental laws by digging bits up as bracken was hardly an endangered species. But before then I had a lot of planning to do on the composition.

This was possibly the most important stage on such a big project. I had a rough idea of the size of the bracken at each of its stages of growth, but it was difficult to juggle them on a blank piece of paper when the exact dimensions may end up being quite different. It is devastating to spend days and days on a painting and then discover that a vital part of the plant wouldn't fit into the available space. There was nothing worse, in my humble opinion, than a page of a botanical study where bits are crammed in willy-nilly wherever there was a bit of room. I had already worked out that I would have to do the study on two separate sheets of quarter-Imperial paper; the first one to include the tight new fronds and then again as they gradually unfurled. The second page would be the mature fern and then the rust-coloured winter bracken.

It would take a bit of thought and many rough-outs before I

could eventually start, but I needed a break. It was late afternoon and I had reached saturation point. I needed space and exercise.

'Enough, Dora,' I told myself firmly, closing the lids on my boxes of paints and upending my brushes in the jam jar. 'You are not the woman you used to be and it's high time you faced that fact.'

Suitably chastened, I staggered downstairs and swallowed a couple of paracetamols for the headache. A short walk through the car park and across the cliffs would soon blow away the cobwebs and free up my cramped limbs.

There was a brief knock on the door before it was cracked open a few inches.

'It's only me, Elizabeth Henshaw. I hope I'm not intruding?'

The look on my face must have spoken volumes, because she held up a placatory hand. 'Don't worry, I haven't come mob handed. I've come to apologise to you for my previous visit.'

Taking my stunned silence as permission to proceed further, she stepped over the threshold. I had to bite back a smile. She looked spectacularly out of place in my humble kitchen in her flowing silk dress, lavender tinted hair-do and double row of pearls, all froth and bustle. I must admit, I was intrigued.

'I realize how wrong I was to have barged my way into your house as if I was on some sort of evangelical crusade drumming up converts for our little church. I'm so very sorry if I offended you, Miss Cummings. Please, will you accept my apologies?'

She had obviously been rehearsing her little speech for days as it had all come out in one breathless rush. By the time she had finished I was dumbstruck. Did I really give two hoots what this woman thought? Not really, but I had to admire her. It had been a fair apology and it had taken a lot of guts to come up here and eat humble pie. I don't think I would have done it half as well, if at all, to be honest. And she had, unknowingly, been on my side in opposition to Flo Jenkins. Perhaps I should give the woman a chance to redeem herself.

'Would a mug of instant coffee at the kitchen table be acceptable while I think about it?' I asked, not willing to let her off the hook just yet. 'Or would you prefer Earl Grey?'

Relief flooded Elizabeth Henshaw's sharp features and I stifled a laugh. 'Earl Grey would be lovely. I put a slice of lemon in, myself.'

'No lemon, I'm afraid. Citrus gives me migraines.' I scanned my kitchen quickly, and offered up a silent prayer of thanks to Janine for having knocked it into some sort of shape. Not enough time had passed for me to have reduced it to my usual chaotic normality.

'My husband is always telling me I charge into situations before engaging my brain. I find it hard to change, you see. I am who I am and sometimes I'm afraid I can appear to have all the empathy of a block of granite. If you can pretend our first meeting never happened, perhaps we could start again. Wipe the slate clean?'

To my amazement, I suddenly realized that Elizabeth Henshaw was nervous. She pushed the mug of tea around and around and stared into its depths as if she expected something to be lurking in there. How far can you go wrong with a bag of Earl Grey? But she seemed to have something more on her mind and she was dithering and I didn't think it was simply the unfamiliar act of apologising that was making her hesitate.

I nodded. 'Okay, fine by me; apology accepted. Just don't expect me to turn up at your next bridge night!'

We both laughed and the tension between us eased a little.

'I hear that the young girl you have staying with you has been doing very well down at the hotel. Selwyn was delighted with her – said he'd never had such a good little worker,' Elizabeth Henshaw said conversationally. 'I meant what I said before. If she wants to take on more work, I'd be grateful if she could give me a hand at the vicarage. You know what these old buildings are like. They seem to attract dust like magnets. I swear it comes out of all that bare exposed stonework, but my husband says that is ridiculous.'

The woman was talking for the sake of talking, and I knew that Janine's expertise with a dishcloth was not what had brought Elizabeth Henshaw to my door, but until she came to the point, I had no option but to play along.

'I'm glad they were pleased with her. She doesn't seem to mind housework, even though I am sure she has a good brain in her head. But if you want her to work for you, Mrs. Henshaw, you'll have to take it up with her. She's only lodging here temporarily. I don't really know the girl, but I feel very sorry for her and would like to help her if I can,' I answered.

She gave me a wry smile. 'If we are starting off again from scratch, would it be possible for you to call me Elizabeth?' she asked coyly.

I moved to shake her hand. 'And I am Dora. Pleased to meet you Elizabeth,' I said. 'Correct me if I am wrong, but I think you still have something else on your mind?'

Elizabeth Henshaw let out a deep sigh. 'You are quite right. Subtle as a cart-horse.' She sighed again. 'I have come to offer you my support at this difficult time – me personally not as part of The God Squad!' She laughed at the expression that crossed my face. 'Yes, I know what they call us in the village.' She hesitated again and finally plunged in. 'You see, I know something of what you are going through at the moment and what will happen for you in the future. Of course, medical science is advancing at a phenomenal rate and my encounter with breast cancer was over ten years ago, so things have probably changed a lot since then, but I want you to know that I am here to help you all I can, even if it is just driving you to appointments or such. All that driving and waiting around can be so draining.' She stopped to draw breath. 'Are you alright, Dora? You've gone very pale. Oh dear, have I put my foot in it again?'

Words choked in my throat. I could hardly breathe. 'What are you talking about?' I managed to gasp out.

Elizabeth Henshaw looked extremely uncomfortable. 'I... I am so sorry. Have I got it all wrong? I believe your girl, Janine, blurted it out yesterday when Flo was having a go at her and anybody else within a ten-mile radius. She said you had breast cancer.'

I dragged air into my lungs with difficulty. Thankfully I was already sitting down, or I think I would have collapsed. In my mind's eye I saw that damned letter and the leaflets I had left on the kitchen table before dashing off to the clinic. They had still been there when I got home, but by then both Janine and my brother were having their ding-dong in the kitchen. I doubt if James would have noticed them as he was too busy roaring at Janine, but the girl would have had ample opportunity to stick her nose in.

'So, now, I suppose everyone knows?'

'No, please be reassured, it was only Flo who had probably had far too many G & Ts and was in a bad mood with Janine for some unaccountable reason. Apparently she had said some rather... derogatory... things about you and, from the sound of it, the girl was adamantly and I believe quite eloquently, defending you. Usually you can hardly get a word out of her, but she stood up for you and I think the bit about the cancer simply popped out. Flo told me about it this morning, mainly as part of a tirade about the cheek of young people these days in answering back to their elders.'

'Then I would be grateful if you would keep it to yourself, Mrs. Henshaw, and to pass on the same instructions to Mrs. Jenkins. My health is a private matter and not one open for discussion around the entire village,' I said sharply. 'You say you only heard about this from Flo Jenkins, not first hand?'

'That's right. It happened yesterday evening and she told me about it this morning. She was very uptight about the girl. She said she would have sacked her there and then if Selwyn hadn't intervened.'

'If you wouldn't mind staying put for a few minutes, I think we both should have Janine's version of what happened. I realize Flo Jenkins is your friend, but I can assure you she is no friend of mine and she has made enough unfounded accusations about me in the past. I think we need to hear both sides of the argument.'

'I couldn't agree with you more, Dora. Flo isn't really as bad as she comes across, but when she takes against somebody, and especially when she is on a drinking binge, it takes a great deal to change her mind.'

'Did she tell you why she had been laying into Janine?'

'No, nothing. And to be honest, I was a bit afraid to ask as she was still in quite a state about it this morning.'

I grabbed the key for the annexe connecting door, gave a quick knock, and let myself in. Janine was lounging in the armchair by the window, writing something in a black hardback book, her brow creased with concentration. She twisted around to look at me.

'Janine, I want you to come into the kitchen. I have a few questions I want to ask you. There is something I need cleared up, and I would like to have the full facts before I take any action.'

If it was possible, Janine's usually pale skin blanched even further. Her eyes grew enormous and I could almost see the 'fight or flight' reflex warring inside her. The fight seemed to win as she put her book down and stood up, her body rigid and her chin defiantly raised. She didn't say a word as she followed me out.

I repeated what Elizabeth Henshaw had told me regarding the row between her and Flo Jenkins and what had been said. 'Is this correct, Janine. Did you tell Mrs. Jenkins that I had cancer? The truth please.'

'Yes.'

'Only two other people know about this, and you are not one of them, Janine. Have you been reading my private correspondence? Is that how you know? And why in hell's name did you tell somebody like Flo Jenkins!

Janine lifted her gaze and looked me straight in the eye, something she rarely did. Unshed tears made her eyes glisten. 'I didn't read anything. I overheard you talking on the phone about it. The walls are really thin and you must have been sitting on the stairs or something. You talk really loud on the telephone, Miss Cummings; I couldn't help hearing it.' I watched a fat tear overspill and trickle down her cheek. Her chin was starting to quiver as she desperately tried to hold herself together. 'I don't want you to die.'

There was a stunned silence.

'Right. Okay. Well... I know I tend to talk louder without my hearing aids in, so that part I can accept,' I admitted in a slightly calmer voice, 'but why should it have come up in an argument with Flo Jenkins of all people?' I could see that Janine was as distressed as I was, though as it turned out it was for different reasons.

'I didn't mean to, but it got all complicated, and I just blurted it out.'

Elizabeth Henshaw turned to Janine. 'What I don't understand is why Flo – Mrs. Jenkins – is so against you, child. She was vitriolic when she was telling me about your behaviour, but Selwyn can't say enough nice things about you. Has something else happened between the two of you that we don't know about?'

Janine looked imploringly at me, silently begging me to let it drop, but I couldn't. I didn't want to punish her for something she may not have done, or at least done in all innocence. And I really wanted to know why.

We waited, and into the silence, Janine muttered out her explanation. She had apparently finally finished cleaning up the kitchen after an evening birthday party. By then it was getting late and she had been the only one left behind. 'I hadn't been paid for the past two nights' work, so I went to the office to ask Mrs. Jenkins for my money.' She hesitated, glancing sideways at Mrs. Henshaw and then back to the floor.

'Go on, Janine. Whatever happened, I want to know about it,' I said.

She took a deep breath. 'Mrs. Jenkins and Clive, the chef, were on the desk…'

'Go on,' I said as Janine hesitated. 'You said they were "on" the desk. How? Were they in – a compromising position?'

Janine frowned. 'Dunno.'

'Were they kissing?' Elizabeth Henshaw asked more bluntly.

'They were doing a bloody sight more than that!' Janine answered. 'And I said it wasn't fair to Mr. Jenkins 'cause he is such a nice man. I told her she shouldn't be doing it.'

I thought Elizabeth Henshaw was going to explode as she tried to swallow down her laughter. 'You are telling me Flo Jenkins and Clive Thomas were having a fling on the office desk and that that's the reason why she is bad-mouthing you because you know about it and she wants you gone before you spill the beans to Selwyn?'

'Yes, but I don't understand what that has got to do with me washing dishes and wanting my pay,' Janine sobbed, tears now pouring down her cheeks. 'And she was saying such horrible things about me and you, Miss Cummings, saying all sorts of disgusting things, and I just got mad and told her to stop... and that's when it came out. I'm sorry. I didn't want to hurt you. Am I in trouble again?'

I took a moment to absorb the image she had conjured up. 'No, love, you are not in trouble. Come and sit down and I'll make you a cup of tea. We could all do with a fresh one.'

'What do you want to do, Dora?' Mrs. Henshaw asked as I busied myself with filling the kettle. 'Do you want me to have a word with Flo? It is totally out of order that she is taking it out on Janine and you because she's been caught *in flagrante delicto*. Really not the behaviour one would expect of a member of The God Squad!'

We both laughed and I shook my head. 'Her affair is her own affair – so to speak. It's nothing to do with me, or you Janine. Not a word to Mr. Jenkins.' Janine nodded but looked unconvinced. 'So, please Elizabeth; say nothing. If you could have a word with Selwyn regarding Janine's pay, I would be grateful. At the moment I don't think I can find the energy to have it out with the woman myself.'

'Selwyn is a good man, and I hate to see him being cuckolded in this way, but be assured I won't say a word about Flo. And I will make sure Janine gets paid with a bonus for taking all the abuse.'

'Thank you, Elizabeth. I would appreciate that.'

'And I hope you forgive me for having once again put my big feet in it, but I have been through it myself, and if you need any help, please don't be too proud to ask. At a time like this you cannot be too independent – I know from experience and I had a husband to run around after me.' She gave me a wry smile. 'You may not think it, but we are very much alike, you and I. We are both strong women who plough our own furrow through life and tend to stand on our own dignity – too much sometimes. I do understand, and I am here for you, if you want me.'

'I appreciate your offer Mrs… Elizabeth… but if you don't mind, I would like to be alone now.'

CHAPTER TWENTY-NINE

I rose the next morning full of purpose and dread. One thing I had to do without delay was to tell Ted Morris about the result of the cancer biopsy before he heard it on the village grapevine. I knew that despite Elizabeth Henshaw's promise to remain quiet, there was no way to keep a secret bottled up once the cork had been pulled. If Flo Jenkins had been in such a rant, there's no end of people who could have overheard her.

I had reluctantly come to the conclusion that my first impressions of Elizabeth Henshaw may have been wrong. I didn't like being in the wrong and it took a lot for me to change my opinions even to myself. But after mulling over what she had said at the kitchen table the day before, I had to hold up my hands and admit that she wasn't as bad as I had first thought. She was still not somebody I would take to be a bosom pal, but neither was she the stuck-up pushy prig that she had appeared to be. Time would tell.

As for Flo Jenkins – she was becoming a thorn in my side, but after Janine's revelation about her having it away with Clive the chef (somebody I had never met but intended rectifying that in the near future) I had a powerful hold over her. A nod and a wink here and there should be enough to get the message across to her that I knew all about it, though I still found it hard to imagine Flo Jenkins's ample body spread-eagled across a desk in a moment of passion. Blackmail may be too harsh a word, but if it came down to that, I would not hesitate to use it. She had bad-mouthed me enough and it was time it stopped one way or another.

I rummaged in the top cupboard for a jar of last year's blackberry jelly. It had been a bumper year for blackberries and I just couldn't let them go to waste. So, I had tediously sieved out as many pips as I could as I hated spending days trying to prise one loose from between my back teeth. They were not where they should be. Janine must have moved them during her purge of the kitchen and it took me another five minutes to locate the two remaining jars. I seemed to spend half my life looking for things and, after Janine had got loose on my house, I would never find anything again! I checked the tops and neither appear to have developed any mould.

I had been worrying about how I could break the news to Ted. He wouldn't have known that I had a cancellation appointment the day before, so he would not be expecting news for a few days yet, but he had been so kind to me that I felt I should tell him as soon as possible. But how exactly do you tell someone? Do you charge in and baldly say – yes, it is cancer, but it's not terminal and I've opted for surgery? I didn't know him well enough to know how he would take bad news, though he had seemed a pretty level-headed person so far. I had to take into count that he had only recently got over a big heart attack, so would it be best if I skirted around the subject in an attempt to soften the impact? It was proving harder to break the news to someone else than it was hearing it for myself!

In the end I decided to pin my hopes on the pots of jam easing me into the subject.

Ted answered the door after a short wait. His eyes lit up with obvious pleasure. 'Dora Cummings. I wondered when I'd be seeing you,' he said, opening the door wider. 'Come on in. Can I make you a cuppa?'

'That would be lovely, Ted,' I answered. 'And I've brought you some blackberry jelly. I should have made some scones to go with it, but it will keep until I've made a batch and I'll send Janine down with them.'

'Oh, now you are spoiling me, woman. I like a bit of clotted cream on my scones, but the doctors would have a fit if I told them that. Now, sit you down and I'll make us tea. Then maybe, if you've time to spare, you would be so good as to accompany me on a little walk down to the beach and back. I must admit I'm a bit apprehensive about doing it on my own just yet.'

I watched him fussing with the kettle and cups. He had certainly spruced himself up since the last time I had visited him. Even though he couldn't have been expecting visitors, he was dressed in a clean shirt and knitted tie and a warm woollen cardigan with no holes in the sleeves. His hair was neatly combed and there was good colour in his cheeks.

When we were finally sitting with our cups in front of us, I told him the news as briefly as I could. He listened in silence and waited for me to finish. 'Well, from what you told me before, it is what you expected and from the sound of it, the outlook is very hopeful,' he said. 'If an old crock of a man like me can do anything to help, Dora, you know I am here for you, lass.'

'Thank you, Ted. And thank you for the "lass" as well. It's a long time since anyone called me that! And once we've finished our tea, I'll be happy to promenade with you. We should set all the tongues wagging nicely. We could even make it a daily thing and wait to hear how wild the rumours get. It could be fun.'

I didn't miss the twinkle in his eye.

'I will have to have a word with Janine when I get back,' I said as we sauntered down the lane arm in arm. 'She's got the idea in her head that I am about to keel over and die. I should have done it yesterday, but I had been just too drained.'

'The girl seems to have taken quite a shine to us oldies,' he said chuckling. 'What are you going to do about her when you have to go into hospital and the like?'

'To be honest, I am rather at a loss to know what to do, Ted. I've grown to like her and she respects my privacy now that the lines have been drawn. I thought I was a pretty good judge of character, but my confidence has recently taken a bit of a knock on the head. I must admit I don't yet fully trust her. It's not her fault – she was raised differently.

'My niece is coming down next week, so I'll ask her opinion and then make up my mind. And of course, it is up to Janine what she wants to do.'

'Oh, I think I can tell you that now. She wants to stay. She's not said as much to me – well she's hardly a chatterbox is she – but you can see it in her. She's come out such a lot in the short time she's been with you, Dora, she sometimes even looks happy.'

'She may be an odd one, Ted, but she is still a teenager. They are not created to be happy.'

When I got back from our walk and had left Ted dozing contentedly in his chair, I called around at the annexe and gave a knock. Janine opened the door and stepped back to allow me in. Her face was twisted with a worried look, so I quickly put her mind at rest.

'You are not in trouble, child,' I said. 'I thought I should explain to you about my cancer so that you don't think I am going to drop dead at any moment. And I also want to know what you want to do about working at the hotel. You don't have to if you don't want. Mrs. Henshaw said she would be pleased to have you help her at the vicarage with some cleaning and I'm sure there are others who would be just as keen. It is up to you whether you want to beard the dragon – I mean face up to Mrs. Jenkins – or tell her you quit. Your choice.'

'I'm supposed to be going in tonight, so I guess I'll see how it goes. I can always leave,' she answered chewing her lip.

'Mrs. Henshaw is having a quiet word with Flo Jenkins. If that doesn't have the desired effect of the woman winding in her neck, then you can quit there and then. You don't have to take any more abuse from her. You hear me?'

After I explained about the cancer, she looked relieved.

'So, am I staying then?' she asked. 'If you like I can look after you when you come home from the hospital; make you food and clean the house and that.'

'I think Tiffany is all fired up to do something like that, but she does have a busy job and will need to get back to London. When she comes down next week we can all have a chat about it, alright?'

We left it at that. Over breakfast the next day, Janine told me that not only had she been paid for her work, but Mrs. Jenkins had been conspicuous by her absence. Clive the chef had merely winked at her and nothing more had been said.

We both took Ted out for a short walk and then I continued with painting my bracken fronds which were rapidly unfurling. Janine had got on with whatever it was she did to occupy her spare time. Tiffany rang to say she would be arriving sometime in the afternoon of Tuesday and that there was no need to do anything. She would do a quick shop in the lovely delicatessen down the road from her flat and the booze was already crated.

All seemed well until the front door bell rang at 9.30 on Monday morning.

I opened the door to two police officers, and a rather scruffy overweight woman who was clutching an official looking manila folder.

CHAPTER THIRTY

'Mrs. Dora Cummings?' the male police officer asked.

'It's Miss,' I answered with a weary sigh. I hated having to correct people who automatically assumed that a woman would be a missus as I always felt as if I was taking part in an old *Dick Emery* sketch, so I usually ignored it. But as this seemed to be an official visit I thought it was important we had things correct from the start.

'Sorry – *Miss* Cummings. I am Constable Phil Dawkins and this is Constable Pat Matthews,' he said indicating his colleague. 'And this is Mrs. Osborne, who is a social worker from the local authority's Children's Services. May we come in?'

I took a moment to steady myself. They loomed in front of me, all flack-jackets and equipment which made them look ten feet tall and the size of a mountain – each. Beside them the social worker – who was no shrinking violet in the matter of size – was diminished to normal proportions. When I had gathered my wits, I showed them into the living room. They towered over me again until I urged them to sit down. I felt slightly less intimidated.

I wondered if I had time to dive for my hearing aids. No! A sign of weakness!

'What is this about?' I asked, though the mention of a social worker had given me a mega-sized clue.

The policeman took the lead. He was early middle aged and going grey and thin on top, but he still had a boyishness about his features. It was difficult to say whether he had a paunch or not because of all the paraphernalia draped about his person, which must have acted like a corset. He looked vaguely familiar. I tried to concentrate on what he was saying. 'We have received a report that there is a young girl living on these premises who has possibly run away from home. Is that correct?'

I didn't see any point in denying it as they were obviously well aware of the facts. 'Yes, there is. She was living rough and I took her in for a few days. What's wrong with that?'

'You cannot just pluck people off the street, Miss Cummings,' interrupted the policewoman sharply – her tone was that of a parent chastising a two-year old for stealing a sweet. She didn't look much older than Janine and was wearing far too much heavy makeup. 'The child is underage and you should have brought her in to the police station.'

I took an instant dislike to the woman. Twenty-three years of working with the police had dispelled any vestige of awe one might have felt in their presence. She was probably barely out of training school, and had yet to learn the fact that automatic respect for the police no longer applied; it had to be earned. 'To what purpose?' I asked shortly.

'To be put into the care of the proper authorities,' the social worker answered. I had already forgotten her name.

'And what would you have done with her?' I asked.

'She would have been put into temporary accommodation while enquiries were made, and then either returned to her home or put into a children's home or into foster care if deemed appropriate,' she answered primly.

I nodded my head wisely. 'Would you be talking about these famous children's homes where kids are jammed together four to a room, or kept in totally inappropriate premises like empty caravans and barges because the care service is bursting at the seams and cannot cope? Where drugs and alcohol and petty crime are the norm? Where she would be left to twiddle her thumbs all day while you make up your mind where best to dump her?' I asked scathingly. The woman bridled with offence but didn't have the nerve to correct me. Even I watched the news, though I would never in a million years have expected to be involved in anything to do with child care! 'Instead of subjecting her to all that, I invited her to live in a self contained annexe to my own house in a pleasant village where she has been earning her own pocket money doing little jobs for local people. She is safe, clean and fed. Can you honestly tell me that you could provide anything better?'

The social worker sniffed. 'She is an underage vulnerable child. There are rules which have to be followed…'

Constable Dawkins interrupted. 'A report has been made by a member of the public, and we are obliged to follow it up, Miss Cummings. Is the girl here? May we speak with her?'

'I'll fetch her,' I said and walked out to the hall. I was shaking with indignation. As I was unbolting the connecting door, the child policewoman came up behind me.

'Are you keeping her prisoner?' she gasped, her face a mask of horror tinged with excitement. I could almost see her brain working, skimming ahead to the awards and publicity she would receive for breaking up a major kidnapping and possible paedophile ring. She really was wet behind the ears.

'We can go around to the annexe the long way if you want, but this is the shortcut. And for your information Janine has a key to her own front door.'

She did have the grace to blush. I knocked the door and walked in. Janine had made no attempt to make an escape and, as we had been speaking in the hallway, she must have heard every word through the thin walls. (If I ever took in paying guests again, I would need to rectify that, quickly.) She stood in the middle of the room, chin up but with a pleading look in her eyes.

'Don't worry, lass,' I whispered. 'Whatever it is, we can sort it.'

We walked through into the living room, together.

Constable Dawkins smiled encouragingly at her. 'We need you to tell us your name and age and your home address,' he said quietly.

Janine shrugged but said nothing.

'You are not in any trouble, love,' he reassured her, 'but we do need to get this sorted out. Let's just start with your full name.'

He waited patiently, and gave a warning glare at the policewoman as she opened her mouth to speak.

'Janine Wallis, and I'll be sixteen on the 11th June,' Janine answered in a hushed mumble.

Constable Dawkins wrote it carefully in his little black pocketbook. 'And your home address?'

She flicked a glance in my direction, and then concentrated on a spot on the carpet. 'I haven't got one. My mam told me not to come back.'

The social worker leaned forward. 'You silly girl, she probably didn't mean it literally. We all say things in the heat of the moment, which we regret later. I'm sure she's worried to death about you.'

Janine sulked silently.

She was reverting to her 'blood out of a stone' persona and I knew that the more they pushed the more she would turn into that stone. She needed defending and it looked as if I would have to do her speaking for her. 'On the contrary,' I said. 'I have already spoken to her mother, and she was more than happy for her to stay here. She said she wanted nothing more to do with the child.'

'We only have your word for that…' the social worker answered, bristling.

I could feel my own hackles rising. 'Are you calling me a liar?'

Constable Dawkins intervened, trying to diffuse the growing tension in the room. 'If you give us your address,' he said turning to Janine, 'we can check whether or not your mother has filed a missing person's report, and we can go from there.'

The social worker weighed into the fight again. 'Our informant was adamant that you, Miss Cummings, due to your advanced age and onset of dementia are barely capable of looking after yourself let alone a teenager, and that you had no experience of coping with children more especially someone from a deprived and troubled background. He said he was reporting it as much for your own safety as for the girl's,' the social worker added, a smug smirk on her face.

The light had started to dawn on me. I ignored the woman and turned to the policeman. 'This informant wouldn't happen to answer to the name of James Cummings, would he?'

The social worker pursed her lips, sucking a lemon. 'We do

not have to divulge his name,' she answered, but I noticed the faintest of nods from Constable Dawkins.

I felt a cold hand twist my gut. I should have known he would never let me get the best of him. 'That man, my dear brother, who is actually two years older than me, wouldn't know his arse from his elbow,' I replied stiffly. 'In the past fifty years, I have spoken with him on no more than half a dozen occasions which I do not think qualifies him to make judgements on my mental faculties or abilities. Do I look incapable to you?'

Constable Phil Dawkins didn't bother to hide his smile. 'I've been trying to place you, and now I've got it,' he said nodding his head. 'Dora Cummings. Of course! You worked in the CID at headquarters when I was a pimply cadet. You put the fear of God into everyone from the chief constable down and it doesn't look to me as if you have mellowed much with age. I still wouldn't want to take you on.'

'Are you going to hold that against me as well?' I asked, my blood so fully aroused I didn't notice the teasing in his voice.

He held up his hands in surrender, a broad grin still on his face. 'On the contrary; you could be pretty scathing when things went wrong, but you were fair, and you often stepped in when some of the older men were winding me up. I never met anyone you couldn't handle.'

His face and name had long ago vanished from my diminishing brain cells, but it was good to feel I had an ally. The social worker coughed and shuffled her folder.

Ex-cadet Phil Dawkins ignored her. 'You are quite right in what you say, Dora – may I call you Dora? – I think every kid in care would give their eye teeth to be in a place like this. But I'm afraid the matter is in the system now, and we have to follow it through. Better go and pack your bags, love,' he said turning to Janine, 'and we'll get this sorted. But don't worry, Dora, I'll keep you posted.'

Janine turned on her heel and reappeared minutes later with her grotty old backpack slung over her shoulder. She left without a word or even a glance in my direction.

I stood at the top of the drive and watched the police car drive away, the small dark figure of Janine wedged in the back seat between the policewoman and the social worker. I suddenly felt alone and miserable, as if it was somehow all my fault that she was going. I, who had never felt lonely in my life, for the first time felt desolate. *So, how much worse would Janine be feeling?* I thought. We had only just started feeling more comfortable in each other's company, willing to give each other the private space we both seemed to need. True I had laid into the kid a few times, but she hadn't borne me any ill will and had seemed almost relieved to be told the boundaries of normal behaviour and she had been doing her best to live up to my rules. I had really felt as if we were making a connection. And now this! Ripped out of a safe haven and thrust into God knows what.

She and I were more alone now than we had ever been.

'I'll fight for you, Janine, somehow,' I promised as the car disappeared from view. 'I'll do my best, but I haven't a clue where to start.' My words sounded hollow even to my own ears.

CHAPTER THIRTY-ONE

I returned to the kitchen, completely at a loss as to what to do with myself. What the hell had just happened? My whole body felt numb and my brain seemed to have stopped functioning altogether. It had been so sudden, completely out of a clear blue sky. Fragments of words and images were whirling around and around in my head, not making any sense.

I slumped down on a chair as my legs started to tremble and I felt as if I was going to be physically sick. Burned into my retinas was the image of Janine in the back of that car. And it *was* all my fault! If only I had left my brother alone, but no, I had wanted to provoke him. I had to admit I had enjoyed hurting him, finally holding my own, but not having the sense to know when to stop prodding and poking. And this was the result. Why had I thought I would get away with it? I knew what he was like. I had spent my childhood suffering from his spite and he had always won in the end. And now it was poor little Janine who was paying the price. Because he couldn't hurt me anymore, he had gone for an easier target – Janine. I was so angry with myself, I could hardly breathe.

I don't know how long I sat there before my body and mind slowly returned to the present.

I tossed our breakfast dishes into the sink. The concept of washing them was way beyond my current ability. How stupidly smug had I been? I had thought that I had dealt with everything so nicely; getting my life back into its normal rhythm, carefully slotting all the events of the past week into their proper places, micro-managing my world as I had always done on its nice straight path. And now, in one fell swoop, my life was back in the washing machine and set on full spin.

I spent the next half hour berating myself loudly, arms waving, temper rising, until suddenly it was all over; burned out of my system, gone. And I was left feeling like a useless old woman and absolutely drained.

The letterbox rattled and I heard the soft thud of envelopes falling on the mat. As I went through into the hall to collect them, I caught a glimpse of myself in the small mirror attached to the wall. I rarely, if ever, looked at myself in a mirror – I am not a masochist. There had been a few unfortunate occasions when I had walked past a shop window and had caught a glimpse of an old woman looking back at me and I had been shocked rigid when I realized she was wearing the same clothes as me – need I say more? Now I glared a challenge at the face staring back at me. It was tired, beaten and haggard. Maybe I always looked like that but the sunlight coming through the window at the side of the door was vicious, accentuating every line and blemish. Where had all those wrinkles come from and the turkey-wattle neck and the black bags under my eyes? I couldn't bear looking at myself any more and tore my gaze away. I was feeling fragile enough without torturing myself further.

I picked up the letters. One looked semi-official and I took it into the front room and slit it open. It was a hospital appointment for an MRI scan in a few days. I threw it on one side and gazed sightlessly out of the window. I felt as if all matters to do with my cancer had suddenly become inconsequential, and were happening to another person with whom I had only a nodding acquaintance. I felt detached from it all.

I blinked at the sun streamed in through the south-facing front window, a blindingly pure light which only a sea vista can create. When I had moved into the house I had refused to put up blinds or net curtains which everybody said I had to do in order to stop the strong light from rotting my curtains and carpets. I had refused. It seemed to me that the villagers were living in hiding, cowering behind their nets, protecting their precious possessions. Perched high up on the bluff as I was, I was only overlooked by the seagulls and my wide open uninterrupted views had been too priceless to cover up. Sod the carpets. Wasn't threadbare the new shabby chic? But now I saw none of it, and my worry for Janine was like a vice twisting my insides.

I was thinking more clearly now that the shock of what had happened was wearing off. In my arrogance I had interfered, thinking that I could change the child's world for the better, but I had only succeeded in making it worse. She was now in the sticky hands of the authorities when before she had at least been free – starving but free. Is that how a caged animal feels? Why hadn't I left everything alone? Why had I forgotten my most sacred rule of minding my own damned business? Why? Would I have done anything about Janine if it hadn't been for that visit from The God Squad that morning? No, I don't think I would. I probably would have sent her off with a few harsh words and not thought any more about her. But I hadn't and this was the result.

My only hope now was that Tiffany would come up with some ideas because I was completely at a loss. That horrible social worker had been right: I had been dabbling in things I knew nothing about. I was a silly old woman.

I gave myself a vigorous mental shake and plunged into physical activity mode. I scrubbed out the chickens coop with such a display of unfamiliar vigour that it sent the girls running for cover. They looked for all the world like three fat ladies wobbling from side to side as they ran to catch a bus. I couldn't help but chuckle. I pushed the Hoover around the living room and moved the dust from one piece of furniture to another until I finally came to cleaning the annexe. I couldn't put it off any longer. The girl was gone and I needed to change the bed so that Tiffany could have a choice of where to sleep.

Despite her hasty departure, Janine had left the place neat and tidy. The only thing out of place was a pile of my *Two Rivers* books left on the table. I sat down and idly rested my hand on them. Janine was the first young person I had met who had read any of my books. I did not do the school literary days or signing of books or public appearances. The only person who knew I was Anna Clare was my agent (other than Tiffany of course), and we had only met once face-to-face and, if she valued her exorbitant fees, she was sworn to secrecy. Janine had been my first encounter with a "fan". I smiled as I remembered the expression on her face that day we had walked to the castle.

A tiny worm of an idea slipped into my mind as I sat there, remembering. I was used to inspiration coming unbidden, sometimes at the most inconvenient of times and from the strangest of sources, and I had learned never to ignore it, either in my paintings or in my writing.

My latest *Two Rivers* book had been lying fallow inside my laptop, three quarters done and stuck in a marshy swamp. I had stopped because I was unhappy with it. I had tried re-organising the plot to make it more exciting, different, but I had still got stuck in the quagmire. It had needed something else, a new angle. Now I felt a familiar swirling in my head of new possibilities and ideas which would create tensions in the cosy balance of the main characters and give the story a new dynamism which would make my readers sit up and think.

What if I added another character? A tall, thin runaway girl with dark spiky hair, a feisty temper and an aptitude for survival at all costs and against enormous odds. As far as she was concerned, rules of behaviour were for lesser mortals. She was her own person, able to take her destiny in her own hands, answerable to nobody – a sort of bad-arse superhero. Remind you of anyone? She would create an exciting new tension and drive amongst the already established gang, none of whom could be described as angels but they were hampered by family and community ties. The new character would be a free agent and she could eventually work her way up to become a loyal and trusted member of the gang, an exciting new second-in-command perhaps.

Maybe, wherever Janine ended up, she would some day read it and see something of herself in the character and perhaps remember me kindly.

The new ideas did the trick and for the rest of the day and long into the night I reworked the plot of the book, slipping the new character into more and more daring escapades. It was as if Janine lived again in my living room. Fiction was so much easier to rearrange than real life. From now on, perhaps I should stick with that!

The next day, Tiffany arrived and was her usual whirlwind of energy and noise, leaping out of the car and engulfing me in a bone-crushing hug. It was so good to feel her young strong arms wrapped around me, squeezing the breath out of me and nearly breaking my neck as she was a lot taller than me. Everybody was taller than me!

I drank in the citrus tang of her perfume (don't ask me the name, I haven't got a clue about such things) and I wanted it to go on forever. It was such a long time since I had had any physical contact with another human being and emotions had been running high for me lately. These days she was the only person I ever touched or touched me. My parents had frowned on any outward demonstration of closeness. They viewed emotional displays with alarm and distaste. And being a single person, there was a distinct lack of opportunity to get into any clinches – well, I could just about remember a few from fifty years ago! I had got used to it over the years and didn't notice anything was missing until someone, usually Tiffany, wrapped me in their arms and whispered silly things into my ear. By the time she let me go, we were both bawling.

'Leave your things for now, Tiff,' I said, excavating a handkerchief from inside my sleeve and mopping myself up. 'Come on in and have a cuppa. You must be gasping.'

She dived into the boot of her car and emerged with a cardboard box, which clinked softly. 'Wouldn't you prefer something stronger, Dodo. We can open a bottle of whatever you fancy and then you can tell me everything – and I mean everything – that's been going on.'

'It's only four in the afternoon, Tiff,' I protested. 'Wouldn't you prefer tea or coffee after your long drive?'

She turned back and pondered my suggestion deeply for five seconds. 'You are right as usual, Dodo. A coffee first, with a bottle of wine on the side. And if you could manage it, a sandwich wouldn't be half bad either.'

A quarter of an hour later, Tiffany was stretched out on the settee munching on a cheese and pickle sandwich. She had always been a pretty girl, and she had put on a little weight since I had last seen her at Christmas, and it suited her. She had long black hair, which waved gently over her shoulders and intensified her eyes which were the colour of harebells, the same colour as her father's. They had been the only thing I had envied of my brother's but his were now as faded as he was. Mine were a grey blue, the colour of a steely winter sea. But even if she had looked like the back-end of a bus, her vivacious personality would always have compensated. She was a girl who had never lacked for friends and admirers.

We talked until the light had started to fade and a couple of the bottles had been slowly emptied. We had laughed and cried and talked ourselves hoarse before we finally drew breath. I am ashamed to say it was mostly about me, but it was cathartic to be able to share all my highs and lows with someone close. Tiffany was an extremely good listener.

'I think I'd better start making us something to eat before I am quite incapable,' I said rising stiffly to my feet. 'My heavy drinking days are long behind me and nowadays I am more likely to fall asleep than become tipsy and I don't want to waste a minute of your visit.'

'I'll give you a hand,' Tiffany said stirring herself. 'I've got stacks of lovely stuff in the car which I should have put away in the fridge, so it will have been nicely pickled and ready to nosh.'

'Just this once, then. I am not an invalid yet, though I must admit I am a little unsteady! Tomorrow, we can fight for the kitchen.' I answered. 'Oh, Tiff, I can't tell you how wonderful it is to have you here.'

She looked at me for a moment and there was so much love in her eyes that I felt I would collapse, but then she deliberately spoiled the moment by pulling a paper tissue out of her pocket and giving a clown-like rendition of trumpeting through her nose. We understood each other perfectly and there was no need for more words.

Between us we just about managed to prepare a palatable meal, suitably washed down with sparkling water in my case and another glass of wine for Tiffany. She insisted on helping with the washing up and we retired back to the living room, she with more wine and me with a small glass of Baileys.

'What are you going to do about the girl, Dodo?' Tiffany asked. 'I don't know much about the care system or the legal implications, but I'll go on-line tomorrow and see what I can dig up. Unless you've decided to let it go? I would have thought you had enough to keep you busy for the next few months without adding more stress to your life. And let's face it, you never could stand being around children.'

I shook my head. 'I miss her, Tiff. I never in my wildest dreams imagined I would ever say that about a skinny scrap of a girl with all sorts of social and behavioural hang-ups, but I do miss her being around,' I admitted. 'I think that by incorporating her character into the latest book, I have come to possibly understand her more and miss her just a smidgen less. Does that make sense?'

Tiffany nodded. 'You feel as if you've still got hold of a part of her. She's not completely lost.'

'I need to know whether there is anything I can do. They made it pretty plain when they took her that I have no right to interfere and thanks to your father, they now think I'm just a doddering old fart who can't even take care of herself.'

'Whilst I'm down, I'm going to have a word with him,' Tiffany said, suddenly angry. 'He had no right meddling and now he has ruined it for you and the girl. I'm going to give him a piece of my mind, the sanctimonious old sourpuss.'

'No, Tiff, let him be. What's done is done and I don't want you muddying the water with your father any more than it already is. But tomorrow, I'd be grateful if you would try and find something out about where I am, legally. Even if I decide not to do anything about it, at least I will have some idea where I stand. Perhaps everyone else is right and I was wrong to bring the girl here, but she was so desperately

204

alone and neglected I just couldn't leave her.'

'The kid's been through a lot by the sound of it and I can understand you wanting to help. I'd probably have done exactly the same thing, Dodo. Only somebody as mean-spirited and petty as my father would see nothing wrong in condemning a child to our archaic and overloaded care system. Some of those places have barely improved since Oliver Twist and the workhouse! And it was certainly not done out of the goodness of his heart. He doesn't have one – I know!'

CHAPTER THIRTY-TWO

Two days later, Tiffany and I travelled to the hospital for my MRI scan.

We didn't talk much on the journey; each of us busy with our own thoughts. Over the past couple of days we had exhausted what little either of us knew on the subject of breast cancer. Neither of us had been through it before and heedful of Mr. Peston's warning, I wouldn't let Tiffany Google it – forgive me if that is the wrong phrase – I would find out soon enough.

It was rather nice being chauffeured around, though. No need to spend precious time hunting for a parking space in the always crowded hospital car park; no need to hunt for my specs so that I can find out which floor I need in the confusing labyrinth of corridors. Tiffany took care of it all.

I handed over my appointment letter to the receptionist and we were told to take a seat in the small waiting room allocated to that department – well, more a partitioned off section of the corridor than an actual room.

Over the past few months I had started to become familiar with the protocol of waiting rooms. I would watch the comings and goings around me, fascinated by the complexity of emotions anxious people show without even realizing it. Sometimes, if the patient quota is of the older generation, one could strike up a conversation and exchange pleasantries and pass what would otherwise have been a boring twenty minutes or more. These days though most people, young and middle aged, have their heads bent over their smart phones tapping away at the keys as a warning not to intrude; or blankly gazing into space with wires dangling out of their ears, a foot jigging to some unheard tune. I had enough trouble hearing my name called even with my hearing aids in, so they must be doomed to spend hours waiting while the nurses strike their names as no-shows off their lists.

It was a very different experience when one has a companion, even if we only sat quietly side by side.

After twenty minutes I was finally called for my scan. Tiffany refused to go off to find a coffee and said she would be quite happy with a magazine. Half an hour later I emerged, my hands clasped tightly over my mouth and tears oozing down the sides of my face. Tiffany was instantly at my side.

'What happened, Auntie Dodo? Was it very bad?'

I shook my head and managed to mutter the word 'coffee' through my fingers. We headed off to the little cafeteria we had spotted on the way in, Tiffany's hand under my elbow supporting me. It was only once we were in the relative safety of the bustling noisy coffee shop that I finally let it all burst out. I tried to control the laughter for the sake of the other people around who were no doubt nursing their own traumas, but by now the tears were pouring unchecked down my cheeks. I could see heads turning in my direction, some perplexed while others were obviously annoyed at my levity.

Tiffany cocked an eyebrow at me as she put our cappuccinos on the table. The poor girl had probably been imagining all sorts of scenarios over the last few minutes seeing the state I was in. Laughter was not what she expected. 'I'm sorry, Tiffany,' I said as I wiped my face and blew my nose. 'I couldn't very well burst out laughing in front of all those poor women who were waiting their turn to go in. I just couldn't keep it in any longer.'

'So...? Tell all.'

I took a quick sip of my coffee to settle myself. It was scolding hot and the pain on my tongue brought me to my senses. 'I can only say that it was the most humiliating and hysterically funny situation I think I have ever been in, in my entire life,' I answered. 'It was so bizarre, like some medieval torture chamber.'

'And you are laughing?'

'In the circumstances, it is the only thing you can do,' I explained. 'For anybody without a warped sense of humour like me, it would probably be quite traumatic.

'It was ordinary enough to start with. I had to take off my clothes from the waist up and lie face down on this bed and put my arms out in front of me as if I was doing the breaststroke. Then it got really weird. The nurse slotted my boobs down into the two holes with funnels, which had been cut out of the bed. I asked her if I could have an aromatherapy massage while we were at it, but she seemed rather shocked at the suggestion.'

'It probably wasn't the standard reaction,' Tiffany said grinning, 'especially from a seemingly respectable lady of your age.'

'What do you mean "seemingly"?' I asked with mock affront. 'It didn't stop there. In front of me, behind protective glass, were two technicians – both male I might add – and there I was, flat on my stomach with my boobs dangling into space. I asked the nurse what would happen if a patient had small boobs. She said it was tricky, but far worse if a woman had big breasts as they could get stuck! Both of us chuckled; I think that by this time the nurse was starting to appreciate my sense of humour. I was told not to move for twenty minutes, but I'm afraid I had great difficulty not giggling. It was all so ludicrous only a man could have thought up such a design.'

'Or maybe there is another hole the other end for men to put their dangly bits through?' Tiffany offered.

We left the cafeteria before we were thrown out and laughed all the way home.

With the MRI scan safely behind us, Tiffany trawled the net – I don't know whether my computer terminology is getting better or worse – for any information about children in care, and while it didn't cater for my particular circumstances, we at least found the route to appeal against Janine being snatched. After Tiffany had gone back home, I would start making my own enquiries as to her whereabouts and make a more informed judgment on my way forward.

Tiffany managed to stay an extra day and we were chatting as we took a leisurely stroll across the cliff-tops. The distant bay and cliffs of Southerndown beach hovered in a soft haze and the breeze was calm and thick with the salty tang of the sea. Beneath our feet, the short turf shuddered as each wave hurled itself against the cliffs below.

The coconut scent of the gorse rose around us and everywhere was the chirruping of grasshoppers and the sweet songs of birds. 'I'm so glad I came, Dodo. I was so worried about you, but I can see I needn't have been. I don't think I could be as cool about it if it had been me.'

I gave her a reassuring laugh. 'If you were my age, you would have an entirely different outlook, believe me,' I assured her. 'As your body goes south, and your boobs sag low enough to rest on your spare tyre and your bum and belly jut out to balance each other, you stop looking at yourself and try to forget what once was. For me, it's hardly earth shattering to have one breast removed – even though it is probably a rather drastic way to lose weight. Nobody will ever see me undressed except for the doctors, and I will be having a false boob to stuff into my bra, so who's to know any different?'

'Well, you never know your luck, Dodo. You are not too old, you know.'

'Look, my girl, by the time you reach your seventies, there are very few people who don't have so many bionic parts that they are afraid to move in case bits fall off.'

'Okay, I give in. But I'll be back to stay for a week when you have your op, and maybe Gina can come down with me as well and we can have a bit of a holiday,' Tiffany said. She inhaled deeply. 'This is one thing I really miss in London. Lovely clean air.'

'There's really no need for you to come down...'

'There is every need – for my peace of mind, if not yours. I fully expect you to be a nightmare patient, so it will probably take the two of us to keep you under control along with replenishing the bottles of wine.'

I smiled. 'I'd love it, my dear. Thank you.'

After we had wandered back home and I had rustled up a prawn salad with new potatoes, Tiffany went off to pack. Just as the meal was ready, she strolled into the kitchen with a couple of books in her hands. 'I didn't know you were into cartoons and illustrations, Dodo.'

I wiped my hands and reached for the books. 'They are not

mine, love. Where did you find them?'

'They were tucked into the bottom of the wardrobe along with this rather disreputable teddy bear which I have never seen before. I only noticed them when I dropped an earring and had to go rummaging. I flicked through – they are very good. Are you sure you are not hiding some new talent from me?' She raised a quizzical eyebrow at me.

'I think this is Janine's book and the sketchpad I gave her. She said she liked to draw, but she never showed me anything she had done and she's not the type of girl you can press.' I flicked through and started to laugh. 'They really are good, aren't they? She's turned my three chickens into The God Squad! You can't fail to identify each one of them; she's captured their characters perfectly. These are far better than I could do. I've always been pretty useless at cartooning – it is a special knack and I don't have it, but it seems Janine has it in spades.'

'There's a story in the back of this book with some more illustrations. It's all about a seagull called Sidney who only has one leg and who wants to run away from his flock. He is fed up with spending all his time mindlessly scavenging through the human rubbish tips. He joins the chickens and they take him on as their bodyguard against a buzzard, a fox and a snake who all making their life a misery. Even though he only has one leg, he is a crack shot with his poo. It is really quite funny and it's all written in rhyme. '

I flicked through the tatty black book. In the front were pages and pages of names and numbers, but in the back Janine had used the blank pages and filled them with her spidery handwriting, all with atrocious spelling but with quite masterful illustrations. 'I had no idea she was this talented,' I said in amazement. 'And this monstrosity is Mr. Boots, her childhood teddy bear. I will have to try and get these back to her, she must have forgotten to take them; which is yet another reason why I have to find her.'

'Do you not think she might have left them on purpose? They were really well hidden. I wouldn't have seen them if I hadn't lost my earring.'

'I'll hang on to them and try and get them back to her somehow,' I mused, but Tiffany's face had taken on her "I'm-planning-something-look".

'What?'

'I may be wrong, but I think this would make a brilliant book for toddlers,' she said thoughtfully. 'Gina has a sometimes friend who is something to do with a publishing company and I think they have a department which specialises in books for young children. I'm not too sure as I've never taken any interest before. Do you mind if I show them to her?'

'Do you think they are that good?' I asked.

'Oh, yes. I am sure they are but don't say anything about it to Janine, I don't want you to get her hopes up. I'd love to be right, as the kid deserves a break, but I'm hardly the expert on little children. I'll bring them back when I come down for your op.'

'Well, they are not really mine to give, but I can't see any harm in it,' I said handing the books over. 'It will probably take me weeks to batter my way through the bureaucracy and red tape to find her anyway.'

We made tearful farewells as I waved her off the next morning. It had been an emotionally exhausting and alcohol-fuelled couple of days but I felt lighter of heart. I can't say I had poured my soul out to Tiff – there were no hysterics or beating of breasts (excuse the pun) – but there had been plenty of laughter and tears and any lingering doubts I still had had been shared and that felt good.

CHAPTER THIRTY-THREE

I mooched about the house for an hour of so, fiddling with this and that to pass the time but achieved nothing. I couldn't settle. My brain was all over the place, repeatedly going over what had happened, what Tiffany had said and how I now felt about – well, everything!

The house felt too empty, too echoey. Over the past week I had lost Janine, someone who had unexpectedly wormed her way through my defences and I had just waved farewell to the only person that I could say I have ever truly loved, my friend and soul mate.

My life had been knocked seriously out of balance and I was wandering into unfamiliar territory. While Tiffany had been there, I had conveniently pushed the horrors of my cancer and its implications to the back of my mind. While she'd been there, a human rock who understood me better than anyone else on earth, I could forget about Janine and The God Squad and all my own inadequacies and laugh until the tears ran down my cheeks.

But now she was gone and I desperately missed her company, the distraction that she had provided and the buzz of having another person to share the little ups and downs of every day, to broaden and challenge my own rather narrow outlook on life

But for all our rather drunken days of setting the world to rights, nothing had actually changed. I still had cancer and the prospect of surgery; Janine was still being dragged around the county in search of a home and I still did not know whether I should wash my hands of her or take up the fight on her behalf. I felt as if my insides had been hollowed out and to my astonishment there had been nothing left. Was this loneliness? If so, then it was a new sensation for me and I didn't like it, not one bit. I had never appreciated the distinction between loneliness and being alone. I loved living alone and would never want to change it, but this feeling of emptiness was something I could do without.

I wondered, with a sick feeling in my stomach, what Janine was doing at that moment. I doubted that it would be pleasant.

There were umpteen things I should have been doing, things left undone while Tiffany and I had idled our way through the days, but now my conscience finally won out and I grudgingly pulled myself out of the chair to get on with some work.

I stripped the bed in the annexe, again. I planted up the pots outside the front door with heartsease pansies I had grown from seed and which were begging to be transplanted – they grew wild on the dunes and had no problem tolerating the salt winds – and sprinkled on some candytuft and Virginia stock seeds. I thought some music would fill the silence but couldn't make up my mind which type I was in the mood for, so didn't bother. I cleaned out the chickens, and did manage to raise a smile as they scraped and scratched and argued around my feet – annoyed that I was not Tiffany who adored them and sneaked them double rations when she thought I wasn't looking.

The pot of bracken which was still squatting on the steps caught my eye. To my horror I could see that the fronds were rapidly unfurling and in another day they would have been too far developed to be added to the tight crosiers which I had already started painting. I hadn't given them a thought while Tiffany had been down. It is one of the great disadvantages of painting flowers and plants – they wait for no man, but I had devised a method of coping when I had multiple specimens all coming to peak at the same time. I dashed upstairs and grabbed my sketchbooks and painting gear. I wouldn't have the time or the composure necessary to do anything finished yet, but I would be able to do a few hours of careful drawing and measuring, along with a quick colour sketch to capture the correct shades of the fresh greens in the new growth. Put together with some photographs and close-ups, they would be a perfectly adequate worksheet for me to use for my finished painting – whenever that was going to be!

It took me a couple of hours to record sufficient detail of two of the best fronds which, despite my reluctance to sit down and work, were a delight to draw and the smell of them was glorious. I mixed a chart of greens for the colour range and sat back, my work for the moment done. The pressure was off. I could relax.

213

In the kitchen I was faced with a sink of dirty dishes from our last breakfast, but I wanted a cup of coffee and a chat, not more domestic chores. I turned my back on them and locked the back door, pocketed the key and grabbing a spare tray of pansies I went off in search of Ted Morris. I shook my head in wonderment; this was something I would never have dreamt of doing only a few weeks ago. Was it becoming too much of a habit, I wondered to myself? Careful, Dora Cummings, you are wandering into dangerous waters.

I gave a perfunctory knock on his back door and walked in, but there was no sign of him. A small fire glowed in the grate and the old clock ticked sonorously on the high mantelpiece. The room seemed to be slumbering, waiting for its occupant to return in his own time. Though it was empty it felt cosy, whereas mine had become cold.

I shouted up the stairs. 'It's Dora, Ted. I've got a couple of heartsease pansies to put in your rockery.'

There was no reply, so I took myself off to the shed in search of a trowel. I was surprised at how disappointed I felt that he wasn't home; a meaningless natter about old times would have fitted the bill; would have taken my mind off things. The shed door opened just as I put my hand to the handle, and Ted shot out and slammed the door behind him.

He looked flustered, almost guilty. 'Dora! I thought I heard someone calling,' he said, swiping his hand through his hair and dislodging slivers of wood chips.

'I've come to beg a cup of coffee, Ted. And in payment I had a couple of leftover pansies and I thought I could put them in for you. Mind out of the way so I can get myself a trowel.'

I tried to push past him but he blocked me off and pressed his back up against the door, barring entry. 'I'll do it myself, Dora, later on. How about I take my favourite girl out for a little stroll instead?'

He was stonewalling me and he wasn't very good at it. I knew it. He knew that I knew, but he wasn't budging. Other than starting an undignified wrestling match, I had no choice but to play along. 'Okay,

I'll just put these in the shade, but mind you plant them and give them a good watering.' Ted almost jumped to attention and rolled down his sleeves. 'I need to explain to you about Janine, anyway. You must have wondered where she was.'

'Aye, I have,' he answered. He collected his jacket from inside the kitchen and pulled the back door shut. 'I'm missing the lass already. She won't be away long, will she?'

He took my arm and firmly led me down the lane.

I knew that the next couple of weeks would be a long period of waiting and I had been thrown back on my own reserves. I hoped the well wouldn't run dry on me.

I had received a letter giving me the date for my operation. It all suddenly became very real. I now had a firm date instead of an event vaguely threatened at sometime in the future. It wasn't something I could keep putting to the back of my mind – it was finally going to happen and I was on a countdown. Probably! I had been warned by people who seemed to be old hands at the hospital system and knew all about its peculiarities, that nothing to do with the National Health Service was ever set in stone. These patients seemed to sense when someone was new and gullible and they took every opportunity to pass on their vast knowledge of horror stories while we sat for hours and hours in various waiting rooms. 'If you get your hands on a bed, love, chain yourself to it,' I was advised on more than one occasion.

For a few days I couldn't stop myself from imagining what I would be doing in hospital at any particular time of the day, but since I had never stayed in a hospital before, it was an exercise in futility and I eventually got bored with it. Let's face it, I didn't know a thing. I packed a small bag ready – enough for a couple of nights at the most, they had said. I had splurged some cash on buying new nightclothes, slippers and toiletries and the latest *Anne Cleeves* paperback – I did love her crusty old Vera stories, and then there was nothing more to do.

I tried my best to wear my body out with housework and vigorous gardening so that I would fall into an exhausted sleep at night – assisted by a few sherries or a Bacardi or two. I had genuinely felt really up-beat and optimistic to both Tiffany and myself before but when I inevitably woke in the dark wee hours, my mind would hook itself on to a stray thought and blow it up to monumental importance and for the rest of the night I would worry away at it until I fell into a dream-ridden sleep, usually just as it was time to get up. I had many such nights and I was sure it had all started telling on my face and temper.

To my amusement, I became (of all things) superstitious, a seeker after assurances! Me – hard-headed Dora Cummings who called a book a book! The sight of a shooting star was surely a sign that everything would be well; a black cat crossing my path or finding a lucky locket I had last worn sometime in my teens when I was sitting exams. They were all omens, or so I kidded myself. Other things – things happening out in the wide world where people and governments fought and bickered over seemingly meaningless things no longer held my interest. The news was always depressing but I had usually felt obliged to watch it in order to keep abreast (excuse the pun once again!) of current affairs but now I felt detached from it all as being pointless. I had turned in on myself, hunkering down into a shell like Herman my hermit crab, keeping out of the way of the world.

Without much hope of getting anywhere, I rather lethargically opened up my laptop to do a bit more writing and to my surprise I became totally lost in it. It was pure fantasy – my fantasy, and it was I who was in control. I had already re-jigged the storyline in the latest book, weaving Janine into the plot as a new disruptive character. She added a dynamic frisson in the group and I thoroughly enjoyed putting her in there and stirring things up.

With days of uninterrupted writing, I soon had the first draft finished. I had enjoyed writing it and I think Janine would have approved. I printed it off and popped it into a large envelope to post off to my agent. She had put up with me for years and, bless her, she still accepted my little eccentricity of refusing to send anything via a distant satellite and the planet Mars.

I drove into town to post the manuscript at the main post office. I never used the post office in the village. The local residents had petitioned fervently to stop its closure a few years before and, because the village was technically classed as a holiday resort, the prospect of the tourists not having anywhere to buy stamps and mail their postcards had won the day – so far. Everybody knew that Rita Davies, who ran the sweet shop and post office combo, steamed open any interesting-looking envelopes to satisfy her curiosity and graciously passed on any interesting titbits. I did not want her prying into my business and announcing to the public far and wide that they had a 'celebrity' in their midst. She would have done it; she couldn't have helped herself. And though everybody grumbled about the invasion of their privacy they did nothing to stop her and accepted her eccentricity as part of living in a small village. They also accepted that she and Mrs. Hardy were the last bastions of traditional village life, for better or for worse. When they went, the village would effectively lose its soul. No more gossips over the shop counter; no more free samples of Welsh cakes straight off the bakestone for favoured customers or a taste of the latest vintage of Alf's elderflower wine which could knock your socks off. Email and Facebook and all the rest didn't quite cut it.

I had popped into Hardy's shop on my way home from town, only to find The God Squad already waiting at the counter. I thought I might have been able to escape undetected, but Flo Jenkins had seen me and nudged Elizabeth Henshaw, indicating with a sidewise nod of her head that someone of interest had entered. I felt three pairs of eyes swivel towards me. I suppressed a giggle, which started building up inside me as my imagination superimposed Janine's cartoon chickens on to their faces.

'Any news of that young girl who was staying with you?' Mrs. Henshaw asked. 'I haven't seen her around lately.'

I had taken the coward's way out and rung Selwyn Jenkins to

say that Janine would not be continuing to work at the hotel, but I had given no further details. Mrs. Hardy would have seen the police car on my drive at about the relevant time and the gossip factory would have put two and two together. I had not added to the speculation, leaving it to them to concoct their own wild theories.

'Typical!' sniffed Flo Jenkins. 'No sooner do you train them than they up sticks and leave.'

'She was washing dishes, Mrs. Jenkins! I would hardly think her departure was going to jeopardise your ambitions for a *Michelin* star.'

Mrs. Jenkins sniffed louder. Mrs. Anthony suppressed a giggle by turning it into a cough.

'Was there a problem, Dora?' Mrs. Hardy asked, one eyebrow artfully raised.

'There was no problem, Megan. As far as I was concerned I was perfectly happy for her to stay longer, but the authorities took her away because she was under sixteen. Sheer stupidity if you ask me as she was only a couple of months short. I've been trying to find out where they've taken her, but so far I have been meeting with the proverbial brick wall.'

They finished buying their purchases and started to leave. Elizabeth Henshaw hung back and turned to me, lowering her voice so that only I could hear. 'If there is anything I or my husband can do, please ask. He can use his position as vicar to cut down most of those stuffed shirts and windbags down at the council offices and we'd like to help. She seemed a very willing child. A little sulky, but a worker, nonetheless.'

I mumbled a thank you and turned away. It took me another minute to remember what I had called in for.

As I wandered up the lane towards home, my mind was wrestling with the unlikely but possible scenario of asking the Henshaws to intercede on behalf of Janine, or at the very least to find out what had happened to her. For the child's sake and my own curiosity, I couldn't let my own pig-headedness get in the way.

Perhaps I would call at the vicarage and ask, without the rest of The God Squad being present.

Ted waylaid me as I drew level with his back gate. If I hadn't known better, I would be inclined to believe that he had a camera-trap set up in his lilac bush. It was my own fault. We had got into the habit of taking a morning walk together which I am sure had set the jungle drums beating overtime. But it was one thing to tease the local gossips, and quite another if Ted was going to start pestering me to join him at every whip stitch. His walks were of necessity slow and unsatisfactorily short, and in order to avoid him I had taken to sneaking down the steep front steps and heading off in the opposite direction. My walks were my solace and my safety valve. Neither could be achieved in the presence of another person.

'I'll stroll up with you to see you to your door, if you like, Dora,' he said eagerly.

'I do know the way rather well, thank you, Ted,' I answered. It had come out sharper than I had meant and I hurried to soften my words. 'It is very gallant of you, but this old soul has a few things to see to. I'll call for you in the morning and we can go for an ice-cream. Alright?'

The injured look remained in his eyes even as he smiled and waved and turned away. I had hurt the poor man by turning him down so rudely. I wondered as I plodded up the hill if I wasn't deliberately keeping Ted at a distance, guiltily using him only when it suited me; afraid perhaps that he may be getting too close, invading my all-precious privacy and perhaps wanting more than mere friendship. There was no denying that he was getting more persistent of late. What was I afraid of, at my age? Was I too independent to spare a few minutes for another human being? Or was there something more? Fear maybe?

I wasn't concentrating as I went in through the back door into the cool of the kitchen. A cup of tea would be nice, I thought and I started to fill the kettle. I suddenly froze. The back door hadn't been locked! I knew I had locked it. Ever since Janine had picked the lock, I had started double-checking every time I went out, even though she was no longer around. I could feel the key heavy in my pocket.

I had often read in thriller stories of terror turning the blood in someone's veins to ice, and I now knew what they meant. Every part of me went cold and chills ran up and down my body. I turned off the tap and strained to listen, but between my tinnitus and the blood hammering in my ears, I couldn't be sure of anything. Were those footsteps upstairs or was it just my imagination? They were too heavy for Janine who was as light as a fairy. Then a loud crash of something breaking echoed through the floorboards, followed by complete silence. There was definitely somebody up there.

CHAPTER THIRTY-FOUR

Oh, God! There *was* somebody up there. Now what was I going to do? My bones were made of rubber and I was on the verge of collapsing. I felt so weak, I did not think I had enough strength to swat a fly let alone confront a burglar. The room started spinning around me, and I clung blindly to the draining board for support. I felt myself sinking into a well of darkness and realized I had forgotten to breathe. I desperately gulped in air.

Think, woman, think! I scanned the kitchen frantically looking for a weapon. I fingered the large bread knife but thought it would be rather overplaying my hand (I didn't want to be prosecuted for murder if I hit a vital spot by accident), and I didn't want to look absolutely stupid if it was somebody perfectly innocent, though for the life of me I couldn't think who would be creeping around my house without my knowledge. Could it be Janine come back? Why would she be searching the house? And anyway, as far as I was aware, she still had her key to the annexe. No, I knew deep down it was not Janine. I was being burgled and I was damned if I was going to let them get away with it. Adrenalin and anger surged through me in seconds. My copper-bottomed milk saucepan was on the top of the stove, thankfully empty. I snatched it up and crept through the door into the hallway. The telephone tempted me and I did consider making an emergency call until I saw the wires lying on the carpet. I had no idea where my mobile phone was and it was sure to have a flat battery.

Later, much later, I would be able to smile at the daft image of myself brandishing a saucepan as my weapon of choice. Fat lot of good that it did me, anyway.

I had always imagined I would be stouter-hearted in the face of an intruder – after all I did have a reputation for being feisty. Over the years, I had considered the possibility of being burgled – it must be in the back of the mind of anyone living on their own, but one which, like dying, nobody chooses to dwell on if they want to keep their sanity. It was easy to scoff at characters on the television while sitting comfortably on the settee, convinced you would never have been *that* rattled or caved in *that* easily. I would have fought and punched and screamed and seen them off with a flea in their ear. But the reality, it turned out, was something different. I was frozen with panic; I had ton weights strapped to each of my legs, and my nether regions were about to void their contents all over the hall floor.

As I crept around the newel post and put my foot on the bottom stair, I saw above me a man's foot shod in a grubby trainer descending the stairs towards me. I lifted the saucepan above my shoulder. The man's kneecaps came within range and I prayed that I would have the courage to wallop him before he walloped me.

'Who the hell are you, and what are you doing in my house?' (Now, isn't that the most ludicrous thing to say?) 'One more step and I'll crack your knee cap like a walnut,' I said as boldly as I could when handicapped by the croaking voice of a centenarian and a saucepan that trembled in my hand.

The man came down another step and I raised the saucepan higher. He peered down at me, an appeasing smile on his face as though I was making a fuss about nothing. 'Hello, there. I'm sorry to have barged in uninvited, but I knocked on the door, and it just swung open, I swear,' he said pleasantly. I was struck dumb, my mouth gaping. He continued unperturbed. 'Perhaps your lock is faulty. You should get that looked at, you know. You can't be too careful when you live on your own and with no immediate neighbours.'

'There's nothing wrong with the door and I know I locked it,' I said, my voice a mere whisper.

He ignored me as if I hadn't spoken. 'I've come looking for Janine, and I thought she might be here.'

'Janine! What have you got to do with Janine?'

His smile broadened, like that of the Cheshire cat and about as sincere. 'I'm a friend of her mother's and we were worried about her. She's got completely out of control now she's hit her teens. We've done our best with her but she's a sly one. She did a bunk as soon as the social services turned their backs. We thought she might have come back here, so I came looking.'

So, this was the mother's boyfriend.

'That's a load of twaddle, and you know it. You could have rung and asked instead of breaking in and searching my house. Where do you think she is hiding – in a shoe box?'

He took another step down; the smile on his face had slipped a little. 'My, but you are a plucky old bird, aren't you?' He took another slow step down. He still towered threateningly above me. 'You're right love, it's not her I want. But that little bitch took something when she run away the first time – a book, and it belongs to me and I want it back. She didn't have it on her when the social brought her back, so it's got to still be here somewhere. Now, either you tell me or I'll tear this place apart. It's your choice love, understand?'

I raised the saucepan higher – the weight was beginning to take its toll.

'Janine took her stuff with her when the social services and the police took her away,' I explained. 'There's nothing left here of hers and I've had no contact with her since. She must have thrown it away.'

His face hardened. 'If that's how you want to play it...'

His foot lashed out but I tightened my grip on the saucepan handle and with a rush of adrenalin smashed it into his exposed leg, with as much effect as if it had been a feather duster. The man charged down the remaining stairs and easily wrenched it out of my hand. He pushed me away from him and with a single hand around my neck pinned me up against the wall.

'Where is it, old woman?' he demanded all pretence at politeness gone. 'You can save yourself a lot of grief if you just tell me where my property is and then I'll leave you alone.' He pushed his face into mine, his breath sour and overwhelming. 'Play it nice, lady, because I am fast losing my patience. I am not someone you want to cross, believe me.'

'Whatever that book is, I haven't got it,' I gasped. He had me standing on tip-toe, almost off the ground, and he was crushing my windpipe. I could feel the blood pounding inside my head.

'It's a small black book – cliché I know.' He grinned, but there was no humour. Black dots were exploding inside my eyeballs as he tightened his grip even further. 'Tell me where it is, or there could just be a terrible accident. There's a lot of inflammable junk in this place, it'd go up like it was bonfire night. Do you get my drift, lady?'

'Janine didn't come into this part of the house. She stayed in the annexe,' I croaked. I hoped he wasn't a mind reader as the image of the black book with Janine's writing and drawings in the back overpowered my mind.

'Well, why didn't you say so before!' He let me go and I sank to my knees, gasping to drag some air into my lungs. 'Open it up right now or I'll bust the door down,' he ordered. He grabbed me by my arm and pushed me forward.

I took the key for the annexe off the hook at the side of the connecting door and opened it. He pushed me roughly inside. 'Sit there and don't move. Old bones break easily, so I'm told.'

I slumped into the armchair and gripped the sides to try and stop the shaking. I had never felt so helpless.

He pulled open all the drawers and tossed the contents into a heap on the floor. He even pulled the unit away from the wall to check behind it. He emptied all the jigsaws out of their boxes and swept the books off the shelves. He was getting angrier and angrier.

I gripped my hands tight to steady myself and tried to swallow the football that had lodged in my throat. My forehead was slick with a cold sweat. I forced myself to calm down. Do something, woman. Take back some control. The only thing I could think of which was within my meagre abilities was to make a mental note of the man's features. Yes, that was one thing I could do. I could give the police a complete description of the man after he had gone – God willing that I would still be alive! He was a shade under six foot, I would say, thin and wiry with a couple of days of stubble blackening his chin and black hair shaved almost to the scalp on the sides and flopping in an unruly mass on top. Surprisingly young, perhaps in his late twenties, early thirties. His face was gaunt and his pale skin was stretched too tight over high flat cheekbones. He had a long, straight nose and pale lips. Cadaverous, would be the best description I could think of. His eyes were brown, so dark that they looked almost black. Would I know him again? Too damned right! I rehearsed his physical description over and over again so that I wouldn't forget. It helped keep the terrors at bay.

Frustrated by his lack of success, the man glared down at me. His face was a mask of fury.

'Dora, are you there?' a voice called.

It was Ted Morris, bless his poor old heart. I could have cried with joy. Even though he would be about as much use as I was in beating off this man, it was comforting to have someone else there. I was no longer alone. My courage started flooding back into my veins. Ted edged cautiously into the doorway and took in the situation with a single glance – me cowering pathetically in the chair with a strange man looming threateningly over me. He raised his stick above his head as if it was a medieval broadsword and charged into the room, rather spoiling his knight-in-shining-armour image by getting the stick caught in the doorway. As the man turned to counter this latest threat, I grabbed a heavy ceramic vase off the table beside me (I had never liked it) and brought it down on his head. It made contact slightly off centre and it was his shoulder that took most of the impact, where it smashed into pieces, but it was enough to frighten him. He pushed his way past Ted and charged out of the back door and away.

I threw myself into Ted's arms, tears flooding down my face and my whole body shaking with shock and relief. I felt vomit rise in my throat and gulped it back. He held me tighter and muttered nonsense into the top of my head. It felt so good to feel safe, to have somebody else take charge and for once to put myself unconditionally in somebody else's hands. I wanted that moment to last forever.

The shaking was diminishing. Ted looked down on me. 'If you are okay to stay here, lass, I'll go out and follow him. He could have a car …'

I pulled him back. 'No, he'll be long gone, Ted, and you need to think of your heart. And your car must have a flat battery after all this time. Just phone the police for me, please.' I could feel my stomach churning. 'I think I am going to be sick.' I managed to get to the little bathroom in time and vomited until there was nothing more to come up, but it didn't stop me shaking, in fact it had made it worse. If I had been wearing false teeth, they would have rattled right out of my mouth.

Ted gently took my arm and led me through to the kitchen. 'A cup of strong sweet tea with a drop of something stronger in it is the best remedy for shock, so they say,' he said. 'You sit yourself down and I'll make one for both of us, then I'll call the police. I've got my mobile.'

I watched helplessly as he took charge of me and set about making the tea. 'There's a card on the table by the phone with Constable Dawkins's number on it,' I said as he placed the mug in front of me. 'Tell him that the man was looking for Janine. He's her mother's boyfriend.'

'Right ho,' Ted said and wandered into the hall. A minute later he was sitting beside me again. He sat opposite me and took hold of my hand. 'All done, lass. I spoke to the man himself. He's on his way. Don't worry, I'm not leaving you. You're safe now.'

I raised an eye at him. There was no trace left of the weak old man who had spent his days huddled beside his cold fireside. 'I don't think I will ever forget the sight of you charging through the door brandishing your stick,' I said, summoning up a weak smile. 'If I wasn't so pathetically grateful, I would accuse you of enjoying yourself, Ted Morris.'

Ted laughed and patted my hand. 'Do you know something, Dora, despite the circumstances which I would never wish on anybody, I think I am. I feel alive again, as if I have been asleep for a long time. And now I have rescued my damsel in distress. What more can a man ask for?'

'Damsel! Me!'

We both laughed. 'That's better, old girl. That's my Dora.'

It was only much later when I was mulling over all that had happened and my own pathetic inability to fight for myself that Ted's words came back to me: *"my Dora."* Oops!

CHAPTER THIRTY-FIVE

Twenty minutes later, there was a knock at the back door and Ted opened it to let Constable Phil Dawkins in.

'She's in the living room, officer,' I heard him say. 'She's a bit shaken up.'

Constable Phil Dawkins entered the room, suddenly dwarfing it with his presence. In my mind's eye I could imagine how a modern police officer, their bodies doubled in bulk with all the gizmos they needed to carry could intimidate rather than comfort. Luckily familiarity had long ago inured me to any such trepidation. His presence was a relief.

'You are looking very pale, Dora. Do you want me to call your doctor for you?'

I gave a short laugh, which came out as more of a snort really. 'You'll never get one just like that; it's not like the old days, lad,' I answered caustically. 'I haven't been hurt, just stretched a bit, but otherwise unharmed. But I can't seem to stop shaking.' I wrapped the shawl Ted had found tighter around me.

'That'll be the comedown from the adrenalin rush. Have you got any alcohol in the house? A drop of the hard stuff will help calm your innards down.'

'Ted has already been plying me with tea and whisky – which I only keep for visitors at Christmas time, you understand; I can't abide the stuff normally, though there's some sherry in the cabinet. Oh damn, I am so angry at myself for being such a pathetic weak old woman. I felt so helpless!'

Ted handed me a glass of sherry and helped steady my hand while I took rather too big a sip. It caught at the back of my throat and I coughed, but I could feel its warmth sliding down right through my insides.

'And another one, old girl. Doctor's orders,' Ted said quietly. 'I'll just go and put those wires back in your phone box while you two have a chat.'

'Don't get too used to bossing me about, Ted Morris,' I muttered to his retreating back. 'This is only a temporary blip.'

'Good,' Phil Dawkins said. He eased himself into the armchair and took out his little black notebook, flicking through to a blank page. 'There's colour coming back into your cheeks now. Ted said on the phone that somebody had broken in and threatened you. Do you think you can tell me what happened now, from the beginning?'

'Yes, um… yes.'

It tumbled out, not in any particular order, bits and pieces falling over each other and sparking off other thoughts, some relevant, others not. 'Oh, I feel so bloody useless and … and angry. I am so *very* angry!'

'You seem to have done pretty well for an oldie. He'll have a sore shoulder to remind him not to tackle you again.'

'I should have done more… at least got my aim straight! I was aiming for his head and missed! How can you miss?' I asked of no-one in particular.

'From what you've said, he was almost a foot taller than you, so there's no shame in not being able to reach. Anyway, hold on to your anger, Dora. Use it to build up your strength so that you can cope with this,' Constable Dawkins said. He was very patient. 'Now, can you give me a description of this man?'

I told him everything I had rehearsed in my head. Even if it was all I had in my weaponry, it felt good to have something positive to say. He seemed surprised at the thoroughness of my description. In fact I was rather pleased myself with my effort. Dementia be damned!

He took out his phone, which every human being on the planet other than me seemed to have grafted to them like an extra limb, and punched in a series of numbers. He held it out to me. 'Is this the man, Dora?' he asked.

On the screen was a photograph of the man who had so recently had me pinned up against the wall by my neck; the man who had terrorised me and turned me into a quivering jelly, stripped me of all my dignity and left me bawling like a baby and puking into the toilet. I would never forgive him. Never! 'Yes, that's him, but he's quite a bit thinner than that.'

'Les Peters,' Constable Dawkins said. 'Cardiff Drug Squad has had him flagged up for quite a while. He's been giving them the run-around for months, but it looks like he's finally made a mistake. We'll have him this time and it'll be a pleasure to show those city boys that we country bumpkins are on the ball.' He did look smugly satisfied as he put his phone away. The animosity between city and rural police was as old as the police force itself. 'Now, about this book you mentioned, Dora. Have you still got it? It is obviously something very important to him.'

I shrugged dismissively. 'It was just a book that Janine had with her when she first came here. I don't think she thought of it as anything special. She used it to draw in and she wrote a little story about my chickens in the back.'

'And what else was in it? Can I see it?'

'There were numbers and names in the front, but I didn't look at them properly. I was more interested in what Janine had been doing. She's a very good little cartoonist.' I would have rambled on longer but I could see Constable Dawkins's mouth tighten as he bit down on a remark. 'I'm sorry, Phil, but I don't have the book any longer. My niece took the book with her when she went back to London so that she can show it to a publisher friend.'

Phil Dawkins rubbed his jaw. 'Is there any chance you can get it back here asap? If it's so important to Peters that he's broken cover to come and find it, it might hold vital information they can use in Cardiff.'

'She'll be in work now and I don't know that phone number or her mobile number. But I can ring her tonight and ask her to photocopy the story and drawings and send the book directly to you. I don't want it anywhere near this house,' I said. Phil nodded and started to tuck his notebook away. 'Now, Phil, tell me about Janine. Has she gone missing like that man said?'

He shrugged his shoulders. 'We handed her over to social

services, and that was the end of it as far as we were concerned. She hadn't broken any laws. But I'll find out what happened as soon as I get back to the station. Anyway, I thought you were all finished with her now.'

'It doesn't seem like it, does it? Whether I like it or not, that girl seems to be tethered to me by a very long piece of elastic.'

'I'll need to take a formal statement from you, Dora, but that can wait until tomorrow. We'll also need to photograph the bruises on your neck, which are coming up a treat. In the meantime, I am going to arrange for a locksmith to come out and change all your locks, if that's alright by you? His name is Ryan Lewis. He's a 24-hour locksmith, and he can be out here today. Best to get it done straight away.'

I nodded dumbly. His words were starting to blur in my mind, what with all the mixed alcohols I had drunk and the realisation that it was over and I was safe. My greatest desire at that moment was to pull a blanket over my head and make the world go away.

'Don't you worry, Constable,' Ted said slipping back into the room. 'I'll hang on until your locksmith comes, and if Dora wants me to stay overnight, I'll be more than happy to oblige. She's done enough for me, now it's my turn to help her.'

'I'll have to call a scene of crime team to come out tonight and take fingerprints and photos and the like. We need to be extra-thorough with this one – Cardiff will be overjoyed to nit-pick anything we do wrong, or find something we haven't done. They'll want to get hold of Peters any way they can. He won't be able to wriggle out of this one easily with you as a witness, Dora. They can hold him on the burglary and assault while they chase up the other charges,' Phil Dawson said. He turned to me. 'You said you saw Peters coming down from upstairs. Has anything been taken from up there?' he asked.

I shook my head. 'I don't know, Phil. I haven't had the courage to go up and look.'

'Do you think you could come up now with me and have a

quick shufti? If he has taken stuff, jewellery and the like, then we can add theft to the charges. We might even catch him trying to flog them.''

With a sigh I heaved myself up from the settee and led him upstairs. In the two bedrooms the drawers and cupboards had been pulled open and their contents thrown everywhere.

'Bit of a mess, but can you tell if any jewellery is missing?' Dawson asked.

'I doubt it. But if you are planning on arresting this man for stealing my jewellery and silver plate, you'll be out of luck as I don't have anything of any value.' I said and stopped abruptly at the open door to my painting room. The breath left my body. I remembered the crash I had heard coming from upstairs. He had swept everything off my painting table on to the floor along with the full jar of dirty water. Everything was ruined and the painting of the bracken fronds had come off worst with the water running in rivers over the water-buckled paper. There was no hope of saving it. It was the last straw. Something broke inside me. I sank to the floor and howled.

Phil Dawkins lifted me gently to my feet. 'Have you got anywhere you can stay while this is all sorted, Dora? How about your fancy man downstairs? He seems very keen.'

I mopped my face with my hanky and managed a weak smile. 'Fancy man, indeed! At my age! I'll stay here, thank you. No man is going to drive me out of my own home.'

'Ata girl,' Phil Dawkins said. 'But it would be best for now if you were out of the house. There's going to be a lot of coming and going, and I think what you need is a hot toddy and bed. You'll feel better after a sleep.'

He shepherded me downstairs and put the proposition to Ted who seemed only too pleased to agree. 'There's a spare bed ready and made up. It would be a pleasure - and just think what the village gossips will make of you spending the night at my place,' he said, his eyes twinkling beneath his worried frown. 'We'll be the talk of the village for weeks.'

232

'Pack yourself some night stuff and go with Ted. Don't worry about the house; I'll be hanging on here while the Scene of Crime boys are here and until the locksmith has done his bit. Ted's job is to look after you.'

Both men looked very pleased with themselves. My nightmare was having the opposite effect on everybody else. Constable Phil Dawkins was relishing a high profile crime bust, Cardiff Drug Squad would possibly catch their man and Ted seemed to have taken on a new lease of life. And the village gossips would be having a field day. Nothing so exciting had happened in Sutton since the *Torre Canyon* had run aground on Tusker Rock in the seventies.

The bag I had packed for my hospital visit was tucked away in the back part of the living room. It seemed to belong to another life. I didn't have the strength left to argue, and allowed Ted to escort me down the lane to his house. He steered me into his familiar kitchen and fussed about making me yet another mug of tea, which I left untouched. I could hear the liquid contents of my stomach slosh about whenever I moved.

'I'll put a hot water bottle in the bed, so you should be comfortable, Dora,' he said. 'I think a little nap will see you right in no time. Is there anything else I can get you, my dear.'

Stop clucking around like an old mother hen, for a start, I thought uncharitably, but I said nothing and simply shook my head. Tears were not far away, even though I thought I must already have used up my annual allowance.

CHAPTER THIRTY-SIX

Janine used the cuff of her sleeve to wipe a clear circle in the steamed-up window of the bus. The windscreen wipers wheezed like an asthmatic as the rain lashed down. She smiled as she settled further into her seat. It was a grey dismal day outside and, other than the miserable git of a driver and her own fuzzy reflection in the window, there was only one other person on board and he stayed right up the back of the bus plugged into his earphones and humming tunelessly, which suited her fine.

She felt smugly satisfied with herself. This time it had taken her a lot longer to escape than she had expected, but she had succeeded in the end. The first time that she had run away she had done so blindly, like a frightened rabbit, without thought or plan. She had grabbed her backpack and thrown in whatever came to hand, obeying some primeval instinct to run and keep running. It had been a miracle she hadn't ended up floating facedown in the river Taff.

This time she was adamant that it would be different: she knew what was up ahead and she wasn't going to make the same mistakes again. This time she would be in charge. She wouldn't let anyone – *not anyone* – stand in her way again. She had been stupid, a weak, gullible child: a little kid running scared.

When the cops and social had turned up at Miss Cummings' house, she had been completely thrown, gobsmacked was not too strong a word to describe how she'd felt though she knew a few riper ones than that. She hadn't been expecting it at all. She had started to relax, to let her defences down. She had thought that at last she was safe, living an idyllic life, which she had never even dreamed of having. And then it had all been snatched away from her and those whom she had trusted had stood aside and let it happen without raising a finger to help. She should have known better. But she had learned the bitter lesson and she wouldn't let it happen ever again.

At the time there had been nothing she could do to stop them. She had been hopelessly outnumbered. But eventually the shock had worn off and her brain had defrosted. She had started planning her escape.

She had had plenty of spare time. After they had left Miss Cummings' she had been driven for hours from one grim sixties building to another until the social worker had finally run out of options and parked her on a stained plastic chair in a corridor in another anonymous building with a packet of crisps and a bottle of water.

'Don't even think of running, young lady, because you won't get out through that door without a code,' the social worker warned. Janine was hating the woman more by the minute. Now if it had been that rather nice policeman she might have had a hope of getting around him, but…

She waited patiently for someone to come through the door so that she could make a dash for it, but her luck was out. By the time they came back to fetch her it was pitch dark and she had pins and needles in her bum.

The social worker loaded her once more into the car and after a twenty-minute drive she pulled up outside a small terraced house on the outskirts of town. The woman who answered the door scrutinized her from head to foot and then, honest to God, she sniffed – that type of sniff like when there's something nasty right underneath your nose, like a baby's dirty nappy.

'It will only be for one night, Mrs. Stevens, we'll pick her up in the morning. They may be able to squeeze her in at Sunnyside tomorrow,' the social worker had said. She was looking decidedly jaded, dark bruises under her eyes, her face grey with fatigue. 'Keep an eye on her, she's as slippery as an eel.'

Janine had been pushed through the door and it had been slammed behind her. The woman made a great show of double locking it and pocketing the key. Simple Yale lock. Janine couldn't stop the smirk breaking out on her face.

'You won't be smiling tomorrow if they put you in Sunnyside. Just goes to show, you can't tell a book by its cover.'

Janine had no idea what the woman was talking about but she was not going to give her the satisfaction of asking.

'You can take your shoes off now and give them to me. You won't get far in bare feet if you do try to do a bunk.'

As soon as she had done, the woman grabbed her by the arm, pushed her up the stairs and shoved her into the top front bedroom of the house – converted cupboard more like – and Janine heard the key being turned behind her. She banged on the closed door. 'I'm hungry. What are you going to do – starve me to death? And I need the loo.'

'I'll bring you a sandwich in a minute and take you to the loo. Then, I don't want to hear another peep out of you, do you hear?'

Janine listened to the footsteps thumping down the thinly carpeted stairs. She could have picked the lock in ten seconds flat but they would only have dragged her back again. And she was tired. She sat on the bed, which rocked even under her meagre weight. The smell of stale piss rose off the duvet. She wrapped her jacket tighter around herself and stared at the ceiling. Her dreams of freedom, which had fuelled her ever since she had been old enough to be aware of herself and her surroundings, had not turned out in the least as she had expected. Her one ray of hope had been with the old woman.

All day she had been trying to work out why Miss Cummings had called the cops on her. She had thought they were getting along well and, to her knowledge, she hadn't done anything bad for days. Admittedly she had thought that the old woman hadn't looked any too pleased when the cops and social had turned up. She thought she had heard her arguing with them but she had been in such a daze that she couldn't recall exactly what had been said and must have been mistaken because she had simply stood aside and let them take her away. But if it had been Miss Cummings who had called the police in the first place, then it didn't make any sense. The more she thought about it, the more confused she got. What really hurt, even more than the loss of her childish dreams, was the possibility that the old woman had betrayed her. She had done her best to behave. She hadn't even nicked any of her stuff like she had first intended. And more than anything, this woman was Anna Clare! She had begun to like and admire her, to feel comfortable in her company and she had thought that the feeling was reciprocated. So how could she have done this to her? Janine scrubbed her hands over her face in frustration. She had thought Dora Cummings was one of those people who believed in plain speaking which had suited Janine down to the ground. Janine needed things to be set down clearly and precisely, like when Miss Cummings had laid down the rules for her if she wanted to stay at her house. At least then she knew exactly when she was breaking them. Now everything was grey and getting greyer. Had she got it all wrong? It was certainly a possibility.

Sunnyside had been a terrifying revelation.

The same social worker had picked her up the next morning and driven a few miles out of town. Sunnyside Residential Home For Children was a grey square slab of a building, which would not have looked out of place as a mausoleum (she had seen some down at the cemetery where she often hid when bunking off school). Mismatched windows and bricked up entrances spoke of countless fruitless lifetimes as it waited forlornly for its final bow. It had a high stone wall around the front with a pint-sized yard and a scrubby hawthorn bush beyond. The single remaining doorway had a substantial security lock, a huge tarnished brass bell and a speaker grill.

'You'll be here for a few days,' she had said as they waited for the door to be answered. 'It's not ideal. You shouldn't be in here really but there's no room anywhere else.'

'Then let me go back to Miss Cummings,' Janine had blurted out. 'Problem solved!'

'Can't be done; you are under age.'

'What is this place anyway?'

'It is really for young people who have behavioural and mental problems and who need constant supervision. They have found you a room of your own, so you shouldn't have anything to do with the others.' The social worker hardened her face as the door was opened and Janine was ushered inside. 'It will only be for a day or two,' she had said with little confidence. Janine wasn't sure, but she thought she detected pity in the woman's face before she turned away.

Two days had been enough. She had been allowed out to 'exercise' in the back yard with a couple of the other residents but it was gloomy and dank and the paving stones were slick with moss, so she had spent most of her time in her room which was almost as bad. There was the smell and the noise and the constant shouting day and night; but worst of all was the girl in the next room crying pitifully for her mother. She vowed she would never ever let herself be caught again and land up in another place like this.

When the same social worker had arrived to collect her, she had scowled murderously at her but the woman had refused to meet her eye.

For the next few days she had felt as if she was the unwanted gift in a kid's pass-the-parcel game. It all started to blur by the end. Most people were kind; some didn't care one way or another and some of her fellow 'residents' should have been locked up and the key thrown away.

The original social worker, Mrs. Osborne she was told once again, appeared on the Monday morning. Janine had been staying with a young woman and her husband in a pleasant little semi-detached house with its own well-tended scrap of garden. It was the best place by far of all the places she had been dumped in and she would happily have stayed there longer.

'I've spoken to your mother and we will be taking you back home this morning,' the social worker said, obviously pleased to be finally getting Janine off her hands.

Janine's head shot up. 'Since when does the old cow want me around? She never has before, so why start now?' she asked.

'You silly girl, your mother wants you back desperately. I spoke to her on the telephone and she seemed like a charming woman and she is very upset at your disappearance.'

'Oh yer! Just not enough to get around to reporting me missing.' Janine retorted. 'She's having you on!'

She needn't have wasted her breath. They had found themselves a nice neat solution – ship her off to her mother. But that didn't make sense either. Why was her mother suddenly so keen to have her back? She had objected to going home out of habit but in reality she had started to lose the will to care one way or another.

CHAPTER THIRTY-SEVEN

Her reunion with her mother had been gooily slushy, full of hugs and kisses, but Janine hadn't been deceived by that in the least even if the social workers were; she knew her mother too well. She had tarted herself up ready to face the social workers with lipstick and thick makeup and both eyes had been more or less in focus.

When she had arrived back in Cardiff, Janine had been handed over like an Amazon parcel complete with paperwork to two new social workers. They had looked just like the one she had been stuck with for the past few days. She wondered if they had some machine somewhere where they churned them out from the same mould, tweaking the details now and then with different clothes and hair colouring. They were as dim as the other one. They had been completely taken in by her mother's act and Les Peters had excelled himself – *give the man an Oscar!* she had thought bitterly. Oh, he knew how to turn on the charm when he wanted to alright, which was what had drawn her mother into his web in the first place. She had felt sick as she had watched the two of them simpering and smiling at the social workers, offering tea and biscuits like they were normal people.

After her mother had eventually signed the papers on the table, missing the dotted line by a good inch as her concentration and focus started to crumble, Peters had shown the women to the door, dragging Janine along with him. He even had the gall to plant a kiss on the top of Janine's head while his fingers dug painfully into the back of her neck. As soon as the door had been closed behind them, he had punched her in the side of the head and had sent her spinning into the wall. Her vision had exploded into a universe of stars. It really had!

At first she hadn't understood what all the kafuffle had been about, she hadn't said a word out of place, but had soon been enlightened, and she had the black eye and bruised ribs to help ram the message home. For some reason which she couldn't understand, it had all to do with that innocent little black book she had nicked that first time she had legged it.

He had kept asking her about the book, on and on, and she had kept denying all knowledge. When Peters had finally ran out of steam, breathing hard, she had slipped from his grasp and found refuge in the small space tucked between the back of the sofa and the battered coffee table and had rolled herself up into a small ball. She had known he was a vicious, dangerous man, but she had never seen him this out of control before. Something was seriously wrong and she was scared.

But he hadn't got the answers he had wanted and Janine was determined not to give in; she would hold out until her last breath if that was what it took. He got himself a can of beer from the kitchen and drank deeply. Temporarily restored, he returned to the fray. He grabbed a handful of Janine's hair and dragged her upright. 'Where have you put it Janine? If you tell me now then maybe I'll leave you a couple of teeth so you can eat your toast, otherwise you'll be drinking your food through a straw; do you understand me girl!'

He shook her as if she was a stray cat. The pain in her scalp was excruciating.

'I haven't got it!' she screamed, again. The tears were very real. 'You've been through everything. You know I haven't got it. I probably threw it away. It was only a book.'

'I know when you are lying, girl, and I'll beat it out of you before the day's out even if I have to break every bone in your body, you can count on that. And if you don't tell me, I'll pass you on to Des Coogan and I can assure you he will get it out of you. I'm not going to let him skin me alive because you are playing some stupid game. This is serious you silly little bitch. Do you hear me? – serious!'

He suddenly released her and slumped down on the sofa next to the prostrate form of her mother who hadn't raised a finger to help her. It had been a hard day for Les Peters so far and he was gasping for a fix. He needed to steady his nerves; chase away the terrors gripping his belly, regain his strength and purpose. Gain control.

Janine took advantage of the lull and scuttled into her bedroom and closed the door behind her. Out of sight, out of mind, she hoped, but she knew he hadn't finished with her yet. She curled up on her bed and hugged her pain. She had managed to piece together some of what was going on from scraps of information that Peters had let slip while he ranted and raved and used her as a punch-bag. The book wasn't his. He had been minding it for someone else, this feller, Coogan; someone who he was very, very afraid of and who was very angry. She thought it was something to do with drugs, which figured. Les Peters would have been a minor player, way out of his league amongst the big boys, useful only for gopher jobs and highly expendable. And he knew it.

She remembered exactly where she had left the book – hidden in the bottom of the wardrobe in the annexe. She had put it there deliberately, not because of whatever was scribbled in the front which she hadn't even glanced at, but because she had hoped that one day she would be able to return to the house on the cliff and go on living with the old woman and doing her drawings, which she had discovered she really enjoyed doing. By leaving Mr. Boots and the book there, she had thought of them as a talismens, waiting to draw her back. She had done it almost without thinking and hadn't suspected then that maybe it was Miss Cummings who had turned her in to the social. Maybe it had been instinct, something she had heard about but was unaware that she had.

Tears streamed down her face as she thought about what she had lost. She had never known anything like it before and hadn't noticed how wonderful life had become until it had all been cruelly snatched away. Her dreams and hopes had been just that – nothing but a fantasy, a stupid kid's fantasy. Since when had anything good ever happened to her? Nobody before had given a damn whether she was alive or dead, but she thought things had changed. She thought she had found someone in the person of Dora Cummings and she had relaxed her guard; she had dared to dream – and this was the result! She felt sick to her stomach. She had stupidly trusted another person and had lost everything. She felt betrayed and desolate. She was more alone than ever before. What an idiot!

It all came down to that damned book.

She knew that she had to get it back; it would be the only way of getting Peters off her case. She could just run, in a completely different direction, up into the hills maybe or over into England, but Peters would still go after the book and that would leave the old lady vulnerable. Until Janine had been dragged back by the social, he hadn't known where Janine had been staying which was why he hadn't turned up at Miss Cummings' house before, but then everything had changed. She had heard him sweet-talking the social workers into giving out the old lady's address – to send her a thank-you note for looking after Janine. And they had believed him! She couldn't believe how gullible adults could be. He had searched through her backpack and come up empty; he had tried beating it out of her and she had said nothing but he didn't believe her. Now he would have to go on the hunt. He had the address for the house in Sutton and he would probably drag her back there and force it out of one or other of them. None of this was the old lady's fault and though she was tough, she would never have been able to survive a beating from Peters. She probably wouldn't have known where the book was hidden anyway.

Janine started making a plan. She had to get away soon, go back to Sutton and pick up the book. She could break into the house without being seen – she couldn't risk Miss Cummings ringing the police on her again. She would tear out the pages of drawings from the back of the book, contact Peters on his mobile and get the rest back to him – leave it at a drop off point or something so neither she nor Miss Cummings would have to see him. Then she could disappear properly.

She mulled it over as long as she dared. It seemed to her to be reasonably straightforward, unless Peters of course managed to get his hands on a car and get to Miss Cummings's house ahead of her. It was a possibility, but one which she could do nothing about. She was a frail old lady. Peters could kill her with one swipe of his hand. Janine couldn't live with that on her conscience.

She started to feel tired, what with the monotonous drone of the bus and the stuffy fug inside. She curled up on the seat, her head resting on the rolled up sleeping bag, which had once belonged to Peters.

She smiled to herself as she relived her escape. She had crept into the living room of the flat where both her mother and Peters were lying sprawled on the filthy sofa, eyes closed and white powder dusting their nostrils. Peters had taken all her money when he'd rifled through her backpack, so she had felt no guilt about emptying her mother's purse. She nicked his gold lighter off the table (it was only gold plated and rubbed thin in parts) and dusted the sticky carpet with the remains of his wraps, which would really piss him off when he woke up. She grinned at the thought. Her clothes were already stuffed into her backpack and, together with the sleeping bag she had tossed them out of her bedroom window, which looked down on the overflowing waste bins below. Unfortunately, it was also three storeys up with no way down without breaking a leg, so she had to take the risk of sneaking out through the flat without waking them. It would probably have taken a Sherman tank and a brigade of infantry, but you never know.

She hesitated beside her mother's slumped figure – not a thing of beauty; mouth open with a trickle of drool seeping from the corner, her mascara smudged into panda eyes and her features slack and grey.

Janine gently touched a curl that had flopped over her mother's forehead. 'Bye, Mum,' she whispered. Her mother did not stir.

She had caught the Vale bus but she hadn't dared go straight to Dora's house while it was daylight. If Peters was on to her, then it would be the first place he would go and lie in wait. She just had to take the chance that the few grey cells that Peters still had were stuffed with enough drugs so that he didn't get there before her. She also couldn't risk Miss Cummings seeing her and raising the alarm. She planned to get off in the little village downriver from Sutton. It had a small grocery shop where she could buy food and it was a very manageable walk down-river and across to the cave beside the ruined manor house where she could hole up until night-time. The countryside was a foreign country to Peters, he would never think of looking for her there. She wouldn't have long to wait as it was already dusk. Once it was fully dark, she would break into the annexe in Dora's house and get the book and Mr. Boots. She could ring Peters from the telephone kiosk on the main road and leave the book there and be long gone by the time he got there even if he was hiding nearby.

It had all seemed so easy, then. And she was totally unaware that Peters had beaten her to it.

CHAPTER THIRTY-EIGHT

It was a strange time, that stay at Ted's. I didn't sleep much that night, but closed my eyes whenever Ted poked his head around the door to check on me, which he did so often it had become annoying rather than reassuring. I *cwtched* the hot water bottle to me even after the heat had seeped away. *My adult comforter*, I thought wryly. That, together with the sherry, had started to chase away the chill that had taken over my body. But no matter how hard I tried to clear my mind, my thoughts kept going over and over everything that had happened, what I should have done different, what I should have said.

Every time I remembered those steely fingers crushing my throat, I felt nauseous and I had to continually gulp the sour bile down. It had been embarrassing enough to have fled in tears from my own home without adding to my disgrace by vomiting over Ted's bedclothes. It was all too starkly recent for me to make much sense out of it. Everything was getting mixed up in my mind, real and imaginary. I felt in some strange way that I had let myself down and more than anything I needed time to sort myself out. It was as if some malignant god had decided I was far too comfortable with my life and had swooped down and given it a really good stir. The more I grasped at a solid landmark, the quicker it spun away.

I didn't know where my nice orderly life had gone. Where was the peace and calm that I craved; the quiet steady progress through life that had taken a lifetime to achieve and which I had thought nothing would be able to threaten? Where had it gone? Would I ever get it back?

There were moments during that long night when I wished that I had never set eyes on Janine. Everything seemed to have gone wrong since that one uncharacteristic act of kindness, which had set off a chain of events that had led me from one disaster to another. The girl was a jinx, a bad omen. She carried chaos in an aura around her, shedding sparks to land wherever they may. Around and around my mind went and by the time I had whipped myself up into a righteous fury, blaming her for everything bad that was happening in my life, I was exhausted and thoroughly ashamed of myself. It was hardly the girl's fault. I was the one who had chosen to interfere and why? To make me feel better about myself? Had I really been using Janine to cock a snoot at Elizabeth Henshaw and her pious charity? It had been my choice to take the girl in and mine alone. And it was patently unfair to blame her for The God Squad or my cancer!

Thank God none of us can see into the future. I for one would have pulled a hood over my head and taken out a mortgage on the nearest hermit's cave!

As the first soft grey light of morning slithered through the thin curtains, I finally found my endless night of fretting had dislodged a scrap of courage. If life wanted to throw *cachau poo* (shit to anyone else but it sounds more refined in Welsh) at me, then I was ready to fight my way through. I would not be defeated. I wrapped the tatters of my dignity around me and set off in search of the bathroom. I would do as Phil Dawkins had suggested and use my anger to face the world and just hoped that it didn't disappear as the day progressed.

I was up and dressed before Ted eventually appeared in the kitchen doorway, hair tussled with sleep and with a white stubble misting his chin. 'I was going to be up before you, lass, and make you breakfast in bed. Full of good intentions, me.'

'Sit yourself down, Ted. The tea is brewing and I'll make you some toast or porridge if you want. It does me good to be doing something; if my hands are busy, it helps my mind to settle,' I answered.

At eight thirty, the doorbell rang and Ted got up to answer it. Phil Dawkins and the same W.P.C. who had accompanied him when they had taken Janine away, entered. They sat down at Ted's kitchen table, mugs of tea in their hands, before they got down to business.

'You look so much better this morning, Dora,' Phil said as he laid his little black pocketbook on the table beside him. He handed me two sets of shiny keys. 'I've picked up your new house keys from the S.O.C.O boys, so you can go home whenever you want.'

247

Ted was instantly by me side, patting my hand. It really was getting irritating, but I bit my tongue.

'Yes, I must go back,' I said hesitantly. 'But I have to admit, I feel worryingly reluctant. I know I am being stupid and pathetic. Nobody was hurt and that man could have done an awful lot more damage. But with all those policemen – total strangers – let loose in my house last night rummaging through my cupboards and drawers and no doubt sniggering at my most intimate possessions, I feel as if my privacy, which has meant so much to me for so many years, has been violated! I feel as if my own home has become grubby and used.'

'Let me stop you right there, Dora,' Phil Dawkins said firmly. 'I was in your house the whole time that the S.O.C.O. boys were there last night, and I made sure everything was treated properly and with respect. They had no need to go through your things. They only took photographs of the damage Peters had done which will be used in the case against him, and they took fingerprints off surfaces he might have touched. Once they had finished, I locked up for you but I didn't think you would be very pleased if I woke you up at 2.25 this morning to hand you back the keys.'

'I'm sorry, Phil, I know I'm being silly.'

'Quite the contrary, Dora. Most people who have been burgled say it is not so much the value of what has been taken, but the invasion into their homes and lives that is more upsetting. Which reminds me – I need your fingerprints for elimination purposes and those of anybody else who has visited recently, unless you've dusted them away.'

'I'm not too keen on dusting,' I admitted with a wry smile. 'A month ago I would have said there would only be my fingerprints in the house. Now – I'll make you a list!'

'Even though they were careful, the house is in a bit of a mess I'm afraid, Dora. Why don't I ask Megan Hardy to come up and give you a hand. I know she will want to help,' Phil suggested.

'I'll do it myself, Phil, thank you. I don't want any more nosey parkers ferreting into my business – I'm not talking about Megan Hardy here, mind, she can keep her mouth shut when she wants. It probably looks worse than it is. It'll be mostly putting stuff back into drawers and I can manage that myself.'

'Only if you are sure, Dora,' Phil Dawkins said.

'I'm surprised half the village isn't already outside the door, earwigging. They can't have missed all the comings and goings overnight and they'll be busting their guts to know what's going on,' Ted said.

Phil Dawkins nodded. 'They are already gathered up at your house, Dora. They haven't worked out you are down here, yet,' he said with a grin. 'Don't worry, I'll move them on, but, with your permission, I will be asking Megan Hardy and her husband to keep a weather-eye out for Les Peters. If he's still hanging around – and he'll be keeping his head down for now with all this activity – they'll be the ones to notice him. They can take some of the pressure off you and stop the ghouls who always come out of the woodwork when there's anything happening from bothering you. Nobody in the village wants to get on the wrong side of Megan, not if they value using her shop again during their current lifetime. She'd blacklist the lot of them. Is that okay with you, Dora?'

I nodded. 'If it helps to catch him, then I can hardly object. Now, did you find anything out about Janine?'

CHAPTER THIRTY–NINE

The policewoman, whose name I still could not recall, opened her pocketbook and flicked slowly through a few used pages. She knew she had our full attention and she was milking it for all she was worth. I could not begrudge her that moment of power. I knew and understood her need. Even in the twenty-first century women had to snatch every opportunity they could to empower themselves and during the time I had worked as a civilian with the police, I had seen the constant battle women had to fight against the sexism, which was rife in the macho world of the police force. It had been prevalent 20 years before but it must be a hundred times worse nowadays when women had finally clawed their way into the upper ranks. They had to be tough. There was still massive resentment amongst the lesser able men left wallowing in their wake and I was sure that most allegations of harassment and sexism were still swept under the carpet. She would need all her arrogance and self-belief to survive.

She flicked a haughty glance at me before commencing. She read in the same flat voice she must have practised to give evidence in court. 'Once we handed Janine Wallis over to social services, she was no longer the responsibility of the Police Service. However, the social services contacted us just over a week later to say that the girl had disappeared again after she had been returned to her home address in Splott. It had not been possible to find a suitable place for her in the care system and according to the report of the social worker, the mother had been happy for the daughter's return and the home circumstances were...' she paused for effect '...adequate. When the social workers had returned the next day Janine had gone. There was no sign of her or the man we now know to have been Les Peters. The mother claimed to have no idea as to their whereabouts.'

'So, you dumped her and then lost all track of her,' I said shortly. The policewoman bridled but said nothing. 'That has been the story of that poor girl's life. She has been let down by everyone, and I feel as much to blame as anybody else. I should have kicked up a bigger fuss when you took her. Is she safe?'

Phil Dawkins ran his hand through his short-cropped hair. 'We have no idea, Dora, but from the look of it, Les Peters thought she was headed back here.'

'I don't see why she would have,' I said, 'not after I let her down so badly. I let social services take her away and dump her back with her mother; back into everything she had run away from in the first place and I did nothing to stop it. And I hardly think rescuing Mr. Boots from the wardrobe would bring her all the way back here, not if Peters was on her tail.'

The policewoman snapped her pocketbook shut and for the first time looked directly at me. She had the most beautiful green eyes flecked with gold. Official business done, she let a hint of compassion fleetingly soften her composed features. 'In all fairness, you didn't have any choice. She was under age and the law is the law,' she said, not unkindly. 'Peters' appearance here yesterday changed all that. Up until then nobody had known who the mother's boyfriend was, but once P.C. Dawkins had informed the Cardiff Drug Squad that it was Les Peters who had been staying at the mother's flat, they had paid her a visit. Obviously Peters wasn't there and there was no sign of the girl either. According to the mother – who was pretty much away with the fairies – he had gone out looking for Janine because she had done a bunk again and she had stolen things from him.'

'So where is Janine?' I asked. 'And how did Peters know where I lived? Did Janine tell him?'

Phil Dawkins shook his head. 'Cock-up with the social services in Cardiff, I'm afraid. It seems Peters sweet-talked them into giving him your address, totally against regulations. Said he wanted to send you a thank-you card. Janine hadn't said a word.'

'The only other coherent thing they got out of the mother had been that Peters was threatening to kill the girl when he caught up with her,' the policewoman said. There was now genuine concern in her face, which in a way I found was more frightening than her cool indifference. 'He has got a previous record for violence and I think both you and Janine may be in real danger. He has failed once to get what he wanted and he may be desperate enough to try again.'

'But if Janine left yesterday, before him, where is she now? The fact that Peters has already been here means that he must have got his hands on a car. And if Janine had left as soon as she'd been dropped home, she would have had to thumb a lift or catch a bus, in which case she should have been here by now. So where is she?'

Phil Dawkins shook his head. 'We've put her description out to patrols, but nothing yet. We'll keep looking for both of them. But what about the book, Dora? Any luck? Cardiff is on the blower every five minutes.'

'I contacted my niece straight away when I got here to Ted's. She sent it Special Delivery straight to your station, supposed to be guaranteed to arrive by 9 a.m., so you should be getting it any minute now.'

Phil Dawkins rose from the table. 'I'll just check. Make sure it's not going to be lost under a stack of papers on somebody's desk.'

He went into the hall to make his call while the policewoman – Pat Matthews I remembered in a rare moment of clarity – set about washing up the mugs.

I thought back to that strained conversation I had had with Tiffany the previous day. Ted had ushered me into the unused front parlour so that I could use the extension in private, but I had been conscious all the time of him pottering around just outside the door. The room was dank and dark, being at the back of the house and never getting a glimmer of sunlight. It smelled of damp and mould and heavily scented air freshener. The cold sent renewed shivers through me.

Tiffany had been highly suspicious when I asked her to send the book back, urgently. 'Why the rush, Auntie Do? Gina and I will be with you in another week and why on earth do you need it sent to a police station? It's hardly subversive material!'

'It's something to do with all those names and numbers in the front of the book. Can you photocopy the bits in the back with the

252

cartoons and story and send the original on the fastest postal service. I'll explain everything when I see you.'

'You are scaring me now, Auntie.'

'I promise you, there's nothing to worry about. Did Gina have any luck with her friend the publisher?' I asked in a desperate attempt to divert her very keen instincts.

'Yes, they are very excited. Apparently there's nothing quite like it on the market. She's putting it to her team and they'll probably want to meet Janine and... why do I get the distinct feeling you are hiding something from me Dodo?'

Tiffany had always been a sharp one, even as a child, and my own faculties had not kept pace, quite the opposite. I fobbed her off with a half-truth. 'Well, it's just that Janine has gone missing again, and nobody knows where she is at this precise moment. Maybe by the time you come down next week we'll know more,' I improvised. 'I've got to go, darling, as I'm on someone else's phone. Send the book straight away, please, and don't worry about me. Everything is fine.'

I had put the receiver down before she could interrogate me any further.

Constable Phil Dawkins returned and collected his pocket notebook and tucked it away in one of his innumerable pockets. 'I can confirm that it has arrived and been downloaded to Cardiff; the drug squad officers are in seventh heaven. Apparently the numbers were a simple code, which a ten year old could have cracked. They've got names, dates, everything,' he said, his excitement making him look like a young probationer again. 'But until we catch Peters, I'd be happier if you were to stay with someone rather than be alone in your house, Dora. Won't you even consider it?'

'Absolutely not,' I replied sharply. 'You have fitted new locks, so I will be fine, locked safely away inside my little fortress. Nobody is going push me out of my own house, thank you very much.'

Phil Dawkins grinned. 'I didn't really expect anything different, but officially I have to say I tried. What about asking your brother to stay for a few days to look after you?' He burst out laughing at the horror on my face. 'Just joking, Dora! But I mean it when I say that you are to stay indoors and you are to keep your doors and windows locked at all times, even when you are in there. And no going off on your nature rambles on your own. Do you understand me?'

I plastered a cute pout with a hint of allure on my face. 'Yes, sir,' I answered in a simpering little-girl voice, forgetting the fact that I was in my mid seventies and about as alluring as a mangy old cat. Phil Dawkins had the kindness to grin at me. He didn't believe a word.

'I'm serious, Dora. And I'm dropping off some mug-shots of Peters to Megan Hardy down at the shop. She said she would be ringing you and if there was anything you needed either she or Adrian or Alf would deliver.'

Ted saw them off the premises and I threw my bits and pieces into my overnight bag and was ready to leave by the time he returned.

'You could always stay here, Dora, or I could camp down in the spare room at yours,' Ted offered eagerly.

I patted his hand. 'Thank you for the offer, Ted, but I don't think two decrepit old-age pensioners are going to be a match for hardened criminals,' I said.

'Oh, I don't know, old girl. We saw him off the last time, and now we'll be more prepared.'

'No, Ted,' I said and gave his whiskery cheek a quick peck. 'You are a dear, sweet man, but I'm over the shock now and ready to repel all boarders.' Well, it was almost the truth – at least the shaking had stopped and I no longer wanted to throw up every five minutes. 'Anyway, I have things to sort out...

'Oh, my God! The chickens!' I said in horror. 'They've been out all night with all those strangers coming and going up at the house, they must have been in a terrible panic.'

'I'm sure they'll be fine...'

'Even if they had the sense to go into the coop for the night, the gate would have been unlatched and the fox could easily have got

254

in and wiped them out. I've got to go, Ted.'

'Well, I'm coming with you and between us we can find them and corral them and there's nothing you can do to stop me, Dora Cummings,' he said, picking up his walking stick and taking his old Dai cap off a peg on the back of the door. 'And you'll still need a bodyguard to repel boarders if your policeman friend hasn't managed to shift on the nosey-parkers from outside your house.'

But Phil Dawkins had been as good as his word and the gate was clear of people. I charged around to the back of the house and up the garden steps expecting to be met by carnage. I could hear Ted's laboured breathing far behind me.

He caught up with me as I was unlatching the door of the coop and three hungry chickens almost threw themselves at me. The flags fluttered happily above my head, stirred by the squally breeze coming off the sea.

'What's the verdict?' Ted gasped.

I was bewildered. 'The gate and the coop were all closed up and the chickens are safe and sound, if a little aggrieved that they haven't been fed yet,' I answered. 'I know I didn't do it, and I hardly think the S.O.C.O. team doubled up as chicken farmers in their spare time!'

'Panic over, then,' Ted said, easing himself down on one of the plastic garden chairs while he got his breath back.

'Come on in and have a comfortable sit-down, Ted. I'm sure your cardiologist wouldn't approve of all your dashing around the place,' I said, ushering him inside. 'Oh, and I meant to ask you, Ted – why were you up at my house yesterday evening in the first place? I am so very glad you were there, but you had only just met me in the lane.'

Ted shuffled his feet like a bashful teenager. 'Oh, it was nothing. I was just dropping off a little something I'd made for you – as a thank you for your help and all that.' He patted his pockets as if it would magically appear. 'I know I had it with me when I arrived, but what with everything that happened after, I can't think what I did with it.'

He was obviously embarrassed and so was I. 'There's no need for presents, Ted. It's what friends are for,' I said, feeling the heat rise into my face. I really didn't want any more complications in my life and the giving of presents was a step too far for my liking.

'It'll turn up, I expect,' Ted said and turned away. 'You promise you will ring me if I can be of any help.'

I said I would, both of us knowing that I wouldn't. I wanted to be alone. I smiled to myself. Wasn't that Greta Garbo's famous line – "I vant to be a-l-o-n-e" – but I owed him a cup of tea first.

CHAPTER FORTY

I dumped my bag on the floor in the living room and would have loved to have slumped into the armchair with a reviving glass of sherry, even though it was only mid-morning. I felt wiped out and was starting to shake again. But I knew that if I did that, I would be there for the rest of the day, just getting more maudlin and depressed and scared. Action was what was needed. I would normally have taken off for a long hike in the bracing sea air, but Phil Dawkins's words of caution were still fresh in my mind. And from the description of the mess left behind by Peters and the police S.O.C.O. team, I had plenty of work to keep me occupied indoors. Good, I thought. It would give me something mindless to do.

But before all that, I had to see to the chickens. I gave them extra rations as an apology for my absence and a chopped-up apple and a hand-full of dried mealworms, which they usually loved, but the three of them huddled together and turned aggrieved eyes on me.

'Just be thankful you've still got your feathers on, my girls,' I said as I tossed them the last of the feed and went back indoors to change into my working clothes.

The annexe didn't look any better in the light of day and to make matters worse, every surface was coated with a dusting of black fingerprint powder. I took a deep breath, popped a CD of the 1812 Overture into the CD player (followed by a sixties compilation) and polished and scrubbed and sorted like a demon until I was exhausted and nearly fainting. It was the telephone in the hall, which finally brought me to a halt.

It was Megan Hardy. 'I hope I'm not disturbing you, Dora, but I'm just checking that you are okay. I am worried about you up there on your own. Would you like Adrian to come up and stay? He'd be more than willing.' I often wondered if the poor boy – correction, man – had any idea how many times his mother volunteered him for charitable works.

'It's very kind of you, Megan, but I am fine, thank you,' I said, sinking down onto a chair. I was a little giddy which should not have surprised me as my food intake over the last 24 hours had consisted mainly of alcohol and tea.

'You are quite the talk of the village,' Megan continued as if I hadn't spoken. I could hear the barely suppressed excitement in her voice. 'The latest is that you have been murdered and there's even talk of setting up a vigilante group to patrol the village until this man is caught! There's nothing as exciting as this has ever happened in the village in living memory. But rest assured, Dora, Alf and I will make sure you are not being pestered. I just hope the press don't get wind of it.'

Oh, my God, I hadn't even thought of that!

'You could always take a room at the Seaview for a couple of days. You'd be safe there,' Megan Hardy suggested. I could hear the chuckle in her voice.

I barked out a laugh. 'I'd rather stay put and tackle the whole of the Mafia with a tooth-pick than have Flo Jenkins gloating at my feebleness. I can manage on my own, thank you, Megan. I am not leaving.'

'I know you value your independence and all that but it is at times like this that you need to swallow your pride and accept the help when it is offered. Please, Dora, ring me if you need anything. I'll give you another ring at the same time tomorrow, if that is alright.'

I told her it was, anything to get rid of her, and it was only when I put the phone down I realized I was shaking even worse. It was hunger; only hunger, I told myself.

'You are not kidding anyone, least of all yourself,' I said out loud. I often talked to myself when I was alone, usually swearing at some minor mishap (words people probably thought I didn't even know), but now it was a comfort. Because I had to admit it to myself, I was afraid; afraid that for once I didn't know if I could cope with all that was happening, afraid of the unknown. The previous day's events had brought home to me the reality of my weakness and my age. Even when I was younger I had thought myself quite capable of defending myself, but of course I had never had to put the theory to the test. Now I knew different. And it seemed that on top of everything else, I was the latest hot gossip in the village. With so many people wanting to stick a finger into my life, I had never felt so alone, so vulnerable. I was starting at shadows, sure there was someone lurking in the scrubby bushes out the back, behind the chicken coop, under every stone. I couldn't shake the feeling that I was being watched.

As I turned to pick up the little wicker basket I used for collecting eggs, I noticed a package lodged between the legs of an old chair which was a dumping ground for coats and scarves and the like. It was loosely wrapped in crumpled newspaper and inexpertly tied with string. I tried to unpick the knots so that I could reuse the string but they were too tight and I had to resort to a scissors. Inside was the most delightful carving of a common tern, its arrow-like wings outstretched as if just about to launch itself into the wind. I remembered Ted coming out of his shed with shavings in his hair and wood dust covering his cardigan. I had no idea he was artistically minded. In fact I had never given him much thought at all other than as a fellow ancient neighbour. But it seemed that Ted Morris might have other ideas. This carving had been done with love and skill. It was no mere thank-you gift for a bit of gardening and the occasional stroll beside the sea.

I felt a little less alone and smiled to myself. I would have to give the matter of Mr. Ted Morris some serious thought before things got too far out of hand – when I had the time. Ted Morris, you old rascal! Who would have thought?

I went out to collect the eggs. It had rained heavily in the night and the sky was steel grey with a heavy drizzle sheeting across a sea that was the colour of wet cement before drifting inland. Above my head the local heron flapped sedately eastwards, bound for the last of Henry Davey's prize koi carp. Janine would have loved him.

The light inside the coop was dimmer than normal because of the dull day and I had to collect the eggs by touch, but when I got to Sandi's nest, I could feel that instead of an egg there was a scrap of white paper. I took it outside into the light, but without my glasses I hadn't a hope of reading the tiny writing scribbled with a blunt pencil on what looked like the back of a till receipt. I grabbed my specs from the kitchen and squinted at the writing.

Meet me at the Red Kite cave.
URGENT. BRING BOOK –
bottom of wardrobe.

Unless the chickens had learned to read and write since I had been away, it could only have come from one person – Janine. It hadn't been there the previous morning or I would have noticed, so she must have been put it there sometime during the night when she couldn't get into the house or the annexe because of all the police activity – and the new door locks. She knew I would be sure to see it first thing in the morning. I was a couple of hours late.

I switched on the kettle and slipped a couple of slices of bread into the toaster almost as an involuntary action, like breathing. My mind was elsewhere. Everything that was happening was hinged around that book. Janine had run away again and seemed intent on getting the book back. It could have just been for the story and the drawings, in which case she could have knocked on the door and asked for it. She wouldn't have known what the names in the front were about and I wouldn't have thought she valued the illustrations enough to risk a beating from Peters if she was caught. But by the urgency of the note and her hiding away, it looked as if it was because Peters was desperate to get his hands on it and was going to use Janine to show him where it was. She must have known he was on her trail but may not have realized that she had already been overtaken. Quite what she intended doing with it, I couldn't for the life of me fathom. She was risking a lot to get it back – did she just want to hand it over to the man? She would have no idea that I was no longer in possession of it.

The toaster pinged and the kettle switched itself off. I made my tea and nibbled the dry toast. I pondered how I was going to get to Janine without being seen. I needed to tell her what was going on before she put herself in danger. I had no doubt at all that Peters was somewhere watching the house. My shoulders itched at the thought. He would know if I tried taking the car out and it would be too dangerous to even think of walking over to the other side of the river. I wasn't hesitating because of Phil Dawkins' warning, but because there would be very few people out and about in this dismal weather and the Downs and river banks were full of deep hollows and gullies where Peters could waylay me and nobody would be any the wiser. Or he would suspect that I was heading out to meet Janine and would simply follow me to her.

I needed to get out undetected. I needed someone else with a car which would not raise a red flag to Peters. Ted had had his licence taken off him when he'd had his massive heart attack and, although I knew he would be willing to risk it, I was not. Megan Hardy was alone in the shop and couldn't leave. A taxi would be just as useless. It was rather a chastening thought to realize that I had nobody to ask. I hadn't been aware that I had so completely cut myself off from people that in a moment of crisis, I had no-one to turn to for help; it had crept up on me over the years and I had never noticed.

There was a perfunctory knock and Elizabeth Henshaw's face peered around the door.

Oh, be careful what you wish for, Dora Cummings, I thought. You brought this one on yourself. On the other hand, my mother used to say you had to do your best with whatever was to hand – even if that might be Elizabeth Henshaw!

'It's only me, Dora. Megan has told me about the break-in and that she is keeping an eye on you, so don't worry, I haven't come to interfere. You know where I am if you need me. But I wanted to tell you about that young girl, Janine. Norman, my husband, has been trying to sort it out with social services but he says it is like wading through treacle. Can I come in?'

She had remained hovering in the open doorway, obviously uncertain of what sort of reception she might get. I waved her in and poured her a mug of Earl Grey while refreshing my own.

'This was on your doorstep, Dora. A bit dangerous – you could have tripped over it.'

She handed me a rock. It certainly had not been there when I have gone to feed the chickens. I took it from her and turned it over in my hands. Set into the top of the rock, polished by the rain, was a beautiful ammonite, almost complete.

'I noticed you have some of those fossils in your front garden. Somebody must have moved it around here for some reason,' Elizabeth Henshaw said sitting herself at the kitchen table.

'Yes, I do, but this is not one of mine,' I answered. The image of that little boy in the sun-drenched quarry sprung into my mind. 'Jimmy. It must have been young Jimmy Farr,' I muttered.

Mrs. Henshaw coughed to bring me back to the moment. 'I don't want to pry, Dora, but I suspect that all this terrible business is in some way connected with the girl?'

I stared silently into my mug and finally looked up. I needed an ally and Elizabeth Henshaw was all that was to hand. 'Yes, it is, but I am not allowed to tell you much. The short version is that there is a horrible man searching for Janine because she took something that belonged to him and he wants it back. When the social services dumped her back in her home, she had obviously refused to tell him where it was and she ran away again before he could force it out of her. He must have assumed she was headed back here. Janine doesn't know that he has already broken in and searched the house. I am sure he is still hanging around and the police are very anxious to catch him.'

'He won't come back here, will he Dora? Are you safe here all on your own? Oh, my dear, you must come and stay at the vicarage until this man is caught.'

I shook my head. I couldn't even imagine being caged in with Elizabeth Henshaw 24/7. Surely a fate worse than death? 'That's very kind of you, but it is not why I am telling you this.' I took a deep breath and continued. 'I am in a bit of a pickle. I just found this note in the chicken coop. It is from Janine and she wants me to meet her. She's in hiding over the other side of the river. I need to warn her that Peters is already here and she needs to keep well away until he is caught.'

'You must tell the police, Dora.'

'Knowing Janine as I do, she will disappear into thin air as soon as she sees a policeman,' I said, turning my mug around and around as I hesitated. I had to force the words out. 'I need your help, Mrs. Henshaw. I know I have got a cheek to ask as we have never really hit it off, but I am afraid for Janine's safety.'

'The name is Elizabeth. Go on, Dora, go for broke; tell me all.'

I managed a wry smile. 'The police have told me not to leave the house, so they may be spying on me and will stop me.'

'There *is* a police car parked over the road.'

I nodded. It seemed Phil Dawkins had got his way – for now. 'If I try leaving in my car, Peters is probably keeping a lookout somewhere and he will simply follow me. And if I try and walk across to where Janine is hiding, there is so much open ground that he would see me a mile off and do exactly the same thing. I need to get out of here unobserved and I don't know how.'

Elizabeth Henshaw was silent. We both looked earnestly into our cooling mugs of tea. 'You could duck down in the back of my car and I could drive you out of here,' she suggested at last. There was a conspiratorial gleam in her eye.

I shook my head. 'He may already have noticed your car coming up here and would follow you on the off-chance. I can't risk it.'

She was silent for another minute and then said triumphantly, 'Then we must create a diversion and mobilize The God Squad. I'll get Flo and Jemma to bring their cars up – leaving room for me to drive out, of course. They can come into the house and give the impression that you are inside entertaining them, while I sneak you out in the back of my car. He won't be able to keep an eye on all of us, so there's a high chance that he won't try. What do you think?'

'Oh, no, I don't think so, Elizabeth,' I said quickly.

'Why not? It's a brilliant idea and it could work. Neither this man nor the police will even suspect that you had left the house. The girls will act as if you are still there.'

'Please don't take this the wrong way, Elizabeth, but I wouldn't like strangers to be roaming the house when I am not here.' I conveniently put aside the fact that quite a few strangers had done just that the day before.

Elizabeth Henshaw laughed. 'Afraid they'll nick the silver, Dora?'

'No, of course not, but I live very privately here and the thought of Flo Jenkins picking through my things…'

'I quite understand, and if you would feel better, then ask Ted Morris to come up and keep an eye on them. You want help, Dora, and I am offering it. Have you any other alternative?'

I had to give in. I didn't have a choice. 'Do you think it will work?' I asked uncertainly.

Mrs. Henshaw beamed. 'We can only try, my dear. And I am sure that if the police come knocking, the girls will be able to concoct some story to sidetrack them. We are all avid readers of detective novels, you see, so between us, I am sure we'll be able to fabricate a credible story. And I am the wife of a vicar after all, and extremely respectable. Who would dare suspect me of subterfuge?'

She gave me a wicked grin. I was beginning to realize that I had seriously misjudged Elizabeth Henshaw.

CHAPTER FORTY-ONE

Everything moved at a ferocious pace and without a hitch. W.I. training obviously prepared its participants for all eventualities, from jam making to organising a break-out under the noses of both criminals and the police alike. In total obedience to their commander-in-chief, the rest of The God Squad arrived with their vehicles and were waved into their correct parking spots by Mrs. Henshaw. Fast on their tails came Ted Morris, puffing mightily from taking the lane at too fast a pace. They must all have had a hundred or more questions, but Elizabeth Henshaw fobbed them off with a flap of her hand and a vague promise to fill them in later. Ted raised a quizzical eyebrow at me, but held his peace.

Soon my house was bursting at the seams.

Elizabeth Henshaw was firmly in charge. It was rather a strange and amusing sensation to watch her ordering people around inside my own house. I had no objection, for now. I had asked for her help, after all. 'As you can see the rumour mill has got it wrong once again. Dora is very much fit and well, but has had a nasty experience at the hands of a vicious lout,' she said nodding briefly in my direction as if nobody there knew who I was. 'We need to create a diversion, to give anyone watching the impression that she is still in the house, when in fact she and I have a mission to accomplish and we need to get away without arousing suspicion. This will be your task.' *Bring on the drum roll*, I thought.

I waited for Flo Jenkins to make some snide remark, but other than the startled look from her brutally plucked eyebrows, I thought I detected just a hint of respect in her glance – it could have been indigestion! Mrs. Anthony, Jemma, patted my arm and quietly said, 'Good for you, Dora. We'll see to things this end, don't you worry.'

I pressed close to Ted as I was passing and whispered into his ear, 'Keep an eye on them, Ted, and make sure they don't go snooping. I wouldn't trust Flo Jenkins not to rifle through the drawers in search of mischief. I don't want them anywhere but in the living room or the kitchen. Make them tea or something; I think there's some cake in the tin. Nothing more. Understand?'

'Are you going to tell me what it's about, Dora? You know Constable Dawkins told you to stay put.'

'I'm fine, Ted, and Elizabeth Henshaw seems to have taken on the role of my personal bodyguard. Oh, and by the way, thank you so much for that beautiful carving. It is absolutely stunning. We will chat again, I promise.' I gave him the most reassuring smile I could conjure up and then escaped, hurriedly.

Outside, the clouds had thickened and the drizzle had gathered into a steady downpour. I switched on the main living room lights. If Peters was watching, he would see people moving about inside which would hopefully be enough to allay any suspicions he may have.

As far as we were aware, we left the house undetected. I lay flat across the back seat of Elizabeth Henshaw's ten-year old Golf and after some very un-Christian language when the engine refused to catch (which made me have to stifle a giggle), she eventually managed to negotiate the lane without bumping into anything. I think I have already mentioned that there is a blind bend at the bottom of the lane – we took it with a screeching of stressed metal and a list of forty-five degrees. I was almost thankful that I couldn't see where we were going, because judging by the bumping and rolling I was being subjected to in the back seat, Mrs. Henshaw had seen the *Italian Job* too many times and adopted the persona of Michael Caine! The policeman in his car couldn't possibly have missed her, but stayed at his post.

'I think it's safe for you to get up now, Dora,' she said eventually. 'There's nobody has followed us from the village. I think we've done it!'

I cautiously raised my head and peered through the back windscreen. Against a stormy backdrop, we appeared to be the only car daft enough to be out in such awful weather. The road was already starting to flood but Elizabeth Henshaw valiantly ploughed her way through the puddles, which rose up in spectacular sprays on either side, as if she were intent on parting the Red Sea. If all of this sounds a little frivolous to you, put it down to delayed shock, car sickness and hysteria.

Elizabeth Henshaw did not know Merthyr Mawr village, so I directed her along the main road which bordered the river, over the bridge at the boundary of the next village, then a sharp left before speeding on through the narrow country lanes at an alarming speed. We were heading back the way we had just come, but now we were on the other side of the river. I wasn't quite in time to warn her about the little hump-backed bridge, which straddled the second river crossing. I swear all four wheels left the ground and my teeth clashed together with a thunk as we landed. I had just had a glimpse of the river, which had risen dangerously high and I couldn't for the life of me remember when the next high tide was. Hopefully we would be in and out before the lanes flooded. By the time she slowed down enough to cast a swift glance at the thatched cottages, I was feeling as if I had spent a lifetime on that back seat and would have bruises in the morning.

'I didn't know this existed,' she said in wonder as she skewed around the sharp corner beyond the church and exited the village. Blink and it was gone. 'I must bring Norman one day,' she said gaily.

By now I had lost the ability to speak.

We barrelled along the narrow lane towards the sand dunes, punishing the suspension on her poor car as she jolted in and out of the deep potholes, which lay completely invisible underneath the floodwater. The rain was still coming down in stair-rods and her wipers were on full speed, but thankfully we met no-one. It would have been a head-on collision.

Elizabeth brought the car to a slithering halt in the sand-strewn car park. I fell out of the back door, thankful to be alive, and led her towards the ruined manor house and the cave entrance beyond. The overhanging trees leaked rainwater and added to the deepening gloom, but the force of the rain was lessening. The smell of brackish water, rotting leaves and an earthy mushroom smell pervaded the undergrowth. The cave entrance was no more than a darker shade of dark behind the dripping foliage.

'Janine,' I called. 'It's Dora Cummings. Are you here?'

I peered into the entrance. I had to straddle a small stream of water, which poured out of the cave mouth and instantly soaked away into the sand. I called again, the sound echoed faintly back at me. 'Janine, it is Dora and Elizabeth Henshaw. We are quite alone.'

A grey shape appeared deep in the gullet of the cave. 'I don't want her here,' Janine muttered. She looked just as wretched as she had when I had first seen her, but now her clothes were black with water not dirt. Her face was hidden inside her hood, which had done nothing to keep her dry.

'I couldn't have got here without her help, Janine. She and her husband have been working hard to find a legal way for you to come back and stay with me. She's on your side, Janine. She is not the enemy.'

Elizabeth Henshaw raised an eyebrow at my unfortunate choice of words.

Janine shrugged her thin shoulders and glared threateningly at her, but let the matter drop. She pushed back her hood. Her lips were blue with cold. 'Then you've been wasting your time. I've only come to get my book back, that's all. If you give it to me, I'll be off. It's all I've come for.'

'There's a slight problem there,' I said. The rain had eased to a heavy drizzle and I was already soaked right through. 'Look, I've brought Mr. Boots, but can we go inside out of this rain and I'll explain about the book?'

'It's raining in there as well; it's coming through the roof,' Janine said miserably, grabbing Mr. Boots to her as if she could wrest some warmth from his raggedy body.

'Limestone, I'm afraid. Very porous,' I said inconsequentially.

'Where's the book? I asked you to bring it.' Her face was a thunderous scowl.

That's my girl, I thought, but before I could answer Elizabeth

Henshaw stepped in.

'We'll all get pneumonia if we stand here much longer,' she said. 'Everyone get back in the car and I'll put the heater on full. There's a blanket in the boot. There may be one or two dog hairs in it, but it will do. You need to get out of those clothes, child.'

Janine glanced at me as if seeking reassurance. I nodded. 'Get in the back and we will talk. You can trust Mrs. Henshaw. She has been very kind and to be honest, it is all getting beyond my ability to cope with on my own.' I never thought I would ever make that admission to anyone, and in front of Elizabeth Henshaw of all people!

With a ferocious glare at me, Janine dragged out her backpack and dived headfirst onto the back seat. I slipped in beside her and helped her strip off her sodden clothes and wrap herself in the hairy tartan blanket. I was horrified at the ugly purple bruises on her white skin and, without the hoodie hiding her face, I could also see her left eye was blackened. My heart cried for her. In a voice husky with tears I explained about the visit of Les Peters and that the police were in possession of the book. Janine slumped into silence.

'Why did you come back for the book, Janine? Did you know what was in it?' I asked.

'I only wanted that book,' she insisted. She burrowed deeper inside the folds of the blanket. 'I didn't know what it was when I took it; it was just a book with some empty pages. Les went ballistic when I said I didn't have it. He said he was supposed to be looking after it for some mates and that they'd kill him if they didn't give it back. I've never seen him so scared.' Janine shrugged. I had missed that shrug.

'So why go to all this trouble to give it back to him?' I asked. 'You don't owe him any favours.'

Another shrug. 'I thought that if I could post it to him or leave it somewhere for him to pick up, it would get him off both our backs, then I was going to disappear. But when I got to your house last night there were police everywhere and I couldn't pick the lock. I didn't know what else to do, so I left the note and came back here to the cave. But there's no point now, is there? You could give me a lift into town and I can catch a bus from there.'

'Nonsense!' I said sharply. 'You are coming back with us, child.'

'Why? So you can turn me in to the social again?'

'That was none of my doing, Janine, please believe me. I was as shocked as you when they turned up.'

Janine looked sceptical.

Elizabeth Henshaw put the car into gear and looked around. 'Miss Cummings has been trying hard to find out where they had taken you and how to get you back. She would hardly have done that if she had been the one to report you, would she?'

Janine shrugged but said nothing.

Mrs. Henshaw drove back carefully down the twisting lane. Alarmingly we could see the river rushing along beside us, just a couple of inches from overflowing its banks. As I hugged the sodden bundle to me, I knew I had made my decision and I knew that, deep down inside, it was the right one.

'You are not going anywhere, Janine. You are coming home with me, permanently if you want.' I held up a hand to stop any protests, though to be honest I don't think there were any forthcoming. 'Whether we like it or not, we are both in this together. We were rubbing along reasonably well before they snatched you, and I think once all this is over, we can do so again – but of course the decision is yours.'

'Why are you being so nice? I thought you'd hate me, after all these problems I've caused you.' a muffled voice asked, followed by a sniff which could either have been the result of an allergy to the dog hairs, an embryonic cold or as I rather suspected, Janine was desperately trying to snuffle back the tears.

I spoke to the top of her head, which was all I could see. 'I cannot for the life of me understand it myself,' I whispered softly, 'but I do know that the chickens have missed you and have practically stopped laying. I miss my eggs in the morning.'

My weak attempt at humour went unnoticed. 'Won't the social

come and take me back again?'

'I've been thinking about that,' I answered. 'The house is in rather a strategic position up on the bluff. If we barricade the lane and loosen a few slabs on the steps, we could hold out for a month or so.'

I was rewarded by a tiny giggle.

Elizabeth Henshaw turned in her seat and talked to us over her left shoulder, oblivious to the road ahead of her. 'You've only a few months to go before you are sixteen, and if the social services think they are the experts in procrastination, then they aint seen nothing yet.'

'Look out! The bend!'

She yanked the wheel hard left, away from the railings and the flooding river, and after a brief fishtailing, brought the car under control. 'Norman is always telling me I don't concentrate enough when I am driving,' she laughed. 'He usually refuses to come in the car with me.'

'Now you tell me!'

CHAPTER FORTY-TWO

We needn't have worried about Peters spying on us in the car, as three wet bodies and a heater straining at its highest setting had steamed the windows up perfectly. By the time we pulled in to the lane and squeezed into the parking space at the top, the rain had almost stopped and a wet wind was chasing it further north. A watery sun was shyly putting in a late appearance.

'What now, Dora?' Elizabeth asked.

'Firstly, get this child into a hot bath and some dry clothes. Then I'll ring the police to tell them she's with me.'

I felt Janine suddenly tense beside me. 'Don't panic. I'll ring Phil Dawkins. You met him before and he's a nice lad and is really on your side. I've known him since he was only a year or two older than you, and we can trust him.' I hoped: I knew how hidebound the police command structure was and junior ranks were to be seen and not heard. 'We have to know what is happening with Peters. They may even have caught him by now.'

I could tell Janine was less than enthusiastic, but since she was only dressed in her pants and a scratchy old blanket, she didn't really have any alternative.

'I'll let you into the annexe and you can shower and join us or take a nap if you want, while I see to my little army of minders. There are some of your clothes in the chest of drawers – I found them in the washing machine after you had gone – so at least you won't have to appear in public wearing my old things.'

After depositing Janine in the annexe, I followed Elizabeth Henshaw into the living room. I have to admit I hadn't given my house guests much thought while we had been gadding about the sodden countryside, but I hadn't expected the sight which greeted me.

Jemma Anthony and Flo Jenkins sat together on the settee. The coffee table had been pulled forward while Ted had drawn the armchair closer and sat facing them. They were busily playing a card game of some description with my box of kitchen matches deputizing for money and if my eyes did not deceive me, it was Jemma Anthony who was winning. Empty mugs littered the table and a packet of chocolate digestives lay open at the side, crumbs mingling with matchsticks.

They started guiltily as I entered the room. Ted rose to his feet. 'Ah, Dora... Just passing the time. Nothing to report, old girl', he said, trying desperately to gathering up the clutter on the table.

'Less of the "old girl" if you don't mind Ted when we are in company,' I said shortly. I turned to the remainder of The God Squad. 'I want to thank you all for coming at such short notice and manning the fort. It was very kind of you.'

'What is it all about?' Flo Jenkins asked. 'It is all very intriguing and Ted hasn't said a word.'

'Elizabeth can fill you in while I make a telephone call.' I escaped to the hall and left Elizabeth Henshaw to do the explanations – as far as she knew them anyway.

An early dusk was descending by the time I returned to my living room. I drew the curtains and switched on a couple of side lights. I hoped the wiring was up to the overload. They all looked expectantly at me. I was at a bit of a loss as to what to say. I had already thanked them, but from the look on their faces it didn't seem to have been enough. What more could I say? I was grateful to them, I really was. In my time of need they had come up trumps, but now I wanted them gone. Was there any polite way of saying thank you but get out? A 'please' tagged on the end might do it, but I doubted it. There were so many unspoken questions on their faces. Perhaps a quick explanation and then they would go.

'I have contacted the police and they will be coming to interview Janine later this evening,' I said.

'I knew that girl was trouble,' Flo Jenkins sniffed, a smug I-told-you-so expression on her face. 'If I had known this was all for her benefit ...'

'You wouldn't have come,' I finished for her. 'But you see, Mrs. Jenkins, Janine is not the problem here, she is the victim and she

273

has the bruises and black eye to prove it. I got away without any injuries, thanks to Ted's intervention, but there's no telling what that man would have done to the child if we hadn't gone to get her. I don't think you could have lived with yourself if Janine had come to serious harm.'

'Well… err… no, of course not,' Mrs. Jenkins stuttered. 'I didn't know the circumstances…'

Behind her back, timid little Mrs. Anthony was applauding, silently, at Flo Jenkins' discomfort.

'Even here she is in danger, as possibly am I. The man who broke in here is a "friend" of Janine's mother, and the police want to get as much information about him and his associates as they can. He is a violent man and has already beaten Janine and threatened far worse, so they want to arrest him as soon as possible. By creating the illusion that I was still at home, we have managed to bring her here safely without him suspecting.'

'You think he is still around?' Mrs. Anthony asked timorously.

'Undoubtedly, so the sooner he is caught the better.' Nobody was moving – for them this must have been like a reality television programme! They were not taking the hint. 'Once you have gone I will lock up securely and wait for the police to arrive,' I added brusquely.

Ted, bless him, recognised the stoniness in my voice. 'It was the least we could do to help, Dora. I'm so glad the lass is alright,' he said quickly rising from his seat. 'And unless you need me to stay, I think I will be off.'

Jemma Anthony scooped up the cards and slipped them into her handbag. 'It has been very pleasant, and I think we may have enlisted another recruit for our bridge night, Elizabeth,' she said, smiling fondly at Ted. I filed *that* little nugget away for another time.

Once everyone had departed and the house was silent, I gathered up the empty mugs and biscuit packet and took them through to the kitchen. There was a tentative knock on the back door. Janine stood there with an armful of wet clothing.

'Come on in, child,' I said ushering her over the doorstep.

'And if you don't mind, I'll go and have a hot shower myself and find some dry clothes. Dump yours in the machine and make yourself something to eat. Oh, and lock the door behind you. Just in case …'

'Bit late for that isn't it?' Janine asked with a grin.

'It will look good when Constable Dawkins comes. And before he does, we need to get our stories straight.'

'Why?'

'Well he did give me express orders not to leave the house, so the least said about our little jaunt the better. Don't mention it unless you have to. You made your own way here, okay?'

'Isn't it illegal to lie to the police?' she asked mischievously.

After a quick snack of poached eggs on toast, I made us both a large mug of hot chocolate with mini-marshmallows floating on top and we retired to the living room. It was cosy with just the table lights on and the curtains drawn and the soft shadows camouflaged the bruising on Janine's face.

She peered at me over the lip of her mug. 'I didn't want to be any more trouble to you,' she muttered. 'I was so confused, about you, about everything. The only thing I could think of was to grab the book and then disappear. You wouldn't even have known I had been here.'

'I'm very glad you didn't – disappear that is. I was worried about you and we couldn't seem to get any information as to where you were.'

Janine buried her face in her mug. I could sense the tension in her, but thought it best for her to speak out in her own time, if she wanted. The silence stretched and was becoming uncomfortable.

In hardly more than a whisper she muttered, 'I am scared, Dora.' Tears glittered in the corners of her eyes ready to overspill.

'So am I, child,' I admitted. 'I have an inkling of what Peters is capable of after he broke into my house, but I have never had to face physical violence before. When I was younger I might have been braver, but old age comes with its costs and I shrink from things I would once have tackled head-on, regardless of the consequences. Now, those consequences can have serious repercussions on old bones and I get fearful.'

'I would never put you down as timid, Dora,' Janine said with a watery smile.

'Timid and introverted. I hadn't realized how much I had shut myself off into my own little shell, happily trundling my way through what is left of my life. Which was all very well when my life was peaceful and tranquil, and I made sure I kept it that way, but not very good in an emergency.'

'Until I came along and spoiled everything…'

'Yes, Janine, until you came along. And it was I who chose to take you in, even though it escalated from what I had first intended – just a sandwich and then sending you on your way. Now, I do not regret it for one minute. It has just taken me time to adjust – it is all happening too fast for my poor old brain to keep up. But we will get through this – together.'

'You can be the brains and I'll be the brawn,' she grinned.

'If that's the case, then I am afraid we will fail on both counts.'

A rim of marshmallow froth stuck to her top lip and I laughed. She wiped if off with the back of her hand and smiled back.

'I have some good news for you that you might like,' I said. I had been agonizing when best to tell her about the book, and whilst we were in limbo, waiting for the police to arrive, it seemed to be the right time. Maybe lift her spirits a bit. 'It is about that little story you did in the back of the book – well, I didn't know if I would ever see you again, or even find out where you were, so I read it. It was so funny, and especially the way you had given each of the chickens the character of one of The God Squad. I was laughing out loud by the end.'

Janine was horrified. 'You didn't show it to them, did you?'

'Of course not! But I did show it to my niece who was staying here at the time – in fact it was she who found it – and she asked if she could take the book to London when she left. She has a contact in publishing who knows somebody, who knows somebody else and so on who specialises in children's books. That's why I no longer have the book – it went to London. I knew how good they were, and my niece was also blown away by them, and she said she would try and find out if they were possibly good enough to develop into a children's book. I could then have more leverage with the authorities to tell me where you were. Nothing like the possibility of some good publicity to get them moving.'

'You sent them to London!' I couldn't tell whether she was pleased or not. Her face was slack with shock.

'I'm sorry if I did wrong, but you do have a wonderful natural talent for cartoons and story telling. I thought there might be a chance you could make a bit of money out of it, or at the very least find out if it was worth working at as a career, or something. You could have your independence.'

'But they were only some quick drawings...'

'I don't want to get your hopes up, nothing may come of it, but, Janine, in my humble opinion they were brilliant, and – '

There was a loud banging on the front door, which made us both nearly jump out of our skins. Thankfully we had finished our drink or we'd have been covered in molten marshmallow.

CHAPTER FORTY-THREE

I fiddled with attaching the latch-chain, as per instructions, and opened the door a crack. I hadn't done that in twenty years and I felt a fool and a coward but I knew it was good sense. The figure of Constable Phil Dawkins filled the sliver of space and I could see another man behind him in the darkness.

'Glad to see you are taking precautions, Miss Cummings,' Phil said formally. 'May we come in?'

I closed the door, slipped off the chain and ushered them into the living room. 'Miss Cummings, this is Detective Inspector Tom Rowlands from Cardiff Drug Squad; he was already in the station going through the book and wants to interview Janine about Les Peters. You left a message that she was back with you.'

Phil Dawkins was obviously nervous and stiffly correct. Detective Inspector Rowlands was a man in his mid forties, already developing a drinker's paunch, with the dry wrinkled skin that marked a heavy smoker and the start of broken veins across his cheeks. He had thinning crinkly hair, which still held the hint of ginger peppering the grey. His brief handshake was slightly damp and I had to resist the urge to wipe it on my trouser leg.

The Detective Inspector sat in the armchair leaving Phil Dawkins to fetch one of the dining room chairs. Janine cringed in the corner of the settee nervously biting on the skin of her thumbnail.

'May I smoke?' he asked, taking out a packet of cigarettes and a lighter and obviously not expecting a negative reply.

'No, you may not. I do not allow smoking in my house,' I answered. He looked rather taken aback and reluctantly returned the cigarettes to his pocket, a scowl on his face.

Nah, I thought. Janine can do a far better one than that, but I held my tongue.

'I need to ask the girl about any names spoken or the identity of people she might have seen visiting Peters when he was staying with her mother, so if you wouldn't mind leaving us, Miss Cummings, we will get straight on. Time is of the essence,' he said shortly.

No way was I going to be dismissed like that in my own home. 'No, I will not leave you, Detective Inspector. As you very well know, Janine is not yet sixteen, so I believe I have the right to remain here as a "suitable adult". Am I right in that, Constable Dawkins?' I said, deliberately turning away from the senior officer.

'You have that right, Miss Cummings,' he answered with a twinkle in his eye, and a deadpan expression on his face.

Rank alone did not impress me. Having worked at police headquarters where every policeman was of some sort of rank above constable, I knew only too well the propensity of some to use their rank at every opportunity. Such men liked to intimidate, both the public and their fellow junior officers, and I had a feeling that Detective Inspector Rowlands was one such example. And while poor Phil Dawkins was hamstrung by his rank, I was not.

'Would either of you like a cup of tea or coffee before you start?'

'That would be very nice, thank you,' Phil answered.

'Janine, you can help me, lass,' I said, unwilling to leave her alone with Rowlands.

Five minutes later we entered with a tray of mugs of tea and I sat down on the settee, as close to Janine as I could without actually sitting on her lap. It didn't look as if anyone had spoken during my absence.

'Now you may proceed, Detective Inspector,' I said coolly. He glowered at me. There was no need for words. We had taken an instant dislike to each other.

He clicked a finger at Phil Dawkins and pointed to the coffee table. Phil, his jaw tightly clenched, dutifully laid down a couple of bulky folders. 'Take a look through these photographs, Janine,' Detective Inspector Rowlands said, finally acknowledging her presence, 'and tell me if you can identify any of the men here who may have visited Peters at your flat or you may have seen talking to him.'

For an hour and a half he fired questions at Janine, badgering her for names and dates of anything which might be construed as suspicious, until the poor child was wilting.

'I think that is enough, Detective Inspector, it is very late and the child is exhausted,' I said, finally calling a halt. 'I think you should leave now.'

He glared furiously at me but he could tell that on this I would not be moved. He gathered together his papers and photographs. 'Dawkins, take these out to the car,' he ordered. 'And when you get back to the station, you can contact social services and have the child taken back into care…'

Janine shot upright, every fibre in her body tensed ready for a speedy exit.

'Over my dead body!' I roared, putting out a hand to hold Janine physically in her place.

He sneered at me, insolently eyeing me up and down. 'That could be arranged.'

'I'm not going anywhere with you or social services. If you try, you can kiss goodbye to me fingering Les Peters or any of the others,' Janine said fiercely. 'They can't force me, can they, Dora?'

I glared at the Detective Inspector. 'Last time the police handed Janine over to social services, they were so totally inept that it resulted in Janine being severely assaulted and fleeing for her life. I am sure there is a case for negligence here if I wished to pursue it on her behalf. And unless you want to take personal responsibility for her safety, then I would suggest it doesn't happen again. I think the wisest option would be for her to remain here.'

'I *am* staying here,' Janine said firmly, 'or you'll have to arrest me.'

'You've been watching too much television, girlie,' Rowlands sneered. 'Please yourselves, but you do realize, Miss Cummings, that it is you who is putting the girl in danger with Peters still at large. Have you plods even had a sighting of him?'

Phil clamped his teeth on a retort. 'It is a vast area…'

Detective Inspector Rowlands waved a hand for him to be silent. 'He'll be on his toes now he knows the police are involved, so there's not much risk. Anyway his only use to us is if we can lean on him to inform on the rest of them. He's just small fry – we are after the big boys. Uniform can go after him at first light.'

Phil Dawkins paused in the doorway, his arms full of files and folders. 'Will you be giving us men for that, sir,' he asked. 'As I said, it is a vast area of dunes and woods. You could hide an army in there.'

'You'll have to scrape together what you can,' Rowlands answered shortly. 'You could always speed up the process by sending the girl out in plain sight, flush him out from wherever he is hiding, make it easier for yourselves.'

Before Phil Dawkins could answer I exploded. 'Use her as bait, you mean! We are talking about a fifteen-year old child here who has already been beaten by the man. You cannot seriously be suggesting...'

Detective Inspector Rowlands dismissed me with a wave of his hand. 'It was just a thought.'

'And if you want to stay in your chosen profession, you should have kept it as just that; the press would have a field-day.'

Before the man could reply, Phil Dawkins turned to me trying to defuse the growing tension. 'We'll be along in the morning to get that written statement from Janine,' he said. 'But with all due respect Sir, I do think a car should remain stationed outside. Peters has shown us how vicious he is. He is unaware that we are in possession of the book and still believes that either Janine or Miss Cummings has it. He probably thinks all this activity is just normal coverage because of the break-in.'

The Detective Inspector's face had turned dark with fury. 'Are you telling me how to run this operation, constable?' he spluttered. 'Tomorrow morning I will be taking down a sizeable drugs ring. Have you any idea of how much organisation that takes – no of course you don't! You plods can't even find a single man amongst a herd of sheep. We don't have the time or the manpower to play nursemaid to a couple of civilians who have expressly stated that they want to stay put.'

I resisted the temptation to correct his English regarding the collective noun for sheep, but it was only by a small margin. Any more insubordination and I thought he might blow a gasket.

However, I hadn't finished with him yet. As he hauled himself to his feet, I blocked his path to the door. 'So, while you are off playing at being *The Sweeny* you are unwilling to ensure the safety of a vulnerable young girl because you cannot be bothered to give her some protection. Rest assured, I will make it a matter of record when I make my statement regarding your refusal. As I say, her future wellbeing will be solely down to you, Detective Inspector Rowlands.'

I heard Phil Dawkins chuckling quietly in the hallway. The Detective Inspector was breathing rather heavily.

'Quite the Miss Marples, aren't you,' he said snidely. 'DAWKINS!' he bellowed. Phil appeared, straight faced and standing stiffly to attention. 'Get a car stationed at the bottom of his lane tonight and in the morning you can start earning your pay packet and find Peters. Will that satisfy you, *Miss* Cummings?'

He did not wait for a reply but stormed out of the house. Phil Dawkins threw me a wink and followed behind.

I was completely exhausted but still so hyped up with the adrenaline pumping through me that I knew I would not sleep for hours. I poured myself a sherry to take up to bed with me and I thought that perhaps I could read a couple of chapters of my book, though I doubted I would be able to concentrate.

'You can sleep in the spare bedroom for now, Janine; it's best if we are within shouting distance of each other. I'll dig you out a t-shirt you can wear as a nightie.' She seemed reluctant and hung back as I went around turning off the lights. 'Is there anything else you need?'

'I'm sorry for all the trouble I've caused,' she murmured. She kept her eyes on the tips of her toes. She looked terribly young.

'I've told you, we are in this together. What has happened in the past can't be undone, we have to work with the situation as it is and deal with it as best we can – together.'

'And if he comes back?'

'This time, I will be ready for him.' Though exactly how that would be, I had no idea.

'Can I sleep with you, Dora?'

'That, my child, is one step too far. I've slept on my own all of my life, and I fully intend continuing the tradition until they put me into my coffin.'

CHAPTER FORTY-FOUR

I cracked my eyes open before dawn. They felt gritty as if I had been hit in the face with a handful of sand. What little sleep I had managed to get had been next to useless, but during the night I had been able to turn a few ideas over in my mind. It never ceased to amaze me how fertile one's imagination becomes in that half dazed time between sleep and insomnia. Anything is possible. Solutions to problems shower down like falling leaves only to disappear five minutes later, elbowed out of the way by yet another stupendous idea. As I lay there summoning up the energy to lever myself out of bed, fragments of the night's brainstorming surfaced – not in any particular order. I discarded one idea after another until finally only one possible candidate remained. I would have to polish it up over a mug of coffee.

One thing I was determined on – Les Peters was not going to best me. I would fight him to the last drop of my blood. A snippet of Shakespeare came to mind…

I had barely taken a sip of my coffee when there was a knock on the back door. Constable Phil Dawkins, the woman police constable who had come with him before and a pimply youth whose helmet was so big for him that it was only held up by his ears and nose, huddled on the doorstep. It was still dark, raw cold and though it had stopped raining sometime in the night, the air was sodden.

'Where's the rest?' I asked as I invited them in.

'I'm afraid this was all I could scrape together for a search team,' Phil said stepping inside. 'The D.I. took everybody else off to help with the raids and only left a skeleton staff at the station.'

'Three of you!' I blurted out.

'Don't knock it, Dora. I had to fight to get these.'

He re-introduced me to Pat Matthews who no longer looked as patronizing as on her first visit, and the pimply youth (who looked even younger without his helmet) as Jonathan Shiers.

'It's his first day on the job, so be gentle with him, Dora,' Phil Dawkins warned with a grin.

'Is he old enough?' I uttered and the boy flushed red with embarrassment. I held up my hand to him. 'I do beg your pardon for my crassness, constable,' I quickly said. 'You can take it as a sign of my senile old age that I view anybody under the age of sixty as a child. Janine is trying to re-educate me. How about some chocolate biscuits to go with your cuppa by way of an apology?'

We all laughed and the tension eased. They squeezed into the kitchen for tea and toast or rather doorstops as I couldn't find the bread knife and had to use an old blunt one instead. They didn't seem to mind.

'What is your plan of action, Phil?' I asked. 'With only three to cover such a vast area, you've not got a hope of finding him.'

'It would have to be a lucky strike, I'm afraid,' he agreed, 'but we plods are going to have to do our best. Rowlands would love nothing better than to see us fail.'

I picked up my cold cup of coffee and took a sip before shoving it into the microwave. 'That is something which is not going to happen,' I said rejoining them. 'Rowlands may think he has bigger fish to fry but I have no intention of letting Les Peters get away with terrorising both Janine and myself. I want that man caught and I think I've got a plan which may work'

Phil Dawkins raised a sceptical eyebrow. 'Okay, spit it out. I'll listen to anything right now.'

I took a deep breath ready to repel the refusal I fully expected. 'We could form a posse.'

'No,' Phil Dawkins said firmly.

I ignored him and continued. 'We can mobilize the locals to help. They all know the area and would immediately notice if anything is even slightly awry. Peters would never suspect some old age pensioners tottering out for their morning constitutionals, he wouldn't give them a second glance. Everybody has a mobile phone these days, and if you exchange numbers, Phil, you can co-ordinate them and cover a far bigger area. You could lay down the law firmly, and make sure they understand that Peters is dangerous and is not to be approached. What do you say? How about we show the city boys how to do a proper manhunt?'

'Who is the "we" you are referring to, Dora?' Phil asked incredulously. 'I don't want to be rude, but you are firstly a civilian and secondly a woman of-a-certain-age. There is no "we". There is no *you* either!'

'You can't do anything with just three of you, Phil. Admit it! With extra feet on the ground and everybody equipped with their mobile phones, we have a much better chance of spotting him. Then you can go in for the kill.'

'There is no "we",' Phil insisted and Constable Pat Matthews grinned behind her hand.

There was an awkward silence. 'It could work, Phil,' Pat Matthews pondered tapping her bottom lip. 'So long as everybody is fully aware that they are only there to keep their eyes open, I can't see any harm in it, if they are willing to do it, that is.'

'No...' he said, but I could tell he was weakening.

It seemed my posse idea wasn't so barmy after all.

Phil Dawkins sighed heavily. He knew when he was outnumbered. 'How many would you be able to rustle up?' he asked.

I grabbed a sheet of paper and a pencil. 'There's the three from The God Squad, and maybe the reverend and Selwyn Jenkins will join their wives if they can get away; then there's Megan and Alf from the shop if they can arrange cover, along with their son Aiden who works from home. Then there's Ted and me and Janine. With luck we could muster at least ten extra pairs of eyes and that's without any other volunteers who may be up for a little adventure.'

Phil Dawkins scrubbed his chin as he considered the implications if anything went wrong.

He was teetering on the edge and I gave him a gentle nudge. 'They would just be out walking with their dogs or anything else on a string ...'

'Alright, ask as many as are available to gather here for a briefing. The last thing I want is someone going off all gung-ho and getting themselves or me into trouble. They will be coming of their own volition, not at the request of the police. Make that plain, Dora. I've still got a few years to go before I can retire and I would really like to collect my pension at the end of it! We can split them up into smaller units, and Pat, Jonathan and I can be the co-ordinator for each.' He sighed heavily. 'And while we are waiting for you to call them, Pat can take down Janine's statement so that we can get it typed up and signed when we get back to the station.'

There was another knock at the back door. I opened it to young Jimmy Farr, his face flushed and breathless from running. 'Is the copper here, Miss?' he gasped.

I ushered him into the crowded kitchen.

He stood instinctively in front of Phil Dawkins, bursting to tell him something but suddenly shy and very small in a room full of adults.

'Spit it out, lad,' Phil Dawkins said bending down to his level and drawing the boy to him.

I nodded to him for encouragement. It all spilled out in a breathless torrent. 'Well, it's like I know all the local cars in the village, and I heard about the bloke who broke in and nearly murdered Miss Cummings, and I've been around checking to see if there's any strange cars and I found one up on Marine Drive hidden around the side of Mr. Pugh's garage, out of sight, like...'

'Was there anybody in it?' Phil asked eagerly.

Jimmy shook his head.

'You didn't by any chance take down the number, did you?' he asked.

'Course I did, mister, what do you take me for, an idiot?' Jimmy Farr answered indignantly.

'I expect it's either stolen or borrowed, but I can get the P.C. in the patrol car to go up and disable it so that Peters can't make a quick get-away. You all carry on, I won't be a minute,' he said and started to walk into the living room. He turned to the boy who seemed a bit deflated by his reception. 'Well done, lad. We'll have to recruit you when you are a bit older. But shouldn't you be getting home now? Do your parents know you are out at this time in the morning?'

Jimmy Farr preened with pleasure. 'Nah, they won't have noticed, mister. Can I have some of that toast, I'm starving.'

Pat Matthews ruffled his hair as she got up and he blushed red to the roots. 'I'll go and get Janine's statement whilst everything is being sorted.'

'She's in the spare bedroom in the front. Just give her a knock and tell her that if she's not down for breakfast soon, we'll be out of bread!'

While Jimmy Farr tucked into two rounds of toast liberally spread with butter and jam, I got on with ringing around the likely deputies for the posse. Even though it was still an unearthly hour in the morning, Elizabeth Henshaw was more than agreeable and said she would drum up the others of The God Squad. I had just got through to Megan at the shop when Constable Matthews came thundering down the stairs.

'I can't find Janine anywhere,' she said worriedly. 'Have you seen her?'

None of us had. We had been so busy hatching our plans in the kitchen she could easily have slipped out unnoticed. I checked in the living room and rechecked upstairs and even unlocked the annexe and peeked inside, but there was no sign of her. As I passed back through the hallway, a sudden gust of wind blew the front door open a couple of inches. I knew that I had locked it properly the night before, and I had even put the security chain on, and I hadn't opened it since. All the traffic had been through the back door.

I was horrified. I joined the others in the kitchen. 'She's not here and her backpack is missing and the front door is open. She's managed to slip out right under our very noses. She could have been gone hours.'

'Why?' Phil asked. 'What does she hope to achieve?'

'She could be running off again. That idiot Rowlands did practically threaten her with being sent to the social services again so she's disappeared before he can get at her.'

'But I thought she wanted to stay with you, Dora.'

Constable Pat Matthews suddenly put her hand over her mouth as an explanation occurred to her. 'Or, she's putting herself out there as bait,' she said. 'You said she was here when Inspector Rowlands suggested she be used to flush him out – now she's gone off and done it herself. As you said, she wants to stay here but she'll never be safe while Peters is on the loose.'

'Great, now we have to search for two people! Where the devil do we start?' Phil groaned. 'Can you think of anywhere she might have gone Dora?'

'I don't think she is making herself a target to get Peters. She is on her own and is six stone dripping wet. What could she do? She's taken all her worldly goods with her, so I think she is simply getting away, afraid I'll go back on my word and she'll be taken back into care, knowing that there's nothing I can do to stop it from happening again.'

'Where would she go then?'

I needed to think quickly and clearly, two things, which did not work so well in my age and everybody was looking at me for the answers. 'If she thinks that the house is being watched – and from what Jimmy says his car was parked not far away – then I don't think she would have gone out of the village to the east. There's only the coast road that way which is pretty open and runs quite close to the cliffs. Peters would be able to stage an accident very easily and toss her over.'

The young constable blanched. Phil Dawkins pulled out his radio. 'I'll get the patrol car to keep watch on that road anyway,' he said.

'I think she's headed for town, maybe to catch a bus out of the area. She wouldn't have to take the road; she'll have gone over the hill at the back and cut across the river at the stepping stones – there is a reasonable track which cuts overland into town. I showed it to her when we went to the castle.'

'Depending on when she did a bunk, she could be half way there by now,' Phil said angrily running his hand through his hair and making it stand on end.

'No, I don't think so, Phil,' I said laying a hand on his arm. 'She may have left here in the middle of the night, but once she passes out of the village there are no more lights. It is pitch black from there on. Even I wouldn't be able to make my way across the dunes and the river in the dark and Janine is no country girl. She'll have had to lie low until first light – in fact until right about now.'

We all turned to look out of the window at the gently strengthening light.

'And Peters is no doubt doing the same,' Phil Dawkins muttered dragging on his coat. 'So we go after them both. Rowlands may only want Les Peters and is willing to sacrifice Janine as collateral damage, but Peters is a dangerous and desperate man and still thinks that Janine has got the book. We need to move, now!'

The room was suddenly a swirling mass of activity. The door opened and Ted Morris was nearly mown down in the rush.

Phil grabbed him to steady him. 'I haven't got time to explain at the moment, Ted. P.C. Matthews will fill you in on what we have in mind.' So saying, he grabbed the young probationer who was milling around in total confusion. 'You and I will drive down the road in the hope of catching a glimpse. Pat, Dora and Ted will stay here and co-ordinate the searchers as they arrive. Dora, you do not go anywhere!'

Before I could protest, he was gone. Pat Matthews and I stood motionless, mouths open, aghast that we had been dismissed from the search.

CHAPTER FORTY-FIVE

'Oh, I don't think so, Mr. Dawkins!' I muttered through clenched teeth. Anger had lit a match under my brain, which was now firing on all cylinders; thoughts clear and actions co-ordinated. 'Pat, you fill Ted in on the role of the search teams. You two can stay here and co-ordinate them. I'll get a jacket and boots and my mobile phone and then I am going after Janine, the same way she probably went – overland.'

'I can't let you do that, Miss Cummings! Phil Dawkins would hang me from the nearest tree.'

'Don't worry,' I answered over my shoulder, 'there aren't any tall ones this close to the sea. I take full responsibility for my own actions – Ted you are my witness to that, aren't you?'

Ted looked completely bemused. 'Will I be incriminating myself if I say yes?'

I sat to tug on my thick walking boots. 'You stay here and brief anybody who turns up that they are to take a nice morning stroll out towards the estuary and river and keep their eyes peeled for this man, Les Peters,' I said pushing a copy of the photograph Phil Dawkins had left. 'They need to ring Constable Matthews on her mobile if he is spotted – give him your number, love. Under no circumstances are they to approach him – just ring the sighting in. Are you clear?'

Ted Morris nodded.

I was ready for the off. 'I'm going to try and find Janine before she does anything stupid. I have a horrible feeling that she has gone armed – I couldn't find the bread knife this morning and it has got a vicious point. If she has taken it, I pray it's only for self protection and she isn't going to tackle Peters herself.'

Pat Matthews shrugged on her coat. 'Well, you are not going anywhere without me. Other than arresting you and cuffing you to the AGA, it's the best I can think of right now.'

I paused in the doorway, suddenly wracked with doubt. 'What

if I am wrong and she hasn't headed into town? What if she's gone through Ewenny and out on to the A48 and has hitched a lift to never-never land? What if Peters went off in a completely different direction and she's following him? I couldn't live with myself if something bad happens to her because I thought I knew best – again!'

Pat Matthews shook her head. 'It's all we've got right now. And it was Janine who decided to take things into her own hands and do a bunk. This is our best option – we have to go with it.'

'We'll have a pretty good view from the top of the bluff behind the house, right the way up the river valley and over to the dunes. If we see either her or Peters, you can radio it in to Phil in the car. If she is out there and has crossed the river, it's a long way around to the other side by road; we can cut her off quicker by going overland. And if Peters isn't on her trail, maybe the search teams will get lucky and spot him.'

I scrambled up the steep grassy slope behind the house on all fours, with Constable Matthews close behind me. After all the rain, the closely cropped grass was like trying to climb up an icy ski slope and for every four steps gained, we slid back down two. The chickens came fluttering out of the coop into their run, clucking hopefully.

'Sorry, girls, I can't play with you now. Things to do.'

'What do you mean, play?' Constable Pat Matthews gasped.

Her sarcasm was obvious but I chose to answer as if I had not noticed. 'Oh, they've got an old tennis ball and they love a game of football,' I explained.

The Pat Matthews snorted in disbelief. When this was all over, I would have to disabuse her of her scepticism. I didn't think my chickens were unique, but they were rather special and were quite nifty around the pitch.

We finally reached the top of the bluff. I was quietly pleased that I wasn't panting as much as the constable until Jimmy Farr joined us. He hadn't even broken sweat. I had forgotten all about him.

Pat Matthews grabbed him by the arm and spun him around, nudging him back towards the house. 'You can't come with us, lad, you'll have to go back down – you can help Mr. Morris,' she said firmly. 'I've already left myself in for a tongue lashing by disobeying orders, I really don't want to jeopardise my whole career before it has started by letting you get involved too.'

Jimmy Farr wriggled out of her grip. He scowled at her and he looked remarkably like a cartoon character from the Beano. 'You can't stop me being out here, and I can help. I can run faster than any of those oldies you've got out searching. Faster than both of you, too. I can scout ahead and report back. It'll save you a lot of leg-work.'

As I gathered my breath I pulled him toward me. I had to admit he had a good point. 'You go just as a scout then, Jimmy, you can be our advanced party. You promise me you will not go anywhere near either of them; you will simply report back to us where they are.'

Jimmy Farr's eyes glistened. He was off like a whippet from the gate.

'*If* they are together that is,' I said to his retreating back.

Pat Matthews slid down the bank in his wake. 'I'm dead,' she groaned. 'I am totally dead.'

I raised my binoculars to my eyes. They weren't my most powerful pair, but they were lighter to carry and the nearest to snatch. Please, please, please be right, I prayed silently as I started scanning the lumpy dune banks edging each side of the road and down to the river. Phil's car, its lights flashing, was already disappearing around the far bend, half a mile away. On such a drab, miserable morning, nothing else was stirring.

Going down the hill was more treacherous than climbing up. One slip and we would have got to the bottom quicker than anticipated, with twisted ankles and bruises at the very least. By the time we staggered out into the dripping bracken at the bottom, Jimmy Farr had re-joined us.

'I seen the two of them over the other side of the river, Miss,' he said. 'I don't know if the girl knows he's there, though, 'cause she isn't hurrying or nothing. The man's creeping along, like, hiding in the bushes and behind the bits of old walls.'

'I'll radio it in to Phil. It looks like your hunch might have been right,' Pat Matthews said.

I groaned with relief. 'I'll phone Ted and tell him to keep the search teams in the house. No need for them to come out now unless things change.'

With no need for stealth, we charged along the road until we could cut down through the bracken towards the river. If I had had enough breath, I would have laughed at what a sight we must have made – an old aged pensioner, an eight year old boy and a rather less-glamorous-than-normal W.P.C.

We ran on through the low dunes until the castle loomed above us, black with wet. Three black crows watched us with sharp flinty eyes from the top of the bastion tower. One cawed a harsh warning. It sent ice crystals shooting through my veins.

We ran down the lane towards the river and skidded to a halt. In front of us the apron of sand, which was used as a sometime car park by walkers, had become a shallow lake. The stepping stones across the surging river – normally standing a good few inches above the water – were being lapped by muddy brown water.

'It's all that rain from yesterday and last night, it's still feeding down from the hills inland. Even though the tide is going out, there's more to come down the valley. It can only get worse.'

'We are not going across that,' Constable Matthews said firmly. 'I'll radio Phil that it's up to him to get them from his side…'

'Nonsense! Janine and Peters made it and they are not that far ahead. We can't wait. All this will soon be under water. It's now or never.'

'The boy stays behind…'

Jimmy Farr dashed out from behind us and splashed his way to the first stone. 'Try and stop me,' he grinned and flung himself onto the stone, hopping with gazelle-like dexterity from one to the next until he was across.

'I'll go next,' I said shouldering my way forward. The river was in full flood, churned brown with the silt from upriver and capped

294

with white crests, like a hungry beast as it surged towards the sea. Incredulously the writer part of me filed the image away in a distant part of my brain for future use. 'It helps not to look at the water itself, just concentrate on each individual stone. They will be slippery, so make sure you're feet are firmly positioned before you jump to the next.'

I had to concentrate hard at taking my own advice. There was still a stiff gusty wind blowing from the previous day's storm, which threatened at any moment to throw me off balance. It was an inelegant crossing to say the least, but I did get safely to the other side where Jimmy Farr waited, grinning with delight at the comic spectacle.

Pat Matthews followed gamely behind. She was quite a bit taller than me, so the span between the stones was not such a problem, but as she reached the end her eye was caught by a large tree branch racing towards her on the flood. Her foot slipped and she went in. She managed to grab hold of a hank of reeds half submerged in the surging water. But the current was strong and threatened to break her grip. Jimmy and I waded into the reed bed and grabbed one of her hands, pulling back with all our meagre combined strength. Just as I thought we were losing the battle, Pat Matthews managed to get a foothold in the muddy bottom and eventually, between us, we managed to haul her out on the bank like landing a large fish. She was very wet and very muddy from her knees down.

'Are you alright to carry on?' I asked.

She nodded. 'I should be asking you that! I am decades younger than you and decades older than the boy,' she gasped. 'Give me a minute to catch my breath.'

'I don't think we have a minute,' I said anxiously peering along the flooded track. In parts the deep puddles had joined together to form large ponds, reflecting the steel-grey of the sky. 'She could be in danger. We have to go on.'

'I'll run on ahead and see where they are,' Jimmy offered, itching to be away.

Before he could run I held him back. 'Keep hidden, Jimmy,

use the hedges for cover. And use the higher edges of the track. There will be lethal potholes under the water and you could easily break a leg.'

'Don't worry about me, Miss, I can take care of myself,' he answered proudly and was away.

CHAPTER FORTY-SIX

Pat Matthews staggered towards me, water oozing out of various parts of her soaked uniform.

'Well, we can't get any wetter. Muddier maybe,' Pat Matthews commented.

We staggered as fast as we could along the flooded track but the ankle-deep water slowed our progress. The cold from the river ducking had leached into my bones and felt like daggers slicing me apart. I was struggling, near to exhaustion when Jimmy splashed his way back to us.

'They are on that white bridge, both of them,' he gasped. 'And the girl's got a knife…'

'I'll find out how far away Phil is and warn him,' Pat Matthews said unclipping her radio and thumping at the buttons. She looked back at me in disgust. 'The radio is out, waterlogged I expect. It looks like we are on our own.'

She took out her baton and extended it with a flick of her wrist. I wished I had thought to bring something, but I hadn't. The best I could do was pick up an old tree branch lying at the side of the track.

They were in the middle of the swingbridge, Janine facing Peters with my bread knife clenched in her hand. Peters had his back to us and the noise of the rushing river had drowned our approach, but Janine saw us and gasped. We probably looked like creatures from the depths. Peters was quick. He launched himself at Janine and easily prised the knife out of her hand while wrapping his other arm around her throat in a half-nelson.

'Let her go, Mr. Peters,' Constable Matthews shouted. 'It's over. Give yourself up.'

Les Peters swung himself and Janine around to face us. Janine's backpack formed a wedge between them and he was struggling to keep hold of her. His initial shock wore off quickly and he grinned. 'And who's going to do that, darling? You is it or that little shrimp and the old biddie?'

Pat Matthews hesitated. This was an armed man holding a young girl as hostage. Was she brave enough to take him on alone? All thoughts of the training she had had in unarmed combat melted away like summer snow. She didn't think she was ready for this. Perhaps he would just give himself up… He confirmed her worst fears.

'I wouldn't come any closer, not unless you want to be responsible for her lovely little throat being cut,' he said confidently. He looked wild, his eyes glittering unnaturally, his face dark. He started dragging Janine backwards to the far side of the bridge.

'Think about what you are doing, Mr. Peters,' I said, evading Pat Matthews's grip and edging up on to the bridge. 'There are reinforcements on the way. You have nowhere to go. And if you harm her you will be in much worse trouble than you already are.'

Peters barked a humourless laugh. 'You think so, old woman? You don't know nothing…'

'So far they can only arrest you for the burglary at my house. Kidnap and attempted murder are an entirely different ball game. And you have three witnesses now with more on the way. Let Janine go, Mr. Peters. She doesn't have your precious book, the police already have that. They are rounding up your people as we speak. She is no threat to you.'

He pulled harder on her neck until she was almost on tip toes, the knife resting on the white skin of her throat.

'She's not lying,' Janine screamed. 'I haven't got the book. Please let me go…'

'Oh, I don't think so,' he said smiling wolfishly. 'They can't do anything while I've got you. You are my passport out of here, so, I'll just say cheerio…'

As he let the knife slip a fraction, Janine heaved herself up higher, using his restraining arm as a lever, and smashed the heels of her heavy boots – my old walking boots I noticed – into his shins. Peters yelled in agony and Janine broke free, rushing over to huddle behind us just as we heard the sweet sound of the police siren blaring on the other side of the river.

298

Pat Matthews pushed us all behind her and edged forward, her baton raised, but Peters stood his ground and challenged her with the knife. It was a stand-off.

'You've got nowhere to go Peters. Be sensible and give yourself up,' Pat Matthews said as Phil dragged the police car to a slithering halt, blocking the other side of the bridge. The flashing blue lights lit up the scene like a surreal tableau.

Peters looked desperately over the railings at the surging river. 'Don't be a fool,' Phil said. 'The river is on the ebb and swollen with rainwater. You'd be across the Bristol Channel before they even mount a search for your body. You wouldn't stand a chance.'

The man was certainly no fool, neither was he suicidal. He realized that he had run out of options. The fight went out of him and he collapsed on the deck of the bridge, rubbing his legs. The knife clattered to the ground and tipped over the edge into the river.

Phil Dawkins strode onto the bridge. 'He's all yours Constable Matthews. He's your first collar. Well done.'

Pat Matthews was cold, wet, muddy and barely able to suppress her delight as she cuffed him and yanked him to his feet. She read him his rights.

'You and I will take him down to the station. Constable Shiers, you will stay with Dora, the boy and Janine and I'll get the patrol car from the village to come down and collect you all.'

Phil Dawkins had pushed Les Peters into the back of the car and handed Pat Matthews the silver survival blanket from the kit in the boot. 'Bit early for a swim, isn't it?'

Pat Matthews, swathed in silver in the back seat of the car and grinning like a fool, gave me a nod as they screamed out of the village. Sometimes, I thought, that was all it took – a silent exchange of acknowledgement and perhaps respect.

Some of the residents of the village had filtered out of their scattered houses to see what all the kafuffle was about. As the police car headed back into town, I was oblivious to their stares. All that mattered was that Janine was safe.

Janine and I slumped down on the wooden bench on the village side of the bridge. I had not let go of her, afraid that she might take off again, disappear like a puff of smoke. We were both crying and laughing at the same time while a mystified Jimmy Farr looked on.

Constable Shiers hovered uncomfortably between us and the local population.

'Why, Janine?' I murmured. 'Why did you go off on your own like that? You could have been killed.'

'The whole mess was all my fault,' she sobbed. 'If I hadn't run away in the first place, none of this would have happened. I just wanted to get as far away as I could. I didn't want you or anyone else getting hurt because of me so I just took off. I thought I could just disappear.'

'But you knew Peters was out there somewhere.'

'I didn't think he'd even have his eyes open at that time in the morning,' she answered. 'I was already down on the road by the time it was getting light. I thought I had given him the slip. How dumb was that!'

'And now? Do you still want to disappear or would you rather come home with me?' I asked. I had a lump in my throat as I waited for her answer. I had missed the girl so much – it had felt as if a part of me had gone missing.

'They won't let me, will they?' she asked miserably. 'That policeman said…'

'It is not up to him. The choice is yours, Janine. Stay and fight or surrender and give yourself up to the powers that be.'

'You really want me to stay with you? After all the trouble I have caused?'

I didn't trust myself to speak, I merely nodded.

She held my eyes for what seemed a millennium. Then her face broke into one of her rare beaming grins. 'They won't stand a chance, Miss. I'm game if you are.'

CHAPTER FORTY-SEVEN

The patrol car which had been guarding the eastern exit to the village arrived quickly, scattering the local residents to the periphery. More had joined them as news had spread and now included most of the population.

Constable Shiers, relieved to have a definite role at last, opened the rear door and ushered the three of us inside and told us to put our seat belts on. He bent down to whisper to me. 'It was my first day,' he admitted, blushing bright red. 'I didn't expect it to be this exciting.'

I didn't have the heart to disabuse him of the realities of policing: he would find out soon enough. He slipped into the front passenger seat.

Jimmy was fidgeting as soon as we left the village behind. 'Can we have the siren on, mister?'

'It is not a toy, lad,' the driver said over his shoulder.

Jimmy repeated his request every few minutes, irritating everybody in the car, until we were on the coast road headed for Sutton. 'Please, mister; just once.'

With a resigned nod, the driver gave a blast of the siren, sending the quietly grazing sheep and their lambs diving for cover in the bracken. Jimmy glowed and sat back, quite satisfied. We all heaved a sigh of relief.

The house was bursting at the seams by the time the police car dropped us off, even though I had rung Ted to tell them all was well and they could stand down. Most of the erstwhile posse had turned up; Elizabeth Henshaw seemed to be in charge – no surprise there – with Flo Jenkins and her husband Selwyn, Mrs. Anthony, Ted Morris and both Megan and Alf from the shop. I was under no illusion that their attendance was out of concern for either me or Janine – where better to get the full story than from the horse's mouth? My little home, which not so long ago had been my private sanctuary, now seemed to have become open house. But I was being churlish. They had come at my request, at a god-awful hour of the morning and though we hadn't needed to use them because of Janine's pre-emptive strike, they had been under no obligation to comply. I had never gone out of my way to socialise with them and I wondered whether I would have done the same if it had been Flo Jenkins who needed help? To my shame I didn't think I would.

Elizabeth Henshaw leapt to her feet. 'Here we are, all safe and sound,' she announced. 'We are all so relieved. You look dreadful, Dora, come and sit down.'

If I looked as bad as I felt, then her description was probably perfectly accurate. Whatever strength had been keeping me upright for the past few hours had gone and I felt drained and shaky. I would have loved nothing better than to crawl into bed, but there were things to be done. The three of us took off our boots as I pattered into the living room to confront them.

'Could one of you fix some breakfast for Janine while I go up and change into some dry clothes? She must be starving. And you, Jimmy, need to ring your parents and tell them where you are.

'It's alright, Miss, they won't mind,' Jimmy replied.

'I insist, Jimmy, otherwise you will have to go home right this minute. The telephone is in the hall.' He looked as if he was still going to argue. 'Please. Do this for me.'

He dragged himself into the hall as if he was walking to his execution.

Janine was hovering behind me. She disliked crowds just as much as I did. And every eye was fixed on her. 'You can slip into the annexe and take a shower to warm up,' I said manoeuvring her out of the room. 'You needn't come back in if you don't want. You and Jimmy can stay in the kitchen.'

She took down the spare key and opened the annexe door and turned to face me. 'Thank you,' she said simply.

Elizabeth Henshaw brushed past headed for the kitchen. 'I'll put the kettle on. You must be gasping. You must tell us all about it, when you've changed.'

I resigned myself to having to face them and tell them what had happened. They deserved that much at least. But first I needed a hot shower and some clean clothes, as I suspected I still smelled of the river mud that had coated my boots and trousers.

'Come on, Dora, don't keep us in suspense,' Megan shouted up the stairs after what she must have calculated was a reasonable amount of time.

I faced myself in my dressing table mirror and dragged a comb through my hair. My skin was an unhealthy parchment colour and dark shadows under my eyes looked like smudged mascara. My hands shook with reaction and fatigue. 'You can do it, old girl, you are on the home straight now,' I told my image. Blank eyes accused me of lying.

Ted met me at the foot of the stairs with a mug of tea in one hand and a plate of biscuits I had never seen before in the other.

'I was so worried about you, Dora. Tearing off like that as if you were fifty years younger. You could have done yourself no end of damage,' he said, concern clearly etched on his face. He put the mug and plate down on the telephone table and took a deep breath. 'I have to talk to you. Dora. I can't wait any longer.'

He ruffled his thick white hair and then gripped me by the arms as if to stop me from escaping. Laughter and shouted questions rang out from the living room. We both ignored it. 'I know that now is probably not the right time, but I'm a bit confused about where we stand with each other, Dora. You see I've been wanting to have a chat with you for ages, but it never seems to be the right time and when it was the right time I just clammed up like some adolescent kid. The scare you have given me has brought it all to a head.'

'Talk to me about what, Ted?' I asked. I had a pretty good idea what was on his mind, but I did not want to say something in case I had read everything wrong and come to the wrong conclusion, making an idiot of myself. I needed the poor man to spell it out, no matter how embarrassed he felt.

'I think you are a very special lady, Dora Cummings, and,

well, I've been thinking, there's me rattling around in my house and you rattling around in yours. At our age I was wondering whether you might consider us getting together…'

He was starting to flounder so I held up a hand to stop him. Thankfully the entertainment going on in the other room would be masking our conversation. 'Well, you certainly pick your moments, Ted Morris,' I said. It was my turn to hesitate as I tried to drag my exhausted thoughts together. 'You are a dear, kind man and I love you as a friend and confidante and I hope that that will never stop. But if you are hoping for it to progress into a bit of romance, then I'm afraid I am not your girl. Please believe me, I am flattered, but it could never happen.'

Ted hung his head. 'I am always too cautious. This time I've left it fifty years too late,' he said with a wry smile.

'Maybe, but I doubt it. Not that I wouldn't have been tempted when I was in my twenties, when all my friends and colleagues were marrying, having children and affairs and divorces. Then I felt I was the odd one out and may have been pushed into marriage just in order to conform. When you are young, it is a powerful driving force. But as time went on, I never met anyone I liked or trusted enough to give up all that I already had in order to commit myself to a different life. I have never regretted that life, Ted, and now I am far too old to change just for the sake of change.'

He didn't look as deflated as I had anticipated. 'We can stay friends though?'

'Of course, Ted, there's no question about that. But unless I am very much mistaken, I have noticed a certain widow has been giving you the glad eye. You could do a lot worse than Jemma Anthony.'

His eyes crinkled up with relief and joy. 'You don't miss much, do you, old girl?' he laughed. 'Who would have thought it, aye? Two gorgeous women to choose from at my time of life!'

Thinking about the image of myself I had just seen in my bedroom mirror, the word 'gorgeous' was not one, which came to mind.

Janine joined us from the annexe and Ted left us together. I had forgotten about the paper-thin partition wall between the hall and the annexe, and realized she must have heard every word. But if she had, she gave nothing away.

More raucous laughter erupted from the living room. 'It's Jimmy,' Janine answered to my unspoken question. 'He's putting himself out there as the hero of the day. He's got a really good imagination, that boy, but not up to Anna Clare's standards.'

CHAPTER FORTY-EIGHT

We entered the living room together. Sure enough, Jimmy Farr was centre-stage and his audience was enraptured. It went quiet as everyone turned toward us. Flo Jenkins heaved herself out of the settee, never an easy job even for a person of lesser stature. She stood in front of Janine who had frozen beside me. I could feel the tension fizz through her body. I felt her fingers nudge mine and I squeezed them gently.

'As everyone here will tell you, I don't often admit to being wrong, but in your case, child, I think I owe you an apology. I have read you wrong. It was a very brave thing that you did.'

Janine gaped at her in disbelief. 'But I didn't...'

'You should have seen her give that man a clout, both feet, nearly got his knee-caps and all while he had a knife at her throat too,' Jimmy Farr piped up.

'Come in and sit down, both of you, and tell it to us from the beginning,' Elizabeth Henshaw urged.

Selwyn vacated the armchair to me and Janine perched herself on one arm while Jimmy took the other one.

I took a few gulps of rather strong 'builders' tea while I recovered from the shock of hearing Flo Jenkins admit any failings, especially in public. She rose a smidgeon in my estimation.

'Well, once again I am in your debt, and I thank you all. You have been very kind to...'

The door flew open and in charged Tiffany my niece, quickly followed by Gina, her beautiful wife. They stared at us and we stared back at them. Nobody spoke. It was Tiffany who thawed first.

'I must say this is not what I expected!' she said.

'What are you doing here, Tiff? Have I forgotten you were coming or something?' I asked. 'Not that it's not lovely to see you, but...'

'You were being so cagey on the phone when you rang up and asked for that book. I knew there was something major you weren't telling me and that if I said I was coming down, you would only fabricate some ridiculous excuse and get yourself all worked up. So we packed our bags and came.'

'I can see that!'

'And from the look of this gathering, something has definitely been going on, so I think it is about time that you came clean, Dora Cummings. And while you are doing it, Gina and I couldn't half do with a coffee. We drove straight down, no stopping.'

Elizabeth Henshaw rose to her feet. 'We are all waiting for the full unabridged version, so I think we can replenish everyone's cup, open another box of biscuits, and then Dora can tell us all in one go. How does that sound, my dear.'

Once everyone was settled back down with their refreshments and more chairs had been pulled around, I introduced Tiffany and Gina to the eager audience.

'Are you sitting comfortably, children? Then I will begin...'

It took some telling and I knew that within 24-hours the story would have been embellished beyond all recognition. I even had to admit to Tiffany that I had been attacked in my own home, at which she puffed out her cheeks, got very red, and I knew I would be in line for a right telling off when we were finally alone.

'So where is this famous black book then?' Elizabeth Henshaw asked.

Before I knew what she was doing or could stop her, Gina dug a handful of papers out of her gigantic tote bag. 'These are photocopies of the stories and illustrations from the book. My friend Stella Shaw took a look at these and fell in love with them. She said that there's nothing quite like it on the market – it's a cross between a cartoon strip and a story rather than a traditional illustrated story. It would appeal to a wide age group, from toddlers to older children who can read it for themselves. And it would be a terrific marketing ploy that it was written by someone of Janine's age. She wants to meet you, Janine. She was very excited.'

Janine's eyes had got rounder and rounder until they seemed to take up her entire face. She opened her mouth to speak, but was too overwhelmed and just stared.

'May we see them,' Elizabeth Henshaw asked and snatched the papers up off the table.

Janine's look of horror was probably replicated on my own face. I watched Elizabeth Henshaw flip slowly through the pages, her face expressionless, giving no hint of what she was thinking.

'I take it I am Shirley, the fluffy one with the attitude?' she said stonily. She glared at both of us. The silence stretched sickeningly. 'I think they are bloody marvellous. You've got me down to a T,' she said, laughing hysterically. 'I always wanted to be famous, now I've finally made it as a chicken!'

The others crowded around to have a look. 'That's me,' Ted said roaring with laughter. 'I'm Sidney, the one-legged seagull!'

'He is the hero of the story,' Janine explained quietly.

Everybody laughed as Ted puffed out his chest and mimed preening his non-existent feathers while hopping around the living room with the aid of his walking stick.

Flo Jenkins had been silent. 'It could have been worse,' she finally admitted. 'All in all, Janine, I think you have been very restrained. I can live with being Cilla.'

While they fingered their way through the loose pages, Tiffany took me on one side. 'I must say, this has all come as rather a surprise. I thought that your goal was to become a reclusive genius living in splendid isolation on the top of the bluff. If it is alright with you, Dodo, Gina and I will stay over until your op next week, but by the look of it you will have plenty of support.'

For a moment I didn't have a clue what she was talking about. Then it dawned on me. The mastectomy! I had forgotten all about it.

'Is that next week?' I gasped. So much had happened in the last week that time had ceased to register. 'Well, yes, um… yes, that's fine, Tiffany. Of course you can stay. When exactly is my op?'

Tiffany laughed. 'You have pre-op checks the day after tomorrow, Dodo, and then your op is two days later. Will you be okay?'

'My blood pressure might still be slightly raised, but after what we've been through, it should be a walk in the park!'

'Auntie Dodo, you are priceless.'

Printed in Great Britain
by Amazon

83827944R00180